NEGATIVE INTIMACY
— SEX, LOVE AND SWORDS —

About the author

Christine Le Gardé came from a humble farm background and has grown up to be an angel in disguise, for many people, befitting her Libran personality. From an incredibly young age, she started her first charity venture, teaching dance at age twelve, out of the garage, to local children. She went on to become a ballerina, often flying across the stage in a tutu and wings, or entertaining crowds in modern dance and ballroom shows. Graduating top of her class at university, she then became a rising star in the retail marketing landscape, enjoying some wonderful international adventures. Christine gave away the corporate life when she became a mother and stepmother, pivoting her personal aspirations to focus on her family, becoming an author, and guiding women and families through divorce and domestic violence disputes as a volunteer McKenzie Friend.

Christine Le Gardé

NEGATIVE INTIMACY
— SEX, LOVE AND SWORDS —

Vanguard Press

VANGUARD PAPERBACK

A CIP catalogue record for this title is
available from the British Library.

ISBN 978-1-80016-041-5

Vanguard Press is an imprint of
Pegasus Elliot MacKenzie Publishers Ltd.
www.pegasuspublishers.com

First Published in 2021

Vanguard Press
Sheraton House Castle Park
Cambridge England

Printed & Bound in Great Britain

Dedication

To my darling children, Panda and Angel

May you always be happy, courageous, and kind, and always safe.

I hope your adventures together are rewarding, your future partners loving and your lives blessed with good fortune.

Acknowledgements

I would like to thank all my family and friends who have made this book possible.

Firstly, to Dallas, my husband and white knight. Thank you for believing I had it in me to produce a novel on a subject so close to my heart. Your constant support, love, banter, dancing and coffee breaks kept me sane.

To my mother and father, I love you both, as you have been my guiding lights, teachers, and confidants my whole life.

Maryanne, Taz, Theresa, James, Patricia, Rhonda and Leonora… Thanks for being a part of my colourful life.

Chapter 1
Marketing Yourself

It's late Saturday afternoon as I return home from a birthday bash for my best friend, Sophia. The breeze coming through my car window and caressing my face, is unusually warm for this time of the year in Victoria, aptly known as Canada's 'Garden City'. Deciduous trees lining my street are starting to turn vibrant sheds of red, orange, and yellow, signifying autumn is upon us. I pull into my driveway then activate the garage remote. As the door rolls up, I wait to see if my Labrador Mia and ragdoll cat Benji will be greeting me. They did not disappoint. We performed our customary pats and hugs, then they fell in behind me to go inside the house. Flicking the fan on as I walk into my master bedroom, I flung my handbag on the TV unit narrowly missing the antique silver-plated candelabra. I sat down on the end of the bed and removed my white stilettos, wiggled my toes to get the blood flowing, and then pulled the hair band out of my hair to relieve the headache I had from the combination of wine, sun and cigarettes at the party.

I had a great time at Sophia's place, but was spent, and in need of a nanna nap. Crashing backwards onto the soft welcoming folds of my king-size bed, I closed my eyes and breathed a sigh of relief to be home. Truth be told, underlying my lack of energy was an emptiness that evolved from a lengthy period of single life. I was the second oldest of my group of girlfriends, at 33 years of age; my best friend Sophia being older by just three weeks. All my girlfriends had married over the previous five years. Male attention coming my direction only seemed to be based on lust and ego, which for me certainly aren't suitable attributes for longevity.

Lying comfortably on top of my doona, I closed my eyes and

thought... *Yet another social function where I was the only unwed female and of course, not an eligible bachelor in sight. These days it seems at every party... it's always the same.*

Reacting to this thought, my stomach tightened as a spasm shot across my lower abdomen. My inner voice continued... *What the hell is wrong with men? I have everything my girlfriends have to offer and more... I'm sexy, educated, have a great job and I own my own house.*

I exhaled heavily in despair, my mind in a state of bewilderment over what men wanted in a partner or wife. I sighed and drifted off to sleep, visualising the party's many moments and conversations, like I was watching a movie, playing in my mind.

The movie began with Sophia opening her front door, despite me being thirty minutes late to the lunch. But she wasn't upset, greeting me at the door with her usual infectious warm smile. We hugged liked sisters.

"Happy Birthday girl," I said, giving her a kiss on the cheek and handing over a big bunch of pink and white roses.

The flowers were wrapped in clear cellophane tied with a black and a hot-pink ribbon as well as a white lace ribbon encrusted with diamantes at the bottom. These three colours combined with some added bling were my signature brand, and all my friends knew it.

"They're just beautiful Ariel, thank you," Sophia commented, taking a moment to inhale the heady aroma.

"But wait there's more," I said smiling and cheekily raising my eyebrows, as I pulled out from my handbag, Sophia's favourite aperitif: a 750ml bottle of Midori.

"Wow that's really generous of you... bestie," she said, totally surprised at receiving a second present.

"I haven't had a glass of Midori and lemonade in like... forever. I think the last time was at my wedding wasn't it? I reckon we should crack it open and have a cocktail together just like old times," she continued, taking the bottle from me with her spare hand.

"I'd love to! Do you have any lemonade?" I replied, crossing the threshold into her house, and following along behind her.

Sophia and I had a deep affection for each other; we had met through a mutual friend when we were just eighteen and had been inseparable ever since. We were the very best of friends. Ushering me through the house, Sophia continued…

"I'm glad you're here girl, I've missed you. The gang's in the kitchen, cooking. They won't let me lift a finger, which is a big concern as you know none of them are great chefs, except for Nona."

To get to the kitchen we had to walk through the family room, past the outdoor barbeque area, where it looked to me like the menfolk were drinking and watching football. John, Sophia's husband, was splashing a little beer on the meat, which was sizzling away on the barbeque hotplate. As I turned my back and walked into Sophia's kitchen, I heard one of boys yelling at the TV. "That wasn't a forward pass ya dickhead, it was a clean try! Argh… come on… No! You should be bloody well sacked."

The kitchen was chaotic and filled with party napkins, balloons, plates, drinks, a large chocolate gateaux, lollies, snacks and food everywhere. After all, half of the guests were Italian; the other half a mix of mostly Australian and Greek. I counted fifteen females, in their element preparing the party food. Plates of food covered every benchtop, the sink was full of dirty pots and plates, and footprints of all shapes and sizes smeared on the floor. The smell of Italian pasta sauce simmering on the stove whet my tastebuds, as I knew Sophia's Nona made the best spaghetti and meatballs.

"Hi everyone, can I help anywhere?" I broadcast, stepping into the kitchen. They all knew I wasn't what you'd call 'domestic material' or a whizz in the kitchen, so I was happy when the replies came back… "All good here," from Vanita, and…

"We're just about done I think," from Sophia's Nona.

"I'll be happy to stand back here then and watch," I followed up.

Kids were sporadically coming in and out of the kitchen for drinks and snacks, running back out to the movie that was playing in the rumpus room.

I poured myself a glass of wine and as I took a sip, Tracey came around the corner behind me. She had been attending to her kids in the hallway bathroom.

"Oh my God! I haven't seen you in ages," she said, tapping me on the shoulder and throwing her arms around me. We hugged jumping up and down like schoolgirls, and half my wine was on the floor by the end of the embrace.

"You look fabulous as usual," Tracey continued.

"Thank you. You haven't aged a day," I said.

Tracey had moved up the coast two years previously after falling pregnant to Fabio, who in my opinion, was a dickhead and a liar, so I hadn't seen much of her.

"So, give me the goss. Who are you seeing these days?" Tracey enquired.

"No one, but I have gone on a few dates lately," I responded, knowing this would spark her curiosity, as I was dying to tell the girls about my recent escapades. Tracey's perfectly manicured eyebrow slowly raised at my comment.

"You can't leave us old maids hanging, tell us all the juicy details. Remember, we chained and married women live boring lives, and from time to time we need some spice," Tracey said, grinning like the Cheshire cat.

She grabbed my hand so I couldn't escape the playful interrogation, which prompted all the womenfolk in attendance to stop what they were doing, and close in around the island bench in the middle of the kitchen, where Tracey had pulled me. My wine glass was refilled by Rachel as Tracey poured another round of drinks for the girls. Vanita echoed Tracey's request spouting, "Yeah… tell us…"

"I'd love to hear it," Rosa joined in.

"We want all the gossip, right down to the sex scenes Ariel," Emilia said excitedly.

With the hens gathered round, they began thumping on the island bench like a mob of protestors and chanted… *"Tell us… Tell us… Tell us!"* after which, a huge belt of hysterical laughter erupted from the mob.

Looking left, I noticed a picture frame sitting on top of Sophia's fridge and the movie running in my dream, suddenly ground to a halt. Everyone at the party was frozen still as time stopped. I gazed deeply at the photo, beaming inwardly with joy. It was a picture of the six of us at my 25th birthday party at the Sheraton Hotel. As I examined the image closely, there were no voices or noises, just a silence all around, and everyone had now disappeared to leave me completely alone in a dark room. My mind began to wander, as I reminisced over our interwoven lives, regretting that those days had passed. I scanned my girlfriend's faces with a proud sense of sisterhood, and took a moment to reminisce…

Since the age of eighteen, these girls had been my closest friends. From our twenties on, and for years after, we painted the town red every Friday and Saturday night. We were like the United Nations, each one being from a different nationality, and this made for interesting times when meeting boys. I was known as the Canadian dancer, Sophia was the cute elfin Italian girl, Tracey was the tough-talking Texan, Rachel was the Aussie hippy chick, Vanita the sexy Asian, Rosa was the dark-haired English masseuse, and Anika the blonde Polish bombshell. We always had great fun, and loved to dress up, dance all night, drink wine, puff cigarettes, and club hop together. And what was our mission? Ahh yes… to check out the talent! I was like the rock star of the group. Being one of the elite dancers in the 'Capital Tease Burlesque Show' that travelled around the big clubs, everyone knew me, and the younger dancers all wanted to be just like me. It was because of my evening gigs that we usually received free drinks, never paid club entry fees, nor queued to get in anywhere and were always treated like VIPs at the clubs I worked. Some owners even sent limousines to collect us so we would patronise their establishments. Those were the good old days! We had so much fun. Now life was, well… different…

As we passed the age of twenty-five, our 'sex and the city' lifestyle began to slow down as one after another of my girlfriends fell in love, got married and had kids—all virtually within three years of each other. After that, they bought houses and acreage, and moved further and further away from one another, both socially and physically. These girls' nights became less frequent and stopped completely by the time I was twenty-eight, although we reunited once every six months or so, and Sophia's birthday was just one of those occasions. As each of them chummed up to their partners, married and became stay-at-home mothers, I often wondered whether my girlfriends ever missed our former life. The reality that these fun days were over hit me quite hard during my late twenties, and more than once I did get a little depressed about my dearly missed girlfriends and those bygone days. However, they never knew how I felt, and I didn't think it fair for them to be concerned, as each now had their own lives to lead.

As I returned the photograph to the top of the fridge, the movie slowly kicked back into motion. Now back in the present… the girls' laughter slowly subsided as all eyes focused on me for some intimate details. I then coyly answered…

"Let's just say… I could whinge all day about this subject, but there really are no good men left in Canada and dating sucks. Let's leave it at that," I declared, staring at a number of disappointed faces.

I thought it wise to bend everyone's focus away from my love life, so that I didn't become the centre of attention at my best friend's birthday bash. There were several faces I didn't recognise so I wasn't overly comfortable in spilling the beans to an unfamiliar audience. I'd rather update my trusted girlfriends in private. The kitchen fell silent for a few seconds as I had put a dampener on the banter with my 'no kiss and tell' attitude. An almost inaudible statement then came from one of the women I didn't recognise.

"I'd hate to be on the dating scene. I just don't know what I'd do or say, as I haven't been on a date in ten years. What about you?" the woman asked Vanita, with a hint of disdain in her voice.

She looked maybe five years my senior and said this looking in my direction, peering straight through me with an expression that showed she was glad not to be in my position at her age. I understood the reasons for her remark and my eyes dropped to the floor in embarrassment. Even though she made these comments under her breath, everyone heard it, which brought the group sex chat to a screaming halt and everyone returned to finalising the food platters.

About ten minutes later, as the party food was rolled out like a banquet for the birthday feast to begin, I went to the outside bar fridge and picked up a Coke before grabbing a seat at the outdoor table. As I bent down, a rather large Italian man named Mario, whom I'd introduced to my girlfriend Trish twelve years ago, said to me in front of everyone, "You look lovely as usual. So lovely, I wish I'd married you, not my wife." Then he began laughing like he'd made a funny joke.

He stepped sideways behind me to allow me to get into my seat but did this for kicks so he could rub his torso and pelvis against my backside. I embarrassingly made light of his joke replying, "Lucky me!" as I slipped into one of the chairs next to Sophia's husband John.

"Let's meet up for coffee next week at La Roux Patisserie," suggested Mario, beating his chest in front of the other men. The voice in my head declared... *Like you would ever have a chance, you idiot!* But I was more diplomatic in reply...

"Yeah sure, I'll tee it up with Trish... I'd love to shout your kids to a babycino," I said, in an attempt at sarcasm. A few seconds later, I detected a very unpleasant odour and realised it was Mario's sweat; he stank like he hadn't showered in weeks. I quickly made an excuse to John that I needed to sit in the shade and strolled up to the other end of the long table to seat myself at the only other vacant chair, which happened to be at the head of the table. Rosa's husband, Trevor, who was at the direct other end of the table asked in a rather loud voice, "So Ariel, has any lucky son of a bitch nabbed you yet?"

"No... can't say there's been any developments on that front," I replied. Curiously, I found that males questioned me more often than females about why I remained single, and on this day, I felt I was becoming a bit of a star attraction. I felt like a female comedian on stage at Comedy Central entertaining guests over lunch about my online dating dalliances. I've found that married people, in general, love to hear stories of strange encounters, internet dating, single life and sex, and especially when socialising and drinking wine. Probably because, secretly they'd love to play in an R-rated movie of their own, completely opposite to the lives they now led.

I then caught everyone's attention when Vanita, one of my oldest university friends and the most stunning Asian lady I'd ever known, asked me from across the table, "Ariel, I heard you started online dating."

"Well, you could say my love life got really interesting about four months ago when I signed up to Executive Introductions. Do you know that site?" I asked.

"Yes, I've seen their ads on TV. Don't they say it's one of the largest online dating portals for professionals with thousands of new members joining every month?" Vanita replied, in a marketing tone.

"I don't know their stats," I responded. "Why online dating? Surely you could just go out and pick up, like old times?" she said with a grin.

"I don't really have the opportunity to meet single men in my line of work, and as all of you are now married and don't go out any more, my rationale was that it opened up opportunities I wouldn't otherwise come across. I wanted to improve the odds of finding that needle in a haystack by using a big dating website in this country," I said, hoping I didn't sound too desperate.

Sophia's tradie husband John, then chimed in, "I'd think you'd be pretty popular on a site like that Ariel. I reckon all you'd need to do is put up your old modelling shots; or better still, why don't you use that photo taken from that advertisement of you at the gentleman's club you managed? Using those, you wouldn't need anything else to pick up a date. You'd be beating them off with a stick." His tone was supportive and complimentary. John was like a big brother to me.

Then poured forth plenty of other suggestions from and between the guests about what to put online. A good ten-minute debate raged on the best type of photos to snag the right man. It was a funny light-hearted conversation. For me, it was quite enlightening to hear everyone's differing perception of my 'plight' and what they thought 'sells best' to procure a date online.

As she had held her tongue for most of this conversation, Sophia piped up at the end. "I don't think you should put up any photos. That way males aren't choosing you because of your looks. I'm really worried about the psychos out there with possible bad intentions that just gawk at your photos! Your last two serious boyfriends just took advantage of your generosity and didn't treat you well. I just want you to be happy and find a man that will treat you right," she caringly said.

I stretched across the table and gave her a big hug. She was my confidante and my rock. Sophia had a beautiful soul and was like an enchanted fairy with her elfin face, long black hair and glowing skin.

"Thank you all for your suggestions, but I've tried out most of your ideas already. I am changing my profile as I learn more about the site and its members," I said graciously.

"So, what exactly does your profile say?" Rachel asked.

Feeling a little embarrassed about exposing my online alias, and hoping they wouldn't laugh, I answered, "My profile name is 'ThePinkLioness' after my favourite wild animal and colour. Then there's a teaser or sales slogan beneath that, where I wrote... *Single, Attractive and Independent*, as I believed this described me to a tee in short."

"Well, I'd respond to that kind statement if I were online. What else is on there?" Mario enquired.

"If a gentleman were intrigued and wanted to know more after seeing my photos and reading this slogan, a more detailed description could be viewed by clicking on my profile name. There are also a range of drop-down boxes to choose from that describe various characteristics. I selected boxes to show I was Caucasian; I had blonde hair and blue eyes; I was 5 foot 6 and of slim build; I voted conservative and was in an executive corporate position. There were a few more descriptors, but I can't remember them all," I explained.

"Well, that all sounds like you... are you sure you want men to know all those details?" questioned Rosa, who had recently married her reiki instructor and ran her own hairdressing business.

Recalling a few more elements of the profile, I added, "It's a tough decision about what to put in and what to leave out. I remember now that I also indicated I had pets, and in the relationship status section I chose that I was single, never married, with no children and would be open to a relationship with a male who had children."

"Are you really sure you want to date a man with kids? That brings a whole new range of complexities like ex-wives into the picture," enquired Lisa, Sophia's cousin.

"Well, I'd prefer a man without children, but I figured that realistically, men in my ideal age bracket – let's say thirty-five to forty-five – would more than likely have children, and cutting them out only limits my options," was my considered answer.

A Greek friend, Spiros, owner of a tobacco shop, and probably the shadiest person in our circle of friends then asked, "Is that all you put into your profile? Cause I've been on that site before and you also have to write a blurb about yourself."

"Spiros do tell more. Why would you need to be on a dating website? You seem to meet women all the time," Vanita teasingly said.

Spiros quickly deflected that line of questioning, as his new lady friend was sitting right alongside him, throwing daggers back at Vanita.

I quickly jumped in to help Vanita off the hook. "I can't remember exactly what I wrote, Spiros."

"Log on to the site through your phone and read it to us then," John's twin brother, Anton, piped up.

"Oh... Okay then, it seems none of you are going to let this go, so I'll get my phone from my bag inside. Please feel free to talk about me amongst yourselves, while I'm gone," I said sarcastically.

I then stood up, walked inside, and pulled my iPhone out of my black and pink Juicy Couture bag. Finding the dating app, I touched the screen and immediately logged into my account. As I was walking back out to the table, Rachel, seeing me at the sliding security door impatiently said, "Well…? Tell us."

"Okay. Okay… let me sit down first, but I'll need a fresh drink before I totally expose myself to all of you," I replied, raising my empty glass.

"So… this is what I wrote for my description…

I'm an old-fashioned girl, but I am not desperate to get married and I don't need to be called every day. I have a degree in International Business & Law from UBC. I consult to a range of retail businesses in the areas of branding, advertising, and product development. I was a burlesque entertainer and singer. I love Latin dancing, socialising, swimming, skiing, good food, motor bikes, fashion and enhancing my business knowledge and debating on world affairs. I am a genuine person and believe I am a diamond in the rough. 'Players', or men who have no kind of responsibilities in their life, need not apply. Please note I am not domesticated and therefore will not do your washing, ironing and daily cooking for you. "

Vanita, who was usually quickest to respond, then summed up:

"Well, that sounds like you all over. Particularly the part that you are not domesticated. But I don't think men are going to like it."

"Show us the pictures," blurted Mario, but I abruptly shot that idea down with a very firm, "NO!" and then… the movie within the dream I was having… faded completely, as I fell into a very deep and comfortable sleep.

Chapter 2
Snakes in the Grass

In the middle of the night my dream returned, and the same movie started up again during the wee hours. This time I was standing at a lectern making a public speech and showing my Executive Introductions profile page on a big screen, to a room full of unknown and faceless people, and I was marketing myself for a date.

"You can see how I have loaded four pictures instead of six. I did this so I didn't seem desperate to show who I was. The first three images are without makeup, showing me in the morning, at noon and night. Then, there is one of me in a sexy red dress from a spring carnival party, which was taken the year before," I explained.

Coming from a sales and marketing background, I thought all the traits, qualities and images displayed on my dating profile would make me stand out from the thousands of other women on the site who, in my opinion, generally looked contrived as they often posted glamour shots with packed on makeup but their profiles contained little real detail about themselves.

The 'pouting glamazonian' type image of a woman, always made me chuckle about the lengths some went to in order to obtain a man! Many profiles made me question whether these women were actual living people at all as they posted photos that had to have been taken up to a decade before. Even worse, a number of them looked like they were downloaded directly from some random soft-porn website, and who knows, the real entities behind some profiles could well have been transsexuals, or crooks posing as blonde Russians to scam money into a bank account in Cameroon. While there may have been many unsavoury characters on the Executive Introductions site, I forged ahead to create a unique sketch of myself.

My style was to provide potential suitors with an authentic profile, to portray what I looked like every day. In other words, cut through the crap from the onset and hopefully deter those men who were only looking for a trophy to stroke their ego and be easy to conquer.

I took this approach as I'd never really been 'goo gar' over men. In general, as a species, they annoy me. Don't get me wrong… I like them, but I don't need one just for the sake of having one beside me in bed. I've been very successful in life, and have stood on my own two feet, despite my underprivileged childhood years. I was raised in welfare housing. I had to sacrifice and push myself hard to obtain financial independence, and by the age of twenty-five I had succeeded. So, I certainly did not need a man to provide for me. In fact, I wanted to be independent of a man, and definitely not live in each other's pockets. But at the same time, I wished for a partner to share life's beautiful moments and someone to create memories with.

I've often wondered how I developed this stand-offish attitude and took a somewhat cold position on matters of the heart, particularly regarding men, relationships, the sanctity of marriage and gender roles. I think generally people are a product of their environment and are also a reflection of the chances they take. I'm also a big believer in destiny and karma, which shapes our paths in life regardless of what course we take.

"So, get out there and sell yourself online… the right way," I said with some relief as my presentation concluded, and I received a standing ovation for a good thirty seconds. Still in my dream state, the movie played on, but I now drifted back to Sophia's birthday party.

"Tell us more about your life and dating encounters online, Ariel," said one of the audience members. Everyone gradually took their seats and I continued speaking, this time to my friends.

I went into some detail and explained that after setting up my profile and going live, I received a lot of 'kisses'—around a hundred and fifty or more, and approximately forty emails from various men on the site. These 'kisses' were an indication that men were interested in me. The emails meant these men had paid extra to communicate directly with me for a date, so Executive Introductions certainly did well from my profile. I must admit, this new source of attention fanned my ego, and I looked forward to my late evening cyber sessions. It was like a nightly buffet of potential suitors as I checked, read and answered my various enamoured emails. The whole process was very entertaining, and I imagined, there would be people meeting each other this way that went on a date every night. Thoroughly enjoying the attention, and regaling people at Sophia's party, I continued, "Within a relatively short time, I had met four 'men with potential' for actual dates, and I saw a couple of these on more than one occasion. The most memorable of these was a man called Amos, whose profile name was 'AutoMoto007'. He was an ex-go-kart champion, and a classic car enthusiast in his late forties. He owned a software investment company. His photo on the website had him standing beside a black Cobra car. He literally hounded me with kisses every couple of days for weeks and sent me nine emails in an unrelenting attempt to make me correspond. However, although I couldn't put my finger on it at the time, there was something about him that deterred me.

"Finally, one Saturday with nothing to do, I answered his email, which was time stamped at 7.25 a.m., and agreed to accompany him to Cirque du Soleil at three thirty that afternoon. I figured why not go to the latest risqué circus for a treat? I turned up at the admissions office at three fifteen, grabbed the ticket he'd left for me and went inside to find my seat and meet Amos. He looked like his photos, seemed nice enough and was pleasant in his conversation during the performance, so I agreed to have dinner after the show.

"During the 'get to know you' conversation that is a precursor for every date, I asked Amos how long he'd been married, as his profile mentioned he was a divorcee with no children. As an outcome of this exchange, I discovered that Amos had ex-wife anger issues and unwisely thought that our first date was an opportunity to rant about his barren wife and the excessive property settlement she received, following their eighteen years of marriage. I also discovered that Amos was a nerd who loved computers, sound systems, remotes, large TVs, video games, Marvel superheroes and car paraphernalia.

"Being preoccupied in talking about himself, he really didn't ask me any questions at all, so I just let him drag on. The real kicker came during dessert when he proceeded to launch into a highly inappropriate conversation about sex. After dinner, he literally asked me straight up for sex because he'd paid for the show tickets. My reaction was totally predictable... *What a pretentious dick!*

"He was totally oblivious to his insulting jibes but didn't stop there. He proudly informed me, thinking it was going to be a turn-on, that, 'I'm afraid my manhood will break you'. There was no way this guy was getting to any base at all with me, but at the same time I was somehow intrigued and kept listening just for a laugh.

"He went on, 'I need to let you in on a little secret before we have sex, my dear. I'm allergic to latex... so, I have to use cling wrap. I hope you don't mind'.

"After hearing this announcement, I arose from the restaurant table, and, holding back my laughter, briskly walked to my car to get the hell out of there. Driving off in a real hurry, I sporadically snorted at Amos's unusual disclosure, the entire way home.

"Funnily enough, years later, Amos and I ended up working together at the same business, which was 'oops' awkward, to say the least! But that's another story...

"My next dalliance was with 'SurfingClown', who presented himself as a sports teacher. He loved to surf and boasted about his talents in the kitchen; he didn't mind cleaning the house; he was a pretty good dancer and had two children from a previous marriage. I met 'SurfingClown', otherwise known as Travis, at the Bourbon St Grill at the shopping centre complex where I was contracted as the Redevelopment Consultant.

"Travis was about fifteen centimetres taller than me, with

blonde hair and a well-toned physique. He was casually dressed in a Broncos jersey and he walked with a slight limp, which apparently stemmed from a surfing accident in Hawaii two years before. The date itself wasn't too bad as conversation went smoothly. We participated a couple of times in the freestyle Latin dancing entertainment and played a couple of rounds on the poker machines.

"Even though I felt no sparks at this early stage, Travis seemed nice enough. So after dessert was served, and whilst he was visiting the little boys' room, I considered that I might just agree to a second date. Then, the waitress arrived with the bill and placed it on the table next to Travis in a black American Express folder. Travis stood up and with a cool attitude started patting his pockets for his wallet.

"'Oh, shit, I think I've left my wallet at home,' he said, a little too calmly. He then shrugged his shoulders and glared at me with a dumb yet mischievous smirk on his face. I immediately knew he had done this before, as there was no genuine panic or embarrassment in either his voice or his actions.

"'Really, are you for real?' I said, more alarmed at his bad acting than the incident. Travis said nothing and started to move away from the table like he was preparing to do a runner. "Well, I didn't bring my purse either, so we're in a difficult predicament," I said, boldly lying to see how he would react. He bolted without a 'thanks' or 'farewell.'

"You must have been livid Ariel. I know I would have been," said Tracey, saying what the rest of the party were all thinking.

"I would have chased after the S.O.B. with the knife and fork in hand just to scare him," responded Vanita making a widely crazy face whilst holding up her cutlery for extra impact. Everyone cracked up at the hilarious visual.

"I just paid the bill feeling a little bit embarrassed and thanked my tenant for their delicious food and service.

"For a man not to pay on a first date is a big no-no, for me and as far as I am concerned, it sends up roaring red-alert warnings about their character and how they treat women," I said, to bring this part of my story about Travis to an end.

"Surely there's loads of executive type men out there who are normal people wanting to find true love," suggested Rosa, the ever optimist voice of the group.

"That's what I thought when 'Stud009' otherwise known as Stellan, contacted me. He was the third gentleman I went on a date with. He lived on the west coast, was European, had a two-year-old son and owned a business that was based around environmental considerations like recycling, which he had built from scratch. He was about six feet tall, with dark hair and olive skin; he was incredibly handsome with the square jaw line I loved and built like a body builder.

"Our first date was at Lux, a lounge bar on the popular waterfront strip. We flirted allusively, with our conversation flowing freely over a couple of drinks; all the while he was making it clear he was very into me by touching my leg and stroking my hair. I admit that his gorgeous European looks combined with his being a successful businessman was enticing. He also dressed in a casual Armani suit, which was a turn-on for me, so I was definitely into him.

"Throughout our two-hour encounter, several people from various walks of life came up to say hello. It turned out that he was very well known and had developed celebrity status at that bar. Stellan invited one of these 'visitors', to sit with us for a drink. I thought asking a third wheel to join us was a bit strange when you're on a first date, but I brushed it off.

"A threesome… Now this is getting interesting," said Mario, intentionally to provoke cheers from the boys.

"Why Mario… is it a fantasy of yours for a three-way with another man?" I trajected, to shut him up so I could continue with my sitcom.

"The man introduced himself as Baxter, explaining he was an aspiring fashion designer and close personal friend of Stellan. I was drawn to his flamboyance, colourful conversation, Mardi Gras gossip and 'loose lips' in relation to my suitor. He was a surprising bonus to the evening.

"From this date I realised that Stellan had a great business mind, an eye for detail, and owned a business that turned over more than $10 million a year. Ventures he considered investing in had to relate to saving the planet, recycling, or construction. He was also spontaneous, obviously capable of making decisions on the fly and went out and just did things; he told me he loved taking risks.

"For example, since he was now running out of time to be a father, he told me he wanted a child before he turned forty-five. So, he asked a female friend Ellen, who was a cabaret singer and single, if she'd be interested in having a baby with him. She agreed and they proceeded through IVF. So, Stellan and Ellen, moved into the same house and now raise their son, purely as friends. The benefit for Ellen is that she doesn't work, as Stellan pays her a salary of some $80,000 a year to be a stay-at-home mum. A unique situation, and one that a lot of women would love to be in, I'm sure.

"At around ten p.m. I thanked Stellan for the date and left to drive back home. He asked me if I'd be interested in getting together again over dinner. I accepted his invitation and we arranged to meet the following Saturday night at the popular La Boca Bistro at seven thirty p.m. But Stellan called me the very next morning, saying, 'Hey sexy girl! I found your watch on the floor after you left the bar last night'. Not realising I'd lost it, I panicked as that watch had been a present from my godmother and was very expensive with diamonds in the face and on the band.

"I gratefully answered, 'Ohh… thank you so much… it was sweet of you to ring me first thing. I'm driving out your way tomorrow morning for a meeting at eleven thirty, so I could pick it up after that?' I had butterflies jumping up and down in my stomach, as I was more than excited to be seeing him again, so soon.

"'Great. Why don't you ring me after your meeting is finished? I can meet you at my apartment. It's not too far from where I'll be spending my afternoon," Stellan replied.

"I answered, 'I thought you lived in a house on acreage with

Ellen?'

"'I do, but I also have an apartment for when I'm in town,' he replied.

"'Okay, perfect! See you then. Thanks again for picking it up, and please text me your address when you can'. I hung up the phone, all excited.

"After my meeting the next day, I arrived at Seagate Apartments just after two p.m. Stellan's apartment was on the 15th floor and overlooked Fisherman's Wharf. The view was spectacular, and his choice of interior design was impressive. We chatted for a few minutes and he then took my watch out of the cutlery drawer in his kitchen. I thanked him for looking after it and said that I had to be on my way for a four thirty p.m. event at the Grand Pacific in town.

"He walked me back down the hallway to the front door of the apartment. But, before reaching the door, he grabbed my hand, spun me round to pull me towards him, and as we stood there, pelvis to pelvis, he landed a sultry kiss on my lips. I eagerly responded to his feverish touch, kissing him for a few minutes whilst my hand danced around, caressing the muscles of his upper torso. His muscular frame turned up my body heat to 'extreme'.

"In this steamy tryst Stellan then suddenly slammed me, a little too hard for my liking, against the wall in his hallway. I was off kilter but went with the whole teasing fantasy romp thing for a minute or two before I left. He slowly ran his hands up and down my body whilst our lips remained joined. Stellan was very passionate, but could have been a little less dominant, and more sensual. When he went to undo the zipper of my black jeans, I quickly pulled out from the kiss and pushed his hand away.

"'Stellan, I like you, but I'm not prepared to sleep with you… yet. We only met two days ago', I said, stepping out of his personal space.

"'Come on baby… we're two consenting adults, and you know you want it', he replied, pulling me back into his embrace and locking lips with me again. My emotions took control of me as he was very sexy, and I did want him. He slowed the kissing down and turned me around to press me up against the hallway wall. This pace was nicer I thought; he even did a bit of a stripper dance in front of me. His hands moved up my chest slowly and across my nipples before he squeezed my breasts between his fingers. He took my arms and lifted them up above my head. I closed my eyes and rested the back of my head against the wall, enjoying the lighter foreplay. He then ran his hands seductively down my arms tickling me as he went, kissing my neck the entire time. I was putty in his hands, and I felt the sex kitten inside begin to purr. I envisaged him teasingly make his way down my body, slowly unlocking my pants and then fingering me until I went off. But my lustful thoughts were abruptly interrupted when Stellan's hands suddenly clamped around my neck, making me gasp for air. He still had his lips pinned to mine, but in an instant the whole situation had completely changed. It was crazy. He wouldn't let go of my neck or get off me. I freaked out trying to push him away, but he had me pinned and his strength was much greater than mine. After about twenty seconds, I used a solid upward thrust of my right knee between his legs. He keeled over stumbling backwards, which gave me the space to quickly open the door and escape. I never looked back, and he didn't come after me.

"While I initially thought Stellan had potential, I wasn't into suffocation as an aphrodisiac… so that was the end of that!

"'BladeRunner' was another man I dated," I said to my audience as I went on to recount this entanglement. He was the closest guy I'd come across to being normal. His real name was Jaxon. As us singles do, I googled him and found that he owned his own logging and wood panelling business. A staff picture on their website showed my Aunty Geraldine had worked there in the financial department. She informed me that Jaxon was forty-seven, extremely well off, and that his company was worth about $50 million. She went on to say that he was funny and kind; that he had been a great boss to her, and she thought he would definitely stimulate me intellectually. From the internet research I performed, it seems Jaxon was involved in business association forums and had been a regular guest speaker at various events. Geraldine commented that she didn't know why she hadn't thought of pairing us up earlier.

"For our first date we organised to meet up at the café in the Butchart Botanical Gardens on a Sunday afternoon. At first impression, I noticed that he was taller than most; he had red hair and was conservatively well dressed and well spoken. He was not a stunner, but had attractive eyes, freckles and a cute smile with dimples. His eyes captivated me as they were light blue with flecks of yellow around the pupil. Jaxon was very attentive, so when I spoke, he looked straight into my eyes as though he hung on every word and no one else mattered. It was a nice date with coffee turning into an early dinner, and a few hours later we had made a second date on the Wednesday night to see a movie. We got on famously like two old friends and ended up going on several dates over that month.

"I went to his house near Victoria Park once and even met his three-year-old daughter on that occasion. He had admitted on our second date that he'd only recently broken up from a long-term relationship with his partner called Elisa, a hairdresser and model.

"Their relationship had lasted just four years, and during that time Elisa had cheated on him, thrown back his gifts of diamond jewellery, apparently wailing that the stones weren't big enough. She'd also supposedly embarrassed him at a number of business dinners by getting very drunk and acting inappropriately and in an unladylike fashion. Furthermore, she was making it difficult for him to see his daughter. Preventing access and using a child as a weapon was abhorrent, so I felt sorry for Jaxon missing out on his daughter growing up.

"For our next date, we made plans to go watch the Monster trucks clash at the stadium. This type of event really wasn't my cup of tea, but I had never been to a 'petrol head' venue, or event for that matter, and thought it might be a hoot to go at least once in my life. Then Jaxon called me one hour before he was due to pick me up.

"'Ariel, I'm sorry, I have to cancel. I'll call you tomorrow." He clicked off the phone giving me no reason at all, and no chance to respond. I didn't receive a call the next day, which irritated me, and I thought it was unusual and rude. But a couple of days later, I left a voice message inviting him to contact me.

"Jaxon eventually got back to me a week later and after the normal hello, small talk and pleasantries, he informed me that… 'Elisa heard I was dating someone, and she contacted me last Sunday, so we've been talking about getting back together'.

"'Well… my question is… *are* you getting back together?' I snapped at him.

"'I think we will. I have to give it a go for my daughter's sake', he said with a tinge of guilt in his voice.

"'Okay best of luck and remember to buy her a bigger diamond next time', I said sarcastically, but obviously hurt by his sudden change of mind.

"Clicking the phone off to 'BladeRunner', was the end of that relationship.

I was still in the middle of my dream, the sounds of people at Sophia's birthday party became much more evident, and I finished my speech by saying…

"I'm poised to go on my next internet date in two weeks' time with Journo48. So, who's having the next party to hear the conclusion?" I asked the group, from my chair at the top of the table.

My audience were gobsmacked; they shook their heads, laughed and chatted amongst themselves about the craziness of the men I had met in the internet gene pool. At least the last few months of my life had provided them with some entertainment. I was sure that my dating stories would be relayed to their various extended social circles, like handing out pieces of delectable chocolate from a gift box of scandalous affairs.

I was awoken out of my dream by my alarm clock buzzing and signalling it was six thirty a.m., time to rise and shine. Mia did her usual bark upon hearing the alarm go off; her way of letting me know she wanted to go outside.

Chapter 3
The Laws of Attraction

Following my online experiences, I analysed each of these dates and drew a few conclusions. Firstly, from my limited experience of dating wealthy men, I developed the opinion that with excessive money, there definitely comes a price I wasn't willing to pay. They seem to have a need for control, either through sexual or financial dominance, and they were also weirdly prone to being attracted to drama queens.

Secondly, I reasoned that most eligible men were probably already taken; mostly married, and therefore not online. Finally, knowing that I was already quite comfortable and financially secure, I began to develop an attitude that having a man was not the be all and end all to life. It seems that most men just annoyed me with their egos, shortcomings and chauvinistic demands.

After a few months of, not so great dates… well, let's be honest, rather scary and tragic experiences, I decided internet dating may not be the best place for me to meet a love interest. But at least I could say I tried. My mother had often told me Mr Right was just around the corner, but I wasn't heartbroken that my 'shining knight' hadn't appeared. So, I figured destiny would eventually lead me along life's path, and what would be, would be.

After being dumped by Jaxon for a drama queen hairdresser, I sat down at my computer with the full intention of deactivating my dating account. I logged in, and was ready to shut the app down, when I noticed I'd received a new email from someone calling themselves 'TemptingAsSin'. Staring at the email subject line, which read *'Greetings pretty girl'*, I debated whether or not I should open the message, as for the foreseeable future, I was no longer enthusiastic about this method of dating. But the little voice in my head got the better of me, saying, *You may as well just read it, there's no harm in that!* So I clicked, and this came up…

Hi Pink Lioness. Pleased to make your acquaintance. May I say, your profile stands out showing you are not the run-of-the-mill feline. I saw your profile a few days ago but I couldn't find my credit card so I had to race out and get a money order, send it to Executive Introductions and wait a couple of days to purchase a membership so I could contact you. Hopefully, you can envisage the comical angle of this… me running to my local post office the moment I saw you online. In conclusion, I'm a better boxer than I am a runner. Am away this weekend at a symposium. So hopefully that gives you enough time to consider my profile and respond accordingly. P.S. Love the red dress.

Kind Regards,

TemptingAsSin

After an introduction like that, I couldn't help myself. I immediately looked up his profile and smiled as I read it, thinking, *Wow, is he for real? And he's got a doctorate!*

From his photos he was a young-looking, forty-year-old, with a boyishly cute dimple in his cheek, thick black hair styled in a taper cut, brown eyes and nicely contoured arms with a tattoo of a winged skeleton on his left bicep. I couldn't help myself, so I excitedly looked up the rest of his profile.

I'm like a good recipe: add the perfect ingredients, match with a charismatic bottle of wine and enjoy the sensory sins of taste temptations. My favourite book and movie genres are action, memoirs, sci-fi, satire, and thrillers. I keep fit doing a bit of boxing and engross myself occasionally in the world of medieval combat fighting. I have a dual degree in psychotherapy and law and a PhD, so I help people have happier marriages or a better divorce and function as co-parents if they separate. Yes, I know this sounds cheesy, but I aim to positively impact everyone I meet. I am a pretty good golfer and poker player, and live life grabbing every intimate pleasurable moment. I'm also a proud father to twin girls.

I closed the email, logged off the Executive Introductions site and went to bed with the image of 'TemptingAsSin' implanted in my head. In that period just before one falls asleep, the mind tends to wander, and I mulled over his email lines with butterflies in my stomach. Before drifting off, the last thing I remember was questioning my decision to cancel any further internet dating.

I woke up the next morning around six, with the thought running through my head that for most of my childhood, my parents had drilled into me to marry a doctor or a lawyer.

This guy had both studies in his background. I didn't know what a psychotherapist did, so I googled it.

The article read… *A psychotherapist uses talk-therapy to assist patients in unstable marriages or acrimonious divorces, delving into behaviour modifications for stress, depression, anxiety, negative action patterns, and other mental health conditions.*

Ergo, I ascertained, he's a mentor working through personal issues to improve a client's sense of wellbeing.

What a noble profession, I thought.

My mother had worked in the Crown Law Office in administrative support to the public prosecutors before getting married to my father. She always spoke very highly of the lawyers, forensic doctors and mental health experts involved in the criminal trial process. Mum typed and proofread countless murder case affidavits involving many dysfunctional families in turmoil. I had not had the opportunity to meet any such professionals so far, so… curiosity got the better of me and I responded…

Subject: RE: Greetings pretty girl

Date: 7 Dec

Thank you for contacting me. Hope you had a great weekend at your conference. Looking forward to your call as I don't believe in impersonal correspondence. It is not a good method of getting to know a person. Too indirect for me. My number is below.

Regards Ariel 236-418-72060

With anticipation I waited, then two days later I received a reply from 'TemptingAsSin.'

Subject: Hello from Dante Prince (aka TemptingAsSin)

Hi Ariel,

I was briefly at the office on Sunday catching up on work and saw your email. Hopefully, it didn't cross your mind that I was ignoring you. As an old-fashioned kind of fellow, I would not leave you hanging. Tis a shame people believe manners and respect are trashy things of the past. To me there's nobility hidden behind these special acts.

I'm a psychotherapist (not a psycho) rushing about saving the universe from yet another divorce going to court, so you can rightly assume I hold onto my optimistic side for self-preservation. Well, if I do not hear from you today, I will text tonight. Hopefully, you're up for a chat and a laugh. Have a great day.

Dante

The following night I received a telephone call from Dante at around seven thirty, which lasted about an hour. The night after that, he called me again, and we talked for even longer, ending with a dinner invitation for the following Saturday night. After hanging up, I crossed my fingers and logged back into Executive Introductions to deactivate my account. I then cancelled on Journo48, so I wasn't doubled booked for Saturday night.

The rest of the week went incredibly fast. Christmas was two weeks away and everything was in full swing at the shopping centre. The centre's redevelopment launch had gone well, and Christmas events and promotions were being pumped out daily, and well into each night to keep people shopping.

I loved this time of the year, with the lights, the hum of the busy shoppers and mostly the Christmas songs. I had the best job making people happy and inspiring them to shop for their loved ones. 'Joy to the World' was definitely in full swing. Plus, Dante had asked me out… Yeah! So, all seemed absolutely perfect.

We were meeting just ten days before Christmas, so it goes without saying that I rode the festive spirit all week. Saturday morning and afternoon seemed to go really slowly as my anticipation grew for our date that evening.

I decided to wear a sexy black beaded and sequined dress that finished halfway down my thighs, with thin straps that crossed at the back and followed my hourglass figure. It was hard to find a little black number that wasn't 'run of the mill'. Thankfully I had found the dress shopping at a boutique the day before. I also wore thick black woollen stockings, and to keep warm, wrapped myself up in an angora cardigan covered over with a floor length black cashmere coat. For this special occasion I wanted to appear sexy, sophisticated, and enchanting, with a hint of playful to go with it.

Finally, it was time to head off, and I rang Sophia while driving to the meeting place.

"Hey girl. I'm on my way. Wish me luck," I said.

"I'm so excited for you. This one sounds perfect," she replied.

"I know… but I feel I shouldn't get my hopes up too much. I can't talk for long as I'm pulling onto the freeway. Remember to call me around seven thirty, so I can use you as my excuse to exit in case things aren't going well," I blurted out rapidly, trying to get off the phone to concentrate on the merging traffic.

"Will do, stay safe and call me in the morning," she said, and clicked off the phone.

I veered onto the Victoria bridge, destination the Grey Street dining precinct. Fifteen minutes later, I turned into the car park. Stepping out of my car, I put the heel of my high heeled boot to the bitumen and pushed myself out of my dark pink metallic sports Nissan. A light rain was falling like particles of glitter everywhere around me. Walking briskly, I kept my head down and a hand across my forehead to protect my makeup from running. The last thing I needed was to arrive with black mascara running down my cheeks. Moving through the car park as quickly and in as ladylike a fashion as possible, I negotiated around the puddles, but my boots were getting wet, which chilled my toes.

As I'd been anticipating this date for nearly two weeks, I was hoping his online profile was everything his emails and telephone calls had suggested. After several disastrous online dates, my heart sped up with the expectation that I may finally get to meet an intelligent, charismatic, career driven, good-looking single male. Other attributes in his favour were that he was in the age bracket I was looking for; and he didn't live in shared accommodation or at home with his mother. All that's left is to ensure he doesn't have warped sexual tastes, or that his most significant relationship isn't with a PlayStation or beer! I crossed my fingers and hoped for a successful night.

Dante said he was a part owner practitioner in a mental health clinic in the Victoria Park medical precinct and he had mentioned he lived in a condo on the northern lake front. He was born in Canada of Australian parents. His voice was low and sexy smooth like a bar singer. He had shown me he was thoughtful in his spontaneous text messages to me. Just this morning he texted me…

TXT Dante: Roses are red, violets are blue. I've tried on several outfits just to meet you… XXX

Dante was also quite knowledgeable in current affairs and didn't mind a feisty debate over controversial subjects. I respected that he had firm opinions, and these traits attracted me immensely.

Continuing toward the Sussex Lounge, which had a bar that opened onto the main street, I walked out of the alley, and was greeted by Christmas colour and cheery voices from various patrons sitting at the bar. In case Dante was there watching, I shed my cashmere coat, took a deep breath, shook my head to make my hair bounce off my shoulders, and adjusted my dress down in preparation for my entrance into the main dining lounge. I then looked straight forward, smiled and turned the corner into the bustling dining area.

Last night on the telephone Dante had given me the following hint…

"You'll know which table I'm at by what's on it," he said. Personally speaking, I'd feel more comfortable with a little to go on, like… he'll be waiting near the bar, or he'll be wearing a red bandana in his back pocket, so I tried probing him for further information…

"I'm sure the Sussex will be packed, especially as it's Christmas in a week."

"But if I tell you, my attempt at being romantic, which I know you'll like, will be quashed. I'm trying to make a good impression after all. Come on, you know me by now, so you can't think I'm a psycho. Just run with me on this. It'll be fun," he said, in a low, mischievous voice, like it was a dare. This pre-formulated staging had of course ignited my imagination even more and raised my expectations of what else our first date was to entail.

My eyes danced across each table of the packed restaurant, searching for Dante. The noises started to muffle in my ears as I momentarily began to panic. After what felt like an eternity, the realisation that I may have been stood up made my stomach twist and my blood pressure surge. I looked at my watch to see if I was too early. It was 7.06 p.m., so I was only just respectably late. Scanning the room again, my gaze stopped at a table in the far-left corner, which I'd not spotted earlier. There was a Christmas candle glowing red on a black tablecloth, two wine glasses and a wine bucket stand attached to the table. A pink-and-white orchid in a clear plastic sheath was laid across the centre of the table. My heart skipped a beat as that was my favourite flower, but no one was sitting there. I stood on my tiptoes and looked from left to right to find the toilet sign as I thought he may have gone to the loo. I must have looked like I needed help, as one of the passing staff members smiled at me and enquired…

"Are you waiting for someone?"

"Yes, but I don't think they're here yet," I answered, still scanning the room.

I then detected a gorgeous musky aftershave, which emanated from someone behind me. I turned my head to catch a glance, and at the same time felt a smooth strong hand wrap around my fingers. My heart skipped a beat as I turned fully around to face the person holding my hand. He literally took my breath away, making me feel like a giddy teenager on a first date. I raised my eyebrows, giggled to myself and, catching my breath, said,

"Hello, I hope you're Dante?"

"It's a pleasure to finally meet the girl who has been in my dreams for weeks," he said with a glowing smile. He then kissed my hand like gentlemen did in the bygone era. My initial reaction was... *My god, he... is... sexy!* Six foot two, sculptured, tanned, perfectly straight white teeth and wearing washed out slightly ripped-at-the-knee blue jeans with a light pink shirt, a dark grey insulated jacket and black leather boots. I realised right then that he was a good listener indeed, as I had passed comment in one of our initial conversations that I loved a man that dressed in pale pink. Physically this guy turned me on without touching me, and that was rare for me.

"Would you like a drink at the bar or prefer to head straight to the table for dinner?" Dante respectfully enquired.

"I'd prefer to order a drink at the table, that way we'll be away from the noise," I somewhat nervously replied. Secretly I wanted to stay at the bar and slowly enjoy a cigarette over a drink, but he didn't know yet that I was a social smoker. I followed Dante to the table, which gave me a great view of his broad back, toned muscular arms and tight buns. He definitely wore his clothes well. Dante pulled out my chair and gestured for me to take a seat with an inviting "Madam?" And there was a huge grin on his face like he was enjoying the moment. He sat down across from me and ordered from the waiter.

"A bottle of chardonnay might be nice to start with." He paused then looked at me and said, "Oh, how rude of me. Is that okay with you?"

"Chardonnay is perfect," I responded.

Another waiter came over and passed me a menu, which I was grateful for as a distraction to settle my nerves, so I lowered my eyes and pretended to read it. In a very short time, the drinks waiter returned with the bottle of chardonnay and filled our glasses.

Looking at one another, we clinked our glasses together for a toast, but just at that moment my mobile phone rudely interrupted us. I half bent down to go through my handbag to find the phone, but knew it was Sophia's 'quick escape' call, so I decided not to answer it. When I finally looked up at Dante, he was smirking at me with his wine in his right hand probably realising that I'd just given up my chance of a quick getaway.

"So how was your day today, honey?" he said, like I was already his girlfriend.

From then on, our conversation flowed smoothly and consistently throughout the entire dinner, and by the end of it I was a little bit tipsy, and starry eyed over the gorgeous man sitting in front of me who had won my heart after gushing about his unconditional love for his two beautiful daughters. I was nervous about what the rest of the evening may bring. After dinner Dante suggested, "How about we go next door to the club for a bit of a dance and a nightcap?"

"Love to, but I have to drive home, so I'll be drinking soft drinks from here on," I responded. "Hope you don't mind?"

His return smile indicated that he was relieved the date was going to continue. He spotted a waiter and made the 'check please' sign with his hands. I excused myself to go to the ladies' room and tried to execute a sexy walk to the bathroom, looking back once to see if he was watching me. He was! In the bathroom I checked my hair and makeup, then quickly rang Sophia.

"So, the date's obviously going well as you didn't answer my call!" she exclaimed.

"Oh my god Sophia, this man is too good to be true. He's sexy, smart, charming, has the perfect dress sense and an incredible body," I said, gushing over him.

"So, you're having a good time then? Just don't rush into anything and call me in the morning," Sophia said, hanging up the phone, so as to not keep me.

"I definitely will," I replied, but she'd already hung up. I closed down my phone, so it didn't ring again and redid my lipstick, then headed back out. Dante was standing up next to the table with my jacket hanging over his arm. As I walked up to the table, he linked his arm around my back and said, "Let's dance, baby girl."

As we stepped outside onto the street it was spitting with rain, but we didn't have to go more than twenty steps to the club's entrance, which was right next door. Dante ushered me inside and navigated through the crowd to an empty table at the front of the dance floor.

"I'll get the drinks... Coke, right?" he confirmed. I sat down nodding to him, as he then turned and walked off to the bar. I watched him for a few seconds then turned my attention to the dance floor. The DJ was playing a remix of the song 'Flaunt It', and Dante returned with the drinks just as this song finished. Then, without giving me a chance to take a sip he asked, "Want to dance?" He stepped onto the dance floor, held out his hand and performed a Latin dance move to entice me.

This made me laugh as I jumped off my seat, held out my hand and replied, "I'd love to dance."

We joined the others on the dance floor and danced and danced and danced. At times we dirty danced, then we danced apart, but I could feel we fit well into each other's bodies. We had so much fun neither of us realised it had gone past midnight, until a crack of thunder broke over the thumping music. This brought us back to our table when I looked at my watch. I didn't know whether to call it a night just yet, and didn't want to seem too eager to leave, but decided to go with the flow for a little longer. By this stage, I was certain of one thing... I was dying for a cigarette, so I finally 'fessed up and said,

"I hope you don't mind, but I'm going to go outside to the courtyard and have a cigarette. I know I didn't tell you, but I smoke socially... sorry." Somewhat relieved himself, Dante replied, "Oh great... 'cause I smoke too, and I didn't know if that would be a turn off for you?" I shook my head, took his hand and led him through the crowd, and out the side door to the courtyard. We had a couple of cigarettes, laughing about each other's dance moves and trepidations about what each of us had expected from the date. There wasn't a lot of room outside, so we ended up having to stand under a tree in the light sprinkling rain. Neither of us minded as we were in our own romantic world, totally oblivious to everything and everyone around us. Dante then commented to me, "I'm heading up to Coles Bay over Christmas, catching up with some old friends... are you doing anything?"

The devilish voice in my head said *I'd like to unwrap him as my Christmas present,* and imagined what his six pack might look like. I then answered, "No, I'll be at home for Christmas as I return to work on Boxing Day."

Looking at the ground, Dante then said, "I'd hate for you to meet someone else while I'm away." Looking back at me and steeping in closer, he whispered in my ear, "I know it's only two weeks away, but will you go out with me for New Year's Eve? I'd really love to see in the new year with you by my side."

My heart skipped a beat and the butterflies in my stomach made me feel alive. After this question was asked of me, he kissed my neck twice, which sent my body into overdrive. I really wanted this man in a sexual way. But, restraining myself, I replied, "I did have a thing planned, but your invitation sounds more interesting. What do you have in mind?"

Dante replied without drawing a breath, "I'll have to make some calls and will let you know on New Year's Eve before I pick you up. I can assure you by twelve p.m. we'll be seeing fireworks at my place."

This brought a huge grin to my face and I laughingly replied, "Your place hey!" With this comment, my left eyebrow raised and I'm sure my face flushed a tinge of pink as a split-second sex-scene flashed across my mind with Dante making love to me up against a glass door, just as the New Year's fireworks boomed and sparkled in the sky behind us.

Dante then said, "It's getting late, and it's really cold, so it's probably time to go."

Looking at my watch I replied, "Oh wow… it's one a.m. I've had a great time, but time to go." I leant in to kiss Dante on the cheek as a goodbye.

Placing his hand around my waist he said in response, "Do you mind if I kiss you goodnight?"
Before I answered he kissed me so sweetly, so calmly and smoothly that I melted easily into his arms. With a crack of thunder, we were jolted from this passionate embrace and said our quick goodbyes. I ran to the car as the rain started to bucket

down. Sitting inside my vehicle, soaking wet, I reminisced about that parting kiss for a minute or more, and then turned on the car ignition. My journey home was accompanied by the radio blasting out NEIKED's 'Sexual Song'. I drove home happily belting out the tune at the top of my lungs.

Chapter 4
Foreplay Tips

Dante dashed across the street, directly opposite the club's entrance and jumped into his red Mustang convertible, hoping Ariel wasn't watching. He didn't want her to see the dent in the front of his car that was the result of a drink-driving accident with another girl he had previously met online. Once inside his car, Dante checked his hair and face in the rear-vision mirror, and grinned at himself, obviously happy with the evening's result.

His egotistical self mentally summarised how he had performed... *Boy you put in a great performance tonight... she's so sexy and completely fuckable. I was right about this one.*

He then reached for a cigarette from the glove compartment and lit one up, lounging comfortably back into his seat.

His inner thoughts kept coming. *She's definitely everything her profile stated, and she matches perfectly with my research... Jackpot!*

He winked at himself and made a tick sound with his mouth then took another drag on his cigarette, pleased with his new catch.

His inner voice became even more devilish... *She's pretty... Tick! I know she's financially comfortable as she confirmed her portfolio of properties... Tick! We could be looking at the next Mrs Prince if she plays her cards right.*

He took another long drag of the cigarette and flicked it out the window onto the road, then started the engine. He knew he'd had too much to drink, but was on a total high and began driving, unperturbed by the law.

Pressing down on his indicator and pulling out of the parking spot, Dante's conversation with himself finished with... *Just a mental note to call Brett in the morning and cancel the Christmas trip. I need to make sure no one else catches this barracuda.*

The next morning Dante rang his best friend Brett and got his voice mail. The message he left was…

"Brett, I finally met Ariel last night and I'm having second thoughts about going on the Christmas trip. Give me a call mate."

Immediately after this call, Dante sent me a text message.

It was only seven thirty and I was lying in bed, half-awake and daydreaming about last night. But I was jolted out of my semi-conscious state when my phone chimed, letting me know a text message had arrived, and of course I hoped the text was from Dante. My heart skipped a beat when I saw it was indeed from Dante, and I was on cloud nine that he followed up so soon. I opened my phone, the message reading:

TXT Dante: Hey beautiful, had a great night. Would like to do it again really soon. Thoughts?

I left it for a few minutes, then my reply began as follows…

TXT Ariel: Yes sure. When and where?

But before pressing send I deleted it, as it sounded way too eager, and had no intrigue. Sadly, my next version wasn't much of an improvement…

TXT Ariel: Thanks for last night. I could be tempted.

Still doubtful, I deleted it once again. My brain now went into overdrive, analysing every word I was writing, and I questioned whether this third response was appropriate and conveyed the vibe I wanted. I became frustrated and threw the phone on the bed, deciding to wait a little longer, and hoping a better response might come to me with a little more time and a hot coffee. I commenced my normal morning routine, stepping into the bathroom, where I formulated two possible replies. Then I took a nice long shower, and God, how I love a hot shower! Ten minutes later, I stepped out and slipped into my robe, dried my hair and rolled it up on the top of my head in a towel. I walked out to the kitchen, made some toast and a coffee, and whilst sitting at the breakfast bar consuming my morning sustenance, I responded to Dante…

TXT Ariel: Thanks for your text. Yes, I enjoyed last night too, so I'd love to meet up again. Will leave the details up to you.

I floated through that Sunday with ease, doing some domestic chores, before sitting down to produce my weekly report for work. After that, it was lunch with my mum and dad. All the time, I felt very pleased, content and yet excited about what the next date with Dante might have in store.

Returning to work on Monday, our receptionist Julie, paged me about eleven a.m., to let me know of a delivery that had arrived at the centre reception. I wasn't expecting any deliveries, so I was half-hoping Dante had sent me something, being the thoughtful gentleman, he was.

As I approached the reception, I could see a pretty bouquet of Christmas flowers sitting on top of the counter. There were white lilies, red roses, pinecones, berries and greenery spray, bulging out of the vase, which, since I assumed it was for me, put a huge smile on my face.

"You're a lucky girl. What are these for?" Julie asked. I looked around in the bouquet for a note and found a small white envelope stuck to the side of the vase. The handwritten note read:

Meet you at five thirty tonight for dinner and a movie at the Cineplex at your centre.

Instinctively leaning in and smelling the flowers, I couldn't help but think *Wow... he must be really keen... these cost a pretty penny.*

"Don't keep me waiting girl! Spill the beans. Who are they from and what does the note say?" Julie said, like an excited schoolgirl. Julie was in her mid-fifties, with long dark-brown hair always worn half up, and half down. She was a grandmother of three, had worked at the centre for twenty-five years in customer service and had a heart of gold. Some staff thought she was too needy, but I found Julie to be overly kind and I noticed that she always wanted to do her very best.

I responded to Julie as I picked up the bouquet and began to walk back to my office. But not wanting my personal life to be splashed around the lunchroom any more than necessary, I looked over my shoulder, saying, "Just a friend is all I'm going to say... sorry."

Back in my office, and after I got over the initial excitement that I was going to see him again that night, the reality struck me that I didn't have time to go home to change my outfit into something more flirtatious than my work uniform, which was red and orange with yellow swirls. I believe it was a copy of an American Airline uniform for flight attendants. I quickly thought to myself *Shit! Think fast Ariel… you need a new dress, makeup, shoes and a hairbrush.*

Picking up the office telephone, I rang Louise, the store manager at Zara's Fashion House downstairs in the shopping centre and frantically informed her of my dilemma.

"Louise I desperately need your help. I have a special event to go to tonight. Could you send me up the long sleeve figure-hugging black dress in a size eight that I saw last week in your new arrivals section, and a pair of black strappy high-heels in a size seven, and some matching jewellery please?"

"Sure can, where are you going?" Louise happily questioned.

"On a second date. Thank you so much for your help. Please put it on my account and I'll come by tomorrow and pay for it all. Got to go as I have makeup and hair to organise. Hope I can do it all in time!" I replied, as quickly as I could to get off the phone. Louise was laughing at me as I hung up. Next, I rang Jacinta at MAC Cosmetics and booked in at five p.m. for a mini makeover. With the essentials covered I raced downstairs to the pharmacy and bought a hairbrush.

At 5.25 p.m. I walked through the doors of the cinema with a skip in my step, confident that I looked quite presentable considering I had all of twenty minutes to pull the whole ensemble together. Dante was waiting by the stairs, leaning on the rail. He was looking straight at me as the doors opened and as I walked over to him, he didn't once take his focus off me. The smile on his face told me he was very happy to see me. We embraced in a quick hug and greeted each other.

"We're going to see an action film in IMAX. Hope that's okay with you?" Dante enquired.

"Thank you that sounds great… I haven't been to the movies

in ages," I replied. He ushered me up the stairs. As I passed him, he grabbed my arm and we walked hand in hand up the thirty-odd stairs to the second floor of the cinema. Dante escorted me to a table in the corner bar area and then left to order pre-movie wine and food. He returned with two takeaway drink cups in his hands.

"Here's a hot chocolate to warm you up before the movie," said Dante, sitting down across from me on the bar stool.

"Thanks. A hot chocolate is my second favourite drink after a hazelnut latte."

"I'm not a fan of coffee," he said as we both took a sip breathing in the chocolate sensation. "We've got a few minutes before the theatre opens, so I'd like to know more about you."

"What would you like to know?"

"Tell me a bit about your parents."

"Well, my mum's name is Denise. She's been a stay-at-home mother as long as I can remember, and she's your conventional housewife in every sense of the word. We are remarkably close," I said pausing for a moment thinking fondly of my mum and taking a sip of my drink. "She's always been there for me, ready to listen and provide her two cents' worth on life's rollercoaster."

"I can't wait to meet her. Do you think she'll approve of me?"

"Mum is happy if I'm happy. So yes, I think she would."

"What about your dad?" Dante asked fidgeting on his stool.

"I don't know about by father," I said, shaking my head slightly, knowing Dad never likes any man I bring home.

"Tell me about him so I can find some common ground for when we do meet each other."

"Dad's the man of the house, a traditionalist, who believes boys and girls live by different rules. He's as tough as nails and stubborn."

"I'm intrigued; what are the different rules?" enquired Dante.

"In a nutshell, boys can do what they want, but girls can't," I responded, raising my eyebrow and pouting my lips, indicating to Dante that Dad and I have never seen eye to eye on this subject.

"What does he do for a living?"

"He's retired now but was a builder back in his day.

Unfortunately, he was struck down by a major illness when I was fifteen."

"That must have been hard on your family if he was the only wage earner."

"I'll just say that his challenges definitely drove my need for financial security from a young age as we were relegated into a much poorer existence after this happened."

"At least your dad is still alive; mine died when I was five," said Dante, as a depressed look came across his face.

"I'm so sorry, what happened?"

"I'd rather not talk about if you don't mind... My aim is to find out more about you. What's your earliest childhood memory?" enquired Dante, deliberately steering the conversation away from his personal life.

"I don't remember much about my childhood, apart from dancing, singing and being on stage," I responded, going through my thoughts to come up with something more interesting.

"Come on, there has to be something unique or quirky you remember?" he said sipping his hot chocolate wanting to keep me engaged.

"Okay, okay... let me think... I've never been asked this question before on a date."

"Surely there's a memory about... playing with... boys?" he said teasingly.

"I got one, but I don't think it's what you're after."

"Give it to me," he said, leaning back on his stool.

"I was about four years old and wore my favourite costume which was a baby pink ballerina tutu. My brother was seven and on this particular day had three mates over: Adam, Ben and Oliver. We were all outside playing tag. It was Adam's turn to be 'up.' The four of us were running away from him around our farmhouse. I was laughing gleefully because I loved the fact that I was outrunning the boys. I bet if my father saw me, he would have said something like 'That's my girl... keep running. No boys for you!' Anyway, I remember yelling out to Adam, "You can't catch me, nan a-nan-a-na!" Then the boys all ran off in another direction down to the cattle shed. I stopped near our outside incinerator for a drink of water out of the garden tap which was attached to the wall of the farmhouse. I turned on the tap and leant forward holding back the tulle of my tutu and caught the water in my mouth. It was really cold, and my feet were getting dirty as the water hit the ground. As I was drinking, from the corner of my eye, I saw a large black snake moving down the bricks of the incinerator wall. I remember the hair stood up on the back of my neck," I stopped for a second shrugging my shoulders and neck as telling the story had brought back the exact feelings I was describing. Dante sat patiently waiting to hear what I did. I continued after the cold shiver had finished.

"I was struck for a split second consumed with fear, and I recollect just staring at the snake as it made it's way onto the ground near me, my heart racing. I said, "Daddy" in a really quiet voice thinking the snake wouldn't hear me, but my dad would. My feet wouldn't move me to run away... I held my breath and started to see black dots flickering like stars in my eyes. I was saying "Daddy... help me" in my head, but I don't think the words were actually coming out of my mouth. I looked to my left feeling a bit giddy, picked up my brother's shovel... stared straight into the eye of the serpent and yelled, "Die you evil snake!" as I brought down the shovel head and cut off its head. I then ran away as fast as I could screaming, "Daddy, Daddy, there's a snake in the grass."

"So at least I know now to call on you if I have a snake problem?" Dante said, as the theatre doors opened signalling the movie would be starting soon.

We walked into the IMAX theatre holding hands and looking forward to watching our first film together.

Dante called me every day after our second date up to the day before New Year. He had invited me to his place for New Year's Eve, but now upped the ante by asking me to spend the weekend. His plan was to have dinner first, and then go out from his place for drinks and to watch the fireworks.

I was very excited about the plan, but also conflicted about spending the entire weekend at his condo. We had only met three weeks ago and been on just two dates, so I let my conscience decide. The good girl versus bad girl thoughts that pop up occasionally streaming in my consciousness went something like this…

Good Girl: "Isn't this step rushing it just a little too soon?" Bad Girl: "Maybe, probably, yes… but who cares… why not just take the risk?"

Good Girl: "I don't know the guy; we've only met twice?"

Bad Girl: "It's not like he's a psycho or murderer… He's a divorce therapist for Christ sake…. so it'll be okay. You can handle him. Let loose… you always do the right thing. Go get your freak on."

Good Girl: "But, should I have sex? Doesn't that make me look too easy?"

Bad Girl: "You know you're gonna let him have you."

Good Girl: "Should I give Sophia his address just as a precaution, or should I just tell Mum?"

Bad Girl: "You're a big girl now… don't tell anyone. Go away and have a secret 'dirty' weekend."

Needless to say, my bad girl won the day. I daydreamed a lot throughout the week, about what clothes and lingerie sets I should pack, and about what sex might be like with the self-proclaimed 'TemptingAsSin'.

I drove downtown to his place at the lakefront straight after work on New Year's Eve. It was a Friday, so there was peak-hour traffic all the way which delayed me by up to twenty-five minutes. So, I sent Dante a text:

TXT Ariel: Am stuck in the car near Central Station but should be there around 7.45 p.m.

TXT Dante: Can you pick up a bottle of your favourite wine and a Mars bar?

I stopped off at the drive-in liquor store for a bottle of chardonnay and then stopped again at a gas station for the Mars bar. I finally reached Dante's condo at 8.00 pm on New Year's Eve. His front door was open, and I could hear the song 'Shake It' by Metro Station playing in the background. I knocked first, then stuck my head through the door space and looked around but couldn't see Dante. I knocked louder on the door and stood there waiting. The music got to me, so I ended up dancing to the music on the spot at the front door, shaking my head and bum like the song says, singing the lyrics in my head.

Whilst dancing like a teenybopper, I noticed there were two wine glasses next to a candle burning on the kitchen bench. The heater was on giving the area an inviting, comfortable feel. The living room was directly in front of the kitchen bench, and was filled by a blue leather couch, a coffee table and a huge TV and stereo, but Dante was still not in sight. I knocked even louder on the door a third time, saying, "Hello, can I come in?"

"I'll be out in a second, come on in," Dante called out, from somewhere in another room. Within about ten seconds Dante walked out of his bedroom sipping a glass of water dressed in a bow tie, no shirt and a cooking apron, nothing else. I was caught off guard and blushed, but a primal sexual flame was ignited inside me, my eyes burning a ray into his naked body.

"Cooking up a storm, are we? Shall I shut the front door or are you expecting others?" I asked, hoping to lighten the steamy sexual tension, as I stepped into his abode.

"Yes, yes and maybe… no, only joking," Dante said with a cheeky grin.

Walking over to the kitchen window I noticed the apartments next door were very close and had their kitchen window at the same height as Dante's, so you could have a conversation with them without yelling if you wanted to. I turned back towards Dante who was standing at the entrance of the kitchen watching me.

"Dinner smells good, what are we having?" I asked.

"Well, you're having satay chicken and rice, but I'm planning on having you," he said with a sexy, arrogant ease. Trying to contain my excitement, I changed the subject and asked…

"Where would you like the Mars bar?"

"In the freezer please. I need it to be hard and cold for when I eat it… from inside you," he divulged.

But ignoring his verbal tantalising, I glided past him to place the Mars bar in his freezer compartment, my breasts lightly brushing across his exposed back as I did so.

"Would you like a glass of wine to start off the evening?" I suggested.

"I'd love some wine but allow me to open it. How about you sit up here, while I organise our drinks," Dante directed, at the same time pointing to the kitchen bench top. He moved toward me, gave me a soft wet welcome kiss and proceeded to lift me gently onto the white Caesar stone benchtop, which left my legs dangling. He then turned away to get the bottle opener from his cutlery draw. I watched as he methodically inserted the corkscrew, then slowly but firmly screwed it into the cork... I thought to myself *If this was all planned... its working!*

He then poured the wine into the prearranged glasses he'd already set up and lifted up my glass to give it to me, finally positioning himself to stand in between my legs.

"Cheers, here's to a delicious dinner," he said holding my bemused gaze with a devilish twinkle in his eyes. We both took a sip and talked about our respective days. At the same time, Dante finished off the chicken meal in his half-naked ensemble. I couldn't help sneaking a peek whenever he turned his back to me at his naked bottom, arms, back, muscly legs and the dark angel tattoo on his bicep. I was definitely smitten.

I also noticed a tattoo of a red lion in a fiery yellow shield with a golden crown on top on his right shoulder. It looked nearly identical to my family crest... *Was this a sign from the universe?* I asked myself, hoping it was.

"That's an interesting choice for a tattoo," I said.

"You like it?" Dante asked.

"Yeh I do. It reminds me of something," I said, not wanting to give it away just yet.

"I got it a couple of weeks ago, just after we met. I had faith you'd like it," Dante said throwing me another gorgeous smile. He had muscles in all the right places. Just looking at him aroused me and pushed the fleeting nervousness I had about the tattoo out of my mind.

"Dinner will take about fifteen minutes. Would you like an entrée?" he asked.

"Sure, I'm a bit hungry," I replied softly. Dante then put his arms around my bottom, drew me closer to his body and kissed me. At first lightly, then he opened his mouth and played with my tongue in slow motion, moving his hands up my back motioning to pull my shirt off. I raised my arms over my head to help him take off my skin-tight top. With my naked top half now exposed to the evening air, my nipples gradually became erect and more sensitive.

Dante threw my shirt to the floor and bent his head slightly to start sucking on my right nipple. With his left hand he massaged my left breast. Then he swapped and sucked my left nipple. He smelt so good. The sensorial combination escalated a growing heat between my thighs. I wiggled my legs a bit and Dante removed his hand cupping my breast, sliding his palm from my nipple to over my shoulder blade, steering me to arch my back, which pushed my nipple further into his mouth. I dropped my head back in response to the intense feeling.

My thighs spread further apart, but gripped his waist showing him I was wanting more. He lightly kissed me from the side of my neck down to the collar bone, across my breasts from one to the other and down the centre line of my stomach to the top of my jeans holding my back in different places as he repositioned himself.

As his lips reached the top button of my jeans, he bit the material and tugged it down with his mouth in a suggestive manner for a few seconds, his breath blowing hot on my skin, increasing my growing hunger for him.

Then he suddenly licked my stomach in an upwards motion landing on my right nipple using his exposed tongue in a circular motion so I could watch him excite me. I attempted to grab him to pull him in closer, but he continued his foreplay saying, "I haven't finished playing yet." He then gently ushered me backwards so that I was lying on his cold stone benchtop. He undid my belt and slowly pulled it out of the loops, throwing it downwards to his left on the blue tiled floor. Next, he undid the button and slowly pulled down the zipper on my white Versace ripped jeans, exposing my white lace underwear. As he kissed the top of my pelvic bone, I squirmed and arched on the benchtop, wanting more.

Dante commenced pulling off my jeans, just as the rice cooker bell went off signifying the rice was cooked. So I lay there, not moving, but questioning whether I should pull up my jeans and sit up or not. But in a deep voice Dante directed me to…

"Stay there, don't move." He dashed across the kitchen, turned off the power point and raced back to completely disrobe me of my jeans. They were thrown to the floor whilst he expertly manoeuvred my G-string off with his teeth and hands. He caressed my body up and down with his smooth strong hands for a few moments, deciding what his next move was going to be.

I wanted to string out the anticipation for my own selfish reasons as clearly, he was into pleasing me and I had an idea of what I wanted him to do to me. So, I sat up naked, grabbed my wine glass and took a sip to plan my own moves.

"Well, I think it's time we removed your apron now that I'm so unprotected," I said.

Dante undid the neck-tie of his apron string, and the black apron fell to the ground exposing a very well-endowed erect boy. I had strategically positioned my pussy just on the edge of the kitchen bench knowing Dante would step back between my thighs placing our private parts together. He kissed me passionately again, then moved down to my neck kissing me, pressing my boobs together and sucked both nipples. Then he stopped, jokingly saying, "I think I'd like my dinner wine now."

"Huh?" was my dumfounded reply as I wondered, *why the hell would you stop now?* Dante stepped back, passed me my wine glass, and then re-filled it. My bad girl thoughts then came to the fore…

Bad Girl: He wants to toy with you, so show him who's better at this game.

So… I acted like his behaviour didn't faze me. I played his little game and joined in the small talk he wanted. We spoke briefly about my drive to the coast and his cooking prowess. But I quickly got bored and became impatient for the second act of this show.

I wanted what I wanted, and I was going to get it, so I launched my own plan. I intentionally grabbed his attention by looking up and down his body like I wanted to devour him, then said,

"Hope you're up for an unconventional drinking game?"

"What are the stakes?" he asked.

"Something you might enjoy! I'll drip this wine slowly over myself and I want you to lick it off me, so it doesn't spill past my pussy," I directed, in a dominatrix manner.

"Wow, I wasn't expecting that. You're definitely… lifting the bar in creating new ways to consume alcohol. I'm certainly up for the challenge," he said, eagerly.

I positioned my crotch just a little off the bench. Then I spilt a tiny amount of wine at the top of my breast and rubbed the liquid into my boob showing him I was open to self-foreplay. He obligingly stepped forward. However, he first took the glass of wine out of my hand, then leant over me, skin to skin, pushing my upper body down with his chest so I was positioned like a ramp. "Stay there," he commanded.

He bent down and hovered his mouth just over where my vagina split, grabbed the wine bottle and ever so slightly tipped the chardonnay bottle downwards a fraction, so a small trickle went down my front in an even pace for him to suck it off my body. He did this action a couple of times, before inclining the bottle more and licking the V at the top of my vagina in even strokes, going slightly faster each time. Before we realised it, the bottle of wine was finished, so I picked up the second bottle. It was a merlot and was pre-opened for airing, so I dribbled it down my body myself. At this stage I was half sitting up on one elbow as I wanted to watch him lick my wet slit. I seeped the alcohol over my breasts, down my stomach, and across my navel so that the oral sex kept going.

Dante took pleasure in teasing me, licking me faster and harder, knowing he was making my mind and body work. He continued licking my clitoris for some time. I rode the wave driving his head down onto my vagina for added pleasure. Then just as my orgasm was beginning to well, he stopped, stood up, grabbed my wrists and pulled me to an upright seated position.

I leant over and kissed him aggressively as my hand made its way down the side of his body and round to the front touching his hard penis. I played with his hot cock for a while, moving my hand up and down as we kissed each other everywhere we could.

I was licking his nipple when he picked me up off the kitchen bench and walked with me in his arms into his bedroom. He placed me on the end of his bed, and I fell backwards, as he spread my legs wide open then licked me up, sucking longingly on my clitoris ahead of fingering me more rapidly.

My heart beat faster, all inhibitions were thrown to the wind as I grabbed onto his head pushing his face into my pink bits, wanting him to fuck me with his mouth and make me come… now. I lifted my bottom upwards pushing my crotch harder against his mouth.

"Just there, please don't stop," I whispered.

He didn't; he stroked me feverishly with his tongue in the one spot and pulled out his finger from inside me. Clasping my bottom with his hand, all of a sudden, he probed his finger up my rear, I squealed a little and then liked what he was doing as it felt even more intense. This was a first-time experience for me.

He found my hand and placed my fingers on the top of my pubic bone and pushed down, building the sensation. Enjoying the new thrill my body circled and rolled with his movements. He would bring me to the edge of climax then slow everything down… making me beg him for more.

"Please… give it to me," I said louder.

Repeating my request, a number of times, he dutifully didn't stop, and I climaxed with my pelvic region convulsing in profound waves of pleasure. He continued to lick my inner parts through the waves. So intense was the feeling, that I finally had to say… "No more, no more."

He stopped, placed himself on top of me, kissed me and then manoeuvred his penis gently to the top of my pussy. He then thrust his member inside of me making me groan and grab his back for more. He was rock-hard and I was in that dreamy land, loving every moment of being fucked by a gorgeous sexy man.

He threw me around the bed from missionary to the pretzel to doggy style, the cowgirl and the man-seat position. For about three hours we pleasured each other kissing, licking, fucking and massaging each other's bodies. I orgasmed three times and was surprised at his stamina; also, the number of times he could come and then go off again with so little time in between. He was primal, a stallion in bed and I'd never been with a man that could keep going for so long.

By eleven thirty, we were both spent, blissfully lying on his queen-sized futon bed with his bedside table lamp on, tickling each other softly. It was at this time that I had a chance to survey his choice of style and bedroom design. Like the kitchen and living room, his bedroom walls were a pale blue, but there was no lightshade; just a bulb hanging from the ceiling. His apartment was sparsely furnished and oh so clean, almost clinical in nature. There were no pictures on the walls or family photos anywhere, and no ornaments, books or health science journals. No clothes popping out of the double-doored wardrobe, no mirrors or anything that reflected that he spent time in his bedroom.

His briefcase was set down on the floor under the window and I thought, *he must be one of those rare clean freak guys who leaves his work at the office, which is a good thing.*

I ended up falling asleep in his arms; neither of us saw the New Year fireworks nor ate the chicken satay dinner.

Dante woke as the last firework cracked in the sky and looked at her sleeping peacefully beside him *and thought… You have her hooked; everything worked!* He got up, went to the bathroom and had a shower.

As he returned silently and still naked back to the master bedroom, he patted himself on the back thinking, *you're still the legend. She's a beauty.*

Chapter 5
Keys That Fit Our Locks

The clock read six a.m.; the early sun and the sea breeze wafting through the window made for a perfect day ahead, Dante thought, appreciating all of Ariel with his eyes… *She's the best one so far.*

Over the next three months I fell head over heels for 'psych-boy', which became my nickname for Dante. He was handsome; his body was like that of an adult entertainer with muscles in all the right places. He was smart, sometimes too smart. He was a gentleman and an expert lover. The sexual chemistry between us was openly evident and we had sex every day when we were together. He seemed smitten, which gave me butterflies and heaps of delightful sexy dreams whenever I thought about him. For the first three months he rang me every night if I wasn't with him, and sent me sweet and sometime raunchy text messages, saying all the right things.

I told my mum over the phone, "Mum, he's the one… I love him, and I believe he's going to propose to me soon."

Mum's more cautious reaction was, "Why do you think that darling? You have only known each other a few months. He hasn't even met us," she declared.

I then blurted out excitedly, "Well… two weeks ago, he asked me to keep the weekend of the 29th free, and last night he asked if he could meet you and Dad sometime next week. Being curious, I asked him why he wanted to meet you, and his reason was that he wanted to ask you both something important."

Mum awkwardly moved around in her chair, repositioned the phone and asked, "Have you told your father?"

"No, I was hoping you could give him the heads up. Please

tell him to be nice and not to interrogate Dante, and if he asks you or Dad for my hand in marriage you must say yes," I begged.

"Well, you're old enough to know what you want, and your father and I know you're very intelligent. If this is what you want, then we're delighted for you," Mum declared.

"Mum, do you think I'm crazy?"

"A little," she replied, shrugging her shoulders.

"He's a co-owner in a therapy clinic, so, he has to be trustworthy, honest and reliable, doesn't he?" I questioned. I was half-questioning his sanity about a proposal.

"You need a career-driven man who's strong, independent and just as smart as you to keep you happy in a marriage. A man with a PhD should be all of these. In fact, he would probably work longer hours than you do, so in all likelihood he should be perfect for you," Mum added.

"Thanks Mum… Love you. Got to go, Mia is barking, and I think I heard a knock at my door. I'll let you know what day Dante wants to come up and meet you both… bye!" I then ended the call.

It was about seven p.m., and I wasn't expecting any visitors considering it was a Monday night. I went to the office window and pulled the curtain slightly to the side to peek at who was at my front door. I could tell it was Dante from his muscular stature and hairstyle, which was exciting, but at the same time I felt a little apprehensive. Dante had not given me any indication he was coming to see me today. He had always meticulously planned every date. I needed to quickly get changed into something not so daggy to greet him, so as I ran out of the office to my bedroom saying loud enough for Dante to hear me…

"I'll be there in a minute."

Dante waited in the dark outside my oversized double fronted mahogany door. This impressive entrance matched the design of my cottage style single-storey house perfectly.

He stood in the dark nervously, his stomach churning; moving his weight from one foot to the other. He had his hands in his jean pockets, and his head was down, looking at the ground.

Dante said to himself… *I hope she takes this all right. She has to…*

as she's gonna have to know. His inner turmoil paused, and his mind stopped the frenetic activity. Then he reasoned… *Don't fucking tell her, why tell her? Let her find out for herself, then explain it away. You owe her nothing.*

I opened the door to Dante, as I said, "Hey you. What a nice surprise, come on in."

I kissed him on the lips and hugged him tightly. The scent of his aftershave smelt so good. He followed me through the formal dining area… paused in front of the fireplace, warmed his hands and then came into the kitchen.

"I thought I'd drop by on my way home from boxing. Hope you don't mind," he said, his voice cracking a bit under the pressure of what was on his mind.

"Not at all honey, I don't mind if you drop in anytime," I replied, totally oblivious to his turmoil.

"Do you want a drink?"

"What have you got?"

"I think there's some red, and a bottle of chardonnay in the fridge," I responded.

"I'll have a red please," he said, his voice softly falling away. I turned to get the wine glasses out of the cupboard, as Dante went on…

"I'm here to make a small confession and I hope it's not going to be a big deal."

My body jerked with a lightning bolt of panic running through me. The kind you get when you feel your heart sink before someone is about to tell you something negative or important! I turned around with the two empty wine glasses I'd retrieved from the cupboard as I spoke, trying to sound confident.

"What's up?"

There was an uncomfortable pause and then uncharacteristically, he broke eye contact with me and looked down at the ground, saying in a little boy voice…

"I really hope this isn't going to be a big deal… I thought you should know… I have to take medication to help me in the bedroom," he declared, like a little puppy cowering down about to be punished. He slowly looked up at me and waited for my reaction.

I tried to process this information without making him feel worse than he obviously already did. All I could think to myself was… *What the hell, what the…! Is he joking?*

I responded by saying, "Really? I mean what exactly happens?"

A spike of anger came into his voice as he replied, "I just fucking said, I have to take a pill to get an erection."

Nervously, I coughed and laughed at the same time, but this didn't improve his demeanour.

"So does this mean you're impotent?" I questioned.

"No, it doesn't mean that! Since when are you a fucking doctor?" he enquired, like it was my fault. By this time the mood between us was ice cold. I hadn't intended to upset him or make him feel insecure. My response was a mixture of embarrassment, disbelief, and sympathy for him as he was far too young, at forty, to have erection issues.

To cut the thickness in the air I declared, "I'm okay with it," and brushed it off as a throw-away line, to help improve the atmosphere. But I read by his body language and the blackness in his eyes that my last comment didn't have the desired effect. I thought to myself, *what else can I do to reassure him he is still sexually attractive to me?*

I walked over to him saying nothing and kissed the side of his neck. I started to unbutton his shirt, and got down to the third button when he flicked my hand away saying…

"I've got to go," as he turned and walked out.

About an hour after Dante had left, I sent him a reassuring text:

TXT Ariel: Sorry I took it badly. I really meant it when I said it didn't matter. I love you.

That was the first time I had said the 'L' word to him.

Dante's phone beeped signalling that a text message had been received. He was still driving home on the highway when he pressed the green 'OK' button to read the message. He had to read the message three times to get the context, then mumbled under his breath, "You lying bitch, it is a big deal to you."

In his mind, Dante was torn between returning one of two very different responses. *I accept she says it's not a big deal and could text back – 'Thank you for loving me', in which case, life goes on for us. Or I reply saying – 'I think you're a fucking lying bitch' which will challenge her lying response, and the relationship will end.*

After smoking a cigarette, he'd convinced himself of his choice. *I think I'll choose the first option.*

I received a text message, that woke me up at one the next morning, which read:
TXT Dante: Thanks for your understanding and I love you too.

However, the sting of our conversation continued in Dante's mind for days afterwards, as previous new girlfriends had ended up breaking it off with him within a couple of months of this flaw being exposed.

I had purchased tickets a few weeks previously for the Michael Bublé concert, so our next planned encounter was supposed to be for this coming Saturday, so I texted back:

TXT Ariel: Are we still on for Michael Bublé this weekend?
TXT Dante: That's fine. What time would you like me to pick you up?

Saturday evening arrived without any communication between us throughout the entire week, but he texted me at five p.m.

TXT Dante: Five minutes away.

A short time later I heard his car horn beeping in the driveway. I looked out the window and saw his Mustang revving out the front. Unusually, he didn't come to the front door, which wasn't a good start. Closing the front door behind me, I lifted my head, put on a smile and told myself… *he's embarrassed, ignore it, everything will be fine.*

I walked to his car, opened the passenger door, and slipped in, leaning over to kiss him on the cheek.

"Hi baby… I've missed you," I said, in a sultry Marilyn Monroe tone. I then recognised a smile of relief wash over his face, and immediately felt that things were good again.

We had a wonderful time together at the concert chatting the entire way back to my place about the set, the songs, and the entertainers. It was nearly midnight when Dante dropped me home. Before I got out of his car, he said, "When can I meet your mum and dad?"

"I wasn't too sure if you still wanted to do that," I replied.

"What's a good time for them?" he persisted.

"How about dinner next Wednesday… say seven o'clock?"

"Seven o'clock it is then," he said purposefully.

An awkward silence fell between us. I was unsure if he wanted to engage in physical activity after the conversation last week. I needed to ignite the sexual chemistry between us, so I instigated contact by leaning over and tenderly kissing his lower neck up to just below his ear.

"Draw your seat back so I can straddle you," I whispered in his ear in a commanding tone. He followed my instruction, sliding the driver's seat as far back as it would go.

I pushed myself up off the passenger seat, crossed over the manual gear stick and placed myself on his lap, facing him. We passionately kissed for a while, the heat between us building, hungering for more intimacy. I unbuttoned his shirt and gently ran my fingertips from the top of his chest toward his navel making sure I came into contact with his nipples. I then teased him by lightly blowing on one nipple before I traced the outline of it with my tongue. I did this to the other nipple. As I focused back on the original one, sucking and licking it, I begun undoing the zipper on his jeans. Dante pulled at the back of my hair lifting my face to his and he kissed me so vigorously, sending me mentally so wild, I wanted to rip his clothes off!

I attempted to masturbate Dante in the frenzy, but he stopped the romp making the excuse he had an early morning start.

Wednesday rolled around and in his unique way, Dante was able to charm my parents. His witty exchanges with my father showed he had listened intently to me over the past few months, regarding topics that might interest my father, like politics, stamp collections, travelling and fishing.

"Would you like a whisky mate before dinner?" Dad asked Dante.

"Sure. I have it neat."

Dad gestured for Dante to follow him into the formal dining for a 'man to man' discussion. Dad pulled out one glass and poured Dante a whisky.

"Aren't you having one, Desmond?" Dante enquired.

"No mate, I haven't had a drink in over twenty years."

"Oh, well then I'll have one for you," Dante said in a chummy manner, taking a sip, savouring the flavour, then mulling the right words over in his head to say…

"Des, I'm going to cut to the chase. I know Ariel and I haven't been together very long, but I love your daughter and I want to marry her," he said, determined to walk away from this with fatherly approval, but Dad remained silent.

"I'm asking you for her hand in marriage," Dante said, trying to prompt a response.

"If she will have you, then the two of you have our blessing," my father eventually replied.

"Thank you," said Dante, very happy with the outcome as he thought he might have to undergo more interrogation.

"Ariel is one of a kind and I want her to be happily married. I'm sure you know already that I expect a pre-nuptial agreement, as I'm sure the two of you would want to protect yourselves, especially as you are a business owner yourself," my dad concluded.

"I assure you, Desmond, that I will take care of her. I was hoping you and Denise might be able to assist me in making my proposal just perfect for your daughter."

"Go on," my father said.

"Ariel has spoken about a possible family heirloom… a three-carat cluster diamond ring. I was hoping to give it to her as the engagement ring as it sounds really special and something she would want to wear as a symbol of our devotion. Do you have it?" asked Dante.

"No. There's no antique ring as far as I know. I'll have to ask Denise," my dad responded, at the same time questioning in his mind why Dante wouldn't buy his own engagement ring.

"Thank you for looking into it. Do you mind if I drop by in a couple of days to see if you and Denise were able to find it?"

"That shouldn't be a problem... now let's go back and join the ladies for dinner as I'm starving," replied Dad.

"Lead the way sir," ushered Dante, happy his plans were falling into place so smoothly. As he followed my dad into the formal dining room, he thought to himself... *now all I have to do is confirm the location is available for the 29th.*

Dinner went surprisingly well with the four us consuming the majority of Mum's roast chicken, veggies and gravy offering. Dad and Dante bantered a lot, and told numerous jokes trying to take out the prize for being the funniest man for the evening. I think Dad won hands down, getting the loudest and longest laughs from us all. By the end of the evening, Mum and Dad were more than happy with Dante dating their daughter.

Dante and I caught up only once over the next two weeks as I had taken on a side-line project helping a friend fit out and launch their giftware business, as well as doing my redevelopment role at the centre. But we did speak most nights on the telephone, even engaging in phone sex the night before the big mystery date he had teed up with me a while ago.

After Dante's voice and instructions had brought me to climax, I put down the receiver, covered myself with my doona, turned the television on and fell asleep a short time later.

I began tossing and turning, waking up around midnight to a confronting murder scene in a horror flick blaring on the television. I clicked the 'off' button on the remote control and sat up in bed stewing over what could be happening today.

In a few hours Dante would be picking me up for the secretive date. It was still dark at four a.m., when I'd had enough of lying there completely awake. I literally jumped out of bed with excitement. Not a creature stirred; there was dead silence and just fog in the air. I turned on the bedside chandelier light and dimmed it to low, which spread a romantic yellow radiance around the room, just enough to enable me to make out shapes.

I stepped into the shower cubicle then turned on the hot water and stepped out to undress. Grabbing the razor from the vanity, I again slipped into the shower then ran the water down my back, resting my forehead against the wall. I was completely enveloped and enchanted by the steam and felt both desirable and relaxed. I sometimes daydreamed about Dante taking me from behind in the shower and felt a zing in my private parts. As this thought passed, I got on with shaving my legs, under my arms and used the trimmer to make my bush almost invisible. After showering, I blow dried my hair straight, then turned the stereo on low, as I usually danced around while dressing for a date.

"Undies first," I said to myself as I pranced over to my underwear drawer. I selected my white lace lingerie, which had a tiny gold bow set in the front of the panties, with a connecting strap across my waist to the bra. The bra was in a V-shape over each breast with a matching cross at the back and front. This set pushed up my boobs and highlighted my slim waist with the undies sitting high on my hips. My presentation wasn't vampish; I just made sure that if my clothes were removed at any point, I'd look 'smoking hot'.

I then realised I should unlock the front door for Dante, to give me more time to prepare, so I stopped the dressing ritual and raced to the front door, clicking off the lock. Dancing back to my bedroom, I ducked into the wardrobe. I'd already chosen the perfect outfit the night before and placed it on a coat hanger in the wardrobe. I had picked out a white above-the-knee-length skirt with the centre ruffle containing small iridescent silver sequins hiding the stitches. I wore a body-hugging black blouse with a plunging V neckline, with a thin black leather tie string across the front to pull the bosom in slightly. This bow would cover up the white part of the bra but gave an indication that there was definitely something worthwhile viewing underneath. To finish off the outfit, I wore a pair of black jewelled open-toe boots with a low square heel to give me a bit of height and a white angora cardigan. The look was casual, but with a hint of fun for getting up so early in the morning.

Right on cue at five a.m. the doorbell chimed, and my heart skipped a beat. I felt like I was about to go on stage and perform, and was both tense and nervous, but extremely excited. Dante opened the door to let himself in…

"Morning, can I come in?"

"I'm in the bedroom; won't be long, just putting my shoes on," which was a white lie as I wasn't quite ready for him to see me. I applied the last touches of light pink lipstick and mascara, turned sideways stroking down the front and back of the skirt making sure it wasn't riding up and it was flatteringly straight, not bulging in any areas. I then exited the bedroom and walked straight into his arms, with our embrace being loving and natural. Dante then led me out the door and held my hand saying, "Are you ready for something special?"

"I am… can't wait," I responded, like a teenage girl about to go to the prom.

We chatted freely, listened to music and told jokes during the drive up through the mountains. Dante kept coy about where we were going. I surmised he was taking me to a winery or lookout in the area. We turned off the main road onto a long gravel driveway lined with pine trees. At the end was a huge log ranch with four private cabins all arranged around a large, manicured lawn. There were horse stables, cattle troughs and horse trails leading out into the picture-perfect acreage. There were no signs of other people. Just grass, horses, cattle, and trees for as far as the eye could see up to the mountains. The ground was covered in morning frost and the smell of cow perfume was overwhelming.

I panicked thinking, *oh my god he isn't taking me horseback riding or trekking up a mountain, I hope? Shit!*

"Well… what do you think?" Dante asked.

"I don't know exactly what to say. Are you showing me this because you bought it, or am I missing something obvious?" I replied; the disappointment in my voice rang clear.

"Just hold your horses," Dante said smirking at me. He

grabbed my hand walked me a few metres away from the car to a swing hanging from a gorgeous old maple tree at the side of the main house. He gestured me to sit and as I did, he turned to face me, dropping down on one knee, and gave me a breathtaking cheeky grin as he said,

"Will you marry me?"

I blushed, smiled and laughed all at once, and was amused by his trickery in making me think something completely the opposite was his plan. I then began to laugh more as he was just millimetres away from a large pile of cow dung.

"Well… will you?" he repeated.

"Yes… of course I will, but I think you need to slowly get up, so you don't end up with dung on your jeans," I said, gesturing for him to lift himself off the ground. He stood, flicked grass off his knees and shooed a fly from buzzing around his face, then pulled out a royal blue box from his jacket pocket. Opening it for me he displayed an impressive diamond engagement ring, sparkling in the early morning sunlight.

The ring was beautiful, with a cluster of diamonds shaped like a flower with the centre stone at least a third bigger than the surrounding white diamonds. It was set in platinum gold, my favourite metal for jewellery. I'd seen the ring before as it was my Aunt Geraldine's, who had told me many years before that she would eventually pass it down to me.

But why, I wondered, hadn't Dante bought a ring himself, and I felt slightly let down that he hadn't done so. But that fleeting moment of sickness in the stomach passed quickly, as I assumed that perhaps Mum and Aunty Geraldine had gotten involved and given it to him. So, I gave into the moment, in which I had just said 'yes' to getting married.

Dante pushed me on the swing as we chatted freely about how he was able to arrange this location. It was a client's ranch, being sold due to a divorce. About two minutes later, a red-and-black helicopter came over the top of the main lodge and landed in a far field to the left of the horse stables. Dante took me on an amazing helicopter tour flying over the beautiful mountains, flora and fauna, rivers, historic sites and finally landing on a helipad on a lake. It was an experience I had never thought to do before. Upon touching down, we were zipped away for a chicken and champagne breakfast at the lake's resort.

After some tussling with dates over the next few weeks, we chose a September wedding giving us five months to plan the nuptials. I was blissfully in love with my sexy 'psych-boy', and things were going just as well at work as I was promoted to a regional role a month after becoming a fiancée. I was thoroughly enjoying the 'bride to be' rollercoaster with my two best friends, Sophia and Tracey, whom I had asked to be my bridesmaids. Together the girls and I searched through piles of wedding magazines for a wedding theme and decided on a design for my wedding dress as well as the bridesmaids' dresses. I settled on a mauve stretch chiffon, V-neck, ruched bodice, with a cold shoulder and gathered skirt, for my entourage. My wedding dress was to be an ivory fully embellished beaded fishtail design with shoestring straps off a heart-shaped bodice to show off my slim figure. I also picked a long veil, which would extend past my dress. We shopped at Fabricland for the material and I hired a local designer to make the collection, which included the boys' suits, and the flower girl and page boy outfits.

I was finally getting married! I loved breaking the news to everyone and it was quite fun telling family over the next few months. First to acknowledge the event was my Aunty Geraldine, who responded to me by saying, "I thought you'd never get married, but I hope the ring was to your liking."

My brother, who had lived in Montreal for the past twelve years and mostly kept out of family affairs, seemed happy enough for me. But my cousin Katherine, with whom I was very close, raised some doubts over coffee.

"Are you sure he's the right one? There's something not sitting right with me."

"Oh really, what is it?" I asked.

"You have only been dating a few months and now you're getting married. It took David and I four years to decide," she said, more than a little concerned.

"When you know, you just know... I suppose," was my considered response, as I tried not to be deflated by her negativity.

"Don't worry, it's just me being protective, as at the same time, I'm happy for you," said Katherine, and my mum's sister Yvonne chimed in with, "So at least you won't be a spinster. You know you gotta try for children straight away, because at 34... your clock's a-tickin'."

Over the following two months I had great fun visiting bridal shows and venue locations, obtaining quotes for the church, reception, flowers, cars, bonbonniere, music, invitations and photographer. By mid-July I had received all the quotes I needed. I booked the Fairmont Chateau for a small romantic ceremony in their rooftop chapel featuring immaculate views of the breathtaking gardens followed by an intimate celebratory dinner in The Chalet restaurant with a crackling fire and floor-to-ceiling windows overlooking a golf course.

Dante had been really busy at work. He missed most of the wedding appointments, so I thought it would be nice to organise a special casual dinner for just the two of us at my place, which was soon to be our place! I messaged him as follows:

TXT Ariel: Dinner... my place... tonight say 6.30?

TXT Dante: Definitely. Can't wait. Sorry have been wedding MIA.

TXT Ariel: Don't worry, lots to talk about re the wedding tonight.

Over chicken pad Thai, spring rolls, and a bottle of Pino Grigio, Dante and I enjoyed a wonderful evening finalising the photographer, the reception package, the menu, music, limos, flower arrangements, the cake and decorations, guest list, invitation templates and readings for the wedding ceremony. It was so much fun. Occasionally he would flash me a cheeky grin and slide his hand up my leg to distract me to get his way on a component of the event, and it worked. Over a chocolate pudding dessert, we tallied up all the wedding estimates, which came to a grand total of $43,000 for 48 guests and included the honeymoon.

Then came the stickiest subject, and one we hadn't discussed until now…

"So how are we going to pay for this?" I said, with some trepidation in my voice. This wasn't going to be easy as we hadn't even discussed our personal financial situations at this point. Being a psychotherapist, I assumed Dante had money, and I knew he rented his apartment and was paying off a car lease, but I knew very little else about his finances.

"Can your parents contribute anything?" Dante asked, pouring himself another glass of wine.

"Maybe… possibly $2,000," I said, as my mum and dad were both pensioners and had no savings. I was aware Dante's mother Sybil, was a widow and also a pensioner, but I popped the question…

"What about your mum?"

"The groom's side doesn't pay for the wedding," he declared, with a stern furrow appearing between his eyebrows, which remained there.

"Traditionally the groom's side pays for the honeymoon," I replied, a little hurt by his reaction.

"Well, my mother can't afford that, and I doubt she'll even come, so I won't be asking her," Dante snapped back, with an emphasis on the word 'mother'.

"Why wouldn't she come?"

"I just know she won't…and my girls won't be attending either," he said in an air of disappointment. I knew by the look on his face not to push for any more information on his guests' attendance.

"Well, then… it's obvious we'll have to pay for the entire wedding and honeymoon ourselves then. What do you think?" I light-heartedly questioned, in an attempt to break the mounting tension. There was silence between us for about thirty seconds. Dante then got up from the table, grabbed a beer from the fridge and returned. Looking at his feet, he took a huge swig of beer and then looked up, glaring straight at me.

For the first time, I was worried. There was a gully between us; something I didn't know about. I had a bad feeling in my stomach as Dante wasn't saying anything. He just glared at me and sculled down his beer. I was too frightened to say anything else, for fear of the wedding bubble exploding in my face.

"Look there's something you need to know," Dante finally said, with an edge in his voice.

"Okay, what is it honey?" I asked, trying to sound calm and supportive.

"I'm a recently discharged bankrupt," he said, shrugging his shoulders and turning away from me on his chair, which left me staring at his back.

"How could you have been bankrupt when you're in a partnership with Helen in the clinic?" I responded, alarmed at his declaration.

"Well… I stretched the truth a bit. She offered me a partnership before I met you. She's given me twelve months to buy in or else she's going to offer the partnership to one of the other therapists. I've been trying to get the money together, but I can't get a loan because of my credit rating."

"Why didn't you tell me this before?" I asked.

"I was afraid you wouldn't like me if I had nothing. I'm sorry I didn't tell you the truth earlier, there just never seemed to be a right time."

"I'm gobsmacked and hurt Dante, and I'm mad you deliberately chose to omit this somewhat controversial detail."

The fun and romance of the night had been totally shattered, and I couldn't look at him. I felt bad for him, but at the same time I was inwardly in turmoil. This placed me in a difficult predicament financially, considering my considerable assets and an impending marriage to an impoverished man who had lied to me.

I supposed I had created this image of what a man with a doctorate would be and have and he seemed perfect. He was too good to be true, or was I just being harsh because I felt cheated out of my rose-coloured world? I certainly had some decisions to make.

"I'll need to digest this, so you won't mind if I sleep on it?"

"I've had a few to drink, so instead of driving an hour home, can I stay here with you?" he asked. I thought to myself… *come to think of it, he's had an entire bottle of wine to himself and two beers in three hours. I haven't seen him drink that much ever. This must have been worrying him.*

"Sure," was my concession, and the only word to come out of my mouth.

I turned my back on him, left the dirty dishes on the table for him to clean up, and went to my bedroom feeling hurt and in turmoil. Dante came in an hour or so later, slipped into my bed and fell asleep spooning me. Needless to say, I didn't get much sleep that night, contemplating… *do I, or don't I marry this man?*

I woke the next morning to find Dante had already got up. I was feeling content that I'd reserved my decision regarding the previous night's disclosure. But I had resolved that I couldn't turn away from the man I loved, just because he was not as financially secure as I was. That would be really shallow of me, considering I'd never looked at any man as a 'meal ticket' to an easier life.

I was, however, most curious as to how Dante had landed himself at the point of going bankrupt. As a couple moving forward, I believed we needed to discuss the subject in detail, so that we were both on the same page. After all, honesty is the best policy, but as I went out to make things right with my betrothed, I felt yet another sting seeing a note stuck to my door, which read:

(NOTE) Didn't know if you wanted to see me after last night. Thought it would be best not to wake you. I have an appointment with a new client this morning. Call me.

Dan

"Coward!" I yelled, crumpling up the note and throwing it on the floor before storming off into my kitchen.

I did calm down throughout the day, deciding to take a more conciliatory approach. I gave him the benefit of the doubt that his note was sincere, and not more lies or just dodging the issue. I also re-examined my expectations of him, since I was surprised, he wasn't more prepared to tackle problems head on, particularly considering he was a psychotherapist who should be skilled in argument, discussion and mediation.

A couple of nights later, we did end up patching things up over the phone. Dante told me he had gone bankrupt because several years back an ex-girlfriend had used his credit card on a holiday to Las Vegas and ran up a $40,000 debt. The bills, mounting university fees for his PhD, and interest all got way out of hand. Then she wanted to separate and take the assets without any responsibility for the debt, so out of contempt for her he went bankrupt, not really realising it would have such a big impact on his financial future. He regretted his decision and felt both stupid and embarrassed in having to disclose it to me, considering his profession.

This sounded plausible and so I accepted his explanation and moved on. After that, our relationship sailed along fairly smoothly leading up to our wedding. Dante seemed happy and I was relaxed. The only downside was my savings were fast depleting as I was the one having to pay for our entire wedding and the honeymoon tickets for a chartered catamaran around the Greek islands.

Two weeks out from our wedding day, Dante gave up his apartment and moved in with me. I hadn't lived with a man since Phillip six years ago. But having Dante in my house made feel so grown up, sexy and a little bit naughty like a young girl preparing to have sex for the first time in her parents' home. It was exciting and I couldn't wait to spend the rest of our lives together. From the outside looking in, we were a power couple: very much in love and with a promising future ahead.

Chapter 6
Love Doesn't Hurt. Expectations Do.

The bridesmaids' car had arrived about ten minutes early catching the groom's bridal party by surprise. They were standing outside in the hotel's garden area containing the flagpole and proudly hung Canadian flag having a cigarette with Dante and drinking a beer each at ten forty-five in the morning. Tracey stared through the tinted window at the boys, saying to Sophia, "Oh shit… Dante looks like he's drunk."

"Really… where is he?" Sophia enquired. She hadn't seen them, as she was being distracted by her pageboy son.

"Over there," Tracey said, pointing by placing her finger on the window glass.

"Oh… You've missed them, they've gone inside," Tracey said, a little disappointed.

"I'm sure he wouldn't be drunk at his own wedding!" Sophia reckoned.

My black stretch limo pulled up outside the chateau's main entrance right on time. I was feeling calm and the prettiest I had ever felt in my entire life. I looked and felt like a princess in my ivory wedding gown, cathedral-length veil, beaded stilettos, and elbow-length gloves, with my jewellery sparkling. My dad was sitting alongside me dressed in his black suit and white shirt with a black-and-silver tie.

"You look more beautiful than ever Ariel. Are you ready to get married… my baby girl?" Dad said, with a tear in his eye.

I looked sideways at my father and for the first time in the frenzy of this wedding, I got a bit emotional seeing a tear roll down his cheek. I'd never seen my father cry. Affecting me, I then also began to tear up and my nose started to run, so I quickly pulled out a handkerchief and dabbed the corner of my eyes, then wiped my nose, trying to breathe a little deeper to calm the nerves and the emotion. I didn't want to walk down the aisle with black mascara all over my face. Not a great look to start off married life.

"Let's get this show on the road," I said to Dad.

"John... Ariel is ready to get out now, if you can get the door, I'll come around and help her out," Dad said to the limousine driver.

Sophia, Tracey and my flower girl Taylah were in the black limo positioned in front of us. The bridesmaids' mauve dresses had turned out absolutely gorgeous. As Sophia and Tracey were both a size eight, with longish dark-brown hair and olive skin they looked like they stepped out of a Grace Kelly movie.

Taylah, my goddaughter, was dressed in an ivory ballet tutu with tiny pink flowers scattered along the bottom tulle. She wore ivory ballet shoes and carried a small flower basket with diamantes and ribbons.

The three girls and my pageboy got out of their vehicle and were standing next to the limousine waiting for me to join them. Dad got out by the rear right-hand side as John opened my door alongside the curb in front of the chateau's entrance to prepare me for my ascent into the hotel and up the grand staircase leading to the rooftop chapel.

"You look beautiful ladies," said Dad as he came around the back of the limo towards them, as proud as punch about his little girl's big day.

"Thank you, Mr D," harmonised Sophia and Tracey.

"You're looking very dapper yourself," said Tracey.

"Thank you, Tracey, I spruce up all right for an ugly duckling," said Dad.

"Sophia can you take my flowers please, so I can manoeuvre out of the car?" I requested, handing the bouquet of mixed white roses and lilies to her.

"Sure. Do you want me to hold up your dress as you get out?"

"Hmmm, no I think I'll be fine," I replied, at the same time winking at Taylah. "If I look like I'm going to topple over flat on my face, someone please break my fall."

I swivelled around on my bottom and placed both feet firmly on the pavement, making sure my heels were not grabbing the beading on the bottom of my wedding dress. Dad held out his arm for me to grab, and I pulled myself up and out of the back seat. It was difficult doing this gracefully with such a long veil attached to the top of my head combined with the heavy weight of my beaded dress. Once out of the limo, the girls fussed about, straightening my wedding gown.

"Thank you for helping me out with everything today," I said appreciatively to Sophia, Tracey, Taylah and Mateo... my little pageboy.

"That's okay, chickadee," Tracey replied, with a huge grin on her face.

Sophia then passed me my flowers and whispered in my ear, "You look stunning. I'm so happy for you." She pulled away, looked over at Tracey nodding at her and then returning her attention back to me said, "Remember, if anytime you need anything, or if you wanna run we gotcha back." She smirked mischievously and began walking into the chateau foyer signalling for the bridal procession to get moving with Tracey, Taylah and Mateo in front of me.

"Shall we?" Dad asked, gesturing that we should commence the walk up the stairs. I smiled at him silently nodding twice in reply. I then took my father's arm for him to escort me up the grand double staircase and down the aisle.

The ceremony was lovely with the ambience being magnified by the natural beauty of the chateau, with the gardens and huge pine trees encircling a water feature and the aroma of the fresh flower arrangements around the venue. The small local boys' choir had angelic voices and were dressed in white robes with red collars. But all that was starkly in contrast to, and entirely ruined by the three drunken larrikins waiting at the altar.

As it turned out, Dante was smashed at our wedding. So were his two groomsmen, Joel and Brett. The three of them had gone out the night before to a bar near the chateau, had dinner, partied, stayed up all night, had Bloody Marys for breakfast, got dressed and went straight to the wedding, after first stopping off at a bottle shop to grab a six-pack of beer. This became evident during the wedding photographs, which were taken by the lake at the edge of the Fairmont grounds.

I was both shocked and embarrassed by their behaviour! Dante was oblivious to my anger. The reception wasn't much better. The three stooges hung out together and my new husband spent most of the afternoon and into the night at the bar. He did dance with me for the bridal waltz for about a minute and a half, then walked off the dance floor to leave me standing alone. Thankfully my father took my hand and spun me around the floor.

Halfway through the wedding reception, Dante did surprise me by jumping onto the stage and stopping the band mid-song. He grabbed the microphone, and yelled, "Where's my new bride?" scanning the room with his hand pointing out to find me.

"Come onto the dance floor honey… everyone… I want to dedicate the next song to my wife," he announced to all.

I walked into the middle of the dance floor.

"I love you… you saved me… so hit it boys!" The band began to play the song entitled 'On Top of The World' by Imagine Dragons. I hadn't realised Dante could sing, but he wasn't too bad at all. I stood in the middle of the dance floor swaying by myself to his serenade. I thought him so gracious, that all was forgiven by this public display of affection for me, in front of everyone.

The day after the wedding, over a buffet breakfast and hot coffees at the Chateau Fairmont, Dante and I reminisced over our wedding. He apologised to me about drinking too much leading into the nuptials, putting it down to being paranoid that I would not show up, and pressure from his mates to participate in drinking games. Towards the end of our meal Dante brought up a discussion he'd had with his mate Joel, on the morning of the wedding.

"Joel asked me if I had signed a pre-nup."

"Really?" I said, acting dumb as though I hadn't thought about a pre-nup. He had no idea how many arguments I'd had with my father over this very topic.

"Why didn't you ask me to sign one?"

"Well… I'm a glass half full, not half empty girl. I hated the thought of starting off our marriage under the proviso that it could possibly fail," I said, smitten with my new husband.

"Exactly. I trust you and you trust me. We're a good team, right?" Dante said.

I nodded.

"You know, just by marrying you gives me 5% of your ass… sorry… your assets," Dante blurted out being cheeky and looking down at my behind.

"You are not!"

"I'm only speaking out as your marriage shrink, darling."

"And what behaviour therapy do you recommend for my ass?" I responded in a sex kitten manner. I then sipped on my latte, waiting. Dante leaned over the table, kissed me softly saying "Let's go back to our room and I'll show you."

I gladly followed him to our bridal suite where he made love to me twice, followed by a hot spa together and then our complimentary, in-room, twin oil massage. We had organised a late check out at twelve p.m. and had lunch in the Wildflower Restaurant before heading off on our honeymoon adventure in the chateau's shuttle bus to the Vancouver International Airport.

Dante and I left on our flight to the Greek Islands at six thirty and set sail at lunchtime the following day to island hop for seven days departing from Paros. Our private double cabin on the 'Lagoona 420 Catamaran' was stylishly decorated just like you would expect on a luxury vessel. It was cosy and had a shower en-suite. The amount of available usable deck offered plenty of room for each of the four couples on board to have their intimate space. The sunset the first night was spectacular as we dined at the rear bar area with the other guests on fresh local Greek seafood cuisine and wine and finished our evening off making love, as quietly as we could, in our cabin till the wee hours of the morning. I felt so free and peaceful, and more 'adult' than ever, as I was now a 'Mrs' in a public setting for the first time in my life. From now on and for ever more, I am… Mrs Ariel Prince.

We pulled into Syros, an island which boasted picturesque Cycladic landscapes. The captain had organised for all onboard to tour around the seaside village for a stint of local shopping and then on to Hermoupolis, the town's central district. This was architecturally fascinating and had a living museum. This place was a walker's paradise with small streets, shops and cafes tucked away waiting to be stumbled upon. For lunch we dined on grilled octopus and sausages, galeos and ouzo, a combination that I would not generally order. But I was having a huge amount of fun immersing myself in the island's culture.

In the afternoon, Dante and I headed down to the rocky beach behind a large cream-and-white three-storey grand hotel. The beach was totally deserted so we took advantage of the secluded romantic setting by setting up our towels and striped beach umbrella behind a large rock configuration and had sex 'seaside spoon' style under our towels on the beach romping around under the canopy of the parasol like young teenagers would, hoping not to get caught. On this occasion, Dante didn't have his medication on him, so it took longer than usual to get him hard, and the act of intercourse didn't last long. But the oral '69' foreplay position on the sand was a thrilling experience with the ocean sounds and sand particles flitting around our skin.

Dante and I had so much fun for the first three days, but I must have eaten a bad oyster, or something else, at our next port of Mykonos, as I felt sick on our return from sightseeing and vomited in our cabin. I had to alight from the catamaran and stay in a hotel in Mykonos for the remaining four days, with half the time spent recovering in bed. Dante chose to continue on with the sailing trip to Delos, Amorgos and Shinoussa to party with the other six guests onboard. I was upset with him, but also realised he didn't want to hang around me and give up the opportunity of a lifetime to see such an amazing part of the world.

On his return from island hopping, we got to spend two more days together honeymooning taking in Little Venice, the ancient Delos tour, seeing the Colossus of Rhodes, which is one of the seven wonders of the world, and attending a cooking class before our scheduled return to embark on our new married coexistence. We were both expected back at our respective work places the day after arriving back on Canadian soil.

About two months after getting hitched, I received the following text from Dante about four p.m.:

TXT Dante: I just resigned. Will tell you more when I get home.

His message was like a bomb had gone off and made me feel uneasy and even mad! I hoped he hadn't been silly enough to leave his job without arranging another one to move to.

Dante arrived home at six. Without saying a word to me, he strode into the kitchen, threw his car keys on the table, grabbed a beer from the fridge and plonked himself on the couch directly in front of the TV. He then placed his feet on the coffee table and turned on the news.

I stood in the kitchen with arms folded, stunned while I glared at him and willed him to say something to me. A few minutes passed before he finally piped up…

"I know you're mad and I knew you would be. I'm sorry. I hate it at the clinic, and I hate my job, so I just quit."

"You've never said anything about hating your job before. Weren't you wanting to buy into the clinic?" I questioned. Dante glued himself to the TV and didn't respond.

"What's really going on here Dante?"

"Okay… Helen and I got into a stand-up argument over client complaints. She threatened to fire me over something I never did, so I resigned."

"Just like that, you resign without talking to me?"

"I didn't have any other option. I won't let her dominate me like that. I have a fucking doctorate. Anyway, it's not like we can't afford it. You earn heaps and your mortgage repayments on the house are pretty low, so we'll survive."

I was fuming inside, but then realised he must have gone through my property files.

"How do you know what my mortgage repayments are? I'm

sure I never told you."

"I don't remember. I'm sure you mentioned it." But, in my head I said to myself... *No, I didn't!*

"So, what are you going to do now?" I asked, rolling my eyes.

"I'm going to study and sit for an exam next year in February to become a court appointed family justice counsellor."

"What will that give you, aren't you already like a counsellor?"

"Adding it to my resume means I can break into the lucrative family court market under Section 10, Part 1, of the 2011 Family Law Act." He went on to explain...

"I've researched the Act, cover to cover, and spoken to the admissions officer. I'm eligible with my current qualifications to apply for the shorter course. A few of my law mates I play poker with have been urging me to do this for the last couple of years as they reckon there's an opening for a 'superior' report counsellor like me. Plus, the courts are overloaded with cases and the attorney general is advertising for casual counsellors to help fill the gaps for court appointed reports and mediation. Babe, I could command up to $3,000 for a private engagement at my office."

"That sounds ludicrous. Families can't afford that!"

"Doesn't matter what they can or cannot afford. Under Section 211, Division 4 of the Act, a judge, in the majority of disputes, appoints a family justice counsellor to prepare a case report to help determine what is in the best interests of the children when parents are entangled in a courtroom war. The Family Justice Services Division of the Attorney General's office will pay upfront if a judge appoints me from their panel. It's only two days' work a week, for a case."

"I suppose if it's something you want to do, who am I stop you? But you need to find yourself new employment," I responded, trying to put my foot down nicely.

"Before you go, the course fee is $2,000. I think it's a good investment so I can open my own practice someday. I'll take Helen, head on, and have this service that she doesn't offer. 'The Divorce Doctors' has a ring to it don't you think, honey?" he enquired, wanting my buy-in.

"Why on earth would you invest in a business that you hate doing for a job? This doesn't make good financial sense to me."

"I can't walk away from all my studies. 'The Divorce Drs' is a unique concept. I'm very excited about it. I was hoping you would support me studying and help pay for the certification. We can put it on your credit card and pay it off. After all, I'd be doing this for both of our futures. I could eventually look after you if we have kids," he said, virtually begging.

I was not happy with Dante's decision to resign. However, I supported my husband's dreams on the proviso he found another job in the meantime. I had major cold feet about going into debt for his business and told him we could talk about it when we were past the newlywed stage and a more solid married couple.

Dante took up two jobs over the next year and resigned from each one. He seemed depressed and his haphazard work ethic began to get on my nerves, which was exacerbated by his regular partying sessions every few weeks with his poker mates. He would leave on a Friday afternoon and return home Sunday, normally with a hangover.

I was concerned he seemed to have lost his way and was intermittently using alcohol to tackle whatever internal struggle he was having. I tried to talk to him about his erratic mood swings a number of times, but he shut me down, strongly denying there was anything mentally wrong with him.

I couldn't help a niggling feeling in the back of my mind that I could be being exploited and used by my own husband. Not wanting to believe this, as I always looked for the best in people, I recalibrated the voices in my head to trust he was possibly going through depression and just needed time and support.

He did persistently badger me about his business plan for 'The Divorce Drs'. I realised his depressive moods were attached to this business dream. This was because every time he raised the subject with me, I dodged it and he would hold a grudge for days and drink and be cold to me.

His grandiose idea was to manage a team of professionals

encompassing the disciplines of psychotherapy, psychology, dispute resolution, court reports, and co-ordinate law practitioners covering family, property and conveyancing. The clinic's target market – apparently with my help – was to be the wealthy clients who required management through an amicable or acrimonious divorce. I thought it wasn't a bad idea, but I had my reservations as clearly, he couldn't keep a job.

On a more positive note, we had an active sex life during this early stage of our marriage, doing the nasty at least two to three times per week. I was surprised at Dante's sexual drive considering his ailment, as our trysts were almost always aggressive and physically active. He certainly loved to perform sexual acts in a range of places and positions, and he relished in extended interactions of cunnilingus stimulation. Sometimes he would tie me up naked on the floor in front of the fire and tease me by eating his dessert, a small Mars bar from my vagina bringing me to my peak before he took me for his own pleasure.

We were heading into our first Christmas as husband and wife and decided it would be a perfect time to introduce Dante's twin daughters, Chloe and Zoe, to me. The girls were eight and lived with their mother, Anna. I knew Dante had not seen much of them as he didn't have an amicable relationship with Anna. Dante had told me on our first date that Anna had fallen pregnant after a one-night stand. They separated when the girls were incredibly young. Apparently, she jumped on a plane and returned home to her parents in California with no warning. Dante believed she did this to make sure he couldn't be a regular part of his daughters' lives. He was supposed to spend half the school holidays with Chloe and Zoe every year, but he reported Anna regularly stopped the time from occurring.

Chloe ended up coming from New Year's Eve till mid-January, but Zoe refused. As Dante had started a job at Central City Therapy, I took time off to look after Chloe. We had a wonderful time together going shopping, to the beach, the movies, catching up with my girlfriends, going to theme parks and hanging out at home., cooking and dressing up. Chloe was a lovely shy girl with long straight dark hair and a dimple in her cheek just like her dad. She was very close to her mother and spoke to Anna every day, but she was strangely more distant around Dante. I put this down to them not having a close father-daughter relationship.

Driving home from the airport after we saw Chloe off, Dante said to me, "That was nice having Chloe with us. Having her around makes me want another child. What do you think?" to which, I responded, "I don't know. I've always feared having children. They're such a responsibility and impact career choices for females, and of course I've always been afraid of getting fat. I don't come from a genetic line of 'skinny' genes."

"You won't get fat, come on. I'm getting old and I'd like to have a baby with you," said Dante lovingly.

"I really don't want to give up everything and become a housewife like my mum did. That doesn't sit well with me, at all," I replied.

"I think you'd be a great mum. Maybe I'll be a stay-at-home dad…" and he paused on that thought. Dante stared out the window as I drove, and his ego got the better of him…

I thought she'd want a baby, like most women do. What's wrong with her? I'd love to give up work to be a stay-at-home dad. Lord knows, I hate what I do. I don't understand, she makes enough money for me to stay at home and she has heaps in property and savings. If any couple could have a kid, it's us. We'd produce a really smart, good-looking boy. He'd take after me of course. I need to convince her to see things my way.

"Please think about it, I really want to have a baby with you," he said, turning to face me in his seat, while lifting my left hand off the steering wheel to hold it in his.

With a weak smile I looked at him saying, "Honey, I don't even know if I can have children. I was diagnosed with polycystic ovarian syndrome when I was eighteen. The possibility of me being able to conceive is very slim."

"I don't know what that is, but it sounds nasty. All I'm saying is let's look into getting pregnant. We could even go to one of those fertility specialists if we had to. Let's look into our options at least."

I admit, I was freaked out and nervous. But I was also thrilled that Dante really wanted to have a baby with me. I thought it was very sweet how thoughtful he had been. He endeared himself to me even more in being the instigator of this discussion as I would never have raised it.

After having this conversation, I did do a lot of research on fertility specialists, falling pregnant, and having babies in one's thirties. I also spoke to my girlfriends about their experiences and took their advice. I was gradually being switched on to the notion of someday becoming a mum. I often caught myself thinking about what fun it might be to have my own little girl.

Four months later, Dante brought up the baby subject again over breakfast. This time around it didn't take him too long to convince me as I'd already changed my mind; I just hadn't expressed my opinion to him yet. We sat at our kitchen bench, and I listened to his many reasons for having a baby, like 'we are both getting old and soon it'll be too late'. Dante at that time was forty-one, and I was turning thirty-five.

"I promise I'll be there to help raise our baby… I love you so much and I want this just as much," he pronounced.

Throughout this performance, I grinned the whole time, then waited until he ran out of convincing reasons, before saying softly…

"Yes, I'll have a baby with you."

"Oh my God, really? You little ripper!" he said, jumping up and down. He lifted me up off my chair and hugged me, whispering into my ear, "I'm so happy. I hope we have a boy!" He then let me go and started walking out of the kitchen saying, "I need to get dressed for work. Let's celebrate tonight. Starting tomorrow you'll have to go off the pill. Oh… and honey, no more wine for you after tonight. We've got a baby to make!"

The very next morning, I happily threw my contraceptive pills in the bin and hoped for the best. Dante had left his script for erectile dysfunction prescription on the bench next to a vase full of flowers he had pulled from the yard. I guessed he wanted me to buy his erection pills from now on. I laughed to myself while holding the script in my hand, as I saw the price label in the bottom corner. It read… $95.95 and from memory a box came with only six tablets.

I said laughingly to myself out loud… "Shit… sex is going to cost me quite a bit."

Surprisingly, after being on the pill since I was seventeen, my periods fell into line quite quickly. After four months of having sex every day, Dante thought we should consider approaching baby making both naturally and with a fertility specialist due to his erectile disfunction and my polycystic ovarian syndrome. We choose a clinic across from our local hospital, which was close to our home. At our first appointment we were taken through the various treatment options to assist us, such as fertility testing, ovulation induction, surgical fertility procedures and IVF. This information session was overwhelming for me. I hate anything to do with blood, guts, needles, etc., and felt nauseous at the prospect. While listening to the doctor, I mentally reconsidered the decision. But after talking it over by ourselves at the end of the meeting, we jointly agreed to begin the fertility testing process as soon as possible so that we knew if we had a chance of conceiving naturally.

Dr Frankes asked Dante to make an appointment the following week somewhere between the 6th and 8th of October to donate a sperm specimen. He also booked me in for exploratory surgery in five weeks' time, on the first Friday in November, to check out my lady bits and uncover any impediments I had to getting pregnant.

Dante definitely had the easier job in 'tossing off' to a girlie magazine, while I had to do the hard stuff from start to finish and go through all the procedures and hormone injections. The thought of all this invasive stuff often made me feel ill. I went by myself for my exploratory fertility testing procedures at the clinic. A pretty red-haired nurse took me from reception to a small cubicle beside the theatre. She ushered me in saying, "Your procedures today will take about thirty minutes, so you'll be out in no time. Can you please remove your clothes and personal items like watches and rings, and put them in the box provided just there beside you? Then you'll need to put the white surgical gown on that I've left just there for you in the clear cellophane packaging. There is also a white hair net, underwear and socks for you to wear. If you have any questions I'm just around the corner. Julianne will come and get you in a few minutes to go over some final paperwork and take some blood samples."

"Thanks," I said, a little stressed at the procedure I was about to go through.

About ten minutes later I was taken into a pathology room with Julianne, where I tried to distract myself by looking away at a flower calendar on the wall, as blood was taken from my right arm. I'd never been comfortable with blood tests and needles. My stomach churned. I also had to give a urine sample.

"It will take a short while to get the urine result and a few days for the blood tests, so if you could please wait for the doctor in your cubicle, that would be great," Julianne said.

"Sure," I nodded, glad to have completed this first step. About half an hour later, Dr Frankes finally arrived. I'd been catching up on my celebrity gossip, reading *People Magazine's* August edition, and was totally consumed by the article entitled 'Brad and Angelina On the Red Carpet'. Brad Pitt was one of my "Hall Pass" guys along with Pierce Brosnan, Mr Sheffield, Patrick Swayze and Cristiano Ronaldo. Even newly married, I wouldn't turn Brad Pitt down.

"I've got some details from your test results that I'd like to discuss with you in my office," Dr Frankes said.

"Oh… okay," I replied in a somewhat shaky voice.

In my head I was saying to myself… *oh shit, something's wrong…calm down Ariel, just go with the flow, find out what it is and deal with it.*

In the short walk to his office, I was so anxious and worked up by my negative thoughts, the angst in my stomach growing painful, that I was on the verge of crying and even throwing up, with that running saliva sensation surging around my tongue.

"Sit down please Mrs Prince. You look worried. I assure you there is nothing to be worried about."

I sat down, took a tissue from the box on his desk, looked straight at him and took a huge deep breath, rolling my shoulders up and back and rocking my head from side to side, I prepared myself for whatever the doctor was about to tell me.

"Ariel, I'm happy to inform you, that you're about two weeks pregnant. Your urine tests confirm this, and your blood work should back this up, I'm pretty sure. Congratulations!"

My eyes welled up with tears and I cried uncontrollably. The impossible just became possible.

Holy shit. I'm pregnant!

Chapter 7
Things Drunk Bastards Say

The pregnancy was going well. I had morning sickness for about six weeks in the first trimester, but I was otherwise healthy; the baby was healthy, and Dante and I were blissfully going on with our everyday lives.

At the twelve-week ultrasound scan, we were informed that the fluid in the back of our baby's neck was a little thicker than the normal expected range, which combined with my age, could predispose our child to a chromosomal disorder such as Down's Syndrome. However, our obstetrician, Dr Smithton, told us not to stress about it at this stage, as he would do another ultrasound measurement at around 18-20 weeks. Even so, we left his office, more than a little worried.

The next six weeks went by for me, like a blur. I was nervous for my baby with occasional feelings of guilt for having a child later on in life. I didn't at all feel old, more like I was still in my twenties, but I hadn't realised that being an older mum meant a huge increase in the likelihood of genetic abnormalities.

I went to the 18-week scan by myself as Dante had an exam on the same day, and was worried he wouldn't pass if he had to fit in the appointment too. The sonographer Bethany said, "Everything's looking fine so far. Your baby is very active today tucking its feet up all the time. I might be able to determine the sex. Do you want to know the sex of your baby?" and without any hesitation I eagerly replied, "Yes please. That would be wonderful!"

I looked up to the ceiling to pray silently to God… *Please God make my baby healthy, and if I have a choice, I'd really like a girl as I don't think I could do this again.*

Bethany put some more gel on my stomach and pressed down

on the side of my belly. The pushing movement hurt, but I held my breath, willing my baby to slow down a little so we could take a peek. Bethany pressed some buttons on the machine to take some snap shots and measurements. She swung the computer screen around to me at the same time as announcing…

"I believe it's a boy. See this thing here pointing at the screen? That tells you it's a boy."

"Wow… that's amazing, thank you!"

"That's all for today. I'll leave the room so you can get dressed," said Bethany.

"Thanks," I replied, with tears of joy welling up in my eyes, although my dreams of having a little girl were dashed.

I snapped out of my self-pity by the time I had put all my clothes back on. I felt a sudden gush of all-consuming joy envelop me as I picked up my handbag to leave. I was finally having a baby and it was a baby boy. I felt different; proud and strong.

I'd almost forgotten about the neck scan results. Bethany walked back in saying, "All ready now. Dr Smithton has received the scans, so you might want to mosey on down to his office for the results."

Dr Smithton put my mind at ease straight away when I walked into his office, saying to me, "Ariel, everything has come up fine with the scan. Nothing to worry about."

"Oh, thank goodness. I've been so worried. Thank you so much."

"From this point I'll increase your frequency of visits. You will need to see me every two weeks and then every week for the last six weeks. Please book them all with my secretary before you leave today. Do you have any questions for me at this point?"

"No… not now, but I'm sure I will, once I get over today's wonderful news."

I drove home and informed Dante, "It's a boy! We're having a son and he's just perfect."

"A son! I'm speechless. That's just what I wanted. Do you mind if I ring some of the boys and go out for a drink with them to celebrate? I'm pumped… a boy! And I think I aced my exam today for the counsellor certification… life couldn't be better," Dante said, placing his hand up for a high five from me.

We had an early dinner together, getting Chinese delivered by Uber Eats and then Dante went out to celebrate the impeding 'heir' arrival with his buddies, and I rang my parents, Sophia, Tracey and Aunt Geraldine to give them our wonderful new addition news. I was in bed by ten, sleeping like a baby.

I heard the taxi pull up outside at three the next morning. I could tell Dante was drunk as he was speaking very loudly to the driver and his speech was slow. I heard the taxi drive off, but Dante hadn't come inside the house. I got out of bed, opened the front door and saw Dante lying on the grass, pants around his knees pissing in the air. This was both a confronting and comical sight. He was so wasted he didn't realise he was urinating all over himself.

"What are you doing Dante," I called out.

"None of your business bitch… leave me alone!" he yelled back.

"Sorry… *what!* What did you just say to me?" I said, enraged at him staying out so late, arriving home absolutely plastered, and then insulting me like that.

Dante got up from the grass, pulled up his trousers and stumbled up the pathway mumbling to himself and completely ignoring my question. As he came through the front door with urine dripping from his clothes, Dante said in a drunken slur, "You're deliberately sabotaging our marriage."

"You're crazy… what would make you think that?" I scowled back at him.

"You're always on my back about my drinking… and my job… and going out with the boys… and spending too much of your money. You're just too fucking controlling… and don't have me start on about your parents," he replied, staring down his nose at me with a bizarre, crazy, contorted look on his face.

"You're drunk and out of line. I've never said anything of the sort to you… ever! Now you want to conveniently blame me for your fucked-up decisions. Grow up. You're being an arsehole!" I ranted, my voice going up several octaves by the time my tirade had finished.

"Fuck you!" he fired back.

"Go to bed and we'll discuss your stupid revelations when you're not so rotten drunk," I ordered, wanting to defuse the tension. I turned and started to walk off to the master bedroom leaving him standing in the doorway.

"Your parents are fucking pigs," he said, as he spun around landing against the wall. He used only his shoulder to steady himself, and then continued as he fell to the floor.

"And frankly, I don't like you very much either, you're a fucking ugly tramp," he declared.

But I ignored his drunken insults.

"I want… out of this marriage!" he yelled, at the top of his lungs and then physically spat at my back. I stood for a moment, frozen, faced with such bizarre and unwarranted hatred. Saying nothing more, I closed my bedroom door behind me.

Dante then stumbled into the TV room. I was full of rage towards him, but I knew that you can't talk sense to a drunk man.

It took Dante near on two days to get over his hangover. By the time he sobered up, he was back-peddling about his behaviour and rapidly apologised. He explained to me he was feeling vulnerable and paranoid, believing he was failing me and that my parents were too much a part of our lives. He also thought I was deliberately trying to get rid of him, just like Anna had done, so that he wouldn't be a part of his son's life.

To me this behaviour was appalling. His reasons for drinking himself into oblivion made no sense to me at all, as I'd done nothing and said nothing remotely close to giving him concerns. However, I turned a blind eye on this insulting delinquent event and thought… *best not to dwell on it, as we are about to bring a child into the world in a couple of months.*

I did speak to my parents about dropping around a little less to give my marriage, and Dante, the space he craved. This made him happy and he seemed more relaxed in his own home. I worked out two things: he wasn't used to having family around as he wasn't close to his mother or sisters, and he wanted to be the 'king of the house'. With Dad dropping around frequently, he was in competition for this podium; both men being extreme alpha males.

At 24 weeks pregnant, I was performing the weekend duty manager role when I felt a pain run across my stomach. There was blood on the inside of my panties, and, in a state of shock, I thought I was about to lose my baby. I immediately called Dante on his mobile…

"Can you come pick me up please and take me to the hospital, there's something wrong… I'm bleeding," I said, distressed.

"Can't you call an ambulance. I'm a bit busy and an ambulance will get you there faster than I can," Dante replied, almost without any emotion.

"Are you kidding… you won't help me? What's wrong with you, this is our baby!" I clicked off the mobile and threw it into my handbag, then radioed security to call an ambulance.

The hospital couldn't find a tear in my womb or the placenta. I was told to stay off my feet for a week and slow down at work. Dante and I never afterwards spoke about the ambulance incident, as I was too focused on keeping our baby well.

At 30 weeks pregnant I went on maternity leave as I was not coping well with the pregnancy and began experiencing false labour pains from 28 weeks.

I went into labour at 39 weeks. Dante went back and forth from the hospital to home during my delivery. However, he was blatantly upset with me that I couldn't perform an all-natural birth like we'd planned and didn't like that his son was entering the world drugged up with pain killers through me. He protested to the doctor at him giving me an epidural block several times. I overruled Dante and thought he was way out of line, and being an absolute control freak, considering *I* was the one going through the contraction pains for twenty-two long hours.

Our son, Christian Lucifer Prince, was delivered by

emergency C-section on the 20th of July at 12.19 p.m. weighing in at 6 pounds, 8 ounces. The unconditional love I felt for him was truly amazing, like nothing I'd ever felt for anyone or anything.

Chapter 8
Roll with The Punches

Dante had finally settled down at Central City Therapy, a highly regarded mental health establishment. However, he was not so thrilled with having to meet productivity targets to keep his job. I imagine this was difficult for Dante to stomach as his prior 'quasi-partnership' with Helen had not been anywhere near as business savvy.

I took maternity leave to look after Christian and thoroughly loved the experience, while Mum came over each day to help look after her new grandson, and we grew very close.

About a week after I gave birth to Christian, I was headhunted by the founder of Burger Boulevard, the third largest burger network in the country. I was offered the position of vice president of global branding, which included a very attractive salary package and additional sales bonuses, paid quarterly of up to $100,000. This three-year contract offer was $60K a year more than what I was on currently.

I called Dante as soon as I got the contract on email to gauge his thoughts about this new opportunity. He was impressed but didn't want me to take on a bigger role that included travel, as he wanted me at home for Christian. He left the decision totally up to me.

I was torn between my existing consulting role that I really loved, and the temptation of transferring to an exciting new challenge in a high-profile role with Burger Boulevard. I wrestled with which one would be the right choice for my career, while still juggling my added new title of 'Mummy'.

My mother convinced me to take up the offer from Burger Boulevard. She knows me too well, and knew I just needed to be told to accept the new challenge and don't look back. I thrived on climbing the corporate ladder and sinking my teeth into the business world of men; this was what drove me.

"Trust your intuition. You haven't been wrong yet," my mother said, adding… "you're more than capable."

I started at Burger Boulevard the second week of October just as Christian turned eleven weeks old, so Mum became Christian's full-time nanny. This new job meant that I was flying interstate at least two nights per week and over some weekends I had to compile reports and planning for my advertising, marketing and operations team of fourteen staff. It was a huge job, but I thoroughly enjoyed the challenge. The role was like nothing I'd ever done before but I learnt a lot from the founder and the president.

Dante and I had some long-term goals in place and had just about everything we wanted for now, but we both worked long hours. I thought there was nothing wrong with powering ahead professionally at this time of our lives.

When Christian was four months old, I had to go on a three-day trip to Quebec to visit some of our stores and meet with an advertising company about a local sporting sponsorship. I was able to get away from this visit a day early as my meeting with the ad agency had been shorter than expected. They had not produced a community sponsorship plan to my specifications, so my having gone there was somewhat of a waste of time. I hoped to get home well before Dante finished work, so I could create a special dinner for us. We'd been like ships passing in the night since I'd started my new job, and most evenings were consumed with Christian. Dante's car pulled up, and soon after, I heard the front door open.

"Hi honey," I said loud and clear from the kitchen.

"What are you doing home so early?" he said going into the study and tossing his briefcase on the desk.

"I was able to take an early flight out."

"Okay. I wasn't expecting you home so early. I brought home a crap load of work to do on an urgent court report. Hope you don't mind," said Dante.

I felt let down, but I understood the requirements of having to complete work at home…

"That's cool. Do you want to play with Christian for a couple of minutes before you start?" I said as I popped my head into the study.

"No maybe after."

"Sure… Christian and I have some things to do around the house anyway. I'm making my famous prawn dumplings in brandy broth. Hopefully you'll be finished by the time dinner's ready. Maybe you'll have time to bath Christian before dinner?" I said hopefully.

Whilst he smiled and nodded at her, under his breath Dante thought *I doubt it!*

In the office, Dante pulled his paperwork out of his briefcase to begin. I went back to my domestic duties and interacted with Christian, who was in the bassinet. I was secretly hoping that Dante and I might be able to spend some 'child free' time alone tonight after Christian fell asleep. I was craving an adult conversation with my husband over a romantic dinner, maybe consuming some wine, which could lead to something even more fun. At this stage, the last time we'd had sex was in March when I was five months pregnant, and I yearned for his touch to reassure me that I was still sexually attractive after having his child.

It was seven thirty and I had just fed Christian, who was napping in his cot. The house was dark except for the light shining out from under the office door. It looked to me like Dante was still working when dinner was ready.

"Dinner's ready. Do you want to join me?" I said as I opened the office door walking in. He had a medical journal open on the desk and was busy compiling a report on word on the PC. I noticed he also had Facebook and Messenger minimised on screen.

"I have about an hour or more to do. I'd rather take my dinner in here and work at the same time if you don't mind," he said.

"Sure," I said disheartened, but not giving up on my plan of a raunchy night of sex with my husband.

I brought his dinner into him, placed it on the desk, gave him a kiss on the cheek, said "Enjoy!" before I left, only half closing the door.

I then left him alone and ate my dinner while watching *Criminal Minds* on TV. At the end of the show, I cleaned up the kitchen and quietly walked along the hallway into our master bedroom so Dante wouldn't hear me. Searching my tallboy, I found my black triangle Lycra harness and chain underwear set with the Lycra choker, which had chains running off the neck and down my stomach. It was from a photoshoot I did a few years back for the Hellfire Club. It was my sexy nasty entertainment look that screamed dominatrix.

I slipped the outfit on, went to the en-suite and applied some lip gloss, deodorant and perfume and excitedly developed butterflies in my stomach thinking about the session I was about to have with my husband.

Glancing at myself in the bathroom mirror, I thought I didn't look much different now that I'd had a baby. I still fit into my clothes, but my boobs were a bit bigger, which was a good thing. A conversation then arose between my two intuitive thought streams again, which went something like this…

Bad Girl: "You're still a catch."

Good Girl: "Stop doubting yourself. There' s got to be a rational explanation as to why Dante hasn't made any advances since early pregnancy."

Bad Girl: "Be sexually aggressive. Blow him under the desk to get his attention and let him know you want him. That's what guys like. The mother in the kitchen and the tiger in the bedroom."

Good Girl: "I hate that saying, surely, woman are much more than that."

After an hour or so, I was ready. I tiptoed out of the master bedroom across to the office door and pushed it fully open, then placed my back against the door frame. I stood there in a svelte sexy pose, my boobs in full view. Dante had his back to me and was engaged in his usual nightly routine of drinking red wine, playing computer games (always based on a medieval theme) and playing Eminem from a CD running in the computer.

"Hi baby, what are you up to?" I asked, but I got no response.

I said it again, but received a shrug of the shoulders and a grunted reply of, "Nothing."

He wouldn't even look at me. He leant forward and turned up the music to a level that would wake the neighbours.

I was both startled and shocked, then infuriated and immediately felt an awful gut feeling that told me we were over.

The thought in my head was silent, but clear: *How fucking rude, you prick!*

The words that came out of my mouth were…

"Why won't you talk to me?"

Ignoring me completely, Dante beat the office table with his hands, to mimic playing the drums for the song he was listening to. Feeling like an absolute fool, I quickly walked to my room and slammed the bedroom door behind me. I then threw myself onto the bed crying. After a while, I tried to analyse what was going on between us and struggled to come up with a positive solution. It was a young marriage, now with a child, so surely there was a solution?

Ever since Christian arrived, I had noticed Dante withdraw more and more from our married life. He didn't help with any of the feeds and outright refused to help care in any manner whatsoever for his son. Christian was still waking two to three times each night for a bottle feed and with my work, I was unable to catch up on sleep during the day. Dante was always making excuses to get out of parenting duties.

His thoroughly odd behaviour led me to the realisation that Dante's attitude wasn't normal for a man who had been the driving force for us to have a child, so that should be the starting point for opening up a conversation.

Coupled with being both physically and mentally drained, I decided not to confront him that night. I was emotionally unable at that point to take on the stress, which would inevitably come out of that discussion. I resolved I needed to get on top of motherhood, change my routines slightly in the next couple of weeks, find time to sleep and then face the challenge of Dante's withdrawal. I never signed up for single parenting and would need his participation to make our lives work.

Being the end of autumn, it happened to be an especially cold night with the temperature dropping to around six degrees, and as usual, Christian's crying woke me in the middle of the night. I got up and passed the office where Dante was asleep in his office chair, then made my way to Christian's bedroom. With Christian on my hip, I made up his bottle and glanced at the clock, which read twelve thirty a.m.

It took Christian about twenty minutes to finish the bottle, but the feed didn't settle him. I sat in the chair trying to gently rock him to sleep, patting his back and saying, "Shhhhh," softy into his ear. I cried a bit over Christian's distress, as I felt exactly the same, except mine was out of exasperation. Christian laid his head on my shoulder and finally went off to sleep some fifteen minutes later. In one long seamless movement I slowly rose to a standing position and walked over to the cot. Pulling the Winnie the Pooh blanket back, I placed Christian into the middle of his bed and pulled the blanket up over him.

Turning to my left I switched off the night light and took a step to walk out of the nursery and return to bed. But the hairs stood up on the back of my neck when I noticed a dark image coming up the hallway and wasn't sure whether it was Dante or an intruder.

I quickly turned on the night light and instinctively grabbed Christian out of his cot to protect him. Christian murmured in his sleep. Dante then appeared out of the darkness at the doorway of Christian's room. His facial expression told of pure anger with his eyebrows drawn in, his pupils black and hooded, and his jaw clenched so hard that his cheek muscles stood out.

I was unfamiliar with this dark phenomenon staring at me.

Dante strode into Christian's room and exploding at me, he accusingly said, "He isn't mine you slut." He was slurring his words and swaying, while reeking of alcohol. Then just an inch away from my face, he bellowed, "You're a fucking whore… I despise you! I despise you."

Startled, Christian immediately woke and began wailing, obviously frightened by his father's yelling. In a panic I froze and didn't even breathe in case some movement set him in motion. I willed myself to not cry as I didn't want him to know I was scared, and I desperately needed to disengage from this nightmare. But Christian's wailing enraged Dante even more. "Shut that fucking bastard up," he said, with disdain. I bounced Christian up and down on my chest telepathically whispering to him, *'please stop crying, please stop crying.'*

"Shut him up or I will," Dante demanded. At the same time, I glared wide-eyed and frightened into Dante's eyes. The petrified girl inside me thinking… *Oh my God! Who is this? What do I do?'*

I was facing Dante with Christian resting across my upper torso, his head on the top of my left shoulder. Shaking, and in fear of our lives, my emotions burst open and I cried uncontrollably. But Dante continued on with his tirade…

"Say something, you fucking whore. Who've ya been fucking?"

"No one… I promise," I appealed, while Christian shrieked.

"I'm sick of hearing that fucking kid. He needs to be put down for good," he said, with an insane look on his face. I'd never seen a violent side to Dante before, but I knew that arguing with him was going to make things even worse, and I knew I couldn't get around him while he was blocking the door.

"Ha! You don't think I can hurt you. I could kill you if I wanted, little girl," he said, wanting to provoke a fight and stretching up tall like a peacock displaying its feathers. I stood perfectly still, watching his bloodshot eyes, which he seemed to be having trouble keeping open. My heart was thumping. All I wanted was to grow a set of wings, fly up into the air and blast us through the roof, away from this crazy man, but we were trapped.

"You, cunt!" he said landing a punch across my right temple and cheek with his left hand. I rolled with the punch to the ground and nearly dropped Christian, who was screaming.

"Take that, ya lying bitch!" he said.

And God it hurt… I'd never been hit before. But the adrenaline pumping through my veins didn't allow me to feel the pain for long. I had ringing in my ears and felt a pain shoot up my neck into my jawline and skull. I was down but went into fight or flight mode to secure the safety of Christian and me.

"Dante, please stop. I'm not fucking anyone," I said getting up, my face awash with tears. "Please don't hurt us. I beg you," I pleaded, getting on my feet, but backing away from him. I put my free hand up like a stop sign, while holding Christian close to my body with the other.

Dante then took up a boxing stance and started making jabbing movements with his right fist in quick repetition. I dropped my hand down as maybe he saw that as a show of defiance. I then watched petrified as he jumped up and down like Rocky Balboa in a training session, which went on for thirty seconds or so. Then his left fist swung around in an upper cut movement, stopping within millimetres of my nose. He snarled at me…

"See, you're nothing… I could kill you in one punch if I wanted." He then resumed his jabbing at me, this time making a noise with his mouth with every jab – "phhh, phhh" – and licking his bottom lip intermittently. Every so often he would step a little closer, while I stepped sideways or backwards to avoid him.

After about two minutes of drunk physical exercise he was panting, sweating and swaying. I could tell he was trying to focus in on me but was having trouble seeing clearly in the dimly lit room. I noticed his movements were slowing down, and his footing was clumsy, but he had me with my back to the window.

"Dante please stop," I implored. I patted Christian's back in an attempt to calm him down as his screaming was ear piercing in the dead of night. Dante's normally brown eyes were still black and possessed; full of rage with a misplaced revulsion of me and our son.

"Please let us go," I begged once more.

"Nope… you deserve everything ya get." He then stopped his

boxing practice, grinned at me and yelled…

"Whore!" while taking a wayward swing at my face again. I ducked and rolled the other way. Then… 'smash' as his fist hit the window. He spun around in the follow through, but lost his footing in his drunken state, and fell down like a tonne of bricks breaking Christian's wooden rocking horse.

I scrambled past Dante's squirming and bleeding body, now crunched up on the floor, and ran up the hallway and into the master bedroom with Christian. With shaking hands, I locked the bedroom door. I then moved into the en-suite bathroom and locked that door. Sliding down the side of the bathtub with Christian crying in my arms, I wept with him. My face throbbed, my chest felt like it had been crushed and my body shook in fear. I sat there listening to Dante banging and kicking at the bedroom door for what seemed like hours.

"Let me in you bitch! You're in my house now."

"I'm gonna get you," he yelled, whilst still kicking at the bedroom door.

My weeping took over from my hearing and my pounding head, but once I was out of tears, I realised the banging on the door had stopped and Christian had fallen asleep in my arms. I sat there in the dark silence for hours until sunrise, my eyelids heavy, with a huge headache and my life spinning around in my head. And I'd just had his baby… this was a huge shock to face.

My best friend had just become my worst enemy and an intruder!

Chapter 9
Secrets of The Past

Without virtually any sleep, I came out of the bedroom at around six on Saturday morning, to find out where Dante was. He had fallen asleep on the chaise lounge right outside the master bedroom. I crept over to inspect the 'thing' that lay in that space. Was this my husband or was I having a nightmare?

Standing there, the scene confronting me was appalling. I found him lying in his own urine. He had vomited everywhere with the spew all over the dusty pink lounge fabric, his shirt and jeans. His swollen wrist had his congealed blood on it, and the vomit smell was putrid. I looked at him with disgust, and a hatred began to boil up inside me.

He didn't know I was there as he was out cold and snoring. I wanted to scream at him, and I wanted to know what drove him to behave like that.

My thoughts of disgust were powerful... I wanted him to feel me rip his heart out and throw him to the curb.

These thoughts seemed to fill me with courage and strength, so I decided to let him sleep it off, and wait for him to wake up before ripping into him.

I was putting the washing on the line when he woke out of his stupor later that morning. He snuck into the master bedroom and into the shower thinking I wouldn't hear him get up. I heard the water in the shower turn on as I came back into the laundry, so I headed for our en-suite bathroom, ready to confront Dante and boot him out. He was standing under the shower with his forehead resting on the tiles, while the water cascaded over the back of his neck and head.

"How dare you hit me, you bastard!" He was startled when I said this to him, but he turned around sheepishly, and stood there naked.

"What are you talking about?"

"What the hell. Don't play dumb with me!" I responded, with rage brewing up inside me.

Sighing he said, "Honey, I didn't hit you."

"Look at my fucking face and your fucking hand and tell me you didn't do this," I howled, my heart pumping faster with his every response.

He looked at my cheek and his hands with a total blankness across his face.

"Don't you remember last night?" I questioned.

"I don't even remember getting home… I'm so sorry," he said, looking down at the ground ashamed.

"You got drunk, cornered me and Christian in his room, hit me across the face and threatened Christian's life! You abused me, oh… and you called me a slut, a whore and… a cunt and you broke the window in Christian's room." Dante didn't look up, just swished the water around on the shower floor with his feet and listened.

"You also said Christian was a bastard child."

"I'm so sorry. I had a feeling something bad had happened, but I didn't know what," Dante said, nursing his throbbing headache.

"It's all a blur… I'm so, so sorry. Nothing has ever happened like this before," he stated, looking up and straight at me.

"What the fuck… are you for real? You don't remember?" I lashed back. "Look at my face, you punched me, and you want me to accept that you don't remember. That's fucking absurd." I blurted, spitting fury at him.

"I'm so sorry baby… I promise it won't happen again… I promise you… please believe me."

"You'd better organise to get the window fixed today, and don't think this is the end of this conversation," I said, storming out of our bathroom, raving mad as I hadn't expected the response he'd given me, and I didn't know what to do with it.

By the time I reached the kitchen my head was in a tailspin. I didn't know whether to jump in my car with Christian and leave or stay. I pulled my mobile phone out of my handbag, walked to the back door, ran around the side of the house and sat at the end of the driveway on the curb. Instinctively, I dialled my mum's number as I needed her advice at this critical point.

I told my mum everything from the fragility of our marriage, his regular drunken binges, us having no sex in nine months, his lack of help with Christian, and concluded with the night's horrendously violent episode.

She listened intently over the phone occasionally saying…

"Please don't cry…

"Go on…

"Hmmmm, I'm listening…

"Really?"

I cried all my tears out of me to my mum.

"To top it all off Mum, his excuse seems to be that he has blacked out and doesn't remember anything!" I said, broken and gutted.

"Is he just totally lying to me?" I appealed, calling on her experience.

"I don't know, love," said Mum.

FUCK! I thought to myself, breathing heavily into the phone, but Mum broke the silence…

"I'm so worried for you. Is there anything you want me to do?"

"I don't know. I don't know what to do!"

"Do you want me to speak to him and find out what, heaven forbid, is going on?" Mum asked.

"No Mum, please don't. You might make things worse," I said. I quickly added, "Please don't tell Dad… I'd hate to see what he'd do if he knew." I reflected on this thought for a second.

"Come to think of it I know exactly what dad would do, and I don't know who would come off worse," I said.

"Maybe you should bring Christian and stay with us for a couple of days to let things settle down?" suggested Mum.

"No, I think I might just drop Christian around to you," I

replied.

"I'm scared if you stay there it might happen again," Mum expressed.

"I need to find out what's going on in his brain."

"You sure about this?" questioned Mum.

"I can't just walk away; we've got Christian. I need to understand and see if I can make things better before calling it quits. Maybe counselling, what do you think?" I asked.

"Okay. But if it happens again Ariel, you must report it to the police. You must!" Mum said sternly.

"Mum, I don't know if I could do that to him. He has said he was sorry, and he promised it won't happen again. It could ruin his career if this gets out," I said.

"You know I don't condone men hitting a woman Ariel. It's up to you what you do about it and your Dad and I will support you whatever decision you make," said Mum somewhat annoyed at me for my lack of decisiveness.

"Thanks Mum," I said.

"It's hard for me or anybody else to give you advice on whether to stay or leave. We don't really know what goes on behind closed doors. It's a very sensitive subject and I'm so sorry it's happened to you. I should have told you some stuff sooner instead of shielding you from men and what they can do," said Mum, like a counsellor.

"What are you talking about Mum? What haven't you told me?" I said, feeling more agitated now.

"I saw a lot of bad things in my twenties working in the Crown Law Offices. Things husbands did to their wives and what some men did to women and children. You remember Bevan, my sister's husband?"

"Yes of course," I responded.

"He hit your Aunty Yvonne a few times when they were living in Belmont Park. I can remember Jordan and Layla came over to stay with us many years ago at the farm. Little Jordan said to me... *'my daddy made my mummy bloody all over'*. I'll never forget those words from a four- or five-year-old at the time. The police were called to the house about eight times from memory," said Mum.

"My gosh, I'm shocked. I'm glad Bevan's dead then… I never liked him. As a child he gave me the heebie jeebies," I replied.

"In those days it was just brushed off, as it wasn't viewed as altogether illegal. More like a dispute, with the husband being the head of the house and responsible for the conduct of the people living in their home. So, everyone let it slide, putting the violent acts down to the husband just correcting the wife's behaviour. That's why so many women got killed in those days. Beating wives up was acceptable in my day. It wasn't viewed as a crime. Most men questioned by the police didn't even deny beating their wife or children, as it was their unwritten right to punish disobedience," explained Mum.

"That's just horse shit. A world built by men, for men."

"Things were very different in my time," said Mum.

"For instance, one of my friends was the daughter of the commissioner and she got a taxi home one night from a function. Well, she was naive, and she sat in the front seat and got sexually assaulted. The police took no action because they said it was her fault, claiming she probably flirted with the taxi driver leading him on. That's why we never let you travel in a cab. Anything like that towards a girl was just pushed aside. That was forty-five years ago. That's how it was in my day, Ariel. It wasn't called violence it was just something that happened, and everyone knew it was happening."

"So, by the sound of it, women, girls and children had no protection from their husbands, boyfriends or men in general and this type of shit was happening when I was a kid?"

"This stuff's been happening long before my time. Most of the marriage laws for the British colonies in the 19th and early 20th centuries gave men the right to hit and sexually assault their wives. I think the laws concerning domestic and sexual violence changed in the 70s."

"So let me get this straight… violence towards women was acceptable for nearly two hundred years… I'm blown away. No wonder boys are saying they are feeling displaced or less of a man. Females, and rightly so, are finally saying "No" to them and they don't like it. I'm surprised women of your generation didn't do more to stop it."

"Have you considered Dante might have grown up in a home where this was happening? It could account for what he did as a learned pattern of behaviour."

"This is all very fucked up. I never considered any of this could be happening. I have to speak to Dante and get to the bottom of this," I responded.

"Okay. Just be careful, please," said Mum.

"I can't have my marriage break up. But then again, I can't live with a person who has violent rages towards me. I never thought this would ever happen to me. This shit belongs in the realm of the poor, or the movies, but not in my world."

"How about I come over and get Christian, instead of you dropping him round? I can look after him for as long as you need. Give you two some time," suggested Mum.

"That would be great, thanks. I'll have him ready in ten minutes," I replied.

"One more thing you should probably know Ariel. Your father hit me once in our marriage when he was drunk, before your brother was born. I chose to stay and he never did it again. Your father grew up in an abusive home. His father was an alcoholic and used to lay into him and his two brothers with a cricket bat and steel-pointed shoes," Mum explained, seemingly happy to get this off her chest.

"I'm so sorry, Mum," I said.

"That's okay dear. It wasn't your fault. It was mine as I spoke up against your father."

Then standing up from the curb of my driveway I said, "Thanks Mum, thanks for listening, I hope you don't think any less of me."

"Of course not. I'll be there in about five minutes." I hung up just as Dante swung open the gate to the front fence.

"I was wondering where you were," he said.

"Well, you found me," I said, walking right past him and back into the house. Dante followed me inside and into the bedroom.

Turning on the bathroom sink tap I began to splash water over my face, symbolically attempting to wash the night's events out of my system and help my puffy red and crying face to go down. Dante came up behind me and hugged me. I shivered and squirmed out of his hold saying…

"I think we need to talk, don't you?"

"I suppose," he replied.

"Mum will be here soon. She's going to look after Christian for a few days."

"You didn't tell her, did you?" Dante questioned, apparently suddenly feeling guilty.

"Of course not! I said I was feeling really tired and needed a few days of sleep and peace."

"I'm so sorry. How are you going to hide the bruise on your face from your mum?"

"Makeup and hair, I suppose!" I responded, in a bitchy tone.

"Thank you. I know how hard this must be on you to not tell your mother. I just don't want them thinking ill of me. This was a huge mistake. I have no words to make things better," said Dante.

Mum arrived and acted like nothing was different to her usual visits. She fussed around with Christian in his bedroom as I packed his baby bag and his bedding into her car.

"You two have a nice, few, relaxing days together. Christian, Pa and I are going to have a wonderful time trying out some new foods for him like roast chicken and beef stew, your father's favourites," chirped Mum, trying to act her way out of being exposed.

After they left, Dante and I sat on our bed face to face, but not touching.

"Have you ever hit a girl before me?" I asked.

"Yes. But it wasn't my fault."

"So you have?" I said, drawing a big breath of air into my lungs in astoundment.

"Well yes. But it wasn't intentional."

"Who was it?"

"Anna."

"Wow...Now things make a little more sense to me." I said, nodding my head up and down in acknowledgement to myself.

"When did this happen and why?" I asked.

"I found out she was cheating on me. I was really drunk and drove over to her house and got into a fight with her new boyfriend. I went to punch him, and she got in the way."

"So, you hit her instead of her boyfriend?"

"Yes"

"Gosh... Was she hurt?"

"No. I don't think so. She screamed at me to get out and so I left."

"Did you have the twins then?"

"Yes, they were toddlers."

"Is that all that happened?"

"When I drove away, I got the drink driving charge I told you about."

"Ahhh, the pieces now fall into place. You didn't fight Anna for custody because you had hit her, and she had a witness. You were studying for the doctorate and facing a criminal charge to boot. So... you did what you did so that it didn't affect your ability to practice."

"I'm not comfortable agreeing with that summation."

"Then you're lying to yourself about your reasons. So, what you've told me is the entire story, the full truth?"

"Yep."

"Have you been violent towards anyone else?"

"Yes... my stepfather."

"Why?"

"He used to beat up my mum and us kids. So, when I was twenty-three years old, I lost it after he stuck a gun at my little sister's head in one of his nightly rages. I karate kicked him, knocking him out and sent the gun flying."

"Oh shit! Really?"

"Yeah, he did shit like that to us all the time. He once hit my older sister with a steel rod and fractured her jaw, and… he used to whip my little sister with rope and rulers until her skin bled. My mum, she suffered terribly. He was a corrections officer and an alcoholic, and often took out his job frustrations on us."

"He deserved what he got then. I hope you kicked his arse, so he never did it again."

"Hmmm," Dante nodded, adding, "Well Mum and my stepdad split up after that."

"I'm sorry to hear that happened to you and your mum."

"You know, my little sister has had a string of bad relationships, and so she's a bit of a junkie now. She's so fucked up because of him.

"My older sister, engaged an attorney to sue my stepfather for psychological damage, but dropped the action after Mum convinced her not to proceed."

"I understand now, why you don't speak to your stepfather. You've never told me anything about him."

"I don't think about him."

"So it sounds like there are a few things we don't know about each other."

"Maybe."

"Are you happy in our marriage, Dante?"

"Well… yeah… I think so."

"That wasn't very convincing."

"Well, if you want to know, sometimes I feel less of a man around you. I didn't think your job or what you've achieved would impact me, but inevitably they do. You are like a 'property gold lotto winner' who is also extremely successful in your profession and you earn shit loads of money doing it. I'm a bit jealous and envious."

"Are you saying, that, through no fault of my own, I inadvertently make you feel less of a man because of my assets and my job?"

Dante just nodded in response.

"So the way you feel, and your actions last night are somehow my fault?"

"No... It's hard to feel like a real man around someone who doesn't really need a man."

"I'm sorry that what I've got makes you feel like that. I don't want you to feel inferior to me. We are a partnership. What can I do to make you feel better about us?"

"Well, what about we open a joint bank account? After all, we have been married for nearly a year."

"You know this subject is touchy with me. Why do we need this when I've already given you the supplementary American Express card which gets paid out of my account?"

"Married couples join finances. That's just how it goes, and I don't understand why you don't see your position on money is unusual."

"I'm not overly comfortable with this, but I'll do it for us, if it will make you happier on one condition... only half our wages go into this joint account and this account then pays all our household bills."

"I think that definitely is a step in the right direction. We can go down to the bank this week. I think you could also help me get my credit rating back."

"How?" I said, feeling uneasy with where this compromising was going.

"If you put me on your mortgages then I get my rating back. What do you think?"

"I'm not giving you title over my properties," I asserted.

"No, I just go into debt with you silly. In essence, if you don't pay, the bank comes after me. So, I'm doing you a favour in helping you pay off your debts."

"Let me talk to my bank manager about your position, as I don't want your past financial affairs impacting on my portfolio."

"Thanks honey. I really love you."

Dante kissed me on my cheek and then down my neck. He brought his upper body parallel onto mine cradling my back and head with his left arm, he laid me down onto the bed. Speaking into my ear he whispered...

"I want to taste you. Get on top of me and sit on my face."

I knew he was doing this to get back on my good side. I now felt overwhelmingly conflicted and wanted more than anything to push him away in rejection and hurt him as a punishment. The other part of me wanted to be loved and touched as I craved affection to help mend my broken heart. So… right or wrong, I accepted his invitation.

A shiver of arousal flowed throughout my body and out my toes as Dante begun undressing me. This was something I'd always thought about doing as an oral sex position, but I never had the guts to do.

We both dropped what garments we were wearing. Now stark naked I crawled up the bed, mounted his chest, and rested one knee above each of Dante's shoulders. He then manoeuvred himself down the bed slightly, so that my thighs were on either side of his head, straddling his ears. Lowering my fanny down so that my pubis was up against his nose, he aggressively grabbed each bottom cheek with each hand and pushed his mouth around my labia.

He began by softly stroking my clitoris with his tongue in up and down movements. I placed my hands onto the wall and pushed my bottom into him in a grinding motion. His flicking tongue stimulated and sucked on my clitoris, then gradually quickened in step with my quicker beating heart and my faster breathing.

"Oh my God! Keep going, please" I said, as my face became flushed.

"Don't stop. Just there!" I said, pushing my vagina harder onto his mouth to control where his tongue was searching, and applying more pressure to my magical spot.

"Oh my God… oh my God… Ah, ha… Yes!" I felt the rhythmic pumping contractions in the outer part of my vagina and all the way around to my anus. The intense pulses continued for a full twenty seconds.

Dante was still licking my vagina until I finally stepped off his face and collapsed onto the bed beside him, silently grinning and thinking to myself… *that was almost pornographic. Carnal really. I like it. I'd want to do it again… a lot.*

"Thank you. That was amazing," I said, as I rolled over and placed my arm across his chest to cuddle up to him. Lying there, I was in two minds as to whether or not, to instigate further sex, but I didn't as I was happily content in my orgasmic afterglow.

A few minutes later Dante got up saying, "I'm going to go wash my car."

"Okay," I said, as I didn't care what he did. I had been more than satisfied.

Chapter 10
Denial is a Dangerous Drug

After Christmas, Dante handed in his resignation to Central City Therapy giving them two weeks' notice. His reasons to me for leaving his job being that he was under too much stress to meet their exorbitantly high monthly budgets and this had caused him to go onto anti-depressant medication. I felt terrible that he was in a state of depression over his work and so I supported his decision.

Dante took up a job with a friend of his, Randall Pointly, who owned a practice close to our home. This was his third job change since we had met. This facility only dabbled in marriage and divorce therapy occasionally, and mainly specialised in mental health disorders and occupational problems. So Dante helped them start up a fully-fledged marriage and divorce therapy service at Pointly Psychology in early February, giving him a month off work to spend with Christian.

Chloe and Zoe came to stay with us for a few days during their spring break in March, and as we had built Christian a small indoor heated pool for his first Christmas, we spent most of this time with the three kids, playing in our new pool as it lightly snowed outside.

For the Sunday we organised a lolly treasure hunt and ice-skating mid-morning and then went out for lunch with my parents at the local pub. Chloe and Zoe had a wonderful time in the kids' play area making friends with three other girls. Dante and I had a few drinks over lunch, so Mum drove us home in our car, while Dad took the kids back to our house in his car.

It had been a long day with the kids waking up at five for their treasure map hunt. I put Christian down to bed at seven and Chloe and Zoe excused themselves around nine, saying they were tired. I was feeling lethargic from the effects of the three glasses of wine at lunch, so I toddled off to bed at around nine thirty, leaving Dante to play his computer games in the office.

I awoke at about two thirty and noticed that Dante hadn't come to bed. I could hear a voice kind of singing and the beating of drums. I made my way out to the office and found Dante sitting in the office chair, with his blue headphones on, singing and playing Chivalry, a medieval warfare game and slapping his hands on the office desk to what must have been the beat of the music.

I tapped him on the shoulder, saying, "Can you quieten down; the children are sleeping?"

Dante stopped, looked at me, screwed up his face and shrugged his shoulders. Then he picked up his glass of wine and continued playing his game. I went back to bed and within half an hour later was in that mind state of being half awake and half asleep and drifted into a dream. I was running away from something in a park, and heard a man yell at me…

"You fucking bitch." My body jarred impulsively, and I opened my eyes, which brought an end to the dream, but in the dark, I could see Dante was standing over me…

"Get up you insolent cow! I'm sick of us and especially your hoity-toity attitude," he said to me, in a crazy skitzy tone. Frightened, I scrambled across the king-size mattress and jumped out at the other side of the bed to put some distance between me and him. He didn't move or make any sound. I ran around the bed end hoping to get past him in the blurry darkness. Dante stepped in front of me, said nothing and deliberately blocked the passageway.

Dante then rammed me. I bounced backwards off his chest, winded, my heart beating so fast I felt the pulses in my throat. He grabbed both my arms, held them down at my sides clasping my biceps to stop me moving and picked me up in the air. My mouth was parallel with his as I dangled in the air. He held me up against his chest, his forehead touching mine.

"Put me down Dante," I appealed. His breath stank. I tried squirming my way out of his grip. My heart was beating so fast, I thought it would explode. Fearing for my life, I was in an utter state of panic. He was so strong, and his grip was crushing my lungs. He squeezed my arms even tighter and lifted me further up into the air.

"Please Dante, put me down, you're hurting me."

"Hurting you. Watch this... Argh!" Dante yelled, as he threw me across the room.

The back of my head hit the glass sliding door and my back followed, bouncing off the glass pane. As I continued to fall, the glass made a pop and a cracking sound. I came to a stop by hitting my tail bone on the single row of terracotta tiles that met the sliding door.

I was crying, my face in between my knees, hands covering my face. I was oblivious about where Dante was. In my mind I was trying to be invisible so he couldn't see me in the dark. The victim within me searching for an answer... *Why me. What have I ever done to deserve this? He could kill me, and I can't fight him.*

Dante gave out a menacing laugh saying, "You disgust me... crying like a baby!"

He turned and walked out of the bedroom. At the door he shouted, "Bitch! You do know... we're over!"

I then feared Dante would go after Christian, and a surge of adrenaline made me spring to my feet. I was not thinking about anything, except, getting to Christian. From my bedroom door, I could see Dante's image stopped a quarter of the way down the hallway to our son's room. He was leaning back against the wall singing something inaudible. Using the walls as my guide in the dark I ran through the formal dining, turned left at the kitchen and sped to Christian's room. I grabbed Christian from his cot and ran back to the master bedroom locking the door behind me.

I laid Christian on the bed and sat beside him in the dark, calming him and myself.

"Shhhh," I said, as I stroked my baby down the side of his face with my fingers willing him back to sleep. It only took about two minutes for Christian to fall asleep again. I walked up and down the side of my bed considering my options, thinking about what to do and what might happen next.

I spoke softly to myself like I was having a conversation with my sleeping child… *You can't stay locked up in here forever. What if he busts down the door? Fuck… call the police Ariel!*

So I picked up the phone on my bedside table. Pressed '91' and panicked, then clicked the end button thinking… *What if the police come and do nothing? He'll get really agro and definitely come after me then.*

I slumped down on the carpet feeling totally defeated and helpless. My back was against the bed where my son was sleeping. I felt trapped and once again was in fear for our lives. If I called the police, I'd no doubt infuriate Dante, and his level of violence towards me would multiply. I thought… *He could take Christian from me very easily considering he knows a lot of lawyers and now judges, being a family justice counsellor. He could also take me for a lot of money in a divorce… Fear, child and money. He's got me right where he wants me.*

I was exhausted and fell asleep with my head on my knees beside the bed. I was abruptly woken sometime later and quickly reached a mental state of sheer panic hearing banging on the door…

"Let me in!" yelled the intruder. Christian woke and began to cry as the pounding on the door became louder. I picked Christian up and tiptoed into the walk-in wardrobe and hid both of us in the bottom corner behind my dresses…

"Ssshhh," I said softly into Christian's ear while swaying back and forth. I needed his bottle to settle him, but I couldn't get to the kitchen.

"I can hear that bastard son of mine. Shut that thing up!" said Dante.

I heard nothing after that and thought Dante had walked away from the door. But five minutes later a different thumping was heard as Dante began kicking the door.

"Pleeeeease… can I come in?" shrieked Dante.

My heart raced, I was frozen to the floor of the wardrobe thinking… *Fuck, he's gonna kick that door in and really hurt us.*

"Sssshhhhhh Christian… please Ssshhhhhhhhhhhh!" I burst into tears. Then a continual banging began that went on for at least three minutes. Then suddenly Dante stopped.

I awoke at six on Easter Monday morning, to Christian's baby squeals, as he was trying to wriggle his arms out of a makeshift wrap I'd put around him from a cardigan just hours before. I then realised I was on the floor in my wardrobe. I packed some bags of luggage and put Christian into the car.

As I placed our bags into the car boot, the twins came out of their bedroom, just as I was about to close the door behind us. I knew from their expression that they had an inkling why I was leaving, as there was no way they hadn't heard the commotion.

"I have to go out. Do you want to come with me?" Zoe shook her head and began to cry. Chloe said nothing and hugged her sister.

"Are you sure?" I asked.

"Yes. I'm going to call Mum so we can go home."

"Okay. I have to leave. I'm sorry. Are you really sure you won't come with me? I'd prefer not to leave you both here?" They shook their heads. I imagined Dante would be even crazier if I took Chloe and Zoe with me as well. I closed the door put the luggage into the boot and drove to my parents' townhouse.

When I arrived, I got Christian out of the car and knocked on the door. There was no answer, and I realised Mum and Dad weren't home… *Shit!* I said to myself. Sitting down in the chair on the front porch, I held Christian in one arm and dialled Mum's mobile with the other.

"Hello, you're up bright and early," answered Mum.

"Mum, where are you?"

"Your father and I are away for the weekend staying with Yvonne. Why?"

"I'm at your house."

"Why so early darling?"

"I… I… I just needed your help with something."

"Oh, sorry darling, can it wait till Monday?"

"I suppose it will have to."

"Is everything, all right?" That's when I hesitated and collected myself…

"Yeah. I'll explain when you get back. Have fun." I hung up feeling very let down and alone. I needed them here. I didn't have a key to get into their place and I couldn't go home. In fact, at this time of the day I couldn't go anywhere. I just sat there on their front porch for what felt like two hours, going over the night's events and feeding Christian.

Fed up with not having anywhere to go, my fearful feelings gradually turned into anger in that it was I who was forced to leave my own house. So I called Dante at eight thirty with the intention of kicking him out over the phone so that Christian and I might return.

In a frosty conversation that began with my demand for him to vacate, Dante once again turned things around by pleading ignorance, he said he couldn't remember anything about what he did and that I should come home.

I got in the car and headed towards Café San Marco for breakfast. Internally I was fuming as yet again, this violence and abuse was being swept under the carpet by Dante. I stewed over and over what was said in our phone call as Christian and I ate a small breakfast and I sipped on two coffees. But an energy pumped through my veins like a poison, and I just couldn't seem to calm myself down.

I drove back home and arrived just before lunch. Dante was standing in the middle of my parking space when I pressed the remote control to open the garage door. He came straight up to my window and signalled me to open it by tapping on it. Once the window was about halfway down, he threateningly said to me…

"Try that again and I'll take Christian from you."

"Try what again?" I said angrily.

"Intentionally leaving with my son."

I was speechless. This time, I knew that he knew what he'd

done to me. He doesn't 'black out' at all.

Dante strutted away from me confidently and muttered to himself… *"How dare she. She knows I'm the boss now. I'll take her for everything she's got if she pulls this stunt again."*

I stood in the garage wide eyed, strung so high I could explode. I ran my hands through my hair grabbing it to defuse my nervous anger. All the agitated voice in my head could say to me was… *You're so screwed. He knows the family court system. If you leave, he'll take Christian and you to the cleaners. I told you to get that financial agreement signed, but no… you went all mushy on him.*

I said to Christian through the window as I kicked the tyre of my car…

"I'm so stupid. He's got me over a barrel." Christian smiled up at me… oblivious of course, to the conflict going on in his world.

By the time I plucked up the courage to go inside with Christian, Dante and his girls were in the pool together, shooting each other with water pistols. I found a completely empty bottle of vodka on the kitchen bench along with two bottles of wine and two Corona beer bottles, all empty.

Dante and I didn't speak to each other until he returned home from the airport that night, after dropping Chloe and Zoe off at the airport. He was just sitting there watching TV. I walked past him on my way to bed saying, "I fucking hate you. Don't think about coming to bed tonight, or any other night." But he said absolutely nothing in reply.

An anger grew within me and gave me the courage a few days later to address the incident…

"This was the second time you've gotten drunk and attacked me. You say you don't remember doing anything, but I don't believe you. I think you're an alcoholic and I want you to give up drinking for the sake of our marriage and Christian," I said, laying down the law.

"I don't have a drinking problem and I don't recall, as you say, attacking you. I think you're making this up to sabotage us."

"So you're not going to admit to what you did to me last week, despite seeing the sliding door has been shattered?"

"I didn't get that drunk. I only had a couple of beers, and a glass or so of vodka. And as for the sliding door in the bedroom, a bird or anything could have hit it causing it to crack."

"Dante you finished off the bottle of vodka, drank two beers and polished off close to two bottles of wine.

"Nope... okay, okay, I'll admit when I mix spirits, beer or wine together I seem to black out."

"So because you black out, are you saying I'm lying, and this shit never happened to me?"

"I think you may be over-dramatising the events."

"You... you fucking... son of a bitch!" I couldn't get the right words out to insult him enough.

"I don't have a problem, so you'd better not tell anyone that I do. However, as a compromise, I'll give up drinking spirits for you. I won't give up beer or wine."

"Okay then, that's a start. I do think you need to go and see someone about your issues. Will you at least do that?"

"I'll think about it," he said, with a worrying absence of regret.

Over the next few days, I removed all the remaining spirit bottles from the liquor cupboard in the kitchen and placed them on the kitchen bench. I then poured it all down the sink in front of him.

"Will you dump these empties in the bin outside?" I asked him, pointing at the five empty spirit bottles and handing him a black garbage bag.

Standing at the garbage bin with Mia beside him, Dante fumed internally, *How dare she say I'm an alcoholic. She's just a fuckin liar. A drama queen.*

We no longer had a safe relationship space as I struggled internally with my failed marriage. So for the rest of the day, I ensured we ate separately, mobilised ourselves to be in different parts of the house and hardly spoke two words until we met up in the kitchen before heading to bed.

That night, he demanded I fund him into The Divorce Drs business, or he would consider leaving me. I was reluctant to do this, so I suggested he put forward a proposal to Randall Pointly that he operated his own specialist practice within Pointly Psychology. He could pay rent and a small percentage of profits back to Randall, as the business relied on him for everything to do with the court reports, which was increasing turnover due to new referrals to his business.

Dante did bring the idea up with his boss, but Randall was greedy and didn't want to share the profits. However, he did agree to allow Dante to put on a personal assistant and employ a casual marketer to promote the new service.

But Dante was so obsessed with owning his own business that he resigned from Pointly Psychology, without ever discussing it with me. One Thursday evening, he announced to me, "I've resigned. I finish tomorrow. We need to discuss me opening The Divorce Drs business starting on the first of May. That gives me twenty-eight days to find an office and fit it out."

"Dante, I'm not funding you into a business. You should have talked to me about this. I'm sorry."

"You're fucking kidding me. Don't you realise I own half of all this now? I've been contributing to the household, I'm on all the mortgages and I'm wanting to do this for us."

"Dante, you can't hold down a job. You were at Pointly's for all of... what? Six weeks by my quick calculation! I'm not investing money to give you a job in a career you seem to hate. That's money down the drain as far as I'm concerned."

"I can't believe you. You're supposed to support me."

"I've supported you plenty. I just don't support bankrolling a bad business venture."

Dante went to his end-of-work party the next night. I had no idea where it was being held. He arrived home still intoxicated at eleven on Saturday morning, with a female accompanying him.

"Hi. I'm Sara, a work colleague of Dante's," she said to me at the door, while holding Dante up. Sara was a large girl, mid-thirties and was wearing a baggy purple jumper and grey track suit pants.

"Okay," I said, looking at Dante and shaking my head.

"He fell asleep at my place. He wanted me to drive him back to the office to pick up his car, but I didn't think he should drive."

"Bye Dante. Stay in touch," Sara said, as she quickly departed. Dante then stumbled through the door, looking down his nose at me, but didn't say a word. I left him in the foyer and went about cleaning the house. Dante continued his binge drinking and TV watching throughout the day. There was minimal conversation between us, just the odd question here and there. By four in the afternoon, I said to him...

"Please stop drinking Dante, you know what happens when you get drunk."

"Don't be silly, nothing's gonna happen, I'm pacing himself," he said, slurring his words, while heading off to the toilet. He couldn't even walk straight.

He ended up consuming a further 2½ bottles of wine and some beers. I went to bed around nine fifteen after feeding Christian his night bottle but was awakened several times between ten thirty and eleven thirty by Dante singing loudly with his earphones on. He didn't know the neighbourhood could hear him. I was understandably concerned about having to approach him in his drunken state considering what had happened to me the last time. Christian was by now awake from the noise and was crying, but I managed to calm him down by putting him in bed with me. I lay in bed for hours listening, waiting and worrying that my intruder would show.

At one thirty a.m. on Sunday morning, I couldn't hear Dante singing any more. Shutting the master bedroom door, I went into the office and found him asleep in his chair with a glass of red wine still in his hand. I removed the glass from his grip trying not to wake him. I failed. He opened his eyes, yawned and moved to get up. Neither of us spoke and I quickly exited the room. He followed me out, so when I reached the master bedroom door, I turned to him and said...

"No... you have to sleep in the spare room. Christian is asleep in our bed."

He stopped an arm's length away from me and pointed to the

master bedroom, indicating his preference to sleep in there. But I refused…

We were in a Mexican standoff. He stood still for a moment contemplating his next move, then suddenly he leaped at me slamming me backwards into the door. He put his hands around my neck and squeezed it cutting of my air supply.

"I'll go where I please," he said, with a snarl on his face.

He then released his grip and struck my forehead with the palm of his hand, ramming the back of my skull into the heavy timber door.

"Take that, bitch! Why can't you be more like Charlotte," he said as he turned and staggered down the hallway banging into the corridor walls as he went.

That night I didn't sleep. I had an egg-shaped swelling on the back of my head and a huge headache. Although my mind was fried, I settled my heart by making up my mind that this denial could no longer go on. Violence was unacceptable and living with an alcoholic was no way to live for Christian and me. I said to myself… *Three strikes and he's out. I should have followed through and tossed him out the first time.*

In the morning after I packed up his clothes, I went to the office to close down the computer and pack up Dante's things as I planned to leave them outside the front door. It was then that I noticed a string of messages on the screen on Messenger that were between Dante and some girl called Charlotte Palmer. I read the conversation with fury swelling in my breast.

CHAT Charlotte at 8.11 p.m.: How's your evening going?

CHAT Dante at 8.15 p.m.: Working, listening to music, having a glass of wine. Ariel just brought dinner.

CHAT Charlotte at 9.27 p.m.: Wattya listening to?

CHAT Dante at 9.49 p.m.: Now – Nickelback – Burn it to the Ground.

CHAT Charlotte at 9.50 p.m.: You're a worry. LOL.

CHAT Dante at 10.10 p.m.: Want to catch up Monday or Tuesday? XXX

CHAT Charlotte at 10.13 pm.: Of course. Call me.

"Who the fuck is Charlotte?" I said out loud, slamming Dante's papers onto the floor instead of into his briefcase.

I strode out of the office like a mad woman and threw open the door to the spare room. "Who the fuck is Charlotte Palmer?" I screamed at him.

Dante straightened up quickly and said, "Why do you ask?"

"Just tell me who she is."

"She's my personal assistant. We're friends."

"Of course… she's just a friend from work. My arse! You either give up alcohol completely and go to AA or you can pick up your shit and get out. It's either your family or alcohol. Your choice. I have your bags at the front door!"

Chapter 11
Divide and Conquer

Dante and I separated the following evening on the 20th of March, after I arrived home from work. As I stood outside at the barbeque, I recalled his parting words to me were…

"I love you, but I'm not in love with you."

I was so hurt and sobbed terribly, as I realised our family, our shared future and I, weren't enough for him to give up the booze.

Dante left, clicked down the lock on the sliding door to the outdoor area and deliberately locked me out of the house, leaving Christian inside by himself. When I realised what Dante had done, I jumped the side fence using a ladder from the garden shed and knocked on our neighbour's door. I had never actually met them, just said hello in passing, but I now needed their help.

"I've been locked out of the house… could I please use your phone to call my parents?" The young Asian lady happily obliged, and stepping inside her home she asked, "Are you okay. You look like you've been crying?"

"I'm fine, but thanks for asking."

My mum and dad came straight over. I told them everything that had happened, and Dad was, of course, furious. He wanted to belt the living daylights out of Dante. Mum stayed the night with me. I was so stressed that I couldn't resist the temptation to go back to my vice, so I drove to the local gas station and bought a packet of cigarettes. I had not smoked for more than two years, but by God I felt like one tonight.

I drowned my sorrows of my imploding world with a bottle of red wine and half a packet of cigarettes sitting by myself at the barbeque area after Mum had gone to bed. I began to question all the things that I had, up to that point, refused to acknowledge. My very own inquest began…

I can't be the only girl he's intimately abused. That Rosalie chick he was seeing before me, I'm sure he mentioned she went crazy and attacked him. I bet it was the other way around. And there's more to the Anna and the twins' story. Did he hit me because he'd been cheating? How much of his past has he covered up? Nothing adds up. He omits stuff, then he gets caught and turns everything around, blaming everyone but himself. He fucks with your mind and makes me think I'm crazy. Is he somehow mental or deranged? Should I be worried?

I tortured myself till around midnight going over and over my short marriage trying to work out what had gone wrong in the two-and-a-half years, and I concocted scenarios of what Dante may have done in his past, in order to make sense of what he did to me. I made some mental notes to investigate certain people and events, utilising social media platforms to gain information. Specifically, on Anna Harper, Rosalie, Charlotte Palmer and Joel and Ivana, who were Dante's best friends and Christian's godparents. I was hell bent on digging up his past to help me understand his behaviour towards me, and could hopefully use that, if the divorce proceedings, which were no doubt coming my way, got out of hand.

The next morning, my mother informed me she was moving in with me for a while. I knew she and Dad were concerned for my health and safety, and I was relieved to have my Mum's support, especially while I couldn't effectively look after Christian. Later, I called up my boss at Burger Boulevard and asked him for a week's leave due to my separation, which he agreed to, no questions asked.

At this point, I was an emotional, mental and physical wreck. But I was determined to embark upon a fact-finding mission. I found Anna Harper through Facebook. She was short like me, very skinny, strawberry blonde bobbed hair, high cheekbones and I thought quite pretty. To start, I sent a friend request to her in the hope I could communicate with her via Facebook. I also found her profile on LinkedIn, as Anna worked for the government, overseeing homeless shelter projects.

I didn't have Rosalie's last name, but I knew she had worked for Samsung. I contacted the company, but no one by the name of

Rosalie worked there. I contacted the building manager at the apartment where Dante used to live, to ask if they knew Rosalie's last name as she had at one time lived there with Dante. Unfortunately, the man didn't remember her last name, so it looked like Rosalie might be a dead end.

I then called Ivana and found out that Dante was staying with them.

"Did he tell you what he did?" I enquired.

"No, he didn't elaborate too much to me last night. All he said was the marriage was over, as there were too many problems and he wasn't in love with you any more. I'm so sorry Ariel," said Ivana, sincerely.

"He spoke about other shit, but I took it as him just mouthing off with his elitist attitude. I went to bed and left the two boys up drinking and playing pool."

"So he didn't tell you exactly what went on? No doubt to save his reputation with his friends."

"So what happened?"

"Ivana, he has been getting drunk and violent towards me since Christian was born. Three times now. Hitting and choking me on the weekend was the last straw, so I threw him out."

"Oh no Ariel, I'm so sorry to hear that. You know, I'm not surprised I should have given you the heads-up long ago, but Joel told me to stay out of it. He protects Dante. I won't."

"Please tell me what you know."

"I know Dante beat up his ex-wife Anna, really bad. He put her in hospital, unconscious, and I imagine there has been others after her. I should have told you earlier as it sounds like he's gearing up to ruin you. He's talking about taking you for everything you have. Be careful, as he's hell bent on destroying you financially. He reckons he's going to take half your properties in the divorce and also go you for spousal support."

"Oh my God. What do I do? Why on earth does he think he can just have my assets, they were mine, way before we met? And what the hell is spousal support?"

"My advice, get a good lawyer and contact Anna. She might

tell you a lot more than I can. I'll come and see you tomorrow night after work."

"Dante never told me he was married to Anna. When did they get married?"

"Don't know when. I know they married in a quickie ceremony blind drunk in Las Vegas."

So, it wasn't her who run up the credit card, it was bills for their wedding - I thought.

"Thanks Ivana. I really need a friend at the moment."

"I'm so sorry pet," she said.

"Thanks for being honest with me, as I know you're in a hard spot."

"We'll talk more tomorrow night. See you then."

My next task was to track down Charlotte Palmer, so I rang Pointly Psychology, but was told by the receptionist that Charlotte had left the company. I pulled up Dante's Facebook profile and found her as his friend. Clicking on her profile the first thing I noticed was that she looked like me with long wavy blonde hair, about my height and she had two children and had 'it's complicated' ticked under her relationship status. I looked at the first couple of posts and saw...

Finally having lunch with Dante. Our first real date XXXX

She had checked into Seaport Cafe about thirty minutes ago. I was furious and thought *he was cheating on me with her... what a creep. So he did hit me because of her.*

"That lying son of a bitch" I said, out loud. I felt like I was going to throw up. I had to sit for a moment and take in some deep breaths. I had a coffee and a cigarette to calm my nerves. It dawned on me at this point that Dante will probably be big-noting himself to Charlotte by paying for their lunch date, no doubt, with his Platinum American Express card, making himself out to be well off. My mind was running hot and I thought... *What bullshit...More fool her...* she wouldn't know his card was a supplementary card attached to my account.

Thinking a little clearer, I said to myself... *Watch this 'psycho-boy'.* I then phoned the American Express customer service line and requested an immediate stop to that card, then chuckled to myself imagining his reaction when the card was declined.

I thought *I'd love to be a fly on the wall. This is going to be just like you see in the movies, so I imagine...*

"Sorry sir, your card has been declined," the waiter would say.

"Try it again... there's no limit on that card," would be Dante's reply.

"Okay I'll run it through again sir..." then... "Sorry sir, it has come back as declined. Do you want to pay by cash or another card?"

Dante would be red-faced for sure, clenching his fists under the table.

And that's exactly what happened, as Dante slammed his fists down on the top of the café table, making the empty plates and cups lift off.

"That fucking bitch."

"Sorry sir. Are you all right?" asked the waiter.

"Charlotte can you pay for this? She's cancelled my credit card! I'll pay you back later."

"Sure," she said, pulling out her wallet from her handbag.

"Don't worry Dan... she's just being a cow because you don't want her any more."

I then decided to send a message to Dante.

TXT Ariel: You were cheating on me with her, Have a nice lunch. Your remaining belongings will be in the driveaway at five p.m. Come pick it up. Don't try to enter my home or I'll call the police. I've already told them what you did to me on Sunday.

TXT Dante: I did nothing to you. I want to see Christian tonight.

TXT Ariel: Not a bloody chance in hell, you violent, lying prick. Your dirty past is out. I know what you did to Anna, your wife!

TXT Dante: You can't stop me from seeing my son. I'll be sending you an email with proposed custody orders.

For Christian's safety, this worried me, so I certainly couldn't agree to Dante having any contact at the moment. I rang Bexley Ramsey Lawyers and made an appointment for the following Monday to obtain legal advice.

After dinner, I tossed up which girlfriend to call as all of them were unaware of my situation. I opted not to call any of my friends in fear of how they might react to the news of my impeding divorce, and my lack of openness with them about remaining in a violent marriage. I was sure they would be supportive, but maybe not quite understand the chaos I'd been living through.

I ended up dialling the number of a long-time work associate of mine called Harvey, who had given me my first corporate job as his Assistant Retail Manager when I was just twenty-three years old. Harvey was my mentor, my only male friend and had provided me with many a wise word throughout my adult life. Harvey listened to me for more than an hour, while I wept over the phone to him. At the end of the call he said, "I think we should go for a long ride on my Harley. It'll make you feel better… what do you think? Are you up for it?"

"Sounds perfect."

"I'll call you… take care beautiful girl."

Three days later, I received an email from Dante…

Subject: Custody

Date: 24 Mar

Ariel

I propose visitation begins next week from Monday to Wednesday on a bi-week cycle. In three months, the time starts graduating by one night every quarter giving me Monday to Sunday bi-weekly within a year. This will be seen by the courts to be a suitable regime. Please confirm your acceptance by close of business tomorrow. In addition, I note you have been contacting my family and friends intentionally slandering me. You are on notice and I instruct you to refrain from this disrespectful conduct or I will sue you for defamation. Do not forget, I also studied law at uni.

Dante

I knew I had to choose my words carefully, as I was very nervous, he was pursuing me for Christian, considering his negative attitude towards our son in our marriage. I responded…

Subject: RE Custody
Date: 25 Mar
Dante

I do not agree with your proposal as I do not even know where you are living, and I imagine wherever you are it is not a suitable, stable residence for a child. You have no income to financially support Christian. You are also a violent drunk with no experience raising a baby as you have had nothing to do with Christian since he was born, and you never believed he was your child anyway.

Ariel

I thought, *That should shut him up for a while!* as I closed down my computer to take Christian to a doctor's appointment.

I was wrong. Dante's response came earlier than I expected…

Subject: RE RE Custody
Date: 26 Mar

I have moved into short-term accommodation renting a granny flat for the next ten weeks until we sort things out. It is twenty minutes from you. As I am not working, I require you to pay me $700 a week for my living expenses. As a partial settlement, I have withdrawn half of the money from our joint account. I will be forwarding to you tomorrow my proposed property agreement. Should you not agree to this proposal, I will have no choice but to make an application to the court. I will as a part of this application request an order requiring you to pay my legal fees and spousal support as urgent procedural orders. For the record, I do not have a drinking problem and have not been violent.

Dante

After reading this message, I was infuriated and thought to myself… *Lying son of a bitch! How fucking dare he think, he can take my money. He couldn't hold down a job. The prick lived off me. He's* *contributed, what… maybe $6,000 to an account with $65K in it. Over my dead body. I've got to get to the bank before he does.*

I didn't reply; instead, I ran to my car after asking Mum to look after Christian. As I went, I called my bank manager Malcolm to tell him I needed to see him urgently. I arrived at my local bank branch in record time.

I stood outside Mal's office as I could see he was in there with someone. He waved at me through the glass gesturing to me he would be five minutes by displaying his five fingers. I sat in the chair opposite his window biting my nails in a state of panic that my bank accounts were just about to be drained by Dante. A few minutes later Mal opened his door, letting his customer out and waving me in.

"What's up Ariel?" Mal said.

"I need to close the joint account immediately. I also want to close down my other two accounts and move all the money into a new separate account under my name please."

"Okay, let's look up what's in the accounts and the best way to make the most from the money." Mal said. He then typed some data into his computer.

"It's none of my business Ariel, but is there something wrong?"

"Yes. I've separated from Dante and want to move all my money out of his reach as he took $30,000 already without me knowing," I said in a panic.

"I'm sorry to hear that. I hope you don't mind me saying, but I didn't trust him when you brought him in to change all your mortgages over to joint names. I thought it was unusual for you as for years, you have been so vigilant with your property portfolio. Anyway, you have $30,000 in the joint account, $60,256 in your personal everyday saver account and $105,423.17 in your term deposit."

"Okay, then. Can you close them all and reopen new ones?"

"You won't get the interest on the term deposit as it hasn't matured to reinvest," explained Mal covering off his legal requirements under the bank's terms and conditions.

"That's fine. Just close it please," I urged, desperately wanting to disconnect everything from Dante's reach.

"I don't recommend you put the $90,000 into an account with an Eftpos card for security. How about I open an everyday account with an Eftpos card, and you have, say $5,000 in it. With the rest of the money, you put it into an online saver account. If you want to access it, you transfer the money you need back into your everyday account."

"Sounds good," I said, somewhat relieved.

"It still is a lot of money to be sitting idle Ariel. How about you put more into the term deposit. Then it's totally secure."

"Okay. Best to leave $10,000 in the online account, $5,000 in the card account and the rest as you say in the term deposit."

"Sure. This is going to take a while. How about you go get a coffee and come back in twenty minutes to sign all the paperwork."

"Will do. Thanks Mal. You're a life saver. Can you please close that joint account immediately, so he can't take any more money."

"Already done, see you in twenty.

On my way home, after signing all the required bank forms and doing a small grocery shop, Dante sent me another text message at 2.14 p.m.

TXT Dante: You fucking cow. You won't get away with this.

My heart was racing. Paranoid thoughts began running through my mind making my stomach churn. It was then that my conflicting thoughts appeared…

Good Girl: Oh, shit what's he going to do now?

Bad Girl: Nothing, he can't do a thing to you.

Good Girl: What do I do if he turns up at the house?

Bad Girl: Call the cops on him.

Good Girl: He could attack me again.

Bad Girl: Don't let him in the door, better still slam the door in his face and hope you break his nose.

Good Girl: Have I done anything illegal?

Bad Girl: It's you're bloody money. Stuff him!

Six days had passed since Dante and I had gone our separate

ways. But I was still walking on eggshells, looking over my shoulder everywhere I went, in fear of Dante following me or turning up at home. I considered what moves I had available to me at this point. I concluded Dante was weak financially and needed money, so just rip the band aid off and offer Dante a financial settlement as I was willing to pay him some 'go away' money. I considered what to offer him for two days, bouncing ideas around with my mum. In the end I constructed the following email to him and sent it off, feeling hopeful…

Subject: Separation Proposal
Date: 28 Mar
Dante

As our marriage is over, I wish to swiftly conclude our affairs. My financial separation offer equates to approximately $145,000. You keep your car ($45K), retirement funds ($25K), the $30K you took and whatever money is in your own bank account ($2K), all the contents in the office ($3K), a bedroom suite ($2K) and your personal effects including your wedding ring ($5K). I will transfer a further $32,500 cash to you within 24 hours if you accept this offer. I will refinance you off my mortgages within 60 days. I consider this to be very generous considering you came to the relationship with nothing but debt, and we were only cohabitated for 30 months. You download and complete the legal paperwork for us to lodge. I'm sure either your law studies or one of your lawyer mates can help you with this.

Ariel

Dante replied by shooting back an email in record time…

Subject: RE Separation Proposal
Date: 28 Mar
Ariel

Transfer the $32,500 into the account - BSB 0013; Account: 45623842590666S

Fine, re the refinancing. I want the weekly spousal support for a minimum of 18 months as well. I am opening my Divorce Drs busines with the proceeds from this financial settlement. See… I always get everything I want.

Do you agree to the visitation proposal? I will file for a divorce as I want nothing more to do with you.

Dante

On reading Dante's email, I was relieved he had accepted my offer. I went to the bank that afternoon and transferred the $32,500 to Dante and followed up with an email to him…

Subject: RE RE Separation Proposal

Date: 28 March

Dante

I transferred the money today to your account concluding our financial agreement. I require a signed legal document from you immediately acknowledging our financial agreement is completed in full. You will also need to sign documents for the refinancing. Instead of the spousal support, my offer is you do not have to pay me child maintenance for the next 5 years. I am seeking legal advice tomorrow regarding your arrangements for Christian and will come back to you after this.

Ariel

I met with Ben Ramsey at Bexley Ramsey Lawyers for an hour and half going over my situation and course of action on a white board.

Ben Ramsey's advice at the end of our meeting was… "It's going to cost you a minimum of $25,000 just to get your property finalised by us with the procedural court orders lodged and the separate binding contract to remove any future spousal claims, and you're looking at a further $10,000 for custody orders, or up to $110,000 in legal fees if you have to go to court over the lot. I suggest if he ends up dicking you around over the property agreement, you have us offer him a further $100,000 to walk away, if you want to get rid of him. This leaves you with sole custody of Christian. He just sees dollar signs with you I'm afraid to say… so, give it to him and move on with your life."

"Offer him this," said Dad, who was with me, as he pulled out a $1 coin from his pocket and pushed it across the table with his finger…

"He's not getting another dime from my daughter. I'll see to that."

I felt like screaming at Mr Ramsey, as his advice infuriated me. Instead, I thanked him for his time and told him I'd be in touch over the next couple of days with my decision. He gave me a folder with their costs agreement. As I went to leave, I asked Mr Ramsey, "Out of interest, do you find my case to be out of the ordinary?"

"No, but I'm totally appalled a family therapist and court report writer has acted in this manner. I'm sure he will not want his dirty laundry aired in a courtroom as it could be detrimental to his expert standing with the court," said Ben.

"Can I go to the media and expose Dante?"

"Please don't do that. You'll make it a lot worse for yourself. If you end up in court, you're not allowed to publicise any matter relating to children."

"Thank you. I'll follow that advice as a starting point."

"If you want us to represent you, I think you should go with one of our custody specialists because of your husband's credentials. Valentina Hunter is our best in this area."

"I'll call you in the next couple of days after I have considered all of my options," I concluded.

I left the meeting feeling like I was going to collapse with a heart attack. In the ground floor foyer, I said to Dad, "You go ahead. I'll meet you at the car Dad. I just need some fresh air. I can't breathe." I fanned my face with my hands to cool my body temperature down.

"Don't let him get to you like this Ariel… be strong."

I looked at my father, tears starting to stream down my face.

"No, I'm not strong Dad. I'm not like you."

"Give me your paperwork. I'll take it back to the car," Dad said, so I handed my folder to him.

Dad walked out of the building turning right, while I turned left, to find a fountain just outside the building, where I sat down to digest all this information.

Basically, if I couldn't come to an agreement over our son, or have Dante agree to sign joint separation orders to lodge with the court, as well as get him to sign a binding spousal support contract (BSS) to protect my assets in the future from a spousal claim if he hits hard times, then I was facing possibly more than $100,000 in legal fees, to fund up to a two-year court battle to try and retain my son and my assets.

The easiest road, according to my lawyer, was to offer Dante a huge underserved pay-out to walk away laughing his butt off. Either way, it was going to cost me all of my hard-earned savings as well as a further loan to either go to court or pay Dante out. Both ways, the solution was going to be a hard pill to swallow.

Ben Ramsey also told me that a judge could award him 10-15% of the property pool depending on how much equity growth has occurred in my properties since we married. So, a range of $65K - $170K on top of my current offer for two-and-a-half wretched years together.

There were so many numbers flying around in my head. An all-consuming anger was devouring my mind about to explode like a volcano eruption. I felt unstable.

One positive with Dante being so violent in our marriage, was that the court could give me sole custody. However, as I had no hard evidence like police intervention, a provincial court judge probably wouldn't accept my domestic violence claims. Their role was to consider the best interests of the child, who should ideally have a relationship with both of their parents. A judge could give Dante gradually increasing time with Christian depending on his age and developmental needs, if I couldn't prove he was a risk to my son through his violence and alcohol dependency.

In summation, outside of Dante physically abusing Christian and leaving visible marks at some point in the future, or god forbid, killing our son during one of his drunken episodes, I was told women alleging abuse of any kind in the courts were not looked on favourably. In fact, I could even lose Christian if I pushed the domestic violence angle too hard. Furthermore, despite the abuse to date, not allowing Dante visitations with Christian, would also not go down well in court, as judges frown on women who are not willing to promote the father-son relationship. I was informed I could be branded as a nasty alienating mother, and this would go against me.

So, financially I was being screwed over for marrying the prick, despite him not bringing any assets whatsoever into the marriage, just debt. To boot, the court wouldn't believe me about the violence because I didn't have police reports. The system literally forces both the abuser and the victim into consent orders or face a lengthy court battle with huge legal fees to defend the safety of yourself and your child. You take the risk of possibly losing custody of your child to a violent man just for sticking up for yourself and your child and telling the truth.

"How fucked was this!" I said to the water fountain. I needed a cigarette. I think I smoked about five one after the other pacing around that fountain.

There was a young girl maybe twenty-four years of age sitting on the other side of the fountain eating a muffin. She looked up at me with a startled looked on her face saying, "Are you all right?"

I wanted to answer "No" but, I politely said to her, "Just having a bad day, sorry for the outburst."

"That's fine. I work for a law firm in this building. You're not the first one to be upset around this fountain. I've heard many. Hope things work out for you." She then stood up and walked back into the building.

Walking to my car in the underground car park, absolutely fuming over how much this prick was going to cost me, I couldn't help but think… *Dante was one hell of an expensive fuck! With this pay-out, I reckon he cost $5,000 for each time we had sex. Why the fuck did I ever think marriage was a good thing. He got a free ride, spent my money, beat me up and gets to walk away scot free. This is not justice, this is total BS.*

Chapter 12
Use and Abuse

I spent the weekend chewing over whether I engage lawyers at this stage of our break-up. Going with my gut, I sent off an email to Bexley Ramsey Lawyers.

Subject: Ariel Prince
Date: 2 April
Ben

Thank you for your time on Tuesday. As Dante has not commenced court proceedings I am going to wait and see what he does regarding custody arrangements. I am not going to offer him any further money as you suggested, as so far, he's agreed to my offer except the spousal support issue. I am going to communicate with him myself regarding the finalisation of consent orders and I will request he draw up the BSS contract you suggested. Should Dante make an application to the court, I will retain your firm to represent me.

Regards Ariel Prince

I thought it was now time to track down Anna. In the back of my mind, I knew I had a mobile number written down somewhere. I had asked Chloe for it when she had visited us the first time so Christian could call her when he started to talk. I just didn't know what I had done with that piece of paper.

Talking to myself while pulling out the cutlery drawers… *Where… where did you put it Ariel? It's here somewhere. Think! Remember where were you when you wrote it down? Come on… Oh, I remember, I was sitting in the office when I asked Chloe for it.*

I sprinted to the office and pulled out the three drawers one by one emptying the contents on the floor and then repacking all the stuff back… *Shit it's not here!* I said to myself. I then pulled open the filing cabinet and began going through the manila folders one by one... *My old address book... it might be in here,'* I said to myself, my hands shaking as I opened the page to 'C'. I read down the list of names out loud.

"Catherine... Caroline... Corey... Chance... Charlie..." I turned the page "Cara... Caleb... Connor... Cleveland..." next page... Chloe... there it is... BINGO!"

I grabbed my little pink book, got my mobile out of my handbag in the kitchen, sat outside and dialled Chloe's number. The phone rang for what felt like an eternity, and I felt nervous and scared that she wouldn't answer my call. On the 9th ring, someone picked up.

"Hello?" said Chloe. I froze for a second trying to decide if I should say who I am.

"Hi. I'm after Anna, is she home?"

"Yeah, I'll get her."

I panicked and thought... *Oh shit... oh shit, what am I going to say? Please don't hang up on me.*

"Hello...? Sorry Chloe didn't tell me who it is?"

"Anna, it's Ariel," which was met by a cool silence.

"Why are you calling me?" she finally piped up.

"I don't know if Dante told you, but we're separated," I explained.

"Yes, Chloe told me a couple of days ago. We had the twin's flights booked to spend a week's holiday at the end of this month. He rang and told them they couldn't come as you two had split up and he needed to get himself sorted out. The girls were devastated you two had split."

"Please tell them I'm so sorry. I didn't know Dante had organised for them to come."

"My problem now is that he won't reimburse me for the plane tickets. He's done this kind of crap their entire lives."

An awkward silence fell between us, but I now understood how she felt.

"Anna can I ask you something?" I said sheepishly.

"Depends on what you're asking," came her guarded reply.

"I need to know. Am I the only one Dante has been violent

towards?"

"I've been waiting for this. I'd hoped he would have changed his ways by now."

"So I'm not?"

"No Ariel. Dante hit me a couple of times really bad. I'm sure I copied you in on emails I sent to him."

"I'm so sorry Anna, I didn't know, and I didn't get any emails. He attacked me three times, so I threw him out over a week ago. He would get so drunk, black out and the next day he wouldn't even acknowledge what he'd done, and continued on like nothing had happened, and acted like I was the crazy one," I poured out.

"Dante turned up drunk wanting custody of the girls. I refused, so he knocked me to the ground and repeatedly kicked me. He broke my jaw, nose, wrist, several ribs, and I had multiple head traumas and bruising all over. I probably would have died if it weren't for the two guys in the next-door apartment coming to my rescue," Anna said, then continued, "I'm not sticking up for him, but Dante grew up in an abusive home. He has suffered from depression since he was a teenager. Surely he would have told you about all this before you got married?"

"No, he chose to omit an awful lot of stuff."

"Surely you would have seen all the cuts and burns on his arms from self-harming?"

"I saw them. He told me they were from a motorbike accident."

"Do you know if he's hit any other girls?"

"No. But I wouldn't put it past him, hearing he's done it to you a few years after me."

"Anna, I think Dante is going to take me to court over Christian, can you help me? Will you come to court with me to show I'm not lying, that there is a pattern of abuse?"

"I'm really not comfortable getting involved. I left the country years ago to get away from him. I only have to deal with his abusive communications now from afar. I really don't want to see him and open up all the old wounds."

"Please Anna. I beg you! Christian is only nine-and-a-half

months old. You know he could hurt him if he gets drunk."

"I don't think Dante has it in him to hurt his own child."

"How do you know? Your girls have had very little contact with him because you made it that way for a reason. I'm now in the same position as you. Except now he's a violent alcoholic, psycho master of mind manipulation getting away with beating up women. He's the anti-Christ of his own profession."

Anna went silent contemplating Ariel's request. "I won't come on my own; you'll need to subpoena me."

"So… you will let me subpoena you?" I said, nervously waiting her reply.

"Yeaa… es."

"Thank you so much," I said as a wave of relief came over me. My eyes stung for a second as a precursor of tears bubbled to the surface of my eyelids. I understood how difficult this was for Anna. She was to an extent free of him, but I was bringing her back.

"Do you mind if I call you again? I really don't have anyone to talk to, as I'm really so very embarrassed and ashamed that I let him do this to me."

"That's fine. I understand. I still have nightmares about what he did to me and I'm always worried about what he could still do to me and the girls. He's very capable of using dark psychology techniques to make you think you are crazy. I admit, I feel sorry for you and I'm really sorry I never warned you. I thought about it but gave him the benefit of the doubt that he would grow up and be a man, not a monster."

"Thank you… I realise you don't know me, nor do you have to help me. I really appreciate it."

Then, a brief silence fell between us as we both knew joining forces against Dante would bring on repercussions both positive and negative.

"I'm really scared Anna," I said through the tears.

"I know. All I can tell you is it does get easier with time and distance. Call me tomorrow night, I want to know you're okay."

"I will. Thanks again for taking my call… and for your

support," I said. Over the next two weeks, Anna told me what she knew about Dante's past. She said he had pulled a pocketknife on a girlfriend of hers at a party frightening her, as he believed she was trying to crack onto her. She thought he had stalked her for a few years after they broke up often turning up in her street, and he'd threatened to kill her a couple of times.

Anna said Dante's lawyers used 'insanity' as a defence at his trial, presenting he was not responsible for his actions at the time of assaulting her due to suffering a persistent type of mood disorder and a borderline dysfunctional personality condition.

She confirmed his issue in the bedroom and said he didn't work during their nineteen-month marriage, just studied, drank, partied and played golf. It was she who had supported them by working in a restaurant throughout her pregnancy, and his mother had contributed regularly sending them money. He dodged paying child maintenance by hiding his actual income, and she believed he was currently a couple of thousand in arrears. Anna also said Dante had been verbally abusive and derogatory to her in most communications, post separation.

Anna believed he was an absolute misogynist.

Her traumatic experiences and having to constantly deal with him, she said made her life a 'hell-on-earth,' so she turned to the same sex for comfort. But when she tried to move forward with her life, she said he always flared up, caused trouble, and spread disgusting accusations about her. Dante had threatened residency changes for the girls because of her lesbian lifestyle choice, forcing her to make a dedicated decision to remain single until the twins were old enough to make up their own minds about who they wanted to live with.

I was horrified by Anna's disclosures about Dante's history and told my parents everything. He was an absolute liar and I certainly understood why Anna had turned to females for comfort, because at this point, I too, felt an internal pure hatred of all men, and in particular I feared him.

Dante, after being silent for the past couple of weeks, sent me an email…

Subject: RE RE RE Separation Proposal

Date: 17 April

I have adhered to your request and downloaded the court forms for separating property. There is a section called 'Assets and Liabilities Schedule' so I require a little more information from you to complete it or the court will refuse to accept it. I consider the matrimonial property totals $2.1 million and have penned in the net values for most items. As we have already agreed on a settlement figure, I will only need your bank and mortgage statements to attach to the orders. My new business begins trading tomorrow. I am now the sole Director of – The Divorce Drs. For property division purposes I have set my share value at $50,000 even though it is in a negative operating position.

I want to lodge orders for custody and parenting to wrap up our affairs all in one application, so I propose he spends 50% of his time with me. Once you've had an opportunity to consider all this and sought your own legal advice, let me know what you want to do.

Regards

Dante Prince – The Divorce Drs

Upon reading this, I thought to myself – *One minute he's Doctor Jekyll and the next he's Mr Hyde. At least he seems to be civil and wanting to finalise everything, which is a good thing. Interestingly, he has opened his own practice, more than likely suckering Charlotte into bankrolling it for him.*

I wanted to keep up the pace to get this settled and flicked back within minutes…

Subject: RE RE RE RE Separation Proposal

Date: 17 April

I am a little confused. Why does an assets and liabilities statement need to be added? Your information also does not state that you have agreed to leave the marriage with the $145K in assets. I have attached what I think the values and liabilities should be.

Ariel

Dante's reply came back within 30 minutes…

Subject: RE RE RE RE RE Separation Proposal

Date: 17 April

I was unaware your retirement fund is so considerable. I want a further $10,000 transferred immediately. Furthermore, I want your assurance that if I need more money you will keep my business going for the foreseeable future. I also require the spousal support agreed to before finalising anything.

Dante

I needed to stew on this before responding. I was on dangerous ground. Clearly, he had played nice to get me to expose my net wealth to get more out of me. I didn't like him wrapping Christian into the property agreement; it was therefore fortunate that I left out my two bank accounts and my stock portfolio. This could go on forever if I didn't make things crystal clear for him.

I didn't have time to consider my reply as it was Dad's birthday and I had to meet my parents and Christian for a coffee and cake at Dad's favourite patisserie during my lunch break.

Afterwards we took Dad to Costco for a quick visit to buy him a fishing kit. I was at the tackle box display with Christian when I spotted Zoe first, then Chloe ahead of us in the adjacent camping section. They came straight up with huge smiles on their faces after seeing us. My eyes darted quickly around to spot where Dante was, but I couldn't see him.

"Mum… Mum," I shouted trying to catch her attention, but she and Dad were talking to someone intently.

"Hi Ariel. Hi Christian," Chloe and Zoe said in unison, giving their little brother a big hug in his pram. Both Zoe and Chloe then hugged me.

"How nice to see you both," I said, repositioning the stroller behind my back like a shield away from Dante's vision.

"Charlotte flew us in as a surprise," Chloe volunteered.

"How nice of her… how's school been?"

"Fine, but we've changed schools. Grandpa wanted us to go to a private school," said Zoe.

"I went to a private school. You'll have a ball."

The three of us chatted for a while about girlie stuff and movies.

"Heh! Where's Christian?" asked Chloe, after stepping away from the banter to play with him.

"He was just here," I said, looking frantically around the pram and floor.

"Girls, I have to go," I said, turning to start my hunt for Christian.

"We'll come with you, he can't have gone far," said Zoe.

"Christian... Christian!" yelled out Chloe, as she sprinted off ahead of me down the aisle with Zoe in toe.

I raced up and down two aisles stopping when I noticed Dante standing over in the electronics section, with his back to me and Christian in his arms. Charlotte faced me and looked like she was tickling Christian's belly, obviously watching out for me.

My blood boiled and my face went red because of the internal rage I immediately felt towards Dante and Charlotte. I walked up to them with Chloe, Zoe, and Mum and Dad trailing not far behind.

"How dare you walk away with Christian. No doubt you put the girls up to this to distract me."

"You were right honey. She is crazy," said Charlotte.

Dante stood there grinning at me, not saying anything. But he didn't have to, his alter ego said it all: *I can get to you any time. You're such a joke.*

I turned and spoke to my dad over my shoulder. "Dad, go to the information booth and tell security they are needed here now," and Dad dutifully hurried off.

"Hand Christian back to me or you can deal with security and the cops."

Dante's voice in his head said, *You don't scare me bitch.*

"We've done nothing wrong. Dante's his father and it's pretty obvious you weren't looking out for him," retorted Charlotte.

"How convenient the four of you are here at an outlet forty minutes away from where you live, right at the time I'm here.

What a coincidence," I theorised out loud.

"Daddy loves you boy," Dante said to Christian, kissing him on the forehead. Dante then put Christian on the ground and said, "Crawl to Mummy."

I immediately picked Christian up, turned, and walked in the opposite direction back to get the pram with Mum and Dad coming in behind as though they were human shields between me and him.

Dad could see I was visibly distressed over this interaction and the reality hit him for the first time that I wasn't crazy: Dante was intentionally menacing. We left Costco without buying Dad a birthday present. In the car park I said goodbye to Christian and sent him home with Mum and Dad. I went back to work, brooding over Dante's behaviour.

I decided to reply to Dante's request for more money…

Subject: RE RE RE RE RE RE Separation Proposal
Date: 22 April

I would not be comfortable transferring any more money unless everything is finalised in writing between us. I am sure you understand negotiation principles 101.

Ariel

It was May by the time Dante answered as he had been away on an RV road trip with his new family.

Subject: RE RE RE RE RE RE Separation Proposal
Date: 2 May

That's fine Ariel. All your values are grossly underestimated; however not relevant given the arrangements we have made. Have your lawyer send me copies of the property searches for all your real estate, then the draft orders can be produced. I want my money the day I sign. I'll have Christian overnight this weekend till Sunday afternoon. Organise the car seat, pram, bottles and his clothes.

Dante

The stress washed over me quickly as I thought to myself… *Now he's pushing me for overnight time as a bargaining chip for him to sign an agreement. There's no way I can allow this. I think I need legal advice, but it's too soon to bring in Bexley Ramsey. I need a non-threatening suburban practitioner, that won't flare him up.*

I contacted Miriam Hope at KR Cross Lawyers to correspond with Dante on completing the property searches and the request for overnight time with Christian. Miriam booked me in to meet her in three weeks as she was going away on annual leave in a few days.

She had remarked to me in our initial phone consultation that, "Dante still has parenting rights despite his alleged history of domestic violence, depression and alcohol consumption. I recommend a graduating regime be put in place, which slowly builds up the amount of time Christian spends with his father. You would be seen by the court to be unreasonable to not promote the overnight stays."

"Let me get this straight. I'm viewed as being unreasonable by a judge if I don't allow my ten-month-old baby to stay overnight at his violent alcoholic father's home?"

"In a roundabout way, yes. Unfortunately, no matter how bad a person he's been to you, he still has parental rights."

"This is absolutely absurd! Thank you for your advice. Sorry about getting mad at you," I said, apologising to Miriam.

"I understand. The law is the law. How about I draw up draft correspondence, and you let me know if you agree with the overnight schedule I would suggest as a counter proposal. I can send off the title searches in the same communication."

"That would be great. I must warn you; he may get… agitated dealing with you."

"I'm not a spring chicken in this profession. I'll be fine. Talk tomorrow," Miriam said putting down the receiver and opening a file on her directory named 'D & A Prince'.

Then three days before Dante's proposed overnight time, he sent me a text.

TXT Dante: I have moved in with Charlotte and her parents at

21 Collingwood Drive, Cobble Hill. Her kids are here week about so Christian will have a great time. Charlotte has everything, so don't worry about the car seat, etc. Send me your lawyers' details.

TXT Ariel: My lawyer is away on annual leave.

TXT Dante: Change lawyers! The clock is ticking for you, Ariel. I will email you the orders probably this afternoon. You'll have 72 hours to remit the $10K to me. You have the cash, so shouldn't be any trouble. My business' bills are mounting, so if it tanks, it will be a matrimonial debt under the law, and we'll be back at ground zero re-negotiating my divorce pay-out. The case law clearly shows you are in the business for the good, the bad and the ugly as we're not divorced. My dream is coming together, and the best part is... it's all funded by you which was my plan from when I found you. Lol! By the way, orders for Christian will be included with everything I want or there is no settlement.

After this exchange, I went back into the kitchen where Mum was feeding Christian.

"So, he was cheating! I just got a text saying he's now living at her parents' house in Cobble Hill," I said to Mum.

"More fool her," Mum said.

"Yeah... I'm sure he's lied through his teeth to her too."

"Didn't Tracey move to Cobble Hill?" said Mum.

"She lives near the Divino Estate Winery. I'll have to warn her she may run into him."

"As far as I'm concerned, that Charlotte woman deserves what's coming her way," Mum said, smirking to herself.

"I think it's so funny. She, no doubt thinks, she's scored a wealthy therapist. Reality will hit her sooner or later and she'll come running to me... I have no doubt about that," I said knowingly. "It also looks like he targeted me right from the start too."

"That was obvious to your father and I right from the word go," expressed Mum.

"Why didn't either of you say anything to me?"

"Your father talked to you about a pre-nup, but you said you wouldn't because you loved him. We didn't want to end up being the 'Negative Nancys'."

"I understand, but I would have liked to have heard your opinions, as I was too smitten to see the forest for the trees."

I had to admit, I was upset Dante had moved on so quickly. Furthermore, my ego was bruised knowing he had moved on with a woman, who going by her Facebook, was six years younger than me, which placed her some twelve years younger than Dante.

I resolved that the best thing I should do at this time was to go out and socialise, have some fun and get my mind off the emotional turmoil I was going through. I thought I should 'grab the bull by the horns', turn my current situation into a positive, and be glad I was single again.

This experience made me realise, that what had been drilled into me as a child about girls having to get married, was absolute crap. It's so not the be-all and end-all to life for a woman. So, I signed back into Executive Introductions with the resolution to just date and have fun. No strings attached. Use and abuse, as the old saying goes.

So, that… is exactly what I did.

Chapter 13
Fear Can Paralyse or Motivate

Things were now moving fast and to cleanse myself of him, I decided to get serious. So that night I piled everything relating to Dante into the garage for him to take away on the weekend. Photos, sheets, mementos, our bed, his punching bag, golf equipment, things he had bought me, his books, and everything of his in the office. I tore up our wedding photos and all the photos with him, and ceremonially threw them into the trash.

Going by his pattern to date with Anna, I knew Dante would stalk me. So, I used this knowledge and published my social outings on Facebook after they occurred, as I wanted him to know that I wasn't wallowing at home over him. Indeed, I was doing the exact opposite, and moving on, baby!

However, knowing what he was capable of, I was paranoid about my safety, so I arranged for Mum to come everywhere with me, except work and on dates. I was scared to be out in public by myself in case Dante followed and cornered me. I couldn't overcome the feeling that he was watching me at close range but didn't know if this was complete paranoia stemming from being a victim of violence, or if it was real. From the day we separated my level of fear grew each time I had any form of contact with him. I felt that at any time he could randomly show up and beat the living crap out of me, just because he could.

Following Miriam's advice, I agreed to allow Dante to have his first overnight time with Christian. I trusted that Charlotte would be there and, being a mother herself, would make sure Christian was safe around Dante, especially if he drank.

Dante arrived to collect Christian and without any introduction, just opened my front door and walked straight in, like he still lived here.

"Where's Christian?" he demanded.

"With Mum."

"Well get him, we've got a party to go to."

"I will. But first there's a couple of matters I need to speak to you about."

"Like what?" came his arrogant reply.

"I need you to sign this letter instructing the bank to begin the refinancing process as we've discussed," I said handing him the letter.

"I don't have time for this," he responded, sternly, pushing away my hand.

"Please Dante, you said you would."

"I don't give a fuck about your financial problems. You'll need to find a different way to get me off them."

"Okay then. Will you sign a passport application for Christian so he can travel with me to Colorado?"

"Are you stupid? Do you really think I'm going to let you take off with him?" he replied rudely.

"Sounds to me like you're just being an arsehole because you can," I said, upset he had this amount of control.

"Go fuck yourself. I don't have to do anything. Now, give me my son!" he said roaring it into my face.

"No," I said calmly standing my ground with him invading my personal space.

"Give me my son, NOW!" Dante bellowed.

"No! You get out of my house… NOW!" I yelled back at him, but even louder to make my position clear.

Dante turned around and left yelling at me… "You'll fucking suffer mole. Be afraid, be very afraid."

I closed the door behind him leaving Dad mowing the side yard totally oblivious to the yelling match between Dante and me.

I walked back into the kitchen where Mum had been looking after Christian. The look on her face told me she was uncomfortable with the exchange she had just heard.

"Are you all right love?" Mum asked folding Christian's clothes on the bench.

"I'll be fine, Mum. I'm just a little rattled by his arrogance. I hate having to ask him for help to do something."

"You'll figure it all out. I'm off to do the ironing," Mum said trotting off to the laundry.

I picked up Christian and placed him into his bumble bee space walker, so he could scoot around the house independently while I vacuumed. This job took me about twenty minutes, during which time I was totally distracted by the argument I just had with Dante. When I finished, I went looking for Christian.

"Bubbah, where are you?" I said a little louder than my usual tone of voice but didn't hear the scuffling sound of the rollers on his walker, so I checked in his room. He wasn't there.

"Christian, let Mummy know where you are please." I listened for a giggle or sound as he sometimes hid playing hide and seek with me. I walked around the rest of the house to the front door finding it open and his walker on its side. I felt a sick sensation well up in my stomach as my gut told me exactly what had happened.

"I ran out the front door looking for Christian. "Dad, have you seen Christian?"

"Nope. Why?"

"I can't find him."

"Denise probably has him."

"No Dad, I think Dante's sneaked back into the house and taken him!"

"You need to call the police and I'll organise for a locksmith to come out and change all your locks. You should have done this earlier Ariel," said Dad, mad with me.

I rang the police immediately. They told me to come down to the station as soon as possible to report the incident. Once there, Constable Ian Rogers took me and Mum into a room to take down our statements. I finally told the police about all the violence that had occurred. Constable Rogers asked me "Are there custody orders in place?"

"No," I replied.

"Then he's fully within his right not to return Christian."

"He can't do that. Surely?" Mum questioned.

"Unfortunately, he can and I'm sure he knows this. But I'm quite certain that with him working within the family court environment may work to your advantage here... do you know where your ex-husband is currently living?"

"Yes, of course," I replied.

"Can I have it?" So, I read Dante's address off to him.

"I'm going to go run some checks first, won't be long," he said, leaving the room.

A few minutes later Ian came back saying... "I've checked into him. This guy's a real piece of work," he said, shaking his head.

"Do you have Dante's phone number?"

"Yes," and I wrote it down for him.

"Okay, stay here, grab a coffee or tea from over there. I'm going to see if I can talk to him."

About twenty minutes later Constable Rogers returned.

"Did you talk to him?" I asked eagerly.

"Yes. He's not going to return Christian. He said he's making an urgent application to the court on Monday for sole custody."

"So, he won't give Christian back to me?" I belted out frantically and began to cry covering my face with my hands.

"I'm afraid so. Sorry I can't be of more help," said Constable Rogers, with great empathy.

The constable led Mum and me through the office door, which let us back to the reception area of the police station. Before closing the door, Ian said, "You should go to your local court first thing Monday and apply for a restraining order... and make sure you include an order for the return of your son."

"What's that?"

"It's an order issued by the court to stop threats and acts of domestic violence to keep you and Christian safe."

"Thanks so much, I'll look into that."

"Do your best to stay away from him, Ariel. He's bad news," the constable said, closing the door behind him.

Walking back down the stairs of the police station, Mum and I passed two officers escorting a handcuffed man into the station. He was struggling to get free repeating over and over as he was walked into the station "Take your hands off me. This is police brutality."

I admit, I was intimidated by this man's homeless crazy look and I immediately felt afraid of him. I recall a chill ran up my neck and down my arms as he passed, which really gave me the creeps. I had no empathy for him whatsoever, which was strange as it wasn't my nature to be cold towards another human being.

Walking to the car, it dawned on me that I had somehow crossed into a part of the world I never thought I'd be touched by. I had led a 'cotton wool' existence thanks to my over caring parents' choice to shield me from all the bad stuff. Up until now I'd never had a need to go into a police station, nor speak to a police officer about a personal matter. I was resentful, that where I thought I stood in this world had now been shattered and I felt less of a person as I'd let a form of criminal element pierce my balloon. I also felt embarrassed. And now I needed a restraining order. It all made me feel really nervous, frightened, a little crazy and most of all, alone. How was all this going to go down with my extended family and friends? None of them had been involved in events that even remotely resembled the past year of my life. In fact, no one in my circle was even divorced.

I phoned Dante several times on Saturday and Sunday leaving messages begging him to return Christian. Surprisingly, he answered on my tenth call.

"See, I told you to be very afraid. I can get to you any time, even in your house."

"Please, just return Christian to me safely," I implored.

"Charlotte will drop him back on Sunday night," he relented.

Over the weekend, I did some internet research into this 'restraining order' and thought it was a good idea to kick into action, first thing Monday morning. The problem was I had to work and didn't want to broadcast my 'dirty laundry' to my employer. I resolved that the only option I had was to call work and request a sick day. At least this way, my boss and staff would think I was really sick as I'd never taken any sick days up to that point.

With my Dad by my side, I walked into the court near to where Dante lived at nine on Monday morning, to apply for a restraining order. An armed security guard stood just inside the electric sliding door.

"Who do I ask for?" I said to Dad, walking up to the bullet-proof counter window.

"I don't know. Just ask that lady at the counter."

"The police told me to apply for a restraining order. Can you help me please?"

"Sure darlin. I'll get you the forms."

I was given an official looking government information form and a blank affidavit. The first form was nine pages and had twelve sections to fill out. I was informed that I could fill it out at the table across from the front counter and that I could go in front of the judge this morning, providing that I returned it by ten and the matter was urgent. If I didn't have it back by then, I would have to wait two weeks for the next opportunity.

"Holy shit Dad, what do I do in front of a judge? Maybe this isn't a good idea. I don't know what I'm doing and I'm certain this is going to make Dante extremely mad."

"Ariel you must do this for your own protection and to protect Christian. You have no other choice," said Dad, determinedly.

I remember physically shaking while filling out the lengthy form. I had to detail any events that concerned domestic violence and note any and all previous occurrences, who I was seeking to protect, where everyone lived including Dante, and furnish my work details, etc.

"Dad, this form wants to know my work details. Does this mean my work will find out? I can't have this happen."

"I don't know, why don't you ask when you hand it in?"

As this was the first time I'd ever been in a courthouse, I got to see the judicial criminal processing system close up. But even with a security guard at the door, my personal safety radar was going off. The waiting room had filled up within half an hour and was buzzing with men, women, police officers and what I assumed were lawyers. A film crew began setting up outside the front door.

Then the courtroom door opened, and a female police officer yelled out… "Brooker and Gordon to the courtroom."

The place went silent. "Brooker and Gordon to the courtroom," the officer repeated.

Six people shuffled in through the door. Once the courtroom door closed, the level of noise in the waiting room went from quiet to a cacophony in less than two seconds. More people poured in through the front door veering right to the seating area. It felt like wall-to-wall mayhem, or was it just my naivety at being new to all this? The realisation of what purpose this building represented, made me feel both emotional and threatened. I felt like anyone in the room at any time was going to pull out a gun and start shooting.

Scanning the room, I spotted a door to my left with a stencilled sign in the centre of it. There was a group of men standing in front of it, so I had to move around to read the whole sign, which read: 'Women's Domestic Violence Support'.

With a wave of relief flowing over me, I said to myself… *That must be me.*

"Dad, I'm going into this room for help." Standing next to the security guard, Dad responded by nodding at me and waving for me to go in. Inside, a female social worker sat at a corner desk. She introduced herself as Lucy and handed me a plastic clipboard.

"Can you fill this out please. I won't be long," she directed. I quickly looked over the form, the purpose of which was to collect information about who was utilising this advocacy service. I filled it out in silence but looked up every few seconds to listen and watch another girl that Lucy was interviewing. The poor young girl was wound up so tight, the negative energy inside her revealing her fears. Lucy was trying her best to comfort this young mother who would have been barely eighteen with a toddler sitting on the floor at her feet.

"I don't understand this form," she said, crying into her hands, "can't I just tell the judge what he did to me?"

"Jess, I need you to complete as much as you can, so you are ready when the judge calls us in," Lucy reasoned.

I looked down at the paperwork in Jess' hand. She had attempted the front page, but it was obvious to me she was of poor education and wasn't good at reading or writing. Jess then caught on to the fact that I was listening in stunned silence. She looked back at the paperwork and attempted to scrawl on the form through her tears.

Lucy took this as a sign to move on and help the elderly woman sitting across from me. I placed my form on Lucy's desk and sat down next to Jess.

"Would you like some help?" I asked. Jess didn't look at me, instead, she burst into more tears.

"Please don't cry," I said, as tears brimmed in my eyes as I empathised with her internal struggles. Attempting to shift her focus I said, "You have a beautiful daughter. How old is she?"

"She's fourteen months."

"My son is turning one soon," I said reassuringly, "what's her name?"

"Layla."

"That's a cute name. I'd really like to help you both. Us girls need to stick together you know," I said, winking at her like a sister.

"Thank you, I'm not good with forms," said Jess.

"That's cool, we'll work it out together. Then you can help me with mine," I said, jovially handing her a tissue.

Filling out Jess' form I learnt that her boyfriend named Beau, was twenty. But he wasn't Layla's dad. He apparently took her to a party on the weekend, snorted cocaine, and kissed another girl in front of Jess. Jess got upset and went to the car to leave, but he came bellowing over, which was when she locked the door. He then bubbled over and put his fist through the passenger window and dragged her out of the car, threw her to the ground and punched her in the side of her head before walking off. She said his friends witnessed it but were all high on drugs.

I also found out this wasn't the first time her boyfriend had hurt her. Jess was in shared accommodation in Berkshire Village with her daughter and another female but had no family around. Jess was unemployed, uneducated and was clearly a child herself, facing this ugliness all alone. My heart went out to her. Seeing Jess' frightened state and knowing what it was like to fear for your life because of the actions of an enraged man, planted a seed in my mind and in my soul.

It was obvious that the public needed to be exposed to the truth about domestic violence, and females needed access to better justice and support through these services. However, this court system was clearly overloaded, traumatic and in real need of change.

I was awarded a temporary order that day with a Form 14D being issued, meaning the injunction orders were made without Dante being present giving the police five days to serve him for the next court date set for the 22nd of June.

Besides the injunctions, I achieved something much bigger that day. I walked out of the court better armed for the experience and became much clearer about my own path forward. I was determined to make a stand for myself and, hopefully, other women. I swore to myself then and there, that I would no longer, live in fear of Dante. I wasn't going to crumble and become his victim. Instead, I would go toe to toe and beat him at his own game, whether it be legal chess or mind warfare.

Dante thought I was nowhere near as intelligent as him. But he was wrong… I would just have to reapply my energies to a new field: the law. I figured it shouldn't be that hard. Every time I've changed jobs in the past, I had to learn a new industry and adapt my skills. I was excellent at research, so I resolved to learn the Family Law Act, study domestic violence, custody, parenting, visitation and property, how to build evidence, and profile domestic violence perpetrators. Then my marketing and PR talents would be useful to tell my story to the courts or whoever would listen. Besides legal justice, I wanted negative karma going his way.

While I was in court on Monday morning, Dante wrote me the

following:

Subject: Property and Christian

Date: 7 May

I have made every attempt to separate amicably and it seems, because I have re-partnered you are now angry, choosing to be adversarial denying me access to our son. Forthwith, I reject your offer. Now I want a 30/70 financial split. I will serve you in due course my court application. I am seeking custody of Christian. Family dispute resolution has been booked and the mediator will contact you soon. Correspond with my new business partner, and lawyer – Jackson Naylor. Do not correspond directly with me any more. I told you to resolve matters with me. Lawyers are going to cost you a fortune as you're not smart enough to go up against me. You never were. I'll have your house by the end of this. Lol! I have nothing to lose.

P.S. Charlotte says - Chow Biatch!

At this point, I had to chuckle to myself at his arrogance. But the tide was turning, and despite being informed that it could take a few days to be served, I knew Dante had no idea of the temporary restraining order that I'd just actioned against him.

Chapter 14
Leveraging Children Against Money

Now I knew what I had to do. I needed to come up with a plan and implement it fast. This feeling had been brewing in the back of my mind since I threw Dante out of the house. I needed to speak to Mum and Dad when I got home from work and get them on board immediately, as our lives were about to change. I asked them both to be at my house for an early dinner that night to discuss my plans.

"Mum, Dad, I've got to get out of here. He's coming after Christian and going for sole custody."

"He won't get him, darling," said Mum, without emotion.

"He doesn't want the boy... he's just using Christian against you. No man wants children by themselves. Men would rather be single and screw around," Dad chimed in.

"Well, he's taking me to court over Christian and now wants over $600,000 as a separation cheque."

"But you already did a settlement?" said Mum, checking for confirmation.

"Well, he's found a business partner who's a lawyer and now changed his mind and wants more."

"He can't do that," said Mum.

"This arsehole is only after your money and he's using Christian as leverage. He's nothing more than a bully Ariel. Kick his arse and expose him to the legal brethren. Don't give him an inch," scowled Dad.

"I know. But he writes custody reports Dad, for judges, and he probably knows the legal system's ins and outs by now from his studies. So, I'm in a divorce court on steroids. Normal people don't have to face this predicament," I replied.

"He's just a professional student darling. He may know the theory, but applying the law is very different," assured Mum.

"Well… I know you don't bring a knife to a gun fight, so I'll introduce him to Bexley Ramsey Lawyers now, as I know they'll intimidate him. They have the largest family law department in the county, so he'll be up against them from now on. No matter what way this is going to go, it's going to cost me a fortune. But I promise he's going to go down. He won't win. Time is on my side. He'll stuff up again and I'll get my justice somehow," I said, full of courage and confidence.

"Doesn't your mate Harvey have bikie mates that could sort him out? He needs a good hiding… then he'll stay away," declared Dad.

"Harvey knows the Hell's Angels. But I don't think having him beaten up is going to help any. It'll just come straight back to me… I'm pretty sure," I replied.

"Get me Harvey's number over the next couple of days. This prick needs to be paid a visit and have the shit beaten out of him. Twenty grand, would be a cheap investment. He needs to learn a hard lesson. After that, I'm sure he'll think twice about taking you to court, and before hitting another woman ever again," said Dad with blood and revenge stuck firmly on his mind.

"Don't think I wouldn't love to see Dante beaten to a pulp. I'm just not that kind of person who could be involved with doing that to another human being. I know you want to hurt him Dad, but you just can't."

"Just get me Harvey's number. You don't have to know anything," repeated Dad.

"Anyway…moving on to a different topic. I need to take another path and it is imperative you both be on board, as I can't do it without you," I appealed.

"Whatever you decide to do, you know we are here for you. Do whatever you must… to keep Christian safe," said Mum.

"The best option is for us to move overseas. I'd love to move to Australia, but I can't get a passport for Christian… so, I'm going to follow Anna's steps and move as far away as I can and fast."

"There will be a lot of repercussions. Number one, you'd have to give up your job, and you have commitments on your properties. You'd have to rent a place and you can't do that without a job. I can't see how you're going to do this," Mum said, with negativity creeping in. My mother was never able to see past a problem to come up with a solution.

"Well... I have no choice Mum. My job... well there's not going to be one at Burger Boulevard soon. Clayton and Anne from HR told me last week that I need to pick myself up mentally from the breakup with Dante or I'm going to be out of a job. Imagine what's going to happen when he puts this into court. Having to attend court all the time will impact my job even more."

"Sorry honey... you didn't say anything to us about this... we didn't know," said Mum.

"I don't want to worry you both with more problems. As for the mortgages, they'll take care of themselves and I'll rent out this house to pay for the rent on a new place, or I can even sell it. I don't really care at this point."

"What are you going to do for income?" Dad asked.

"That's the new direction Dad. I'm going to buy a business and move north near the coast. It puts over two hours driving distance between us."

"Terrific. I'd be going back to where I lived for the majority of my twenties," said Mum nostalgically.

"What kind of business?" asked Dad.

"Something in hospitality or fashion, or a combination of the two. That way I would be doing what I love, working with food and fashion."

"What about going back to business consulting. That's what you do best," said Dad.

"I need a business that generates a large income, that could look after us all."

"I think you're making a mistake with a food or retail business. The economy is not good, and people stop spending in these areas when the belt tightens," said dad, in his usual 'negative nelly' position to my ideas.

"What area do you want to move to?" Mum enquired.

"Somewhere around Balmoral Beach," I responded excitedly.

"I think it's a great idea. You need a new challenge and a new life," Mum said.

"So... I need your help; will you move with me?" I asked.

Mum and Dad nodded to each other and then to me.

"Of course. We have nothing but you and Christian here. So, wherever you two go, I'm coming," Mum said.

"Thank you. I know this is a huge thing to ask of you both. But moving and putting distance between Dante and I will stop him in his tracks. Opening his business in Hatch Point means he can't get out of his lease for a few years, I'm guessing," I said.

"I hope you're going to make the bastard pay child maintenance now, instead of letting him off like you did," Dad said.

"You know what, you're right Dad. I hadn't thought about that. Stuff him! I'll lodge an application online tonight."

The three of us sat in the living room discussing our plans and eating dinner, while Christian played with his toys on the floor and watched *Alvin and the Chipmunks.*

Dante and Charlotte were closing up late for the day at their newly opened clinic on Park Lane, when Charlotte asked Dante... "Did you get the paperwork finished?"

"Yeah. I'll need you to witness the affidavit and property application so Jackson can lodge it online in the morning."

"Do you want me to do it now or at home?" asked Charlotte.

"We'll take it home," said Dante.

"So you didn't finish the custody documents?"

"Nope. Don't know what I'm gonna exactly do for that one."

"Don't get mad at me but do you mind if I say something?" enquired Charlotte.

"Why would you think I'd ever get mad at you?" said Dante flirting with her.

Charlotte shrugged her shoulders and then blurted out... "Have you considered the possibility Christian isn't yours? He doesn't look anything like you, and you yourself said 'Satan'... sorry Ariel, was probably cheating on you."

"It has crossed my mind, and it would certainly make my life a lot easier if he weren't. I've had a niggling feeling he couldn't be mine, as we never actually began any type of fertility treatments."

"So why don't you get a parental DNA test done? I looked it up online. It's seems easy, fast and it's only $295 for your peace of mind. We can order the kit tonight and send back the sample by DHL overnight," said Charlotte, somewhat chuffed at herself for making the suggestion.

"Sounds like a good idea. The only problem with your plan is 'Satan' won't let me see him."

"So, when you do, we'll have the kit all ready. At least you can use him as leverage to get more of a pay-out from her in the meantime, even if he isn't yours," said Charlotte.

"Duh! You've only just woken up to that?" chortled Dante, teasing Charlotte for her naivety.

"My strategy with her all along was, to get in, get married, and get out with some of her money." Then Dante said to himself... *Women are so fucking easy, they're all so flaming dumb.*

"I wish I could see her face when she gets served. She's gonna have a conniption over me going her for not 30% but 35% now. She's so fucking tight and wound up over her money, parting with it will hopefully give her a heart attack. That would be a double whammy for me," said Dante.

"Yeah, considering she has said all that violence crap to everyone who will listen. She needs to learn a lesson that she can't go around saying that kind of stuff and get away with it. A heart attack would be karma biting her on the arse. So, what are you going to do with a $700,000 settlement?" asked Charlotte.

"You'll see."

"Come on give me a clue."

"Okay. Besides buying a brand-new BMW, I could look into a hitman. What do you think?"

Charlotte stood frozen to the spot and thought she should consider her response wisely as her reaction could come back and bite *her* sometime in the future. "A bit extreme, don't you think?" she said, in a joking tone.

"I'm not serious. Just wanted to see your reaction," said

Dante, with a wry smile.

Charlotte wasn't really listening. For she daydreamed about what she would do with that kind of money. Images of a huge fancy house, designer clothes, and a holiday in the Bahamas came to mind. Snapping out of it, Charlotte said to herself… *When Dante gets this money, I'll need to convince him to buy a house or condo in both our names. That way, I get a chunk of the money too. I should start looking at properties in the area around the girls' school, then subtly point them out when we're out and about. Hopefully Dante will get the hint and think it's his idea. He's already professed his love for me so I'm sure it won't freak him out. I wonder how long it took him to tell 'Satan' he loved her? Knowing what I know about her, I don't know how he could've ever loved her. $700 grand… will be like winning the lotto. Can't wait to tell Mum about this latest development. I'm finally with an accomplished doctor and we've started a terrific little business venture together. Eventually I won't have to work, and we'll have a huge house thanks to the she-devil.*

"Let's go home… hello. Are you coming?" said Dante, waving his hand in front of Charlotte's face.

"Oh sorry. I didn't hear you. What did you say?" said Charlotte, waking up from her scheming daydream.

"Let's go home and get this affidavit finished."

Charlotte held out her hand for Dante to take it and walk out of the office together. Instead, he came up beside her and flung his arm over her shoulder and squeezed her breast as they left the office. They were both unknowingly separately grinning to themselves, happily daydreaming about how they were going to spend Ariel's money.

I felt uneasy for days, like a sitting duck waiting for whatever Dante was going to do with me and the court. I was also agitated about how he might react when the restraining order paperwork was served on him.

Even though I'd been married to a divorce therapist, I didn't have the foggiest idea what happens when you separate, and your ex takes you to court with domestic violence controversies. Up until now, I'd been praying he was bluffing me. My work was the only place I could stop these worrying thoughts, by applying myself to projects that required all my attention.

It was the day before my 36th birthday. Nathan, my PA, waved at me from his desk mouthing to me… "Can I come in?" I nodded to give him the okay, just as I was finishing up a teleconference call.

Nathan was 21, smart, efficient, half-Canadian, half-British; he was studying Marketing and was a bit of a distraction to my female staff. He resembled a young Luke Gordon in '90210', but with olive, tanned skin.

Closing the door behind him, Nathan said, "Ariel there's a man at reception saying he needs to see you. I told him you were in a meeting and the best thing was to make an appointment, but he's refusing to leave, and demands to see you. What do you want me to do?"

I looked at my Outlook calendar before answering, "I have three minutes before the international expansion meeting for India starts. I'll go out and see him. Did you get his name?"

"No, he wouldn't tell me."

"He probably wants to personally complain about his experience at one of the stores, no doubt," I quipped.

"No, I don't think so. I asked if I could assist him. He said it was personal."

"That's weird. I hope he's not a stalker. I've never had an unidentified male in my entire working history come to my office without an appointment for a personal chat," I said jokingly.

"There's a first time for everything," Nathan said, walking out of my office and returning to his desk.

Picking up my 'India' file, notepad and pen in preparation for my meeting in the conference room, I headed down the corridor to the reception counter. The head chef and operations team were already standing outside the closed conference room door, which was to the left of reception.

With the group of people huddled around reception waiting for the meeting to begin, I was able to briefly take a look at the man who was so desperate to see me. There were two men in the waiting area to the right of the reception counter. One sitting down with a stack of papers on his lap, mid-forties, going bald, black spectacles, and casually dressed in shorts and a linen chambray short-sleeved shirt with navy and white sneakers. The other stood up. He was dressed in a black suit and a white-collared business shirt casually unbuttoned to the third button. He seemed to be in his mid-thirties; with a neat goatee, laptop bag and a presentation folder under his arm. I didn't recognise either of them.

"Which one?" I lent down whispering to enquire from our receptionist named Polly…

"That's him in the shorts," she whispered to me.

"I thought it would be the guy in the suit. Thanks."

The staff waiting for their meeting were getting louder and louder with their banter and realised I was in the entrance way. Since I was an executive in the business, staff politely stepped aside one by one, to let me through the crowd with a domino greeting of nods and, "Morning Ariel."

The man in the spectacles heard my name and abruptly stood up and took steps to shorten the distance between us.

"Are you Ariel Prince?"

"Yes… and you are?" I questioned.

"Jason Bishop. I work for Sharman Investigations."

"I'm not sure I'm the person you want to see here at Burger Boulevard; I look after the marketing side of the business."

"No… you're the person I need to see."

"Okay. How can I help you?"

"You can sign here," thrusting a document in my face with a biro on top of the paper. He did it so forcefully that I had to take a step back to achieve my personal space, as he was right up in it.

"What am I signing for?"

"An acknowledgment that you have been served."

"Served what?"

Jason turned back towards the chair, picked up a reem of paper and spinning back to face me, he said, "Take these please."

He handed the documents to me; I accepted them still playing catch-up in my head about what was going on. I was in an internal state of panic thinking to myself... *Why am I being given legal documents by an investigator?*

"Can you sign the document acknowledging the serve please?"

I scribbled my signature and dated the document with the date.

"Thank you, Mrs Prince. Have a great day!" Jason said, spinning on his heels and immediately leaving the building.

An overwhelming sensation came over me. I felt like I was going to throw up and have diarrhoea all at once. I ran out the office entrance door, down the hall to the female toilets clutching the paperwork in one hand, with my other hand over my mouth.

I made it to the sink just in time to vomit. Then I went into the stall and sat on the toilet. I began reading the first bundle, a hundred-page document entitled 'Form 17 Affidavit' sworn by Dante Prince. There was another cluster of paperwork stapled individually with 'Form ADM880 Application,' then a Form 44 headed 'Notice of Family Violence' and 'Form 13B Net Family Property Statement' in bold lettering in the header.

My stomach was in knots reading his version of our relationship. By the time I reached page 20, tears were streaming down my face over the lies and false accusations Dante was telling the court. I realised I couldn't stay in the loo reading and crying, so I pulled out my mobile phone from my jacket pocket and rang Nathan.

"Hey. Are you okay? The meeting started fifteen minutes ago."

"I won't be able to attend the meeting. I need you to attend on my behalf and give my apologies. Something urgent has come up. I have to take the rest of the day off."

"I'll clear your schedule. Is there anything else I can do for you?"

"Yes. First, grab my handbag and meet me down at my car in two minutes. Then call Ben Ramsey. His number is in my Outlook contacts. Tell him I'll be at his office in an hour. Then call my dad and ask him to meet me at the café outside Ben's office in forty-five minutes. If he asks why, let him know I have a pile of documents I need his help with. He'll understand."

"Okay boss. Will see you tomorrow, I hope," replied Nathan, dutifully.

By the time I thumbed through all the court documents at the café I was red-faced with black mascara running down my cheeks; I felt absolutely gutted over the contents being aired to the court. I was being painted as a scorned, bitchy and vindictive wife pursuing a high-profile career at the expense of his personal progress, and I placed money above my interests in all things including both him and Christian. He alleged that I was verbally abusive to him throughout the entire marriage; that I was financially abusive in not allowing him access to money and had left him with nothing but his clothes, a car, some old towels and his golf bag. Oh... and also that I'd refused him access to his son, topped off with an allegation that I'd cheated on him.

For his so-called 'victimised' lifestyle while with me, he had now upped his demands to 35% or seven hundred thousand dollars, and spousal support of $2,000 a month for three years. He also requested that he pay nothing towards the costs of the raising of our son. I felt an all-consuming burning hatred run through my body urging me to kill him!

I was ushered into the boardroom at Bexley Ramsey and offered coffee or tea, with biscuits while Dad and I waited for Ben. I stood at the huge glass window overlooking the bridge across the river, frozen to the floor but churning inside over events throughout my marriage. I chastised myself over being so stupid and naive to have married Dante in the first place.

Ben was accompanied by a tall, extremely well dressed, blonde-haired woman in a red business suit, red matching shoes and a gold necklace. She was introduced as Valentina, their family law guru, and she sat down next to my father.

"I was just wondering about you this morning Ariel, and how you were getting on. I did some digging on your ex-husband. A couple of people had briefed him for a report and commented they didn't trust him to produce unbiased reports as his recommendations are coming out swaying towards giving fathers custody," said Ben.

"After reading his bullshit affidavit, I don't trust him either to tell you the truth," I replied.

"So, I assume he's made an application to the court?" said Valentina.

"Yep!" I replied, sounding downtrodden.

Ben sat down and quickly scanned through the documents. "He's certainly trying it on and coming in excessively high. I'm surprised he thinks his orders are going to fly with a judge. I notice his application is for property only. He's not seeking custody orders.

"I don't want you to worry, Ariel. We'll let Dante and the court know we are representing you with a Form 11 today. It looks like the first return date is in August, which gives us enough time to compile a solid case. Valentina will go through everything and be in touch. In the meantime, don't correspond with him or his lawyer and don't let him get under your skin. He's just bullying you. I doubt he will try strong-arming us and, in my opinion, what he's got here in this affidavit material is just going to infuriate the judge," said Ben supportively.

"I'll have Miriam Hope send you over all the correspondence she's had with Dante so far and then I'll disengage her," I said.

"Thanks. Can you provide my email address to her please? Here's my card," said Valentina.

Taking Valentina's business card, I said, "Is there anything else I need to do at this point?"

"No. Did you receive a copy of our Client Agreement when you were here last?" asked Ben.

"I think I did. I remember reading somewhere you require $10,000 to be transferred into your trust account to retain you."

"Yes, that's correct."

"Cool. I'll sign whatever you need now and by close of business today you'll have the retainer."

"We'll send a notification we are the attorney's on record to

Dante's lawyer and the court this afternoon. See what he does then," said Ben, raising both eyebrows as though a dance was about to begin.

"Oh, I forgot to mention, Dante entered my home without my knowledge and kidnapped Christian. He then refused to return him when the police intervened for me. I got a temporary restraining order on Monday. I don't know if he's been served yet. The return date for that one is the 22nd of next month."

"A restraining order against a family justice counsellor with an application in the court! That's gold, Ariel," Ben said, laughing.

"I'll get the ball rolling and write to him this afternoon about visitation arrangements. In light of the restraining order conditions, I'll need to seek his undertakings to not consume alcohol before and during visitations and to organise a third party to perform changeovers. Then I'll offer a short daytime visitation once a week.

"Why give him anything at all?" I asked.

"You need to show the court you are promoting sufficient time with his son considering the circumstances. This type of arrangement puts you in good stead with the judge. Trust me," said Valentina.

"Okay. I don't like it. But I don't want to be on the wrong side of a judge."

The next two weeks passed quite peacefully with Dante dealing with my lawyers instead of me. Jackson's correspondence to them was abrupt, unprofessional, and showed the two of them were way over their heads against Bexley Ramsey. Dante was agitated and consumed with flexing his brawn at them trying to get increased time with Christian instead of the three hours being offered.

Their correspondence in return was factual and detailed, courteously putting The Divorce Drs in their place, and obviously making Dante out to be an idiot for his complicated responses; especially over the alcohol injunction in order for him to see his son. He also refused to pay half of the costs for a family report to be completed. He was always crying poor when he had already received $67,500 in cash so far from the separation. He then had the temerity to deny he had a problem with alcohol and violence to my lawyers and refused to provide disclosure documentation for his own property application, which is apparently a normal procedural requirement.

Witnessing this behaviour was like watching a child chucking a huge tantrum on the floor. I thought Dante must have been compiling all the correspondence and just having Jackson send it to my lawyers as he went on and on in great detail about his belief that I had failed to consult with him with respect to matters such as Christian's day care, health issues and his day-to-day care and development. He even questioned why Christian, at just shy of one was not walking yet, like it is my fault.

Apparently, I was not being cooperative in my co-parenting with him and was using the revised minimised visitations to inflict pain on him. '*Wah-Wah-Wah!*' At least I was getting a laugh out of his antics, and it was obvious he still didn't know about the restraining order yet.

After a lot of kicking and screaming, he provided Valentina with the word-for-word undertakings they requested. He then chose every second Saturday for his visitation day until our upcoming court date in August. Pick-up time was ten a.m. from my home and the return time was one p.m., with Charlotte being the person interacting between us.

On the Friday, I received the following text…

TXT Dante: Ariel. I was informed you have filed a restraining order application by the police. I will of course be defending this. I haven't been served yet so changeover will occur. I have called Joel as Charlotte isn't available. He will get Christian from you at 11 not 10 because he's busy in the morning.

They turned up ten minutes late. As Sophia had dropped by, she did the exchange of Christian with Joel. I stayed inside the house, out of sight.

At 1.05 p.m. Christian had not been returned, and my gut told me to be concerned. But I wanted to give Dante the benefit of the doubt that they were possibly just running late. This positivity was just to make myself feel better. I had agreed to the visitation on the advice of the lawyers but knew full well the dark enigma within Dante and his propensity for torment, as well as his all-consuming need to assert power over me.

At one thirty I sent the following text to Dante…

TXT Ariel: Is there something wrong? You were supposed to deliver Christian back at one p.m.?

I received no reply. I then called Dante again at 1.44 p.m., but the call went to his message bank. I began to panic and paced up and down my bedroom. I feared Dante might harm Christian terribly in retribution for my having taken out a restraining order against him.

I then called Joel at 1.54 p.m.

"Hello."

"Joel it's Ariel. Sorry to call you, but Dante's not answering his phone."

"I really don't want to be put between the two of you," pleaded Joel.

"I'm sorry, but can you tell me when you're returning Christian?"

"I had no arrangements with Dante to return Christian."

"What? Dante told me you were doing the changeovers for today instead of Charlotte. Christian was supposed to be returned over an hour ago."

"Shit sorry. I had no idea. I'll call Dante."

"Thanks so much, Joel. So sorry to put you in this position."

"I'm really sorry Ariel, but I'm Dan's friend and I really don't want the same kind of trouble between him and me such as what happened after Anna. Please don't call me again after this." He clicked off.

Ten minutes later Charlotte called to inform me that Dante believed he could not meet the current arrangements.

I hung up on her with no pleasant goodbyes.

"Motherfucker!" I yelled stomping my feet as I shouted. "Arseholes and the law! I have a psycho manipulating the system against me, and paid ones that don't get how unscrupulous and dangerous he is. And then there's the actual law that forces me to go against my better judgement."

I called the police again and spoke to a Constable Justin Ransom. After the introductions and a brief rundown on the events Justin said, "Yes, a Charlotte Palmer called me at one thirty p.m. regarding your text message. She told me her partner Dante Prince had picked up the temporary order before going to your house."

"So they knew about the restraints even before picking up Christian?"

"I believe so. Under the temporary order he can't contact you or come within a hundred metres of your home."

"Don't you see, it was his intention right from the start to kidnap Christian and now the restraint seems to have worked in his favour and stops my efforts to get Christian back. What do I do, Officer?"

"Well, the restraints don't stop you from contacting him."

"I've tried calling several times, but he won't answer. Can you contact him?"

"I'm sorry ma'am, but I can't help you as there are no court orders in place for your son's return and even if there were, you would need to apply to the court for a recovery order."

"But there are contact orders. He agreed to them with my lawyers."

"He says he's only signed an undertaking not visitation orders."

"Thanks for your assistance, Constable Ransom." I hung up the phone and burst into tears, knowing he was enjoying playing these games with me, and that he was using Christian as the pawn in his chess match.

I rang Dante at 3.23 p.m. leaving the following message on his message bank…

"Dante, please bring Christian home as per the agreement. Please don't make this worse." I cried into the phone for about 20 seconds, then stopped as rage filled my mind. "I will get him back Dante! One way or another." I said in a low voice as I was in a bit of a trance, fixated in my mind on doing some real harm to him.

I rang Dad and told him what had happened. His single response was, "I'll get this sorted out darling; don't you worry," and hung up on me.

Dad drove to the police station at five p.m. and spoke to Constable Clara Davies. At first, he was met by a similar position as I'd experienced, which was that they couldn't help me get Christian back. But Dad wouldn't take no for an answer and convinced the constable to contact Dante by telephone. Dante agreed to hand Christian back the following day at five p.m. Clara told Dad that Dante claimed he was never asked by my lawyers to agree to their terms by jointly signing an order, and that it takes two to make an agreement.

When I was told about this comment, I went through the emails and realised Dante never actually agreed to the revised visitation put forward by Bexley Ramsey. His email wording cleverly agreeing only to the various undertakings around alcohol, safety, supervision and his changeover delegate, not the times of changeover.

OMG! He saw the opportunity to take Christian as my own lawyers hadn't put forward actual orders for him to sign. He or Jackson created the legal loophole for him to use. Then my protection order fell into his lap! I thought to myself... *He is so calculating; Bexley Ramsey are going to have to do much better than this.*

Over the next week Bexley Ramsey swiftly kicked Dante's arse over his weekend antics and had him sign interim visitation orders, that would have an impact on his standing as a court report writer, if he decided to pull the same stunt again.

He stupidly made excuses around him being unable to perform the travel for pickups and delivery of Christian and communication issues in terms of the protection restraints, that my solicitors backed him into a corner whereby he had no other option but to decline visitations until after our court date. He looked like an absolute lair to the court if he, all of a sudden, changed his position and could do everything he initially said he couldn't do.

It was the 12th of June, the day before I was to leave for India on a nine-day work trip. The marketing team was all abuzz with the prospect of opening our first international store. There was a lot to be done especially by me. Added to this workload, was all the material I needed to compile for Bexley Ramsey for the property case, to try and keep my assets. This legal work has been consuming my evenings. Hence, the mountain of work on my plate grew exponentially along with my level of stress. I had headaches every day; my eyes stung, and my entire neck and back ached. I had lost about eight kgs from not having the time to eat between work, lawyering and looking after a baby who himself wasn't sleeping well at night. My brain was like mush.

"Ariel, Valentina is on line two, will you take the call?" said Nathan.

"Yes, I will, thanks."

Pressing line 2 on my office phone, I politely said "Valentina, how are you?"

"Good thanks. I wanted to let you know he's filed more material. I thought I'd call you before I send it on email as I don't want you to freak out."

"What's he wanting now?"

"Well, everything and more; you know him."

"Unfortunately, I know nothing is ever enough. What is it?"

"Dante has upped the ante: lodging for sole custody of Christian."

"What an arsehole. He threatened it, but I never thought he'd do it."

"He's bypassed the general family law rules lodging this way. Parents are normally required to attend mediation before being able to make this type of application."

"So how did he get around this? I haven't even attended mediation yet."

"He has obtained a mediation certificate by having Family Mediation decline to mediate, which opened the gates for him to lodge a Form ADM880 applying for an urgent hearing based on the Form 44 family violence notice."

"Are you saying he has told someone at the court I'm violent or abusing my son, to leap over court processes?"

"That's why I wanted to call you before you read these court documents. You know he's a liar and he's going to throw as much mud at the wall to see what sticks. I need you to stay level-headed. We are not surprised by this move considering who he is."

"Can he get away with this? He can't have Christian. Christian is not safe with him and I won't agree."

"Ariel… please understand, this is an intimidation tactic. He's clearly leveraging Christian to get a higher percentage swing in the property case."

"So he's deliberately using Christian against me to extort the $700 grand?"

"He won't get that in a trial. However, a parent with the most custody is entitled to a 5-10% swing in the property pool to assist with the care of children. This means the property split you two already did, is now well below what a court would give him if he had sole custody of Christian."

"Scumbag! Sorry, that wasn't said towards you Valentina."

"I know. It's hard when you're dealing with a clearly deranged man, who's after nothing but money. Read the documents, remain calm and call me tomorrow if you have any questions. And before you go, I'm also sending you a separate email containing a list of questions I need you to answer as fully as possible, to help create your response material to both property and parenting now."

"When will you need this done by as I'm in India for over a week starting tomorrow? I return on the 21st which is the day before the restraining order court matter."

"Can you have it all back to me by the 3rd of July? That gives us a few weeks up our sleeves, as I need to file the final signed material by the end of July at the latest?"

"Somehow, I'll get it done."

"I know you will. Take care and have a great time in India," Valentina finished.

I was pretty much incoherent, and my stomach was in knots

for the rest of the afternoon, waiting for the email to arrive from Valentina. The correspondence was sitting in my inbox when I got home from work. It took fifteen minutes to print all the documents, as there were eighty-seven pages in his affidavit alone, five in the application and he'd lodged another Form 44.

I thought, while waiting for my printer to finish... *This court process certainly kills a lot of trees.*

In Dante's material, he continued spouting on about me being vindictive and a liar. But he now added that I was a mentally unstable drug user with an antisocial personality disorder and anxiety, and in urgent need of therapy. He was spruiking that I was an abusive cruel mother with no maternal connection to our son, as well as an absentee parent who had abandoned Christian to the care of my ill mother, in order to pursue my career. He shouted from the rooftops that I was the abuser in our relationship, having been physically and verbally violent towards him and cited me as a poor role model, since I had allegedly had an eating disorder when I was a burlesque dancer. In short, he told the court that I was a totally unfit, violent mother who alienated Christian from his father from the day he was born. He reasoned therefore, that *he* should be given sole custody, with me provided only limited supervised time, one day per week.

As my blood boiled, I thought to myself... *This weasel has just thrown down the gauntlet for all-out war.*

Chapter 15
Keep Calm and Pamper Yourself

I left the following morning for India flying out on British Airways with Cody, my advertising and marketing assistant. Cody and I made a great innovative marketing duo, and he worked just as hard as I did. Cody was eight years my junior; tall, blonde, blue eyed, lanky; a ladies' man, with excellent taste in high-end brand clothing, and he loved to party, dance and flirt. From the way he presented himself, I was surprised at the start of my employment with Burger Boulevard that he wasn't gay. He came from a wealthy family but stood on his own two feet and renovated properties on the weekends he wasn't working for me.

Our potential new business partner, Krishana Fine Foods, were paying all the expenses for the three of us to meet with them. The owner, Pranava Punjab, was a very wealthy entrepreneur who owned hotels, camp sites and other short-stay accommodations. His latest achievement was building the first six-star hotel in New Delhi. This hotel was going to be our base, so after my recent trauma with Dante, I was certainly very excited about staying in luxurious surroundings while being wined and dined by their venture project team.

It was my aim to complete a strategic branding, marketing and advertising plan to introduce our burger concept into the Indian market, in the seven days we were in the country. Part of this involved meeting with their advertising agency to finalise brand identity and the menu. We were also being shown several possible locations for the rollout of the initial five stores, to test the market over the next twelve months. There was a lot to do and little time, but I was up for the challenge and looking forward to a break from the worries of litigation.

On the plane over, I grinned more than once knowing how furious Dante would be if he found out I was on an overseas trip staying in six-star luxury. I was sure he would lash out and try to place an injunction on me from leaving the country. But too late… I was now on the plane somewhere over the Pacific Ocean enjoying a glass of wine and indulging in a movie.

There were two black Mercedes Benz SUVs waiting at the airport to collect us on our arrival at eight p.m. Each car had two noticeably armed male escorts dressed in military type black uniforms with a red beret. One of the men wore a black turban with a red stripe.

We were quickly shuffled separately into the waiting cars. Their haste in scrambling us into the cars, with one man throwing the luggage in the back while brandishing a revolver was a little confronting.

"Please, please sir… ma'am, we must get into the vehicle quickly."

It looked to me like a military type kidnapping operation that you often watch on TV, except for the 'please, please' bit. I hadn't realised until that moment that India was not a safe place to be a Western person.

Needless to say, we sped away fast. There were cars, buses, vans, motorbikes and three-wheeled taxis everywhere; they were in six lanes all going in one direction with no road rules, and dense smoke-like pollution all around. Further out of the city, as trees started to appear and traffic merged into three-and-a-half lanes, there was a more orderly chaos on the road as pedestrians appeared in the thousands on the makeshift footpaths, often within just an arm's distance of the cars. The paved road gradually turned into dirt with a considerable number of people on tuk-tuks. We passed many local roadside food-stands amongst makeshift homeless camps, with tons of garbage piled up to a metre high, lining the roads. House structures were made of tin, mud, brick or concrete and were sporadically visible along the way. Then there were cows every few hundred metres or so, just sitting in the middle of the road, mingling amongst the people and cars or simply standing outside the front door of dilapidated shops.

I even saw a dead cow in the middle of the street with passersby just going around it. The level of poverty was striking, and like nothing I had ever imagined. I counted my blessings more than once for the life I had and wondered how these local people were ever going to afford gourmet hamburgers.

It took us over an hour to get to the hotel, but I was pleasantly surprised to see a more developed part of India with high-rise buildings, roads, neon lights and uniform streets. However, it seemed to me that nothing was ever finished properly with half-completed pathways, leaning electricity poles and overgrown shrubs and weeds.

The hotel was lit up like a Christmas tree and shone like a star amongst a constellation of concrete compounds. The hotel was squarish with a multicoloured exterior in sandstone, black and brown trim, and was around twelve storeys high. We passed through enormous black security gates manned by four armed guards, and I couldn't help but notice the Indian and Canadian flags flying either side of the entrance.

The hotel manager, Arjun, greeted us in the lobby with great enthusiasm. He was dressed in a light gold satin long-sleeved button-up shirt and black trousers and called us his 'priority guests'. Arjun gave each one of us a hotel room card and allocated a porter each to escort us to our rooms.

The hotel foyer and downstairs bar area were gorgeous, with glass panelled square columns alternating with black walls with ornate mirrors and others with white marble walls. There was a huge black chandelier hanging over the glass reception desk, blue accent lighting in the bar across from the check-in area, and a white marble floor with a black-marble feature tiled area. It was simply stunning! The bar area had a dark grey carpet with the same flower design in white as was on the foyer floor, with square black tables on fancy chrome legs and featured black throne chairs with white flowers displayed on each table. The ceiling was white; the walls had heavy black curtains enclosing the area and tall lampshades glowing a muted yellow.

This opulence got me very excited to see what my hotel room would be like, and I wasn't disappointed. The suite was spacious and followed the same black, white, mirror and chrome finishes as downstairs. My room had a king-sized bed, a TV built into the wall with chandelier lighting throughout and a workstation. The bathroom had white marble walls, a dark-grey tiled floor, white sanitaryware and a huge frameless shower with a white round, standalone bath with black accents. It wasn't going to be too difficult to settle in here.

Cody and I worked every day from eight in the morning until around eight at night, getting the entire concept drafted up and accepted by Mr Pranava Punjab and his team. Every time we left the hotel, we were escorted by a four-man armed security detachment. On one occasion on the way to see a possible site, Cody asked if we could stop at Pahargani Main Bazaar, just to see our competitor's store. Besides being dirty, noisy, chaotic and full of crumbling concrete, it was nevertheless colourful, exciting and packed full of tourists and local shoppers.

Because I was a natural blonde Western female, people often stared, followed and tried to touch me on a number of occasions. The security guards would gather around me when males got a tad too close and pulled their weapons on several homeless men when they wouldn't take the direction to move on. I felt like a celebrity, but also feared for my safety yet again.

Each night our Indian partners would pick us up at eight thirty and whisk us off to an exclusive restaurant in the more fashionable parts of the region. At these places the parking lots were lined with million-dollar cars, while beautiful women draped in jewels and expensive clothing were everywhere; which was a far cry from the hundreds of millions of people living in poverty elsewhere in the country. The rich weren't rich, they were mega wealthy! I was also awed by how many young people there were, much younger than I with seemingly endless amounts of cash, and I wondered how they made their fortunes.

During lunch on our last day in India, we achieved agreement on our burger branding expansion strategy from all relevant financial parties including our Canadian founder and president. This gave me an afternoon off to relax and wind down after such a high-pressure week.

While going to and from meeting rooms throughout our stay, I passed by the hotel spa and dreamed of a massage, so I decided to try it out. Back in my suite, I picked up the in-room phone, called the spa centre and made a booking for two thirty p.m. I then ordered a room service lunch and enjoyed some downtime in my suite.

The spa looked so luxurious. The reception was decorated with a ten-metre cream marble wall with a feature of orange bronze rings falling from ceiling hooks. Cream sofas were lined in front of a gold satin full-length curtain. There were gold vases and vanilla candles and a water fountain on the main shelf with an image of a beautiful, crowned princess. On the floor, there was a shadow reflection of the flower mural from the front foyer.

I was greeted at the Lotus Flower Spa by their receptionist, Alishna, who spoke broken English. With the differences in our languages, it took a while for Alishna to work out that I wanted a one hour, forty-five-minute 'Kaamuk Massage and Vaspiya Shower', which I think was a full body massage and hot rain shower at the end. The package pictures and descriptions sounded very exotic and I needed a little pampering. Upon signing the charge to my hotel room bill, Alishna requested…

"Please wait in our seating area Ms Prince, while we prepare your treatment room."

She rang a small bell in two quick repetitions. A short time later a stunning man in his late twenties appeared in Aladdin type dark-grey pants and a gold unbuttoned vest. He looked like a male model out of a Calvin Klein ad with black hair, golden brown eyes shimmering playfully at me like the afternoon sun reflects off a glass of whiskey, five o'clock stubble, a diamond jawline, and olive skin—like he was half-Indian half-European. He was introduced to me as Armaan, my masseur.

I had never had a male masseur before and must say, I was shocked by the impact his presence had on my inner loins. I then wondered how relaxing this experience would be, being massaged by an absolute hunk of a man that I didn't know.

Needless to say, I now looked forward to this day spa even more.

Armaan escorted me down the corridor and opened the door to my room. It was beautifully designed with a bamboo floor with an open rain shower on the wall beside a door big enough for three people to get through, with a second, hand shower on the right. There was a massage bed in the middle of the room covered with a white towel and four rolled up cream towels; one of these was shaped as a swan with pink petals shaped as three-leaf clovers on each towel. There was also a double-door mirror on the wall at the bed head with a basin and free-standing vanity in front. At the foot of the table was a gold bejewelled console table with a white marble counter, topped by five burning candles encircled with pink flower petals, Evian water and a drinking glass.

Two walls were floor-to-ceiling rosewood panels and the third was a full glass window with a beige roller curtain. An ornate brass bowl sat on the floor next to the bed and a three-tiered shelf sat to the side with many white pump bottles and other oils and creams on the top shelf. The middle shelf had rolled up face towels and the bottom shelf had three orange tea candles. In the background I could hear an in-room music system playing a soft instrumental compilation of rainforest sounds.

"Please ma'am, undress completely. Leave your clothes in this basket. Touch this button when you are ready for me and I will return. Please take your time. There is a towel on the bed to cover yourself," said Armann. Clasping his hands together in front of his chest in a praying positioning he nodded and bowed at the same time, upon leaving the room.

I had never been asked to remove all my clothes for a massage before, but I thought... *I'm in another country... they might do things differently here, so just relax and go with the flow.*

The room temperature was set to a comfortable 22 degrees Celsius going by the electronic remote on the wall. I undressed, taking my shoes off first, then my jeans, t-shirt, and bra and then removed my underwear. I placed everything including my handbag in the adjacent basket. I pressed the button on the wall to let Armann know I was ready and quickly skipped up onto the massage table face down and wiggled to get into a comfortable position as my size 10D boobs always get in the way when lying on my front. I hadn't had a massage since the day before I was married and was looking forward to a totally relaxing afternoon of pure pampering. Although, I must admit I was a little embarrassed about being naked in front of a male masseur.

Armann entered the room about two minutes later, and immediately enquired… "Is the room warm enough ma'am?"

"Yes… thank you."

"I'm going to close the window blind and dim the lights if you don't mind," he said.

"Okay," I said, closing my eyes so I could start to relax, unwind and put my turbulent life to one side for a while. I heard Armann's footsteps go over to the electronic wall panel, then the motor on the electronic blind kicked in, slowly closing out the sun in the room. The lights gradually dimmed down to turn completely off, until the room was lit only by candles. Armann walked back to me with a towel in his hands. Standing over me, he said,

"Can you roll over ma'am?" As I repositioned, he placed a towel over my chest and legs. "Ma'am, can I take the band out of your hair?" Armann requested.

"Sure," I replied, thinking… *this is different to most other massages where I've always been asked to put my hair up.*

Armann carefully unwound the band around my ponytail, then he placed my hands down the sides of the bed asking me…

"Is the music okay?"

"Yes, it's really nice and relaxing. Thank you."

I thought the whole setting was really romantic and luxurious. I was a lucky girl indeed to be experiencing this level of luxury in a third-world country like India, especially in light of my recent chaotic troubles.

Standing to the top right-hand side of the massage bed, Armann put his hands on either side of my head, cupping my skull behind the ears. He ran his fingers to the top of my head through my hair slowly with just the right amount of pressure to make me melt and submit to his control. I felt an immediate release of negative energy rising off my head through every strand of hair he touched. The sensation carried on down my jaw and the side of my eyes with every stroke he performed. He did this movement several times, then began massaging my scalp.

"Are you feeling more relaxed now ma'am?" Armann asked.

"Definitely," I said, with my eyes closed as my mind started to float off into a peaceful space of its own, like an out-of-body experience.

"Mr Punjab told me you been working very hard for him, and I am to pleasure you with massage. I will start with your head first, that way we get rid of work thoughts, so you can enjoy the rest."

I didn't respond as I was in a state of total peace on that massage table. Armann then took a warm towel and progressed to the end of the massage table. He wiped my ankles to toes slowly on both feet discarding the towel when he was finished. He then parted my legs slightly moving my ankles one at a time. He folded up the towel that was covering the front part of my body so that it finished just covering my crotch. I floated for a second as I felt a caressing heat between my thighs and over my pussy, and I thought to myself… *that was weird.*

I opened my eyes to see Armann placing a rolled-up towel underneath my ankles. He then said very softly… "I'm going to begin with an ultra-relaxing foot massage." He spread some warm oil over his hands and started to massage both heels of my feet at the same time, slowly, in circular movements. Then he moved up to the centre of my arch applying a little more pressure with his thumbs on the fleshy underside part and with his remaining fingers across the top of my feet. Gosh it felt good. I had never had both feet massaged at the same time. My mind drifted off into a deeper relaxation with each rhythmical massage stroke.

Armann completed the foot massage by tracing the lines upwards from my heel to the ball of my feet. He then massaged the outer edge of each foot making small circles. These movements released little pins of pain along the bone, but it felt good… pain and pleasure at the same time. His hands were strong and firm and commanded surrender with each touch. I was in heaven. I allowed myself to dream for a brief moment… being in a tryst of lust with Armann on the massage table.

Next, I felt a warm wet sensation on my big left toe. *Is he sucking on my big toe?* I questioned myself. Armann was indeed fondling my toe with his tongue in perfectly timed sensual waves, which tingled my entire body and heightened my sexual desire. I opened my eyes and raised my head off the table an inch to sneak a peek at what was really happening.

Armann gently released his teeth grip from the bottom of my toe; his lips and tongue glided upwards exposing my toe to the air, followed by a cheeky sexy smile that came across his face as we locked eyes.

"You not like this ma'am?" he asked me.

Without thinking too much I responded with…

"Feels amazing," as my body tingled with erotic stimulation.

As I lay there being given intimate pleasure by a stranger, my mind was in conflict as I kind of felt I was doing something wrong. Surely, this shouldn't be happening. But I didn't want it to stop…

Good Girl: "I wonder what Kaamuk means in Hindu?"

Bad Girl: "Whatever it means I like it."

Good Girl: "I wonder what Sophia would think if I told her about this?"

Bad Girl: "Why am I worrying? I should just enjoy. No one needs to know!"

Armann sucked every toe skilfully, giving me pleasure, and turning my body into melted butter in his hands. Grabbing more oil while sitting on the console beside me, Armann squeezed it into his hand. He smoothed it out on the surface area of my right leg from my tail bone to the top of my hip where my underwear once was, using slow, smooth gliding strokes and warming up my femoris muscle tissue, my knee and shin. His hands were warm and gentle. It felt glorious as my body got used to his delicate touch. He then kneaded the muscles of my inner thigh, lifting and pulling it up off the bed and slightly working the muscle tissue deeper. He repeated these movements on my left leg, and I drifted off into a peaceful hypnagogic state where I lost track of time, space and reality.

In this half-awake, half-asleep consciousness, Armann moved his attention to massaging my stomach, obliques and up to my armpits, quasi kneeling on top of me and straddling my hips on the bed. He gently cupped my breasts rhythmically squeezing and massaging his fingers upwards and closing them around my nipples with the warm oil igniting my intimate senses once again. I arched my back wanting more of this pleasure. Armann's hands glided all over my torso, up to my neck, and back down stopping to circle and stroke my nipples. The sexual energy running through my body, and in particular my sacred cave, was engaging in orgasmic realms. My subconscious screamed for Armann to suck my nipples and climb aboard.

With his smooth ripped upper body poised skin to skin on my chest, Armann whispered into my ear… "I want you to turn over," which made my heart skip a beat. I realised then that I was not having a dream! Armann seductively nibbled on my ear lobe then raised himself up off me, sliding off the table.

I rolled over, my body tingling, my mind gobsmacked and horny as hell. I wriggled around a bit to get comfortable placing my cheekbones into the face cradle. I lifted my arms up in a cross position above my head, which tangled amongst my hair.

"Are you comfortable?" enquired Armann, as he placed a warm towel over my mid-section covering my lower back and bottom.

"I think so. Are my arms all right where they are?"

"For the moment, yes. Please relax now. I'm going to re-position the bed for relaxation."

The bed began to bend in the middle rising upwards, so my body was in a triangular position, like bending over a couch. I felt uncomfortable, but as Armann slid his hands smoothly from my ankle up to my groin I moaned with pleasure. He repeated the motion several times and I completely forgot I was kind of arse-up in the air. He massaged to the cheeks of my bottom and lower back, and down to almost teasing my outer vaginal lips, which began to open like a flower. Softly at first, but then with more aggression he released all the pain in my lower back and made my girly bits throb and tingle.

He moved to the front of the bed, kneeled in front of my head and worked his magic on my back, arms and neck for about fifteen minutes. To signify the massage had concluded Armann patted me down with a hot cloth and electronically straightened the bed back to the horizontal position. I didn't get up from the bed. Instead, I chose to linger, thinking to myself… *my mind and body had definitely been soothed and enlightened.*

"I will prepare the Vaspiya Shower for you, ma'am. Come in when you are ready," said Armann. I heard his footsteps as he went over to the wet area. Pulling myself up off the bed I wrapped a towel around myself and tied it at the front of my breasts. I felt younger, stronger, sexy and in control; I hadn't felt like this since my twenties.

Strolling over to the shower area, the whole setting was designed for seduction. There were candles; the room was dark and water sprayed from many directions and dense steam encircled the shower cubicle.

I dropped the towel from around me at the entry, swung open the frameless glass door and stepped into the steam shower, and was immediately enveloped by clouds of sandalwood-scented steam. The hot mist bewitched all my bodily senses, bathing me in exotic indulgence.

I stood under the rain shower, and placed my crossed palms onto the wall tiles, leant down so my forehead rested on my hands to soak up the experience, mesmerised by the water and steam streaming onto the back of my neck and running down my back. I stood in silence collecting my thoughts, recalling the flashes of sexual imagery, the feelings and heat stirred up by the massage. I was busting at the seams to tell Sophia and Tracey about this orgasmic experience.

A few minutes later the door to the shower opened. Armann came inside swiftly stepping in behind me. Body to body, skin to skin. He said nothing to me, he just slipped his left arm around the front of my pelvis, his hand settling on my crotch for a second whilst his other hand cupped my breast. He then began fondling my private parts teasing my body, as my mind was being seduced by the steam and water.

His left hand reached for the detachable hose shower head on the wall, while his other was stimulating my clitoris. He pressed a button on the hand shower turning the spray into a faster thinner high-speed spray. Armann then splayed open my vulva between his fingers on his right hand, and placed the shower head between my crotch, tickling my clitoris and labia with various water spray combinations. He moved the shower head in motions up and down and across like an external vibrator, stopping whenever I made sounds of pleasure.

The repetitive movements resulted in my escalating euphoria. I was enjoying this foreplay so much that I let go of all of my inhibitions and took the shower head off Armann to self-masturbate, thinking... *Oh my God! It feels like oral sex but softer.*

"I want you to play with me... fuck me," I said spontaneously to Armann.

He expertly brought me to orgasm twice throughout the remaining fifteen-minute steam shower. The entire experience had been hot, raunchy and tantric! Being massaged and fondled all over by a gorgeous stranger for nearly two hours! It was then I realised he had been there solely for my own personal satisfaction and gratification, which was empowering. There had been no kissing or penis penetration, but I had definitely been fucked!

I certainly had no idea that what I had ordered at the beginning of my day spa treatment was sexual therapy. Had I have understood the Hindu language, I don't think I would have been game enough to order that service. But I would certainly do it again and thoroughly recommend it to any of my girlfriends.

Mr Punjab took Cody and I out on our last night to an authentic Indian restaurant and the dance club on the fifth floor of the Surya Hotel. We had an absolute ball, and it was a great way to finish off our trip before heading home.

On my return from India, I had several items of correspondence in my letterbox that needed my urgent attention. The first was a letter from the child support enforcement agency. I was elated as I opened the letter as this meant they were finally chasing Dante to support his child. This was going to piss him off to no end.

On reading the contents of letter, I discovered the bastard had informed them he would be earning $10 this financial year. I thought to myself laughing… *What a dick! He's actually going to try it on with me like he did with Anna, for all those years dodging his responsibility. Big mistake buddy! You won't get away with this shit with me.*

I walked over to telephone and called the agency. As I dialled their number, a different line of thought crossed my mind… *Actually… what an idiot, he's just assisted my case big time. A judge is going to see him, 'a family justice counsellor', as dodging his own parental responsibilities, and how can he seek sole care of Christian earning only $10?'*

I went from happy, to mad, to elated reading the entire contents of the document whilst on hold to the agency. Upon answering, a customer service person told me I had to make a Departure Application, to have his $10 assessment deemed at an increased rate.

The second piece of correspondence was an envelope with the government's logo in the top right corner. I always tense up when getting something from a government department, especially when I've had no need to speak to one of their divisions in the last couple of years. It was a notification informing me that Dante had placed caveats over all my properties. I immediately rang my Dad as I didn't know exactly what this all meant.

"Hello, Desmond speaking."

"Dad, Dante's put caveats on my properties. What does that mean?"

"That little SOB! He's freezing your properties. Basically, he's laying a legal claim over them so you can't sell, refinance or transfer title until the matter is resolved by the court," said Dad.

"But he knows I'm in the middle of refinancing him off the mortgages," I replied, raising my voice an octave from the stress.

"Well, you can't now, sweetheart. This is just one of his games to force you into caving. I should have known he'd get dirty like this," said Dad, apologetically… like it was his fault Dante had done this.

"You'll need to contact the bank in the morning, get them to defer your refinancing for now and in court you have to get your barrister to go for the son of a bitch for all costs involved in removing the caveats, for vexatiously stopping your refinance. You have the proof he requested it to be done before he placed the injunctions. The judge will have a field day with this, and you want the judge to be mad at him," said Dad.

"Well then… that's two things I have to make the judge mad,"

"What's the other?" asked Dad.

"I'll bring it over tomorrow for you and Mum to read. I want to see your faces when you go through it."

"Okay. See you in the morning. Don't worry, he's going to pay dearly for what he's done."

A third letter was a notification from the court that the return date for my restraining order application had been set back two months at Dante's request putting it after our property and custody first return date.

Upon reading this letter, I wondered… *how many people working in the family court system have restraining orders against them? Funny you never hear about this in the news. I think there's an evil black serpent slithering around in the background of these courts, cloaking a lot of terrible truths.*

The last envelope was documentation from the mediation service confirming that our matter was not appropriate for mediation. Surprise, surprise… domestic violence, risks to a child, abuse, and the list goes on. Dante had already lodged this in court, so I didn't need it and threw it in the bin thinking… *A lot happens in ten days with Dante on the other side. No wonder he can only earn $10. He's spending all his energy trying to outmanoeuvre me.*

Later that day I went into the office, scanned the child support letter and sent it off to my lawyer Valentina with the subject line: *Psycho family justice expert tells child support his income is $10 whilst contesting for custody – THIS IS GOLD!*

In my inbox I also had three emails from Dante's ex, Anna Harper. I was a little surprised, as I had never received anything from her by email before. I was intrigued to find it was correspondence she had sent to Dante during our marriage. The first one read…

Subject: FW Call to Zoe

Date: 11 December

What you said to Zoe on Monday night is totally reprehensible. You have gone too far this time and broken her heart completely. Why would you nastily inform her you wouldn't be her father any more unless she came with Chloe to visit you and Ariel for New Year's? She came to me hysterical and bawling her eyes out wanting to know what she had done to make you not love her any more.

For the record, the reason why she refused to visit is because her grandfather had booked the girl's tickets to attend the Disney on Ice Show on the 3rd. Chloe was happy to forgo the activity, but Zoe is training to be an ice-skating performer and didn't want to miss it. Picture this: She sobbed so uncontrollably into the night that she even vomited, over your threat to her. This is child abuse and flies in the face of your own profession! You make me sick! You're just a monster in sheep's clothing.

Anna.

I was staggered Dante would retaliate against his own daughter like this. Anna's second email read…

Subject: FW Cancellation of Holidays

Date: 18 January

Are you still that full of resentment towards me that you would do this to them? For Christ's sake, if anyone has a right to be upset it's me. I have done nothing even remotely close to your ever-increasing checklist of bad behaviour. Your numerous violent attacks on me still give me nightmares. Like the time you repeatedly picked me up and threw me onto the ground after I had my appendix out. I'm sure you don't remember turning up at my job drunk and punching me in the car park and of course there was the time you put me in hospital. You left me death threats on my voice mail that were so revolting you were arrested. And your ongoing tirade of abusive threatening rhetoric is usually associated with a person with a mental disorder, not a PhD in psychotherapy. Oh, and there's your forever 'poor me' attitude over child support, and your horrible criticisms over my parenting, plus the years of threatened court action over the girls. Tell me what on earth did I do to deserve all this! I've never understood it.

Anna.

The last email Anna forwarded to me was sent when I was pregnant...

Subject: FW Conversation this evening
Date: 5 February

I have never denied you a relationship with the girls and for years, I have borne all the responsibility and cost for your contact visits with them. Clearly you are doing this to hurt me. Well, you accomplished that as I can't see them ever recovering from your ongoing mental scarring. The way you talk to me and our girls is sinful. Masking your shame by lashing out at them to retaliate against me is not the answer. You had two wonderful gifts given to you that you don't deserve. Their love was unconditional but now they want nothing to do with you. I hope at some point this rips you apart. I will no longer promote or facilitate their relationship with you. I know what you are thinking - breach me. I dare you, do it! – I will have great pleasure rolling out the index containing all the dismal parenting acts you have performed, to a judge.

I've copied all the relevant people in your life into this email like Ariel. I want them all to know you did this! It's been years, Dante. Get some professional help and grow up, or you'll forever remain a monster.

Anna.

Tears were running down my cheeks from the sorrow I felt for us all being involved in Dante's web. God... how I hated him!

In the shower I realised these emails were all sent shortly after I married Dante. I could have made different choices back then with this information, like leaving him before I fell pregnant. He must have deleted the email from my account, knowing he would be exposed if I had the chance to read it. The darker side within me whispered… *Calculating, lying prick. He really needs to feel pain and fear. But how?*

My mind then wandered off as if going away to find a solution to my problem.

Chapter 16
Raising the Battle Flag in High Heels

It was the morning of our first appearance in the family court section of the Victoria Provincial Courthouse. Our hearing was listed for ten thirty a.m. in front of Judge Quintin, and I was escorted by my lawyer, Valentina, her paralegal Jessica, and Peace Thatcher, my gun female barrister.

Peace was striking, with short, black, shining hair, light-blue eyes, diamond-shaped face structure, dark pink lipstick, pearl earrings, dusky pink power suit, Louis Vuitton briefcase and very high beige-coloured heels matching the briefcase handles. She was treated like a celebrity with the suits and other barristers acknowledging her as she walked past.

Peace was costing me $3,500 for today's appearance and $2,000 for her preparation. This did not include my lawyers' attendance fees. Laying out all this money for lawyers was in the hope that Dante would see what he was up against, and to direct the judge to achieve everything my lawyers had asked for; which included the interim orders that pressured Dante into negotiating and settling out of court.

My legal eagles led me through the security bag check as you would at an airport, past a huge wooden carving of the court coat of arms, into the elevator and up to the third floor. The building was very cold with the air conditioning obviously set on full. We passed another security desk manned by four guards. Peace led our entourage into a private room next to the lawyers' photocopy room. This floor had hordes of people milling around outside the numerous courtrooms: some standing, some sitting on the couches, some people even sitting on the floor against walls. With the hard surfaces, the noise was deafening. I was overwhelmed by the sheer number of people in such close proximity. My guess was there were over one hundred and fifty people on this floor alone, when I had naively thought we would be the only ones there.

Looking around there were people arguing, others biting their nails, some looking blankly down at the carpet or paperwork, and people in suits moving between couples. Two very official-looking people on either side of the floor wore black judges' robes and were shouting out, at the top of their lungs, the last names of people to go into the back of the court.

My lawyers had done their preparation for today's session, and for presenting this information to the Judge. But they had not prepped me in what to expect, which totally threw me off. As Valentina sat down, she asked me, "Did you see Dante anywhere?"

"Yes, he was standing behind the column near the lifts when we walked in. He's wearing a dark blue suit, striped shirt and a light pink tie. An ensemble I bought him," I replied.

"Typical" said Jessica, offhandedly.

"What happens now?" I asked, as I sat down across from Valentina and Jessica.

"We're going to go and speak to Dante," said Peace. "Best you stay in here with Jessica till we're called up."

"Okay," I said, biting my lower lip in a nervous reaction that tried to cover up the sick feeling in my stomach, due mostly to being in the same general vicinity as Dante. Peace and Valentina then left the room with some court documents in hand. The two women conversed as they strode around the corner in pursuit of Dante.

"I want to see, if he's open to negotiating the property settlement, today. That way we can ask the associate to stand the matter down for the morning. We'll deal with the visitation and custody issues this afternoon; it should be easy enough for us to achieve Ariel's interim orders. There's no way he's going to get custody, and he knows it. He's being egotistical and arrogant. I can't believe he wants all this aired in front of Judge Quintin," said Peace.

"There he is at the water cooler," Valentina said to Peace.

"Mr Prince. I'm Peace Thatcher representing your ex-wife today. This is Valentina Hunter from Bexley Ramsey."

"Hello, pleased to make your acquaintance," said Dante, holding out his hand to shake hers. She took it as Dante squeezed her hand like he was trying to break it.

"Hey, take it easy there. You don't have to break my hand," said Peace.

"Oh, I'm so sorry, I'm used to shaking a man's hand," said Dante. Peace smiled nicely back at him and opened with, "Will Mr Naylor be representing you today?"

"Nope," Dante said smoothing out his jacket lapel feeling full of confidence about going up against two girls.

"Well, then... I believe there's a good chance we can settle a lot of the issues today especially around property. Do you agree?" asked Peace.

"Well, that all depends on what she's offering?"

"I see you are seeking a further $450,000 in your final orders. We all know you won't get this because of your relationship being relatively short. So, what's your walk-away position to get this done today?"

Dante replied tersely, "$250,000."

"I don't think my client will accept your offer as she has been briefed about the possible range a judge could award you and this is well outside of that. I believe if you are willing to accept 10%, we can draw this up, put it to bed and have you paid tomorrow."

Dante took a few moments to consider his response.

"Tell her it's fucking 250 thousand dollars, or I'll force her to blow everything she's got fighting me through court. Oh! And by the way, tell her I'm still gonna take the boy too. Tell her, I don't give a fuck about her and she's a fucking liar. I didn't hit her or throw her against the door. She'd better see it my way or else I'll string her out through the courts for the next decade to teach her a lesson. She'll lose all of it by the time I'm finished with her. Bitch!" spat Dante at my legal team.

"Thanks for your time. We'll put your settlement proposal to our client," said Peace.

Peace and Valentina walked off, shocked by Dante's level of aggression and unprofessional demeanour.

"He's got rocks in his head," said Peace.

"I told you he was a piece of work. He's volatile and it seems on the surface a very pig-headed unscrupulous man," said Valentina.

"He's just made my job that much easier. I was going to go in civilised, but he doesn't deserve pleasantries. Excuse my language, but he needs a new arsehole ripped to teach him a few lessons on how to play with the big boys and girls in court," scoffed Peace.

"How did you go?" I asked, with a worried look on my face and biting my nail.

"Not positive news, I'm afraid," said Valentina.

"His vernacular is certainly offensive," said Peace.

"I'm sorry. Nothing surprises me where he's concerned," I remarked.

"His offer to settle property is $250 thousand," said Peace.

I immediately felt sick and my forehead and neck ached. I put my hands around my face and eyes, elbows on the table, digging the tip of my fingers down into my scalp, as if to contain my head from exploding. "He's really not going to give up, is he?" I said softly, the tears welling in my eyes.

"I'm afraid not," said Peace.

"What do you really think he could get in front a judge, Peace?" I enquired looking up at her through tears. I thought a barrister would know best.

"Looking at your case, he could reach twenty percent."

I felt rage at Peace for saying this… "How can he be entitled to 10% of my assets for each year of marriage? That's about $400 thousand dollars by my calculations? No! I don't believe it. This is all absurd. How could a judge award him that much over properties I purchased over ten years before we met? I worked my bum off and sacrificed to achieve all this on my own. He can't do this to me; it's just not fair. Where's the justice in this? He doesn't deserve any of it and I won't give it to him," I said, firmly snapping out of my misery.

The anger wanted to explode out of me. I envisaged myself in my head flying across the room outside at Dante in the body of a stealthy shiny black leopard, crashing him to the ground and scratching at his face and chest until he was unrecognisable.

"I'm going to let the associate know we are here and ready to proceed," said Peace nodding to Valentina as if signalling for the battle flag to be raised up the pole.

"We'll just wait in here until we're called," said Valentina.

"In court Ariel, you will sit on one of the chairs behind the bar. Peace and I will sit at the bar. You will not be able to address the judge yourself. Also, the courtroom is set up so the Judge can hear every whisper and word from anywhere in the room," explained Valentina, looking at me as though probing me to ask a question.

I was listening, but kind of not, being temporarily in my own world and thinking only about how much I hated Dante, and the different ways I could fight him.

"Before crossing the threshold into the courtroom, you will need to bow to the judge and then sit at the back of the courtroom until our matter is called up," said Valentina.

"The matter of Prince and Prince… to courtroom 3," a booming voice announced from across the hall. Peace came swiftly into the room. Picking up her briefcase she said, "Showtime Ariel; the judge watches everything, so I need you to be calm, act professional, smile, and… *don't look at Dante*. I want you to sit behind me when we are called up."

Inside courtroom 3, it was really cold. My hands were so cold, I had to sit on them as I sat down in the back row on a dark blue/greyish fabric chair. The judge was hearing another matter. It sounded like the parties had agreed to the recommendations made by the family justice counsellor and were seeking to conclude the matter. The judge seemed happy and politely thanked both parties for reaching an outcome.

The clerk of the court then called up another party… "Matter of Allen and Harper?"

Looking around the courtroom, it was quite impressive. I had no preconceived ideas about what the inside of this courtroom would look like. To me it was very old world, almost regal, set in a tiered system with the judge sitting higher up at the back of the room, looking down upon the proceedings.

The wall panels were floor-to-ceiling, stained oak, finished off with a cream ceiling, matching oak wood for the judge's bench, and bar where the attorneys sat. There was a large glass-etched coat of arms behind the judge and down lighting around the room. The clerk sat to the right of the judge and the waiting parties sat in the general seating area set up in theatre fashion three rows deep, with about ten chairs across.

"Matter of Prince and Prince," called out the clerk.

I followed Valentina and Peace onto the courtroom floor. Peace pointed to the seat where she wanted me to sit. I had a slight ringing in my ears and my heart was beating quite fast. I suppose I was panicking, as I was fearful of what the judge was going to do and say. In my naivety, I wanted him to like me and therefore he might see it my way.

"Appearances please," said the judge in a monotone voice.

"Dante Prince, Applicant, Your Honour."

"Peace Thatcher, QC Inns Chambers for the Respondent mother, Your Honour."

"I see there's a Form 44, a property and a custody application, Mr Prince. Are there any allegations of recent domestic violence?" asked Judge Quintin.

"Your Honour, the mother has made numerous false allegations of violence and applied for a restraining order," responded Dante.

"What are you seeking today regarding the property matter?" asked Judge Quintin of Dante.

"I'm wanting 35% of the matrimonial property pool, spousal support and an immediate payment of $20,000," said Dante confidently, as he glanced at me out of the corner of his eye. I reacted by nervously moving in my seat and rolling my shoulders back.

"What is Mrs Prince's position?" Judge Quintin said, staring at Peace.

"The parties agreed to and completed a property settlement in March, Your Honour, but Mr Prince seems to have changed his mind. On face value, from the correspondence, it seems Mrs Prince would not agree to shared care of their ten-month-old son after he kidnapped the child from her home, so Mr Prince reneged on the property transaction."

"Is this correct Mr Prince?" Judge Quintin barked.

"That is not what happened. She has made up numerous false allegations to ensure I do not see my son," stated Dante.

"Your Honour, if I could please point out a serious flaw in Mr Prince's presentation to this court?" requested Peace.

"Go on," said His Honour, in a curious tone.

"Mr Prince has omitted from his application material his accreditation as an approved family justice counsellor. Furthermore, his business website promotes him to be the country's renowned Divorce Doctor offering separation and parenting counselling services and he has a family law department run by his legal practitioner partner, Mr Jackson Naylor. I believe it should be noted by Your Honour that Mr Prince is not just a psychotherapist, but a highly specialised and court-appointed doctor in the field of managing families through separation and divorce."

I couldn't help getting excited and thought to myself... *Boom! You're fucked!*

"Mr Prince is this correct?" Judge Quintin asked, raising his voice a little louder at Dante in annoyance.

"Yes, Your Honour," he said sheepishly.

"Then you should know better than to come into my courtroom under a deliberate cloak of silence in an attempt to deceive me, Mr Prince."

Dante looked down and moved his paperwork around, clearly not knowing how to respond. His face went red and he couldn't stand still. The courtroom audience of lawyers, barristers and lay people held their breath in suspense as this was getting entertaining; like a train wreck about to happen.

"I am appalled to hear your expert opinion is for a 10-month-old child to have his routines, attachment bond to the primary care giver and residence upheaved with allegations of serious family violence and substance abuse surrounding the secondary parent. You of all people should know better than to come seeking such ridiculous interim orders, Mr Prince and wasting the court's time. Clearly you do not know what is in the best interests of your own child."

"Ms Thatcher are there any allegations of domestic violence against your client?"

"Nothing of any consequence, Your Honour."

"What orders are you seeking?" the judge asked of Peace.

"The normal procedural property disclosure, valuations of items not agreed, and the removal of caveats Mr Prince placed over Mrs Prince's properties."

"Is there a need for caveats Mr Prince?" enquired the judge.

"Yes, I'm entitled to equity in these properties and due to having access to limited financial resources, I've had to take out a loan for my business and for legal assistance with a lending group who required the caveat as proof of my ability to pay. I'm also afraid Ariel will dispose of them and flee the country with my son," replied Dante.

"Why do you have the belief Mrs Prince will leave the country, considering that, by the looks of it, she has a full-time job, mortgages, a baby, two court matters and her parents nearby?"

"She has ties to Australia, Your Honour."

"What ties are those?" asked Judge Quintin.

Peace leaned over to me and asked… "What's he talking about?"

"My dad's two brothers live in Queensland. I have met them once, travelling there when I was twenty years old," I whispered.

"I believe Mr Prince is embellishing the facts Your Honour. Mrs Prince has uncles living in Australia, which she has met on one occasion over a decade ago. My client is not about to sell up and leave the country. In fact, Mr Prince requested to be refinanced off these properties. His actions have put a stop to it just as the bank's documentation was to be finalised. These caveats have caused my client unnecessary stress and fees, when all she was doing was meeting Mr Prince's demands."

"I believe you have placed the caveats irresponsibly with no substantive cause, Mr Prince. You will do all things necessary to have them released by Wednesday next week," bellowed Judge Quintin.

"But Your Honour, I have secured a loan against my equity in these properties. The lender may terminate my loan," said Dante, visibly worried.

"That is not my problem. You should have asked Ms Prince for her consent to the injunctions and then applied to this court for a determination if you were not happy with the outcome."

"Your Honour, I request she pays for the lifting of the caveats then," said Dante.

"Mr Prince, *you* will pay for their removal. It is through your own stupidity they are there in the first place," said the judge.

Judge Quintin then looked down, searching for something in his paperwork. "Ms Thatcher, can you hand me up a copy of your orders please? I can't seem to find them under the mountain of paperwork filed by these two parties."

Peace passed them to the clerk, who passed them up to the judge. The courtroom was silent for a few moments. Nobody moved.

The judge sat reading the orders in silence.

Finally, the judge took off his spectacles, stared down at Dante and said, "I will be making orders in line with the respondent's interim property orders. Hopefully the parties will be able to resolve their differences at mediation or, I suggest for Mr Prince's benefit, private arbitration might be a much better alternative than airing this in a courtroom. It is clear to me that this is going to get unnecessarily ugly for all concerned if it proceeds in court. Now, where is the custody matter at? I have trepidations to even ask."

"Ariel has not allowed me to see my son in weeks, Your Honour," spat out Dante quickly.

"What does your client say to this Ms Thatcher?"

"I believe the mother, through Bexley Ramsey, offered Mr Prince time with his son conditional upon providing undertakings assuring abstinence from consuming alcohol and his girlfriend being present at changeovers and visitations. Mr Prince chose Saturdays from ten a.m. to one p.m. However, then declined to take up this time."

"Why doesn't that surprise me?" said Judge Quintin, rolling his eyes with contempt over this case.

"Do you actually want to see your son?" the judge asked Dante, as though questioning Dante's motives.

"Yes of course, Your Honour."

"Well then, you will provide the undertakings and see your son on… Sundays, I think would be better… from, say ten a.m. till one thirty p.m. The extra half hour helps with travel time."

Dante just sat and nodded.

"That is all I will consider today for these parties."

"Will you take an oral submission to transfer the restraining order matter into this court, in front of Your Honour or can you stand us down for me to fill out and file a Form 27 to be considered today?" enquired Dante.

"I will accept your verbal request. But if I were you, I would consider the implications of such a request and think to resolve the matter quickly. Is there anything else you would like to request Mr Prince?" enquired Judge Quintin.

Meanwhile, I got an impression that the judge just wanted to see the back of Dante.

"Your Honour, I would now like to consent to the standard conditions of the temporary restraining order without admission to form part of the interim orders made today," blurted Dante.

"Okay. Noted. I will relist this matter in three months. That brings it to November giving the parties time to hopefully resolve the disputes, Mr Prince. What dates do I have available?"

"Nothing in November. Your next available date is the 1 December at nine thirty a.m.," said the clerk.

"Is this satisfactory for both parties?" the judge questioned. Dante and Peace nodded and thanked His Honour whilst bundling up their documents for a quick exit.

Dante fled the scene like a criminal robbing a bank and I had no doubt he muttered many profanities about me in his head as he left. There were at least ten lawyers sitting in the back of the court who burst into loud chatter and laughter amongst themselves as he exited the court, his tail between his legs. No doubt they were all shocked by the tiny snippet of dirty laundry exposed in the courtroom today. On our way out, the clerk had to request silence in the courtroom before the next matter could proceed.

Outside the courtroom door, Valentina commented… "That was a really good outcome today Ariel. Judge Quintin went with our orders on both matters."

"My head's spinning. I'm blown away at what just happened. He didn't get anything he wanted. Is that right?"

"Correct," said Peace, nodding at the same time.

"And it looks like the judge really isn't a fan of Dante's, which is a good thing, right?" I asked, looking back and forth between Valentina, Jessica and Peace. They were all nodding with huge smiles on their faces. Jessica laughed a bit and covered her mouth.

"Wow… Thank you, but I'm sure with Dante there's going to be backlash somehow. I'm going to have to brace myself for what's coming."

"Ariel, I've looked at my diary and I'm not available for the date in December, as I'm in another trial. I can refer you to another barrister if you need to take one," said Peace apologetically.

"Thanks Peace. I'll follow up with you in the next few days," said Valentina. "Let's get a cab back to the office. I'm sure Ariel wants to miss the afternoon traffic and get home to Christian. I also need to forward Dante a clean copy of the amended orders handed down today."

At two that afternoon, less than two hours after we left the court, Dante's solicitor sent an email to Valentina letting her know Dante was not available to spend time with Christian that coming weekend.

At four Valentina sent the following email to Dante after

speaking with me on the telephone…

Subject: Photos of Christian on Twitter

Date: 22 August

It has been brought to our attention there are unacceptable photos on Twitter of Christian. Our client insists on their immediate retraction. Failure to adhere to this request will be met with a restraining order application with Christian being the aggrieved. Please advise.

Valentina Hunter

Family Attorney – Bexley Ramsey Lawyers

What's she on about now? thought Dante flicking quickly through his feed. *These are all holiday, beach, party and home snaps. She's crazy!* Dante decided to respond personally as he was too busy for this crap and he didn't want to have to pay Jackson to sort this out…

Subject: RE Photos of Christian on Twitter

Date: 22 August

I will wipe all photos containing Christian from my account to keep the peace. It is unfortunate, but typical of your client's low IQ to raise such a mindless issue. It is bizarre Ariel is following me on social media.

Dante Prince – The Divorce Drs

On the Monday after court, Jackson sent an email off, bright and early to Valentina on behalf of Dante.

Subject: Court Matters

Date: 25 August

My client wishes to resolve all disputes and will issue a 'Form 12 Withdrawal' for each of his court applications. He is willing to do this on the proviso property and custody are treated as contractually inclusive affairs. He agrees to Ariel retaining sole custody and agrees to 'renounce' his paternal role as Christian's father, if your client is open to the following three items:

1. The parties enter into a parenting plan, not legally binding custody orders.

2. A legal agreement stating Mr Prince does not have to financially support Christian; and

3. A BSS contract so Mrs Prince cannot come after Mr Prince if, and when his business is successful. The BSS is to be drawn up by Bexley Ramsey for our approval.

In return, Mr Prince will honour the separation agreement made in March this year. His final requirement is to sever all ties within 20 days.

My client Mr Prince wanted me to quote him word for word (please accept this is not my professional or legal opinion) to make it known to you and your client that; 'she is a pitiful storyteller, and she physically repulses me. She is a vicious, corrupt, and poor excuse for a female, but for Christian's sake I believe I should be the bigger person ending this debacle.'

This offer remains open for 14 days. Should Ariel decline to settle on all the terms above, my client will have no other option but to seek a listing requesting spousal support.

Jackson Naylor Family Lawyer - The Divorce Drs

Dante was conflicted by what he had just done having Jackson shoot this off, aware Ariel would take his boy for good. His alter ego said... *She's such a fucking liar... she'll do anything to destroy my reputation. I'll get her back in time.*

Valentina swiftly responded to Dante's lawyer that I would defend any such application and seek costs when I was successful.

To win his alimony case, he had to prove two things. Firstly, that I had the capacity to pay him the money he was seeking, which I don't, and secondly why it should be my responsibility to support him considering he is a highly qualified individual able to earn a considerable income as an employed psychotherapist.

The Divorce Drs went silent on this subject and didn't respond to my lawyer's counter discussion.

As soon as I read the email from Dante wanting to settle, I rang Valentina straight away, and was ecstatic that it was finally all going to be over. I couldn't believe it. Dante was finally caving. He was prepared to leave me alone, walk with the agreed property and leave Christian with me.

"Hi Valentina, I can't believe it… we won. Please tell him I accept it all," I said, over excited and probably a little bit loud for the office.

"I was as shocked as you. But then again, I think he saw the writing on the wall on Friday and is wanting this to be worked out privately. He would have been in fear of losing his family justice counsellor accreditation seeing how Judge Quintin reacted," said Valentina.

"Before responding, I need you to understand a few things, as it is my advice not to accept his peace offering."

"Oh my God, *why*? I'd be crazy not to accept and finish all this," I said, in a panic.

"The property and BSS part, is all fine. However, there are possible future issues with his custody and parenting plan proposal, and the reciprocal child and spousal support termination clauses he wants."

"But he's agreeing to whatever I want with Christian. I want him to walk away."

"I know you want that, but as your lawyer I have to advise you against it. If you agree to him having no contact, he can use it against you in the future because a parenting plan is not legally binding, so he can take you back to court over custody at any time. I believe without a doubt in my mind that he will do this. Furthermore, if we go back and ask for custody consent orders to make his offer legally binding and on a final basis, I can't see a judge agreeing to no contact."

"But he can't take me back, we'll have contracts, won't we?" I said flustered.

"I'm just saying Ariel, it is a wrong move to agree to this in its entirety. It's a smart move and one only an unscrupulous lawyer would suggest! The termination clauses he wants are solely designed to backfire on you, not him and his business. If one is set aside by a court or third-party agency any time in the next seventeen years, for example, the no visitation order, or you fall on hard times and need him to financially assist with Christian's needs, the financial separation contract is terminated and you will be back in court possibly over spousal support, property and custody with Dante showing the court, you stopped him from seeing his child. He is playing you for a fool. From what I've seen of this man, this is not the last hurrah from him."

"So, I can't accept?" I said deflated.

"It's entirely up to you, but I wouldn't. I'd also suggest you think about whether or not you're really willing to sign on for all of Christian's upcoming expenses. There may be things come up in Christian's life that need a lot of money like private schooling, specialised medical assistance, or private medical treatments. Or what if something happens to you and you have to give up work? He's got really specialised skills and should earn a very decent living in years to come. Maybe even a lot more than you. He is responsible just as much as you are for his child, no matter if he sees him or not," said Valentina in a motherly voice.

"I'll have to digest all of this and talk to my parents," I said, feeling somewhat gutted.

"I'll wait on your instructions. In the meantime, let your bank know the caveats should be lifted by Wednesday according to Mr Naylor. I have forwarded you his confirmation email just now."

On Thursday, my bank informed me the caveats had not be lifted, which once again stalled my refinancing. Valentina expediently wrote to The Divorce Drs putting them on notice to confirm Dante's intentions, or we would proceed to request orders in chambers with Judge Quintin seeking bank damages, lawyers' costs, and breach penalties for non-compliance with a court ruling.

Mr Naylor did some investigating and promptly discovered from his secretary that the release request form had been sent to a misspelt email address. He copied Valentina into the correct communication.

Chapter 17
Instruments of Manipulation

Christian fell ill two days before visitation with his father. He was burning up, was lifeless and clammy. I called a doctor who came by my house. Then at 9.27 p.m. I sent a text message to Dante.

TEXT: Ariel: Christian's sick. I think he could have a bug as he has a fever, is coughing and is off his food.

TEXT: Dante: Are you advising me he isn't going to be available to see me this weekend?

TEXT: Ariel: No. I just thought I should let you know as stated in the orders.

On Sunday morning at 4.57 a.m. I had to send the following text to Dante.

TXT Ariel: I took Christian to the hospital. He was vomiting and I couldn't bring his temperature down. The doctor is worried he may dehydrate from throwing up. He says Christian needs fluids and hydrolytes for at least five days. I have a medical certificate and will send it to you as a separate photo. The doctor's name was Joe Cage. Therefore, Christian can't see you today.

Dante's reaction was to have his lawyer commence an action breaching me over noncompliance with the interim custody orders.

I was ropable over Dante's reaction to his son's illness and hospitalisation. With an ache in my stomach, fuelled by stress and pure hatred for this man, I questioned myself… *Is this really what it's going to be like whenever Christian gets sick if I follow Valentina's advice and reject his offer?' Where the hell does he get off threatening me because his son is sick? He isn't a man; he's a child, throwing a tantrum because he didn't get his toy!*

I didn't know how to handle this situation, so I left it to my lawyers to teach me how best to utilise legal clout.

Subject: Breach Application lodged on Monday

Date: 3 September

In response to your recent breach application, we strenuously deny our client had any control over your son becoming ill. Furthermore, advice was given by Dr Cage at the hospital to keep Christian at home to assist recovery. It is clear, in this instance, Christian was diagnosed with a serious medical condition preventing him from being transferred into your care. Our client had to put Christian's health first and kept you informed as to his condition and treatment. We have included a scan of the medical certificate issued by the emergency department that Ms Prince already provided you with. We recommend you discontinue your frivolous breach claim as it will be defended and defeated. Should Christian's health improve, he will be made available this coming weekend.

Valentina Hunter

Family Attorney – Bexley Ramsey Lawyers

I had to speak to Valentina late that afternoon about minimising my legal fees after receiving yet another bill from them for last week's work. Dante's game plan was clearly to 'court' me into submission. I joked with Valentina about the term 'being courted' now having an entirely new meaning for me. My legal fees had escalated to $70,000 in the four months of litigation with five court applications being defended over custody, property, the restraining matter, the caveat debacle and now a breach. Surrounding these were his constant threats for spousal support, and to pay his business bills; there has also been a threat from my side to apply for a restraining injunction for Christian. Running parallel to these were Dante's offer to settle with a BSS, parenting plan, financial separation contract and his child maintenance exclusion covenant. It was an epic legal circus with me being the trapped underwriter.

Valentina and I worked out, to help contain my costs, that she would forward on to me all the correspondence without reading it and would not respond to anything unless I specifically instructed. I also notified Dante to directly communicate with me on all co-parenting matters from that point.

D-day came with my financial and custody proposals being delivered to The Divorce Drs via email and the post. There was a five-page legal consent order document covering his visitation, sole custody, and other parenting subjects and injunctions. I had offered a full day, one Sunday, for twelve months. Then this turned into an overnight stay until school started. School holiday time was then added, and it contained orders for Christmas and telephone contact, changeovers, and information authorities. The child maintenance subject was left out leaving it up to me to apply for it or not in the future.

The financial separation consent orders were drawn up as per our existing agreement. There was an extensive twenty-page BSS addendum that was to be lodged with the court in conjunction with the two main applications.

I crossed my fingers and toes hoping this was finally it. I prayed Dante would sign the documents and we could all move on. At least this would enable me to focus all my energy on Christian, as his health had deteriorated. Bexley Ramsey sent a follow-up communication regarding Christian as a tongue-in-cheek 'FYI'.

Subject: Christian's health

Date: 5 September

As you have shown no interest in finding out how your son's health has progressed since last Sunday, we are instructed his condition has deteriorated as he has been diagnosed with chicken pox. Christian has visited Dr Stan.

Valentina Hunter

Family Attorney – Bexley Ramsey Lawyers

A few days later, we finally received a reply regarding concluding our disputes.

Subject: Settlement Offers

Date: 9 September

My client rejects Mrs Prince's offers to settle. The timeframe given on the 25th August to accept my client's terms has expired. Please find attached a Form 13.1 issuing a 'Claim for Property and Support'. The court return date is the 24th of September at eleven a.m. My client is seeking a payment of $500 a week and for Mrs Prince to vacate the family home, giving possession to Mr Prince until the financial dispute is resolved.

Regarding your client's recent breach, Mr Prince wants make-up time for the time he has already missed this past weekend and any future visitation removed due to his son being infectious. Upon confirmation of a make-up day and time given for last weekend, I am instructed to withdraw the breach application.

We expect your response by no later than the 19th of September or else we will also request a costs order against your client.

Jackson Naylor

Family Lawyer - The Divorce Drs

I was furious upon reading Dante's rejection. He had pulled out the 'big guns' now with this preposterous claim to have Christian and I evicted from my own house and pay him a wage. "He's a conniving… sadistic… evil *animal*!" I said out loud to Mia and Benji. "… and clearly he has no empathy for his son at all. It's all about getting one up on me."

I phoned Mum and Dad and read it out to them having a hissy fit… "It looks as though it was all just a scam. A farce to waste more of my money on legal fees. He's so infuriating!"

"Yep! Sounds like it's his way or the highway," Dad agreed.

"Don't worry darling, he won't win these claims. The judge will laugh him out of the room, as he's not destitute; he's living with Charlotte and her parents, and he has his own business. It's success or failure is not your responsibility. The judge will tell him to go out and get himself a paying job," retorted Mum eloquently.

"I've resolved that I'll take him right through to a full court trial if I have to. I'll subpoena Anna, Ivana and Joel and his daughters if I have to. I'll bring them all, kicking and screaming. They're all going to tell the truth about him. I hope he loses all access to Christian and his ability to produce reports for the court. He'll dread the day he ever met me!" I said, with so much venom in my voice that I was surprised at what I was prepared to do.

"You go my girl. Kick his arse like I know you can," Dad interjected.

"Dad, I intend to screw him over in so many ways, more than just through the courts. Valentina even suggested last week I should make a complaint to the Psychotherapy Federation."

"You could even use your contacts in the media and do a big expose about him," said Mum.

"Mum I'm going to bury him, if it's the last thing I do on this earth," I responded.

"I wonder how he's going to survive with no money?" said Mum.

"I hope he'll be out on his butt on the street, for all I care. Let's see how long it takes for him to come at me for money. I'm calling Valentina in the morning to instruct her to hold off and tell them on the 19th to... go and screw themselves. I'll take my chances with the judge on these two requests."

Jackson Naylor represented Dante on the Form 13.1 application in front of Judge Quintin. He gave the reason for Dante's absence, as being summoned to appear as the expert witness for a custody trial in another courthouse. Peace was briefed for this appearance and crushed it, hitting the ground running and informing the judge that Dante had no legal standing to have his claim heard, as it didn't meet the 'Moge V Moge case' benchmark for marital compensation.

"What is the $500 spousal support for Mr Naylor?" asked Judge Quintin.

"I believe it consists of $80 for food and groceries, $60 for fuel and vehicle insurance, $250 for a loan repayment and $90 for personal entertainment and the rest is other general bits and pieces," said Jackson.

"What is the loan for?"

"The business Mr Prince and I own together has debts for the initial capital outlays contributed by the directors. I believe this is a repayment of this investment loan back to my client," Jackson said knowing he just sounded like an idiot.

"Do you think your client would be willing to leave his business and obtain paid employment?" asked the judge.

"No, I don't think so Your Honour, as our business is in its infancy stage and would not be able to offer the range of services if Mr Prince had to work elsewhere."

"I can't see when Mr Prince started this business from the affidavit lodged alongside the Form 13.1."

"I believe it's first day of operation was… the 18th of April this year," recalled Jackson.

"When did the parties separate?"

"I cannot remember Your Honour. Maybe my learned colleague could help me out?" Jackson said, handballing to Peace who then asked me quickly for the answer.

"I believe it was the 20th of March," replied Peace knowing she had just squashed his argument.

"I see Mr Prince is also seeking to reside in the marital home and is requesting the respondent to move out, is this still the case?"

"Yes, Mr Prince feels that, as Mrs Prince has several properties, she could move into one of them and allow him, his new partner and her children to live in the home until property is sorted out."

"Where is your client living now?"

"In the home of his new partner's parents in Cobble Hill."

"I am going to stand down this matter for ten minutes while I read each party's affidavits."

We all stood and waited for the judge to leave the room taking the court documents with him. My stomach was tied up in so many knots I had to hold my stomach muscles in to relieve the pain. Everyone in the courtroom waited in silence for the time with an occasional whisper.

The associate lifted her phone, spoke briefly to the person on the other end, then, there were three knocks, and she made her way to open the door for the judge to return.

Judge Quintin was furious, citing Dante's claims in his affidavit that I left him penniless and he was without a reliable income were idiotic considering he had frivolously spent over $65,000 in six months, was not willing to seek out paid employment for a regular wage and was seeking $250 a week for a loan repayment to pay himself and his business partner who just happened to be the lawyer on record for this matter. The judge was further appalled that a family justice counsellor saw it fit to evict the primary carer of a child out of their home for his own benefit when he lived with his new partner and didn't have to pay them any rent or board. He dismissed Dante's application.

The next day, Dante was on fire, acting like he was a lion roaring on top of a mountain, firing off email demands himself, feeling in total control. He obviously was totally oblivious to the caning his lawyer had received the day before.

Subject: Settlement Offer

Date: 25 September

I refer to your client's offer to settle made on the 25th of September. I am agreeable to the financial terms, with the exception that your client pays me an additional $50,000 in cash within five days. I will also agree to the BSS with some minor alterations and will not pursue removing child support claims.

Christian will live with me. My full proposal with respect to visitation for your client will be forwarded shortly.

I will give Ariel the restraining order injunctions she wants for 12 months, not the 10 years she has requested, as long at the wording 'without admission' is included into the order.

Dante Prince – The Divorce Drs

He was never going to agree to change his residency position, and neither was I. This was just another psychological transaction for him to make me go round and round in circles in his little game. I thought to myself… *I should have seen this coming; he's using Christian as his instrument to squeeze more and more money. He'll never sign anything.*

Valentina called, urging me to consider agreeing to Dante's property amendments, but not his residency position. This would immediately settle the financials, the BSS contract and the child support dispute with little expense as all the work had been done, leaving only the custody proceedings in court.

My thoughts were that my lawyers don't know this man, as I do. I now knew that nothing would satisfy him. He was just taunting me and would change his mind again, wanting something different if I agreed. He had nothing to lose and everything to gain. So, I gave Valentina the following instruction…

"Please confirm there will be no further negotiations and that I have instructed you to seek directions to move the matter towards a trial."

I deduced Dante obviously needed money. He had come off his high horse from $250K at the courthouse to now $50K in less than 30 days, and a judge had removed spousal support as a disputed item. So, it's best to reject the lot, as this was in no way about Christian, it was all about the money. The way he spends it, I knew he'd be on his knees for cash in no time.

In taking this tack, at least he could no longer play Christian off against the money. I'd be taking away his power. It's a shame the court system, in its own procedural dealings with parents, indirectly validates the use of leveraging children against money, pushing for custody and finances to be resolved together. Dante has been pointing this imaginary gun at my head since we busted up. I sat back sipping my coffee at my desk feeling relieved I had drawn the line in the sand. My intuitive reasoning revealed just how I thought…

Good Girl: He's now been told, for the last time… I won't pay him, nor will I give him Christian.

Bad Girl: Let's do the courtroom dance… psycho-boy! I've had enough of your fucked-up games.

The next Sunday would be the first time Dante would have seen Christian since he developed chicken pox. I did not attend at the handover, as Dante was now restrained from coming within

100 metres of me. This meant my parents had to perform all the changeovers.

On returning, my parents told me, a professional videographer had filmed the changeover. Apparently, the operator had the camera resting on one shoulder and used his free hand to push Dad over whenever Dad tried to push the camera away. There ended up being a minor tussle between Dad and Dante, with Christian stuck in the middle, which was exactly what Dante had set out to orchestrate, painting 'violent personalities' in my household around Christian. I felt so sorry for my parents, who now unfortunately had to suffer the wrath of Dante on my behalf.

Dante couldn't help himself having his lawyer flinging off a long-winded narrative to Valentina on the Monday detailing how my father had incited an ugly scene, caught on video, insulting Dante and Charlotte and being aggressive with Christian in his arms. It was implied that Dante had observed my dad, on many occasions, behaving irrationally and suggested my father had a dubious police record.

My predictable reaction was to think to myself... *What an idiot! I don't think he gives much thought to his wicked web of entrapment! His own evidence will be used against him if he's stupid enough to hand this up. As for my dad, I'll have to get him to apply for his police records under a Freedom of Information Request for the trial, to prove Dante wrong.'*

Valentina replied requesting a copy of the video, but her plea feel on deaf ears.

Two weeks went by with no litigious correspondence. I gathered Dante was either constructing his next move or didn't have one.

Christian, Mum and I went out late night shopping at a local strip. Mum took Christian and went off in one direction to the supermarket, and I headed off to Toys 'R' Us to buy Christian his first three-wheeler toy bike. I was stopped in my tracks outside the main street's café, to see Dante sitting by himself within a metre of me, drinking coffee at an outdoor table. He had been watching me, grinning with his elbow poised on the top of the table giving me the bird with his finger positioned over the front of his lips.

He watched me turn white, as a blanket of panic came across my face. He knew, and I knew, he was stalking me to terrorise and disrupt my life. I could just hear Dante saying to himself… *You're so fucking ugly. Like a pit bulldog. You need to be trained to know who's gonna be boss.*

I turned around and briskly walked away, past several fashion and jewellery stores, and made a beeline for the supermarket. I looked back a couple of times to see if Dante was following but didn't see him. Upon reaching the supermarket I stood out the front and waited for Mum and Christian to pass through the checkouts.

Dante came up behind me, so close his chest rested against my shoulder blades. He grabbed my arm whispering into the back of my ear… "I know you. I can track you down anywhere. Don't forget that."

I froze; the hairs on the back of my neck rose, sending a shiver down my spine and my eyesight went wavy. I spotted two, armed bank security guards getting out of their van and ran towards them.

"I need your help please. My ex is stalking me. He's standing over there," I said to them, pointing to where I had left Dante.

"He was just there. He's gone! Where did he go?"

"Miss, are you all right?"

"I'm a bit shaken up. He can't come within 100 metres of me."

"Maybe you should tell the police, as we have to get on with our delivery, I'm afraid."

"Thanks for being here. I think my running to you scared him off."

Mum and Christian came out of the supermarket as I left the guards. The promise of a fun night shopping had been completely extinguished, so we went straight home.

Mum suggested he could be tracking me on my mobile phone, as she'd seen a TV programme on ex-partners secretly hiding a tracking app on their smart phone to follow and some could even flick on the ability to record their ex from a remote location. This spooked me as it made sense, so I traded it in for a new one after work the next day and had a new phone number allocated.

Dante haphazardly declined his allocated time with Christian over the next few weeks, which was no surprise! He really couldn't be bothered to see his son, probably because it's more important for him to drink. His predicament was laughable! How can he, as the applicant, get away with seeking custody, when he can't put aside a few hours a week to spend with his child? This was one of the infuriating hypocrisies of the legal system, and it makes you fight these fights.

My cat Benji died, two weeks before our December court date. He died from a devastating virus called feline leukaemia. Benji had been diagnosed with this condition about 24 months ago, when Dante and I were still together, and was placed on medication to help prolong his life. For a week leading up to Benji's demise, he had lost most of his bodily control functions. I was so distressed over the death of my cat, and not in any frame of mind to deal with life-or-death decisions.

My chest hurt constantly throughout this time. It was like lots of things in my world were imploding and vanishing in sequence. I had little control over stopping painful things from happening. I really wanted to run away and start a new life somewhere but was trapped by circumstances. I sent a text message out of courtesy to let Dante know of Benji's passing. Little did I know however, that this glint of politeness was going to bite me severely, down the track.

Three days later, the court informed us that our matter had been adjourned for another three weeks and was placed on a different judge's docket at the Duncan Courthouse. We were being handballed.

At least this gave me more time to go through Dante's mountain of property disclosure documents, to make notes for the trial. His bank statements showed he was living the same pattern with Charlotte as he had with me. He was going to bottle shops every other day and had paid out $800 to play his online games. I noticed his company and trust account statements were missing pages and I saw he had even paid for a DNA test. I immediately thought... *That's probably why he held off lodging for custody, believing Christian wasn't his.*

My lawyers wrote back to Jackson Naylor, requesting more disclosure and explanations based on my many comments, as well as proposing panels of valuers and mediators for Dante to choose from. This meant he would have to cough up a couple of thousand dollars to meet the financial court orders issued by Judge Quintin in August. I knew this would hurt him, and I loved the fact that his own actions were finally going to cost him money.

Dante had Jackson respond by offering to resolve the outstanding property dispute, prior to the parties having to incur costs of valuations. I believed he did this for tactical reasons as disclosure was completed now, and he couldn't come up with the money to pay for half of the costs of the valuations. Secondly, he didn't want the glaring evidence regarding his business, earnings, and alcohol consumption to be placed in front of a judge.

The gist of his latest proposal was that he wanted a further $30,000 in cash, within 28 days after settlement, and also wanted me to agree to an undertaking that the disclosure documents were kept confidential. Hence, I couldn't use them in any further proceedings or in regard to child support. I took the deal on the table. Finally, the battle over my property was all over. However, the real unforeseeable impacts on my life and that of Christian's lay ahead of us, as I once again underestimated my Machiavellian opponent.

Chapter 18
Deflection, Control and Retaliation

The months of litigation had resulted in 174 pieces of correspondence between lawyers and Dante or Jackson Naylor, my lawyers and the court staff, and between my lawyers and me. My total bills from KR Cross Lawyers and Bexley Ramsey Lawyers had reached $119,000. I had settled with Dante at 8.5% of the property pool. Then it had cost me 5.6% of my assets to pay the lawyers to date. This was sitting very close to the 15% that Ben had told me he could be awarded at a trial. So, I had spent the money in its entirety, it's just that Dante didn't get it all. At least that was the positive side to this negative circumstance!

The Sunday after we had settled our finances, Mum and Dad returned home with Christian after his visitation with Dante. I noticed Christian was returned with a mark across his back, like he had been whacked with a stick.

My instinct was to phone the police as I wouldn't put it past Dante to take things out on Christian if he had gotten drunk. But if I contacted the police with something like this, I knew Dante would paint me as a drama queen or say I did it to our son. I spoke to Valentina about the incident and she concurred with my position. She also agreed it was time to subpoena Dante's police records for our next court date.

Dante's play after being served with the police subpoena was to advise us of his intention to seek the court appoint independent counsel to represent Christian's interests and a family justice counsellor report.

Christian developed a scaly dermatitis rash on his back around the mark left from last weekend. I was paranoid Dante would scream neglect from the rooftops. I recalled it looked similar to the skin condition Dante occasionally had on his shins.

My Mum gave Dante the cortisone cream at our next changeover. Dante's terse reply was… "I'll be getting a second opinion for the probable causes of this rash."

I telephoned Valentina from my office at work on the Monday with a very heavy heart.

"How do I cope with Dante's mentality over medical issues in the future? He's turning them into something they're not, making me really paranoid, like second guessing myself over everyday decisions for Christian."

"I'm afraid you just have to ride the wave out. Do your best and just take care of your little boy. He'll run out of wind eventually."

"But I fear any smear of blood, cut, bruise, bump or rash is going to end me up being investigated by police or child services and used to paint me as an abusive mother, which is so far from the truth. This is not good for Christian as I will always have to take him to the doctor to cover myself," I said, really upset and starting to cry. I was overwhelmed by all the legal correspondence and awful allegations flying around me.

"I agree, parenting is going to be hard with Dante. But you have to find some peace and a way through," she insisted.

"Is it possible for me to go for sole custody for medical, at least at trial?"

"I would recommend we wait and see what unfolds."

"I need some help from the legal system. I really fear him. I cannot live a normal life with all these things swirling around, until Christian turns eighteen."

"Leave everything up to us and stop stressing. It's my job to deal with him and sort this out," Valentina declared.

"Oh, by the way, you should know Dante has apparently contacted the day care centre demanding all of Christian's records. They have had their lawyers write a letter to him as they're cautious of any dealings with him," I remembered.

"I'm sure they have come across this kind of request before. I wouldn't worry about it," said Valentina.

My focus at work had begun to diminish, and I became

apprehensive about my future with Christian and what Dante was prepared to do to both of us. Either by reading, digesting and formulating, responding to it and searching for disclosure documents, I became consumed by correspondence. I thought the property matter had been concluded, but it hadn't as Dante was taking his time signing the agreements.

It became evident to me that the legal system itself actually fuelled all this insanity. The costs were enormous. There had been another 35 legal communications over just five weeks, which totalled $10,500. With my funds draining rapidly, I knew I couldn't retain my legal representatives indefinitely. The financial setback was also causing me emotional stress, and I began to crack under the combined weight of the pressure, especially at work. For the most insignificant things, I would spontaneously burst into tears at work, and had to leave on some occasions, so that I didn't disrupt the office and my staff.

My lawyers again wanted me to engage counsel, namely Peace Thatcher to appear for me on the 22nd of December as Valentina believed her expertise would be advantageous.

I couldn't hold back my thoughts... *I saw last time lawyers standing up for the clients at the bar, not barristers. What am I paying lawyers for when they won't want to stand and fight for me themselves? I was aware QCs were instructed for trials. This pressure is doing my head in, 'cause everyone thinks I'm made of money!*

My brain was fried, my inner stability and mental health was becoming fragile. I couldn't believe the effort and sacrifices I'd made to build my wealth could be stripped away by Dante with ease.

I informed my lawyers that I would not be engaging a barrister and urged them to focus on and push Dante to have the property contracts completed immediately, so that I had enough money in reserve for legal fees regarding Christian.

The day before court was a Sunday, so I called Valentina on her mobile instructing her to write to Jackson and Dante by lunchtime that day, in the hope one would be reading their email, agreeing to the independent counsel for Christian and the family justice counsellor, if he put his signature on the financial orders and the BSS contract to hand up to the judge tomorrow.

Dante responded accordingly and copied Jackson and me in...

Subject: RE Consent Orders for Court Tomorrow

Date: 21 December

We can declare to the judge tomorrow a property agreement has been reached. See the signed document attached. Nice doing business with you Ariel.

Dante Prince – The Divorce Drs

He signed it! I cried tears of joy. Finally! He couldn't keep going after more money. We were going to tell the judge tomorrow that an agreement had been reached. I went out that afternoon with a few friends, for a celebration of sorts, and to keep my mind off the fact I was in court tomorrow, and Dante still had 24 hours to somehow create a loophole and change the status quo.

It was my third time in front of a judge. Three loud knocks sounded, and the clerk said, "Please rise; this court is now in session. The Honourable Judge Blake is presiding."

The entire court stood in silence as the judge opened the door and walked across the room to sit at his bench.

"Prince and Prince to the bar," cited the clerk, as we all moved into our positions.

"Appearances please," signalled the clerk.

"Jackson Naylor, The Divorce Drs, representing the Applicant father, Your Honour."

"Valentina Hunter, Bexley Ramsey Lawyers, representing the Respondent."

"What are we here for today?" asked Judge Blake.

"Your Honour, I'd like to request a closed courtroom for all our proceedings for this matter," appealed Jackson.

"And what is your reason for this request?" said the judge.

"The mother is clearly out to damage my client's professional career, our business and embarrass him in front of the court and its waiting participants behind me, with her outlandish allegations and filed material," said Jackson, with angst in his voice.

"I see Mr Prince has affirmed in his most recent affidavit and Amended Orders dated 9 November that he is a psychotherapist, a business owner and a family justice counsellor," said the judge.

"Yes, Your Honour," Jackson said, looking down instead of at his Honour, clearly showing a weakness and disrespect to the judge before him.

"I must refuse this application on the basis proceedings before this court are, in the main, to be open proceedings, not conducted behind closed doors. It is my view there are no extraordinary circumstances here," said the judge concisely.

"Where is the property matter up to, Mr Naylor?" asked Judge Blake.

"The parties have reached an agreement Your Honour."

"Is this correct?" His Honour looked over at Valentina for acknowledgment.

"Yes, Your Honour. Here are the signed consent orders," replied Valentina. As she handed them up to the associate to give to the judge, she said, "The parties have also agreed to a binding spousal support contract, we are just waiting on minor final changes from Mr Prince."

Judge Blake read the financial orders as we all held our breath, hoping he would accept them.

"Good to see the parties have come to an agreement. I am happy to make these orders in chambers once I review the spousal contract. Send it through to my associate by the 5th of January."

Jackson looked back at Dante for a signal this timeframe could be achieved. Dante begrudgingly nodded.

"We will do our best to meet this timeframe, Your Honour," replied Jackson.

"Mr Naylor, your best… will get it done."

"The only additional order we would seek to have discharged in respect of property today Your Honour, is to discharge the respondent from being restricted from dealing with her properties, which are all being retained by my client in the agreed financial settlement at points four through to nine," requested Valentina.

"Are you agreeable to this amendment being made with the final orders?" his Honour looked past Jackson at Dante, wanting to size him up.

"That's fine, Your Honour," stated Jackson after conferring with Dante.

"I am prepared to make those orders by consent," said His Honour. "Moving on… are there any agreements with respect to the children's matter?"

"The parties have agreed to engage a family justice counsellor for a report and are seeking a court appointed solicitor to represent the seventeen-month-old child," said Jackson.

"Excellent, I think a report should help the parents see some reason; I'll recommend one from our panel of sitting experts associated with this court. On the second request, as the parties are both legally represented, I do not feel it necessary to appoint a children's lawyer."

The judge looked over Dante's amended orders to see what else needed to be decided…

"I see Mr Prince is seeking a residency change in the interim, and for any fees associated with the producing of the report to be at the respondent's cost."

"Yes, Your Honour," said Jackson.

I looked down at my feet to hold back the tears. My facial muscles twitched in an effort to hold back uncontrollable sobbing, but I had to wipe away a teardrop that had rolled down my cheek. Keeping my head down, I then slowly raised my eyes to stare straight at the judge and telepathically willed him not to consider Dante's application.

My gut tightened, and I held my breath waiting for the judge's reply to this.

"I am not inclined to consider entertaining any drastic changes on an interim basis such as moving residency, without the benefit of a child welfare recommendation, or a family justice report," said His Honour.

I leaned over so the judge could see me on my chair and mouthed so ever softly… "Thank you," and covered my mouth afterwards in case I had done the wrong thing. Tears streamed down my face and I had to wipe my eyes with my hands to pull myself back together. I looked at Dante and hoped he would see my despair at what he was doing, but his body language showed just the opposite. He was ready to explode, and shot me a death stare, clenching his fists at the same time.

He jumped up from his chair behind Jackson… "But Your Honour, she's keeping my son from me and I demand to be heard. All her wild allegations I completely deny. She's the one physically abusing him; he will only be safe with me," said Dante in a raised voice, his face turning red.

"Control your client, Mr Taylor, or I'll find him in contempt if he addresses me again," bellowed the judge. Jackson's cheeks burned from being scolded by the judge in front of everyone for Dante's outburst.

Jackson turned back to Dante motioning him to sit down and shut up.

"Back to the orders. Mr Naylor, under Section 211 (5) of the Act as the parties have consented the fees for the court appointed justice counsellor will be shared equally."

"Thank you for clearing this up, Your Honour," said Jackson.

"What counsellor is available for this matter?" asked Judge Blake of his associate.

"Noelle Gordon is available on the 11th of February, responded the associate, after checking the calendar.

"Are the parties available for interviews on this date?" asked Judge Blake looking from Dante to me.

We both nodded at the judge as he looked each of us straight in the eyes.

"That's settled. My orders will reflect the parties are to avail themselves for interviews here on the third floor on the 11th."

"Your Honour, I have instructions from the respondent to request an injunction refraining the applicant and third parties from videotaping and recording changeovers. I would like to refer you to point twenty of the Respondent's Affidavit lodged 1 November and point twelve of Ms Prince's orders. I believe there have been safety issues around this behaviour, which place the child at risk on a main road," led Valentina.

Judge Blake sped read the relevant affidavit paragraphs and order.

"It is my view you would know this kind of evidence gathering is frowned upon. It is not conducive to a civil, or safe, transition for any child. I think I will make it abundantly clear to Mr Prince that I am troubled by your overall conduct. I am not supportive of this kind of practice, so I intend to restrain both parties, so this doesn't occur. Am I clear?" asked the judge.

"Yes, Your Honour," said Jackson and Valentina in unison.

"Now, I believe I should see these parents back in court towards the end of March, say the 24th, giving Ms Gordon enough time to file her report. Mr Prince, I will then consider if your residency bidding has any merit. My associate will send out the orders with a confirmed date by this afternoon. Parties... Good day," said Judge Blake, agitated by the confrontation.

It felt like the judge was angry and had banished us.

That afternoon, while in chambers approving all the orders he had made, Judge Blake asked his associate to place our matter on another judge's docket.

Keeping his word, Dante had Jackson send through his signed BSS contract at five thirty p.m. the day before it was due to Judge Blake for me to sign and forward on.

"Just sent you through the BSS contract. I'll need to review the document today and once it's all done, you will need to sign it," said Valentina.

"Great," I sighed.

"Ariel, we have no funds in trust to cover this work."

"How much is this going to cost me?" I asked.

"I'll need a further $2,000 I think," said Valentina, very business-like.

I was silently going insane, like being in a room with no doors.

I thought to myself… *Hold on, you want to double charging me to fix the spelling mistakes you originally made that Jackson informed us he had found?*

"Can't I just read it, and sign it myself?" I said, panicking.

"That's up to you. Unfortunately, you won't know if he's been sneaky and changed something significant," replied Valentina.

"Is there a legal requirement for a BSS contract to obtain a legal sign off for it to be accepted by the judge?"

"No, but when you have lawyers 'on the record' the court assumes, we have perused and advised on all documents going before a court so it's our reputation on the line for a client."

"I will have to see what I can do, as I'm totally out of cash after having to pay for yesterday. I was charged for eight hours of your time, even though we were only in front of the judge for about 45 minutes in total. Your accounts department requested I pay $3,560 by the end of today to cover the current outstanding amount," I said, very depressed.

"I know your legals have been more excessive than most due to Dante's games… I'm sorry Ariel. I will await your further instructions before doing anything else," said Valentina, kindly.

"Thanks Valentina," I said, feeling sick to my stomach that I was being cornered by this vicious money draining legal beast.

"You know, you are strong enough and smart enough to be a self-represented litigant in court, after we get the property done," said Valentina.

"You mean proceed as my own lawyer, against Jackson and Dante?" I said, sounding miffed.

"I really think it would be an advantage for you to self-represent. You could even find yourself a McKenzie Friend to assist," she said, supportively.

"What's this friend, is it an organisation or a person?"

"Normally they're a support person. A McKenzie Friend could be anyone like your dad or a close friend, but usually they're professionals who are experienced in the workings of the court and can guide you with paperwork and sit at the bench with you. They can't speak to the judge though."

"How much do they charge?"

"I've heard some charge as little as $20 an hour up to $100, and there are a scarce few, who may volunteer depending on their workload. Contact McKenzie Friend Inc. I think they are based in Vancouver but have a network of people across all of Canada," said Valentina.

"Thanks. You are very kind to give me that advice considering it would impact you. I really appreciate that you're doing your best for Christian and me."

"I can't impress on you enough. You are so smart, look at how well you've done this far with all your paperwork, investigation, planning and strategy. You're so far ahead of any client I've ever had. Take what you have learnt from me and fight him yourself. You have it in you; to do it for Christian!" said Valentina.

I was in tears on the phone listening to Valentina. She was telling me what my gut had for months, but I needed to hear it from her... "I really didn't know if I was allowed to at this stage of the proceedings, or that I would be anywhere near capable to take over," I replied.

"Yes, you are!" she said sternly, "talk to your parents; I'm sure your dad will help you. Chin up... you'll be fine. You don't need me."

"Okay. I will talk to Mum and Dad," I said, with a glimmer of hope in my voice after hearing Valentina's words of inspiration.

"Speak to you soon Ariel." Valentina signed off, and hung up the phone.

Chapter 19
Mastering the Art of Legal Sword Fighting

After a fitful night's sleep, I awoke the next morning with a few things resolved, but with a weight bearing down upon me. I had a migraine, my stomach was in knots, and my body shook with anxiety. I was internally incredibly stressed as I wrote to Valentina.

Subject: Prince V Prince

Date: 5th January

Please withdraw from the proceedings and lodge the formal paperwork this morning before ten to notify the court. I will use you to shadow me from here.

I will read through, compare the changes Dante has made to your original version and finalise it myself by lunchtime and email it to the associate.

As you can tell, I am bewildered and stressed about my fees costing me over $100,000 with your firm and I have to pay Dante the $30,000 within 28 days of the orders being sealed by Judge Blake. He has accomplished his goal of breaking my cash reserves so I can't afford lawyers.

I note your email yesterday about prepping me for the counsellor interview. What will that cost me? I have to borrow funds from Mum and Dad to help pay for all this and possibly draw a second mortgage on my home to keep myself above water. Can you tell me how much it will cost me for the subpoenas you discussed so they are there for reading material for Ms Gordon?

Regards Ariel

Bexley Ramsey withdrew from the court proceedings leaving me to do the legal sword fighting with The Divorce Drs.

"Hey baby… she's dropped Bexley Ramsey," Dante said to Charlotte as soon as he received the withdrawal notice.

"I bet they've cost her a fortune," laughed Charlotte.

"My strategy at least worked to cut out her legal team for the fight over Christian. They would have charged her to the hilt every time I sent them correspondence. I must say she held on to them longer than I thought she would," Dante said, most pleased with himself.

"Now you can bury her, baby! There's no way she can defend herself through to a trial" said Charlotte.

"I know. I'm going to thoroughly enjoy this now. My bet is she'll probably end up committing suicide when I take Christian from her, she'll be that unstable. I told you settling on property wasn't the end of it. I have my end game in sight," scoffed Dante, elated at his victory.

"What are you going to do to her now?" questioned Charlotte.

"I have an ace up my sleeve. I'm pulling mine out for the family justice counsellor," said Dante, smirking but remaining tight-lipped.

Dante then took his first swing at me in my new role as a self-represented litigant as I hadn't sent the signed contract off to the associate.

Subject: BSS

Date: 5th January

I am concerned you will not meet Judge Blake's timeframe as the court closes in thirty minutes. If you do not have the signed contract to me today, I will consider our deal to have crashed. Dante

I was furious. I thought to myself… *He's impossible! He provides me with a contract virtually the night before it's due with three new pages, which is a lot more than spelling mistakes he said needed fixing. So now I'm waiting on Valentina to call me with her advice on his changes with a bomb clock about to go off in my face in thirty minutes.*

So, what else could I do?

I now had to think, breath and act like a lawyer.

Subject: URGENT REQUEST Prince V Prince; Interim Orders - 22 December; Order 5

Date: 5th January

Dear Associate,

Judge Blake's Order 5 required the parties in this matter to submit a BSS contract by today. The applicant did not provide me with his significant changes until late yesterday. I am seeking leave to file the document by lunchtime tomorrow giving my lawyers enough time to provide me with qualified legal advice.

Regards Ariel Prince

The associate replied just moments later approving the extension.

I co-signed the contract after receiving a detailed letter from Valentina on the meaning and consequences of Dante's changes and submitted it at eleven a.m.

Judge Blake sealed both documents the same day. This was a huge relief. Finally, the haemorrhaging of my assets had been plugged.

Noelle Gordon, the family justice counsellor, emailed me on her first day back at work on the 10th outlining her interview timeline including pushing our meeting out to the 12th of March, and requesting my mother and father attend to be part of the interview process. I had no idea what a justice report looked like even though Dante had produced them, so I was a little paranoid she had chosen to speak to Dante first up on the day.

I spoke to the McKenzie Friend Society who advised me to start putting together a response affidavit with as much evidence as I could find to show Dante was not telling the truth. Following this, I orchestrated a plethora of measures over the next couple of weeks like moves in a game of chess. There were Form 23s to confirm facts, Form 24s, Form 12s for disclosure requests of photos, videos, and recordings and four subpoenas for evidence. Draft witness lists had to be compiled, phone calls made, or letters sent off for documentation to qualify paragraphs in each other's affidavits from GPs, hospitals and other third parties. My aim was to quickly funnel in all this dirt for the family interviewer.

I was on fire doing my lawyering. I needed to do all this to show the court his character, to try and sway the judgement towards my side as the more credible parent.

"Shit!" Dante said out loud in his office, squeezing his hand on his forehead to contain the frenzied explosions going off in his brain.

"What's wrong honey?" enquired Charlotte, sitting at her reception desk at their office.

"Oh, nothing for you to worry about; I'm just going through the subpoena she's issued," Dante said, casually to avoid being further probed.

"Okay babe. Do you want a coffee?" asked Charlotte.

"Yes… that'd be really nice."

Dante's chest felt tight; his thoughts were running wild as he sat down to draw up his own subpoena request list for Jackson to issue… *Shit, shit, shit! How can I contain this? I need to throw suspicion back at her. I'll request her family's police history. There's got to be a criminal among them.*

As I had been including Charlotte on all my emails just to be a bitch, I felt confident Dante had slept on the sofa for a few nights because of this broadcasting technique. He would have had to do some major sucking up and lying to her face.

Dante's physical response was to get Charlotte to ask me to sign divorce papers, at which I laughed my head off.

In a conversation I had with my mother, before heading off to work one morning I related…

"I must admit, I was gobsmacked over how much he had lied in material and in particular his Form 24 Fact Responses, particularly when there's already evidence before the court that he should know is there."

"It's clear all the alcohol must have impeded his memory," laughed Mum.

"He should know I'm more than capable of pulling all the evidence together."

"No, he's just so full of self-importance, that he underestimates you."

"How can he lie so much in these sworn documents… isn't that perjury?"

"Judges aren't stupid Ariel. They'll do something about it. It's their job to find people in contempt of court."

"Yes… but will they do it to one of their own experts?"

Tracey rang me out of the blue to let me know she had a 'friend suggestion' come up on Facebook for Charlotte. She opened her profile and saw the most recent post was a photo of her and Christian with the wording… *My handsome son is going to break hearts… Mum's the word!*

I sent off a scathing email to Dante, fuming that Charlotte was publicly representing herself as Christian's mother and requested the removal of all such public statements.

Dante responded by belittling me for being sensitive and alleging I was stalking them on Facebook. He also informed me he and Charlotte were engaged, so he considered her to be Christian's stepmother.

We had two financial formalities to complete at Judge Blake's behest, to seal our BSS contract on the same day I was to pay Dante out. Firstly, we were to exchange $1,500 as a final support payment to each other. I didn't understand why, but I was just going with what the judge had ordered. The last thing was Jackson was court ordered to produce a legal letter we had to sign with our witnesses, acknowledging the respective payments had been made.

Charlotte sent an email five days before this meeting, letting me know that she had filed the divorce papers. My day could not have been more successful. I got up from the office chair smiling happily over the day's results, shut down my computer, walked out of the office and headed home. As I drove home in the peak-hour traffic, my brain was in overdrive thinking about what had happened.

I began ticking items off in my head… *Property… done… loser husband gone… finally… check! Oh, speaking of cheques, I'll have to make a mental note to let the child support enforcement agency know, that he's to receive a cash injection on the 2nd of February. This is going to be funny. I bet they make him pay me my arrears quick smart. He's going to absolutely spit chips!*

I transferred the $30,000 final payment the next morning to Bexley Ramsey's trust account to be disbursed. I then set in motion, my pay-back plan. After I called the enforcement agency, I looked up who his bankruptcy trustee was and called them. They were incredibly pleased to take my call and learn about his cash windfall.

Unbeknown to me, that very day, the trustee had frozen all the funds. Bexley Ramsey then popped the trustee's injunction documentation into the post the next day so it would reach The Divorce Drs' office by the court-ordered timeframe. They provided me with a copy by email.

I had decided to meet Dante outside the police station for our rendezvous to exchange the $1,500 that the judge had ordered. I was nervous and felt sick at the thought of being anywhere near Dante, especially if he knew I had gypped him at the ninth hour. My dad came with me as my signature witness. We pulled up outside the police station on Monday afternoon and waited for twenty minutes. There was no sign of Dante. I got out of the car and started the journey into the station grounds, but as I got to the fence gate and opened it, there was what looked like a ruckus occurring at the side door of the station. Three armed officers came out with Dante and another woman in tow.

My brain was flicking through a number of possible scenarios. Initially, I thought Dante was being escorted out of the station. But then they could have been following the officers out as they went about their police day. I froze at the gate waiting for what was going to happen. I thought to myself… *What the fuck is this?*

All five of them were walking in my direction. I tried to keep my cool and not look perturbed, but started to panic inside thinking… *What have you told them, to have three armed police officers striding towards me?*

Dad got out of the car, as he realised the police officers were gunning for me and stopped under a tree behind us, in case I needed him. The oldest looking of the male officers said to me,

"Are you Ariel Prince?"

"Yes Officer."

"Mr Prince has asked us to be here as he has concerns you may become violent."

"What! *He's* the violent one, check his police records." I said, enraged at him flipping his appalling behaviour onto me.

"Nevertheless, we are taking his concerns seriously as you can see. Now I believe some moneys need to be exchanged." The officer passed me an envelope. I said nothing as I opened it, fuming inside at Dante's antics. I read the letter Dante had signed and saw a stack of $50 notes inside. I then passed my $1,500 in $100 bills to Dante with my letter.

During this tense standoff, Charlotte had appeared at Dante's side from I don't know where. She tapped me on the shoulder as I turned to go. "What do you want?" I said, stepping backwards to face her. She handed me an A4 orange envelope. I took it and started off again. A woman in jeans, a cowboy hat and a white-and-red striped linen collared shirt, who had been standing in the background, then stepped in front of me, saying, "Ariel Prince you have been served. Please sign here to acknowledge service."

"Okay, I wasn't aware I was being served something else today. But what the hell," I said taking the pen from her and signing my name.

"And what, pray tell, am I being served with?"

"Divorce papers," Charlotte said, putting her hands on her hips and grinning at me like a bitchy cheerleader.

"Is that all? Great, I'm happy to oblige. You've made my year," I said, grinning right back at her as I walked up to the tree where my father stood.

I was still attempting to camouflage my shock at being confronted with three big burly police officers. Dante, Charlotte and the unidentified woman stood around talking with the police officers. Watching this dramatic standoff unravel over little old me, I realised Dante either must be really scared of me, or he thought I was going to be heartbroken and cause a scene about being served divorce papers.

I thought chuckling to myself… *He is paranoid! Good, he should be. Karma will come around one day… big time!*

Dante was flustered on his way home in the car, thinking… *How dare she think she can play games with me… She's gonna pay even more now.*

By the time I arrived home, Jackson threw his latest legal dart at me.

Subject: $30,000 cash settlement

Date: 2 February

Mr Prince has advised me you did not pay him the $30,000 by the court-ordered date. Under Part 10, Division 6 of the Family Law Act, we can seek appropriate enforcement remedies for expenses. It is our position a fair remedy is to apply interest on the outstanding money until it is paid at a personal loan rate of 11.7%. If you refuse, we will seek an urgent enforcement order.

Jackson Naylor – The Divorce Drs

My reply, I thought, was an artful piece of legal artwork. I thoroughly enjoyed sticking it to him as I now knew he had no idea what had truly happened.

Subject: RE $30,000 cash settlement

Date: 2 February

I have fulfilled all the orders made on the 5th January. My lawyers have already posted to you the necessary correspondence within the stipulated timeframe, so your assertions are wrong at law.

Anyway, it is not my issue the settlement money may have been frozen by a trustee. Go ask them for Mr Prince's interest. I have done what I was required to do and had fun doing it.

Regards Ariel Prince

"What have you done, you sly cow!" Dante said, throwing his coffee mug at the wall.

Charlotte ran into his office. "What happened?"

"Just get the fuck out! I don't want to talk about it."

After this, I heard nothing from Jackson or Dante for an entire month. The next time I saw him was at the courthouse for our interviews with Ms Gordon. I dressed conservatively in black trousers and an off-the-shoulder floral shirt with black high heels, with my hair half up and half down, for the casual mum-next-door look. I was nervous as I had opted to go this alone and not outlay further funds and now did not have my lawyers to prep me. I was clear minded about my goal, being simply that I needed her to help me keep Christian safe from his father.

Noelle Gordon was not at all what I had expected. She was quite tall and looked like an older version of Grace, from the TV show *Will and Grace*. She was mid-fifties and had possibly six children or grandchildren, judging by the photographs strewn around her office.

Noelle spent all day interviewing everyone. She had come across as very calm and knowledgeable regarding our case, which meant she would have been the first court person to have read all the affidavits, subpoenaed evidence, applications, reports and emails, from cover to cover. It was evident to me, that no judge had done this so far, despite three of them having presided over our matter to date.

It was an emotional day for me. Noelle and I spent a total of two hours talking in the afternoon. In begging for her help, I cried a few times. Charlotte, at the behest of Dante, had been included in the interview process and his daughters had been interviewed by telephone in the morning.

When we finally left her office at four p.m. it was pouring with rain so I left Mum, Dad and Christian in front of the commercial office building and ran to collect the car, so they wouldn't get wet. As I pulled out of the car park exit across the street, I saw Dante watching me from the corner café, and was creeped out by his lurking behaviour.

My dad received a text from an unknown number that evening.

TXT: Hi Des… it's been a hoot taunting you. But me thinks, it's time you died. Haha

We all assumed Dante must have been drunk and sent it on someone else's phone. His alter ego was now poking its ugly head out, letting me know he could get to my dad as well.

Noelle Gordon published her report just in time for our next court session. I saw the email come into my inbox during a meeting with my product development team. I felt immediately terrified and could not focus for the rest of the team meeting, as all I could think about was that my life rested in this one report. I forwarded the email on to Nathan, asking him to print it off, staple it and leave it on top of my handbag as I was in back-to-back meetings concerning international expansion plans in the boardroom with the executive team all afternoon. I intended to read it straight after work as soon as I got into my car.

That way, if it were bad, no one would see me crying. I had already had a second performance review chat with the President the previous week over coffee. His position was the entire office was still being negatively impacted by my separation and the court proceedings. Apparently, as I was the face of the organisation, the brand and company morale were being impacted by my personal issues. I was given three months to lift company sales and the internal culture and get back to being my 'usual happy, confident, inspirational self' as the president put it, or else I might be up for termination. This conversation had not gone down well, adding significantly to the amount of stress already descending on my life.

My last meeting for the day finished up at six p.m. I sprinted to my office, picked up my things and ran out the door to my car, noticing, as I ran, how huge the document was. I initially thought to myself… *this cannot be good, as she has so much to say.*

The front page looked very court-like, and the second page was a Form 22.2 acknowledging her expert duties to the court and then there followed her qualifications. I began reading the introduction and reached page seven by the time the other executives had made their way out of the office and into their cars, in the underground car park. Fearful of looking a little strange just sitting in my car, I turned on the ignition, reversed and sped a little too fast out of the parking lot and straight into peak-hour traffic. Every time the cars slowed down, I tried to read a little more. It was an excruciatingly frustrating exercise and built up so much internal stress inside me, as all I wanted to do was read this bloody document about Christian's future.

I was so stressed about not knowing what the report said that my stomach felt like I was going to spontaneously throw up from the panic whirling through my head and body.

I couldn't take it any more. I pulled into the emergency lane of the freeway and put the car into park, but kept the engine running. I then turned on the internal light and read the family report on the side of the road.

I highlighted points with a biro to use at the upcoming court date. There were some thirty points that were absolute dynamite in supporting my case. Noelle had also obtained the transcript from Dante's criminal assault trial nine years ago, and medical reports used in his case, which was eye-opening. He had been charged with two other offences: harassment and threatening death, as a part of the same proceedings.

Everything I had told the court about my experiences paralleled or had similarities to Anna's testimony. His own defence evidence suggested he had a mild schizoaffective disorder associated with a questionable delusional system. This enabled him to enter a plea of temporary insanity, relying on the 'People V Serravo' case in the Supreme Court of Colorado. This was introduced years ago, and it investigated whether a person with a mental disorder had the cognitive ability, at the time of the criminal act, to know right from wrong. Dante was acquitted. His review board didn't think he was a threat to society and sent him to cognitive behavioural therapy, as well as Alcoholics Anonymous. He was put on mood stabilisers and an antipsychotic medication. Noelle could see there were recurring patterns of dysfunctional behaviour spanning over a decade and a form of amnesia or delusional trickery too. Utter chaos was all I could think.

Dante, of course, downplayed all of it in his interview. His responses indicated that he had no issues to be concerned about that were worthy of court. He didn't consider himself a violent person now, nor was alcohol an issue, and he didn't believe he had been threatening or abusive in any way to either me or Anna. Indeed, Dante contended that I was apparently the mental case.

Thankfully, Noelle was not convinced and recommended that our son remain living with me with short visits to Dante. I agreed with her endorsements for psychiatric assessments of us both and the appointment of a substance abuse expert. I was not on board with her desires for us to attend divorce coaching and individual therapy.

My eyes were welling up with tears of relief and joy. I lit a cigarette and called my parents from the car.

"Mum, Dad… the family report is in. The god of the court nailed him. She hasn't given him custody."

"That's wonderful darling. Can you drop over a copy so we can read it tomorrow?" asked Dad.

"I can't. The front of her report states it cannot be shown to anyone other than the parties involved and their lawyers. It's an offence apparently."

"That's just ridiculous" said Dad, frustrated with the hypocrisy of the entire family court system.

"I'm so happy, you have no idea."

"We told you, you had nothing to fear," said Mum.

"Yes. I know… anyway, I've got to go as I'm still driving home."

"Okay. Do you want me to drop Christian off to you?" asked Mum.

"Thanks. But I think I'll be at least another thirty minutes in this traffic."

"How about you take the night off. I'll bring Christian around in the morning before you leave for work," said Mum.

"Thanks Mum… that would be great. See you then."

I pulled into the traffic, turned up my stereo and sang along with the music on the radio the entire way home. I remember a thought coming to mind while the radio hosts were talking… *He's going to be so mad he's lost. Stupid SOB… and she's just as dumb. It's going to be a good day in court next week. Can't wait to see him cower in defeat.*

I floated along on cloud nine expecting this court mess to be completely over next week as the appointed 'God of the Court' had spoken, and not granted custody to Dante. Finally, after nearly a year, Dante had been stopped in his tracks by one of his own family justice colleagues.

Chapter 20
Losing My Mind

On Saturday morning I was heading out the door with Christian to meet up with Sophia and Tracey and their kids for brunch. I hadn't seen them since the court stuff had begun last year. I had become somewhat of a recluse to shield myself from all the bat shit crazy, surreal chaos. The home phone started to ring as I grabbed my car keys off the kitchen bench to leave.

"Hello. Ariel speaking," I said brightly.

"Hello. Is this Mrs Prince?" said a man's voice.

"Yes, it is. How can I help you?"

"Mrs Prince, this is Constable Sasha Winters. I have a restraining order application to serve you. Are you able to come into the station today, or could I come to your work to drop it off?" he enquired.

I didn't respond. I was in shock thinking, *oh my God, What, now?*

"Mrs Prince, are you there?"

"This arsehole never stops," I said to the constable.

"So, can you come in or would you prefer I come out to you?"

"Please don't come to my work. I'll get fired. I'll try to get in today," I said squirming with an inbuilt feeling that my world was about to implode.

"I'm on till three so any time before then would be great," said Constable Winters.

"Thank you, Constable."

I clicked off the phone. A pain came across my head and chest like I was being squeezed and I screamed out, "Arsehole!" collapsing onto my knees on the tiled floor of my kitchen.

The voice in my head said as I was crashing down: *He won't stop unless you give up Christian*. I cried uncontrollably rocking back and forth for a few minutes chanting softly "Please let us go, you're killing me. Please let me go. I can't take any more."

When I regained my composure, I texted Sophia and Tracey.

TXT Ariel: "I can't make it, sorry. I have to go to the police station."

I called my parents as I needed Mum to look after Christian and Dad to take me to the police station, as I wasn't in a good frame of mind to drive.

On the way home in the car, I read his application out loud to my father. I was facing twenty domestic violence allegations in just two days in the Western Communities Courthouse. The arsehole had obtained a temporary restraining order against me for destruction of property. Dante had also detailed a plethora of serious claims including stalking, animal abuse, harassment, bullying, defamation, financial abuse, psychological trauma, child abuse, neglect and professional degradation.

By the time I reached reading the end of Dante's document I was crying from the sheer exhaustion born of this endless fight. The fear caused me to hyperventilate. I was confused to the hilt about what I was going to do and how I get off this vile abusive spinning wheel Dante had me on. He just wouldn't stop, and his Machiavellian mind misconstrued everything aiming to damage me, no matter what the cost.

I knew I hadn't done any of the things he had sworn to. But I didn't have the mental or physical energy to focus on this spinning plate on top of the custody dispute, my marriage breakdown, my fragile job, looking after a young baby, my health and my financial predicament. I certainly could not afford to engage the services of another lawyer for this without selling a property or getting a bank loan.

"What am I going to do Dad? How can I fight this with just a day? He's asking the court to make orders that I can't come anywhere near Christian and him. I don't care about him, but it means I can't be anywhere near my son," I said struggling to put the words coherently together.

"He can't get away with it, Ariel. It's all lies," said Dad trying to calm me down while he was driving on the freeway. "I'll pull off the side ramp up here and take you for a coffee. We can go through it all there together and work out a plan."

I didn't hear Dad as my hearing had shut down; my heart was pounding; I was sweating, and I felt light-headed; the chaos going on in my brain halted like I was hypnotised in a trance. Fear was all I felt. It gripped me like a ghost had settled on my bones.

I turned to face my Dad.

He smiled at me saying something that I didn't hear. I stared at him for a short while and said, "I need to go."

Unclipping my seat belt, I then I pulled on the inside door latch of his car and pushed open the car door with Dad still driving. In a split second I shuffled on the car seat moving my knees and bottom over to the left to step out of the passenger door.

Dad yelled at me "Get in the car Ariel. What are you doing?"

I looked back at Dad, tears streaming down my face holding onto the door handle. "It's okay Dad. Please let me go."

I moved to alight the vehicle. "No Ariel! You'll kill yourself," yelled Dad frantically struggling to keep his eyes on the road and me.

Dad grabbed me by my wrist to stop me from fully alighting the moving car and slammed on the brakes. He looked in his rear-view mirror and saw the cars behind him begin slamming on their brakes. He held onto me until he was able to slow down to a complete standstill in the emergency lane side ramp. I was hanging halfway out the door as the car came to a stop.

Dad couldn't pull me back upright, as he thought he would break my arm if he did. So, he let go of my wrist. I fell out of the car onto the grass beside the road, almost lifeless. He jumped out of the car, ran around to me and picked me up like I was a rag doll, holding me tightly to his chest and protecting me.

He whispered, "Thank you God for not taking my baby girl." He began to cry and continued his prayer.

"God, she doesn't deserve this. Please help her. I beg of you. If you need to take someone, take me. Not my precious angel."

Dad placed me in the back seat of his car and drove home in

silence, listening to me as I wept. As he drove, he got worked up mentally consumed with the fact that Dante had finally broken me and pushed me to the brink of suicide.

He resolved to finally do something about him.

I had a splitting headache, lending further to the utter confusion running haywire in my brain. I was melancholy to be still alive, having to face more mental torture from a person whom I truly now believed to be the devil on earth.

I am not a religious person by any stretch, and I am not crazy. I surmised he was using deception, distractions, violence, fear and cruelty to gain intimate control over my soul, desiring my annihilation. I decided there and then to rename Dante, the 'devil'. I would treat him with disdain instead of believing he was going to change, leave me alone and move on with his life.

Mum and Dad did not leave my side the entire weekend. Mum wanted to take me to the private hospital for help. Dad refused, knowing Christian would be removed from my care if it got to Dante that I had tried to take my own life and was in a psychiatric wing of a hospital.

Dad phoned my boss Monday morning as we stood outside the Western Communities Courthouse leaving the message that I was sick and would be back to work on Wednesday.

I didn't know what I was supposed to do for this day in court. I turned up with nothing prepared and I was not mentally up to fight it. I had not faced anything like this before, so I was in the dark about protocol and procedures. I was nervous, nauseous and looked like crap with dark rings under my eyes. A rash had broken out across my collarbone and up my neck and I felt like I had aged ten years overnight. With no lawyer to call or represent me, I was petrified he was going to get me thrown in jail for something I hadn't done.

We were called into the courtroom by a police officer. Dante made his verbal appearance as the aggrieved and then I said, "Ariel Prince, the Respondent, Your Honour."

"I'm going to take a minute to read Mr Prince's application" stated Judge Darby.

I probably looked like a druggie to the judge due to my demeanour and blotchy red face and skin.

"Ms Prince, do you agree to a consent order being made today?"

"I'm sorry Your Honour, what is that?"

"You can consent to the order being given to Mr Prince today with all the conditions he seeks. If you do not wish to, a date is set for a hearing where the aggrieved sets out their case and you can provide yours."

I looked down at my hands thinking for a moment and deciding what to do. The judge, the associate, Dante and the police officer all glared at me, as they stood in suspended animation waiting for my answer.

I looked up at the judge holding back my tears and said "Thank you, Your Honour. I will not agree. I didn't do any of this." I then took a breath and calmly glanced across at Dante.

The judge began speaking to him.

I daydreamed, imagining myself changed, wearing black leather pants and a black vest with huge, beautiful glistening black angel wings and a sword. I shook my shoulders, and the wings expanded gracefully allowing me to fly up and over to where Dante stood. I was so strong I could pick him up with one hand, and I threw him into the wall. I then darted in, to pummel at his chest with my lightning-speed fists. When I stopped, he slid down to the ground. A look of utter fear was on his face, with blood running out of the corner of his mouth. My wings disappeared into my back and I walked back to my seat at the bar like nothing had happened. I snapped back into reality when the police officer sitting beside me, stood up and handed the judge a piece of paper.

Dante controlled the proceedings. The judge looked favourably on Dante who was eloquent and charming with his psychotherapist face on, going through the recent alleged violent acts that met the threshold to proceed to a trial.

Once he finished, the judge said "I can certainly see there are a few incidents here that could be bordering on acts of domestic violence. I am inclined to continue the temporary order for Mr Prince today and set a final hearing. However, as there has been no recent acts of violence towards the named child… I will not be including him on this order. I will keep Ms Palmer on as a named associated aggrieved party for the stalking allegation."

"Thank you, Your Honour" said Dante chirpily.

I was devastated the judge had believed I had committed domestic violence crimes. I sat there looking down, shaking my head. I had always tried to do the right thing, all the time, by everyone who came into my life.

"I will set a hearing date for three months hence. The orders will set out the dates each party will need to file and serve their material on the other party as well as the court," said Judge Darby.

"Ms Prince I advise you to obtain legal advice on this matter."

"Thank you, Your Honour," I replied.

I had difficulty walking out of the courtroom under my own steam. Thankfully, the police officer assisted me, dropping me off with my dad who had been waiting outside.

Dante and Charlotte left the courtroom, arm in arm laughing at me as they walked past.

The following day was yet another day in court back at the Duncan courthouse. This time over Christian. Dante brought Jackson and a barrister, Mr Jason Green, to represent him. The barrister seemed to be on friendly terms with our new judge right from the get-go.

Judge Swanson was informed by Jason that his client would not be consenting to the justice report's recommendations and produced Dante's temporary restraining order as his proof I was a risk to our son. This piece of trash paper formed Dante's interim rebuttal to the report findings, opening the door for his barrister to recommend an alternative arrangement instigating overnight time instead of the day visits proposed in the report.

The judge didn't ask for my opinion. He read the report recommendations and moved to set down interim orders to advance the proceedings.

Judge Swanson made all the justice counsellor's procedurals

orders for the interim, triggering the appointment of psychiatric assessments, and the group and individual therapies, and a substance abuse expert. Barrister Green argued and won, for me to pay the costs for the alcohol expert as I had received the majority of the matrimonial property. He also gave Dante an overnight stay on a Sunday to the Monday bi-weekly, totally against Noelle's recommendation.

At home that night, over a glass of red wine and a cigarette, I sat alone in the dark outdoors. I was loath to realise Dante had smartly out-manoeuvred the 'God of the Court' by bringing in a barrister who was a mate of the judge and deceiving a different court into giving him a domestic violence flag to wave in its face, to remove focus from the fact he had pleaded to episodes of insanity in the past. I don't think the judge even read any part of my affidavit, he just read the final recommendations page by Ms Gordon.

I thought to myself, h*ow fucking corrupt is this system. He's getting the judge to believe I'm dangerous to our son using political ties and lies to trump expert opinion. There's no justice in a courtroom, only magic acts of distraction.*

None of what had happened, and what was happening sat right with me. Dante was hiding behind his mental science practice and harnessing the court structure he worked for, playing his own game of thrones.

Dante did jack up about the substance abuse expert through his lawyer the next day to Noelle and me, touting it was unnecessarily probing into his personal life. I contacted the 'Expert Institute' who put me onto Mr Jervis Fitzroy. Once I had paid his $2,000 fee on my credit card by phone, Ms Gordon then took over, briefing him as to what objectives and reports she wanted.

At the end of March, our divorce was officially sealed by the court. I should have felt great that I was free of him, but my soul knew better.

Chapter 21
Honesty is the Highest Form of Intimacy

Dante let me know he and Charlotte were getting married on the 4th of June. I laughed inwardly for the first time in ages thinking to myself - *how stupid can this girl really be? It would be so good if she falls pregnant and soon, and then it would be gold if he's violent towards her. That would help me and Christian a lot!*

It was going on a nearly a year since Dante had started his fully fledged court assault on me. My body wasn't getting on top of the stressors, so my immune system was pretty much at rock bottom. I had had a sustained chest cough and flu for about four months and my asthma was flaring up, making a wheezing sound in my chest.

I was mentally finding life harder and harder and my mind would wander off contemplating how to escape this hell in the easiest, quickest way possible. These same two irrational answers always came to mind – give in or kill myself.

I was struggling with the huge workload at my work and the travel necessary to perform the job and fitting in all the litigious obligations with Dante firing on all cylinders. He recently had Jackson throw in yet another grenade, requesting arbitration which would mean taking it out of the courtroom and into a 'private court' interaction. I said I would think about it as he needed my agreement to withdraw our matter from the public space and I had to do more investigating to see if it was a good option.

These were all big distractions hindering one's ability to live any type of normal life and remain mentally and physically healthy.

My hands shook a lot and I had migraines by the end of each day. I wasn't eating. Instead, I lived on coffee by day, chocolate, red wine and cigarettes by night. I felt alone, helpless, and depressed. I was full of a gripping, paralysing fear crunching at my stomach 24/7. It was like my brain was foreseeing something unbelievably horrible just around the corner and it couldn't pull the handbrake to stop it.

I had used up all my sick leave and holiday time at work to attend court and prepare legal documents, so I didn't miss important deadlines. I was aware my president was watching the train wreck of my private life, growing more annoyed at my absences and lack of ability to drive his business. He was questioning my superstar status he had initially seen in me.

My dad and I worked every night for two months putting together my defence to combat Dante's restraining order hearing which had been set for the 14th of June. During the day, my dad would track down the evidence I needed and stand in queues at government departments applying for documents. He visited my pet's veterinarian, toiled through boxes and filing cabinets for more bits of paper I needed to prove my innocence.

My response trial affidavit was huge, with forty pages of written response and seventy annexures containing my evidence to squash Dante's domestic violence allegations. This took a lot of man hours and placed huge strain on my body and nervous system.

I had obtained one hour's free legal advice over the phone from the women's legal clinic. They recommended I get a lawyer to represent me as these proceedings would definitely impact the final custody arrangements of the court if I were proven guilty on just one allegation. I obtained a quote from Ruben Creek Lawyers to represent me. Their quote was $15,000. I was out of cash to pay for legal representation and I had too much equity in property to get legal aid. So, I was screwed and forced to go it alone, or I could cave and accept that the order be slapped on me.

I finally understood the heart of this beast of a legal system. Lawyers' and judges' mentality is the public just have to come up with the money because only a legal professional can defend well enough to obtain the best possible outcome. It wasn't their issue that I couldn't afford legal representation, as I'm sure they had never faced this dilemma themselves, and they never will because they are qualified in this field.

The domestic violence trial went ahead ten days after Dante and Charlotte's wedding. I had told my boss I needed the day off to defend myself in the proceedings. I had broken down in his office literally begging for his okay to have yet another absence approved. He had been sympathetic during the discussion, but his body language let me know he was not happy at all.

Dante hired Slade O'Connor, a barrister, to represent him. I had met him before at a BBQ lunch and thought he was intensely attractive, carrying off the cool bad boy image with a Hugh Grant hairstyle, green eyes and black Ducati motorcycle and matching black leather jacket. In fact, I recall we had flirted up a storm in the kitchen that day until the conversation steered around to partners which is when he found out I was married to Dante.

The final hearing in total lasted three hours with Judge Darby's decision coming out at the end. My mum and dad had not been able to attend as witnesses as Mum had had a stroke and was in hospital with my Dad at her bedside. I was there all alone feeling like the court's black serpent was about to strangle me.

When I was on the witness stand, Slade exhaustingly went over every allegation twisting my words and trying to get me to admit I did the things Dante was alleging.

For my return cross-examination, the only thing I did with Dante on the stand, was hand up every piece of evidence, on each and every allegation, and asked him to read the highlighted parts out loud to the judge.

After Dante's witnesses were cross-examined, Judge Darby called for verbal submissions. I had no idea what this was, and was thankful Slade had to do it first. It was just like I had seen in movies. Slade appealed to His Honour to find me guilty based on four admissions I had made during questioning, twisting what had logically happened and skewing the picture for Dante's benefit.

For my final submissions I said, "Your Honour, I said the very first day in court, when you ordered a temporary order, that I had not done any of the things Mr Prince says. I continue to stand by this statement. I believe I have produced enough evidence proving Mr Prince has downright lied to you, for his own personal gain. He's played his poker game, banking on a permanent order to use as a weapon against me to achieve parental residency of our young son. I beg of you, please don't give it to him."

Judge Darby thanked me and deliberated for a few moments before speaking to us. I have never felt so nervous before. I thought I was going to be in so much trouble because of what Slade had said about me.

The judge began bestowing his decision on us: "A court is entitled to make an order if it is satisfied a domestic relationship prevails and an act of violence has taken place and is likely to occur again. In this instance it is clear one exists because the parties were married. An extremely acrimonious dispute over their young child is afoot. I feel I need to say, divorce with a baby involved is tragic and emotionally traumatic. In this case, I'm distressed Mr Prince says he became miserable in his marriage and decided to remarry, with the ink barely dry on his divorce, and wants me to accept he didn't begin with his new wife until well after separation. The facts pointed out here today speak volumes. The new Mrs Prince says she considered herself to be in an intimate union within days of Mr Prince leaving his wife. Therefore, in quick succession, there's been a break down, an injection of a new female partner with other children, and the death of a family pet into the emotional mix," said the judge, stopping to contemplate his next words…

"The aggrieved is highly qualified in the areas of how to handle divorce in a mature and considerate manner, holding a PhD in mental health sciences. He is a family justice counsellor called upon in our courts to help parents sort out disputes based on the best interests of their children and family dynamics, promoting civil co-parenting. There's definitely a lot to be resolved between these two parents. Perhaps with some clear hindsight, Mr Prince would have resolved all of his affairs taking a more considered and compromising approach, before remarrying. Those are my initial considered thoughts, apart from the feeling that the two of you should have taken a cold shower and went your separate ways in the very beginning… I'm going to make an effort to not comment on irrelevant matters, only focusing on acts of domestic violence that meet the legislative definitions. I wanted to voice this now, to point out there's a high level of conflict here that doesn't constitute violence, it's mere ear bashing on adult issues and one-upmanship communication." The judge paused, rubbing his chin.

"Now, this application Mr Prince has filed says Ms Prince is stalking him and his wife on social media gaining access to personal information which she then mishandled or used to persecute the aggrieved and his new wife. Ms Prince says she did not personally go onto either of your social networks. She says it was one of her best friends who told her about the postings and photos. Ms Prince has placed into evidence a text from the best friend Tracey showing how she got access to the information in question. Therefore, I'm not satisfied Ms Prince has acted deceptively or that this falls under an act of stalking. Anyone in the world could have looked at the photographs as they were not protected by any privacy setting. I also accept, that as the mother of a young child, Ms Prince would express her concerns about a third party's public announcement about being her child's mother. I'm sure this would be very upsetting for any new mother whose marriage had recently dissolved.

"The next range of stalking allegations are that Ms Prince is harassing by physically creeping around Mr Prince's yard, peering through their windows because she has made representations to third parties about household items within the boundaries of their four walls. Well, if you can say one thing… Ms Prince has dedicated herself to researching every detail because she needs to have her side of the story heard. She's precocious and thorough, forensically going about this entire case as a private investigator would. I'm satisfied with her explanations for every alleged episode and do make the finding that Mr Prince himself gave all of the information to his former wife through various disclosure processes," he said nodding his head at me.

"The next thing is, Mr Prince says Ms Prince is abusing their young child by smacking or pushing him over leaving bruises and scratches on his legs and arms, and deliberately using creams to irritate his skin. The aggrieved has produced some twenty photos in his efforts to establish a pattern of visible marks and has even included nappy rash. The evidence seems to suggest to me, on the balance of probabilities, that Christian is falling over while playing. Ms Prince has produced multiple incidence reports from the childcare centre, and I have a doctor's certificate here for dermatitis treatment prescribing a cortisone cream. It disturbs me that Mr Prince cannot see logic anywhere in this. He wants to see the worst in the mother of his child. If it is his belief natural options are better than the prescribed medicated creams, then that is his opinion. It is certainly not, abuse or negligence," said the judge matter-of-factly.

"The next complaint is that Ms Prince has made false allegations in the context of the custody matter designed to denigrate Mr Prince and financially ruin his business, namely, The Divorce Drs, knowing he provides services to the very same court community. Furthermore, it is alleged Ms Prince in consulting with lawyers is being defamatory about him and his new wife. I am satisfied Ms Prince has consulted with a few law firms in the past year, as there had been a lot going on. She had KR Cross Lawyers acting for her, then Bexley Ramsey and spoke with Ruben Creek Lawyers about a restraining order application. She approached Sebal & Kingsley, but they refused to act for her due to an existing business relationship with The Divorce Drs. Then there was a Colville Johns who was engaged as a service agent by Ruben Creek. I find consulting with this number of lawyers is nothing out of the ordinary and confidential legal sessions to discuss personal matters cannot be postured as denigration or defamation because you are on the other side of the matter. Mr Prince is saying lawyers, instead of maintaining confidentiality, gossip about cases innately. If this is occurring, Ms Prince certainly cannot be held responsible. I am not surprised she is distressed about all this and feels at her wits' end, placing little faith in the legal profession. So, in relation to that allegation, Ms Prince is entitled to seek legal advice and to legal representation. And I'm not satisfied she went out aiming to crucify his business or Mr Prince's standing as a family justice representative by overzealously soliciting a multitude of lawyers to assist her.

"The next allegation is Ms Prince has made hundreds of harassing phone calls to The Divorce Drs business, verbally abusing their receptionist. I'm fairly sure this is a trumped-up allegation. My reasons for this are, because neither Mr nor Mrs Prince, can show any evidence they rang their phone company to complain and find a resolution to block the person; nor is there testimony from their receptionist to prove she took these hundreds of calls and was verbally abused. I know Mr Prince wants me to believe this happened. But it didn't. Ms Prince says she has never called their business and went to the trouble of tendering her telephone records to prove it. She has sworn under oath she didn't do it, and I believe her," said the judge, taking a drink from the cup of water beside his notebook before he went on…

"The next allegation is that Mr Prince is concerned Ms Prince is going to kill him. In my formidable opinion, I believe there is absolutely no possibility of this ever happening. She certainly seems mad at you, but she's doesn't present as violent. If she were inclined to hurt you the way you believe, I ask… why wouldn't she have already done it, as she would have saved herself all the trouble and the $100,000 in legal fees fighting you in court? This delusion, and that's what it is Mr Prince… a delusion, is just not real. I certainly do not believe Ms Prince has a hit man on her speed dial, nor that she would be prepared to spend even more of her money to take out a person being nasty to her," said the judge, shaking his head in disbelief.

Judge Darby went on with his decision for another thirty minutes addressing other historic allegations. It was gold and music to my ears. Dante was shrinking away in his chair and turning red with rage, as the writing was on the wall.

Finally came the words, "I find I am not satisfied Ms Prince has committed any acts of violence, domestic or otherwise, towards Mr and Mrs Prince and Christian Prince; and on that basis, I dismiss the application. It's evident Mr Prince brought this vexatiously as a distraction from the main custody issue to waste more of Ms Prince's money, time and energy. I find this without a doubt. What I do also find, is that Mr Prince has been less than honest, deliberately leaving out known information and this is very disappointing considering his official position being contracted by the Attorney General's Office to assist families in court."

Judge Darby didn't stop there continuing, "For example, he omitted the police report detailing the damage done to his office and the fact that there were fingerprints left that were not Ms Prince's. I was convinced to issue a temporary order when Mr Prince knew full well the property damage was not done by his ex-wife. Had the court known these details, a temporary order would not have been made against Ms Prince. I apologise to you Ms Prince for putting you through this process; I know it has been emotional and caused you much unnecessary stress."

The judge glared at Dante before making his final statements:

"I've got some real concerns and think it's very disappointing Mr Prince brought this into my courtroom! I am appalled, being a cat lover myself, that Benji's tragic demise fighting leukaemia was twisted for personal gain into a false animal abuse claim. I feel sorry this young lady was forced to relive the death of her pet. I can see Ms Prince's point-scoring concerns. It is a shame Ms Prince was not legally represented here today, as I would have awarded her costs. Good day to you both," said the judge bringing the trial to an abrupt halt.

I left the courtroom first. My heart was dancing, and I was so proud of myself for buckling down under the pressure and coming out the other side conquering the devil. I stood under a tree in the front garden area of the courthouse having a cigarette before I left thinking… *I nailed him; I can't believe it! I should make complaints now to the Psychotherapy Federation and the Attorney General's Office considering the remarks made by the judge.*

"Bitch. You'll never be anything more than scum under my feet!" yelled Dante from the top of the courthouse step. I was startled and brought back to earth by this abuse and ran off to my car.

When I got to the hospital to visit Mum, I gave them the abridged version of the day's events and came out of the visit with a great idea after a conversation with my dad.

"The courthouse will have security footage of Dante's outburst at you," he said.

"Do you think so? I could issue a subpoena tomorrow for the footage for the custody case to show he has broken the good behaviour injunction in the interim orders," I replied.

I put the incident in writing to Dante first, happily laying the trap. He, as expected, denied it in writing, so I copied him on my letter to the court requesting a subpoena for the footage.

Although this entire process had been predominantly negative, it had provided me with a timely insight into a court's expectations for a trial. I was always concerned about the devil using these violence accusations against me for custody. I bet he never saw his own pitchfork being hurled back at him by me in the custody dispute.

Chapter 22
When Thrown Lemons, Make Limoncello

I got fired from my job at Burger Boulevard the very next day after the restraining order trial, taking me from being on a well-deserved high to a crushing low in a split second. The president and human resources manager cited I was unable to perform the required duties of the job to the KPI expectations because of the ongoing legal and personal issues having a negative impact on my ability to attend work, focus and represent the brand.

I know an employer doesn't have to care about an employee's personal life, but I was disturbed that such a large organisation had no sympathy nor support for a highly regarded senior team member going through repeated domestic violence. They surmised their only course of action was to terminate an already vulnerable female knowing this would impact my ability to maintain custody of my two-year-old child.

I was always learning through my management career. This experience taught me to be supportive of victims of domestic violence in the workplace instead of persecuting them further. Psychologically, they had not thought about how this type of conversation can tip a person over the edge. Anne and I had been dancing buddies all those years ago and the president often called me by his wife's name as we spent so much time together. We were all good friends. But at the end of the day, I was just a faceless number. It didn't matter that I had taken their business from the number 3 player to number 2 just with my business acumen.

I felt like the sky was falling, urging me to just give up and hand over Christian for this hellish rollercoaster to come to a stop. My marriage was gone, with me blowing $175,000 in the property deal; Christian had cost me well over $120,00 in legal fees to keep him safe with me in my home, and now my career had gone up in flames. I wanted off this nightmarish ride.

Burger Boulevard had given me three to four months' notice depending on when they were able to find a suitable replacement consultant, taking me out to mid-October. Their callous decision to fire me had been a blessing in disguise in the end. I had wanted to move, and this gave me the opportunity. I drove home, called Mum and Dad and said, "Pack up your house, we're moving to Balmoral Beach in time for Christmas."

That night I poured myself a limoncello and savoured the delicious bittersweet ride.

I spent two months investigating a possible business to buy. I came across Ambrosia Fine Foods & Homewares. It was like a mini marketplace with internal kiosks selling cakes, ice cream, flowers, homewares, kitchen goods, fresh fruit and veggies, and deli items. It also had a small coffee shop. I loved it. I received the financials, ran the numbers, and pinpointed my opportunities for growth. The profit margin was more than acceptable for an income. I made the trip north to visit the premises. It was perfect for a lifestyle change and a far enough distance from the devil.

The universe had aligned, providing me with a door. I just had to take a risk, open it, and close the chapter behind me. I negotiated with the vendor's agent and settled on purchasing the business for $166,000 taking over the 14th of December, giving me a short window to move by stealth so that the devil couldn't catch me.

I needed the custody dispute to go to trial after I moved to Balmoral Beach, so the distance was already in place between the devil and me; this way I couldn't be stuck close by in his web for the next sixteen years by the final orders of the judge.

Our matter was in limbo, waiting on Ms Gordon to finish with the substance abuse expert who had been performing random alcohol and drug checks on Dante so he could produce his findings for a trial. Dante and I had already had our one-hour session with Ms Gordon's appointed psychiatrist, and we were booked in for three group coaching meetings in October. The judge had left our 'privileged' individual therapeutic sessions up to us to arrange.

I needed to pull some strings to chart my course, so I decided to extend an olive branch. I sent an email to Jackson at The Divorce Drs.

Subject: Custody Matter for Prince V Prince

Date: 12 October

Please inform your client I am agreeable to participate in arbitration to settle our custody matter provided he is agreeable to this 'private trial' occurring in January. May I also suggest, we appoint the Canadian Arbitration Society to manage the process and chose an appropriate retired judge to adjudicate.

Regards Ariel Prince

Jackson Naylor accepted my offer on Dante's behalf requesting we jointly write to the society today briefing them on our needs, and that we inform the Duncan courthouse the matter was being sent off for private arbitration. Three days later the Arbitration Society wrote to us.

Subject: Notice of Arbitration

Date: 15 October

Dear Mr and Ms Prince,

We are pleased to confirm your custody arbitration at our office on Forte Street, Victoria. The Honourable Mr Greyson has been selected by our 'Appointing Committee' to arbitrate.

Please find attached our fees, payable within 5 days from the date on this letter. Also attached is our Arbitration Rules and a profile on Mr Greyson. A Preliminary Hearing by tele-conference has been scheduled for the 20th of October at ten a.m., to explore the issues and set dates for information exchange, which will then be confirmed by Mr Greyson issuing the Stage Three 'Scheduling Order'. This process moves the matter along to the Stage Four: Hearing, which has been set for the 27th – 29th January.

We wish you the best of luck resolving your matter.

Regards – The Canadian Arbitration Society

I was petrified as I knew I was going into a blood bath against Dante, but excited to bring this mess to an end as a trial date could be over a year away due to the number of cases before the court. For him, he was just one more move closer in his game of psychological warfare with his end game being his golden financial trophy: Christian. But by the time we went to arbitration, Christian and I were going to be the hell out of here, way out of the devil's grip and I was so pleased about that.

I knew in Dante's warped mind, getting custody of Christian means he gets me paying him a fair whack of child maintenance, and if anything happens to me all my properties go to Christian as well as a $1.5m life insurance pay-out, giving him everything. He even had the gall to tell the justice counsellor that he only married me because I had money, and that he had never loved me. These statements are now in court documents forever. Dante's game plays have never been about actually wanting Christian because he loves him; it's all about destroying me because he feels entitled to what's mine. This frightened me, as greed fuelled by alcohol and an evil mind is dangerous.

I had gone unconditional on my business purchase the 1st of October with the funds to pay the vendors sitting in my lawyer's trust account to pay across in December for my takeover. I no longer needed Burger Boulevard and I didn't feel like I owed them to stay on while they found someone to replace me. So, I quit knowing they had to pay me out the remaining two weeks as per my contract. The president and Anne were shocked as they hadn't thought of a contingency plan if I left early. Nor had they anticipated I would tell my staff the truth about why I was leaving.

My departure sent shock waves through the office as no one had been told that I had actually been sacked back in June and that they were keeping me around till they found someone to fill my shoes. My five senior advertising and marketing staff (out of total team of thirteen) resigned over the following three weeks in protest over the business's treatment of me. It would take Burger Boulevard over a year to replace the lost expertise and I was fairly sure sales would dive and store morale would spiral. It was my department that kept the organisation pumping along, as I had created and nurtured the dream team. Now it was blown to pieces.

I hope the executive team and the founder learnt that people make the business and do matter. The president and human resources manager were fired just short of a year after me because the business tanked post my departure. Throwing me under the bus, as their sacrificial lamb, hadn't worked for them. That's karma!

Who knew that less than four years later, the once mighty powerhouse under my watch, would go into administration, with the brand eventually wiped from the face of the planet?

Leaving Burger Boulevard when I did, gave me time to breath, de-stress, find a house to rent for Mum, Dad, Christian and me, and pack up our two residences. It was an exciting time and gave me a renewed faith that things were going to get better. I felt safe and secure knowing I was finally moving to the place I had always wanted to live as an adult.

I leased a gorgeous soft-pink coloured mansion fully furnished for $1,000 a week. Tenants were moving into my place and paying me $600 a week. So, the rental difference was minimal for me to afford in the scheme of things.

The owners of the place we were moving into had recently purchased it for $2.6 million and they lived next door. The master bedroom was my favourite part of the house. It was on the second floor with an entire wall of glass overlooking an electric-blue-coloured indoor pool, then the road, sand and the beach. I could have fit six king-sized beds in my room and there was a balcony off to one side.

The en-suite had a double vanity; marble floor-to-ceiling tiles; a spa and shower. But the wardrobe was the ultimate girl's place. It was about 18 sqm and set up like a retail showroom. There was a further three huge bedrooms on the second floor and another bathroom. Downstairs was a fireplace; a kitchen; two living areas; an outdoor undercover seating area; an office; a two-car garage plus a fully enclosed front yard with a six-foot brick rendered security fence with security cameras, intercom and electronic gates to keep out unwanted visitors. The house design and furnishings were very 'Gone with the wind'. I loved this house! I was free at last. I could go out and not be scared Dante would be there.

The day before I left my old life behind for good, I went to my local shopping centre for some last-minute packing boxes and tape. There was a kiosk outside the supermarket promoting tarot card readers with twelve clairvoyants on hand. A white-haired gypsy woman wearing a light-pink scarf, and who was probably old enough to be my great-grandmother, caught my eye. I walked over to the booth paid the $15 for ten minutes and sat down at her tarot table. She told me her name was Judy and went on, saying, "I had a feeling when I saw you that you needed guidance as there's a demon hunting you. Have you ever had a tarot reading before?"

"No, I haven't," I said.

"I'll get you to shuffle the cards and choose twelve as we only have ten minutes. These will answer questions from a practical or spiritual perspective. They can reveal the importance of past events, the relative present and may reveal your future. They may answer as yet unasked burning questions," Judy explained.

"Okay, I'm not too good at shuffling, but I'm open to give this a go as I definitely need some… divine intervention is probably apt."

I had nervous butterflies in my stomach as there were two or three dark obscure questions in the back of my mind; I hoped the cards would divulge what I wanted to hear. The cards I chose from the pack were: The Tower; Judgement; The Ten of Wands; The Devil; The Two of Swords; The Ten of Pentacles; The Three of Wands; The Knight of Cups; Death; The Sun; The Hanged Man; and Justice.

At the end Judy asked me to pick one more card. I pulled, The Star.

The psychic intervention revelations I went home with were:

I was right about Dante; he will not stop. Someone within my family circle would pass. I thought this may be my mother or father as they both had heart complications, or my grandfather who was ninety-two years old with dementia. Judy warned me that I shouldn't trust the justice system, and two unspeakable questions of mine were answered... Yes, Charlotte will cop it more than I did, and eventually Dante will pay for what he's done after he marries a wealthy female client who lives on a hill. Judy saw Dante being hit but she couldn't tell if it was fatal.

It's not in my general nature to wish harm on others, but I was delighted and comforted with this precognition as I drove home, ecstatic that I was leaving for good in the morning.

The removal people arrived with two trucks around seven a.m. with two men in each vehicle. It was two days before I took over Ambrosia, so the move had to be done quickly and efficiently. As the truck started to be filled, I packed my remaining personal items into my car which I didn't want the removalist to take on board. Things like jewellery, makeup, toiletries, bank books and personal mementos.

I was looking forward to leaving all the bad memories behind me in this house. I still had to eventually make the decision to sell the house or keep it to rent out long term. I took one last look around the house, picked up Christian and went out through the garage to my car.

Inside the truck cabin, unpacking what looked to be dusty old thick grey and brown blankets was Greg Knight. Yet another extremely bad choice in boyfriends. I had met him eleven years ago. Greg had ended up being a conman who took me for money along with nine others to the tune of some $650,000. He was eventually jailed for four counts of fraud.

While he was in jail, he had tried to contact me several times attempting to blackmail and scare me into sending him money. He even sent goons to my house and he eventually sent Dante a letter telling him I was his girlfriend, and to stay away.

Clearly, Greg was out of jail as he was in my garage.

"Dad... Dad!" I screamed at the top of my lungs running back inside the house shielding Christian hoping Greg had not seen me or my son.

"What?" yelled my father, from inside a bedroom.

"Greg is here," I yelled back in a panic.

"What the bloody hell! Show me, where is he?" Dad said, striding as fast as his legs could take him down the hallway to where I was standing in the office out of sight.

"He's in the back of the truck Dad. He now has facial tattoos and a mohawk."

"Right then… stay here," said Dad, as he bolted into the garage.

"Is that Greg Knight?" Dad yelled like a crazy man, as he stood at the back entrance of the truck with Greg standing in the middle of the cargo hull holding up a bed mattress.

Recognising the voice of my father, Greg jumped backwards startled, dropping the mattress on the floor.

"Get the fuck off this property Greg, or I'm calling the police. You were told to stay away from my daughter," Dad yelled.

Greg scuttled off the back of the truck and walked quickly off the property and down the street.

I was worried Greg saw that I had a child and would sometime in the future use this knowledge for his own gain as criminals do, and that he would have access to my new address considering he worked for the removalist who was now taking all my belongings there. I immediately rang the head office of Faulkshead Removals and asked to speak to the owner to ensure Greg Knight did not get hold of my new address.

I thought after putting down the phone… *All I need at this point in my life, was two psychos coming after me. I certainly seem to attract them. My new year's resolution is to stay away from all men.*

I had seventy-two hours to inform the devil of any change of Christian's contact details going by the interim orders. I sent the following text on the 14th of December just before I left home on my first day of owning Ambrosia…

TXT Ariel: Merry X-Mas and Happy New Year! Our new address is 16 Stevens Street, Balmoral Beach.

TXT Dante: How dare you. You never asked me if you could move.

I took over Ambrosia six weeks before the custody arbitration and was served with Dante's final battle thesis affidavit by registered mail the following week giving me three weeks to finalise and serve my affidavit and witness testimonies on him.

I worked in my business every day and at night after I put Christian to bed, I was my own legal eagle formulating and compiling my response arguments and cross-examination questions. I was up till two or three every morning, and on the road at six back to work, running on adrenaline, coffee and cigarettes.

I couldn't sleep or eat. My brain was on all the time and wouldn't switch off. My body felt like I was under attack from a ghost residing inside my body that wouldn't let me go. I broke down at work a couple of times under the pressure, hyperventilating and crying that I couldn't do it all. Thankfully, Linda, my confidante, and manager of Ambrosia, was there to catch me and build me up, every time I broke into pieces. She will never know how much I appreciated her friendship through this time in my life. She was my only friend in my new hometown.

I had felt alone back in my old house after separation, even though some of my girlfriends were nearby. They hadn't been touched by domestic violence or even been anywhere near a court, so they were absent, not knowing what to say to me. I didn't feel this with Linda. She had a sixth sense of the internal fight going on inside me. She knew exactly what to do and what to say, often kicking my arse back into supermom mode during the day and for the legal eagle at night. She would call me most evenings to check up and have a chat to calm my nerves and talk strategy. I loved her for this.

Linda didn't always agree with my decisions. However, she could see my ex was an unstable, cruel soul. Linda gave the devil too much credit, believing once court was finished, he would move on and focus on being a good father. She refused to believe me that this was never going to happen. Both Linda and Harvey thought I was still in love with the devil because of the amount of time I spent corresponding to him. This was upsetting for me and I often found myself mad at them for not truly understanding my predicament.

There were four grenades I had not expected Dante to throw leading into the showdown in his material. One of his two witnesses was from his mother. I couldn't believe she would compromise herself by choosing her son over protecting her grandson, knowing what Dante had done to Anna. I was devastated reading her horrible fibs at the kitchen table.

I walked outside and lit up a cigarette after breakfast contemplating what do about her. I had never met her, but it didn't fit well with me to burn a seventy-year-old lady under cross examination over her perjury. I knew I had to, but I felt uneasy about it. I felt sorry for her, as I was sure Dante had intimidated her somehow into signing it.

My mobile phone rang. The screen showed me it was Harvey. I pictured him in my mind before picking up the phone. Harvey was quite handsome for a mature man. He was sixteen years older than me and very tall with thick, ash blonde hair. He looked a bit like a cowboy with a sporty build, long legs, broad shoulders and a smile that always brightened your day. He also had light blue eyes similar to my dad's. He was old school charming, a huge flirt and always helped out anyone in need. Harvey loved football and was a pretty good dancer. He loved to socialise and be the centre of attention. He had married Margot two years before I had gotten hitched. She had hated me back when I worked for Harvey, but I never knew why.

"Why hello. The last time I saw you it was pouring with rain and you had me on the back of your motorcycle," I said in a flirty manner.

"Yes. Great times. Isn't it crazy that clairvoyant telling me I was going to help a friend have a baby and then you told me that very same day you were looking to have another baby with a sperm donor? Spooky," laughed Harvey.

"Yeh… I haven't really thought about it," I replied.

"So, when do you want to do it again?" laughed Harvey.

"As in a motorbike ride, I assume?"

"Of course."

"I don't know. I've moved to Balmoral Beach and bought a business."

"Really? Well that just suits my plans perfectly. I love riding out there; the scenery's beautiful."

"I'm afraid I'm pretty tied up at the moment. My arbitration is three weeks away and I'm still trying to finalise my case."

"I'd really like to catch up, I've been worried about you. I can be there today around lunchtime. I'll pick you up and take you out for lunch."

"Okay. I don't think I've eaten lunch in a few weeks. I don't have time to eat much these days."

"Text me your address. I've got a meeting to go to," said Harvey.

"Will do. See you at lunchtime."

I hung up and sent my address to him.

Harvey confessed at lunch that it had been love at first sight for him when I walked into his office interviewing as his assistant fifteen years ago. He had also revealed he and Margot had separated as she had been unfaithful numerous times over their sixteen-year relationship. I wondered why he hadn't told me this in our previous conversations.

I must admit, I had never considered Harvey to be a possible suitor before our lunch get together. I had always thought he liked Sophia more than me when I worked for him. I expressed this to him…

"I always treated Sophia like my little sister, because you were the one, I was head-over-heels for and she was your best friend. I even employed her because you said she needed a job. How could you not see how I felt?"

"Sorry, a fatal flaw of mine is not seeing how people really feel about me."

"So, can I take you out on a real date?"

This question stopped me in my tracks, and he saw the panic

come across my face. I didn't want to damage our friendship.

He expertly manoeuvred his chair from across the table to right next to mine within a few seconds, he then took hold of my face underneath my chin and kissed me gently. I found myself kissing him back, which I didn't expect.

"Please let me show you what a real man can do for you. Just one date. We'll always be friends."

"Okay, but can it be the day after the tribunal on the 30th?"

"You bet. What day is the 30th?"

"It's a Saturday."

"Then I'll take you out on the Sunday so you can have a day's rest and then I promise to get your mind off Dante Prince forever."

I had nodded smiling at Harvey and took a sip of my chardonnay. I had butterflies in my stomach from that kiss.

After my lunch with Harvey, I went on to read the second grenade Dante had hurled. It was a doozy! He alleged I had admitted to him during our marriage that I had committed fraud with Greg Knight. Furthermore, he and Charlotte had personally met up with Greg last year to have my confession confirmed. This made me feel really ill and stressed out, because the devil had purposefully gone out of his way to track down a convicted felon and bring him back into my world. I realised, thinking to myself... *This man was a genuine psycho and Dante knew this! Greg appearing last month couldn't be a coincidence could it? I'm sure they told him where I was living out of spite.*

In Dante's warped sociopathic brain, his argument was going to portray me as a criminal and therefore an unstable 'risk' and poor role model to have custody of our son even though he knew I was investigated and cleared of any fraudulent activity, being found to be the victim of the crime. I issued an 'evidence only' subpoena on the criminal investigator who led Greg Knight's conviction case. I thought, *at least this will fuck up this part of his crazy strategy*! I really shouldn't be surprised at this tactic... Afterall, *he's the one who got his legal team to concoct 'temporary insanity' to get away with beating up his wife!*

The third crazy proposition was that I should be ordered back into my old home and restrained from moving until Christian is legally an adult. He was out of his mind thinking he can remove my civil liberty of living wherever I pleased, but home hop himself with his new wife. He infuriated me!

The last allegation was concerning my sex life. Apparently, according to him, I am a bit of a slut traipsing a range of men through my house in front of Christian. So, my fake dating posts on Facebook made him bitter. Of course, on the other hand, he was painting a picture of stability with a new wife and more children as a better alternative for our son's residence. "What a crock!" I said out loud, amused at the thought of seeing his many facial expressions when reading my posts. He would have been beside himself with jealousy.

There was no doubt in my mind he was going to try to make me cough up who I was having sex with under cross examination to squash them out of my life. Fat chance I'm giving any such information to him. I said to myself, *I'll object… Who I sleep with has nothing to do with my ability to be a parent, Wanker!*

Dante would just die if he knew one of the men, I had slept with was his own barrister, Slade O'Connor. He had contacted me after the restraining order trial apologising, as he had had no idea what the truth was until I exposed it in the courtroom. Slade and I went out on a few dates and I slept with him, to get back at Dante, and because he was cute.

In having a sexual dalliance with Slade, he could no longer assist Dante in anything against me in the future as it would be a conflict of interest. I had pictures of us together to prove it on my phone if I had to. I implied this to him coyly over a glass of wine one night, about his compromised position. He didn't care as he no longer wanted to be associated with Dante, believing him to be a narcissist of the worst kind.

I found Slade's summation of the devil insightful back then, as it was before the schizoaffective disorder revelation had been found by Noelle. Since separation, I had been searching for a box or medical term to categorise him, his personality and his actions; I wanted to make reason out of his obsessive cruelty towards me.

Maybe 'narcissism' was the desired prognosis I needed.

I researched various articles on the internet after our conversation and came across the psychological syndrome of 'malignant narcissism' which was a personality disorder consisting of an extreme mix of narcissism, anti-social behaviour, aggression, and sadism. These people are grandiose and always ready to raise hostility levels. They undermine families and any organisations in which they are involved, and they dehumanise the people with whom they associate. These individuals are the most dangerous type of narcissist as they can be destructive and abusive; they always want to dominate others and win. Furthermore, they lack a conscience; enjoy damaging because they can, and interactions with them are likely to be harmful as they cannot maintain healthy relationships. The malignant narcissists are human parasites feeding off their prey, raging, crying and throwing tantrums like children because they believe they are entitled. They are generally a product of their childhood environment, which would normally be filled with abusive and traumatic attachments.

A few bloggers compared this type of individual to devil-like humans throughout history such as Christian the Great, Adolph Hitler, Napoleon Bonaparte and the devil in the bible. This syndrome has no cure for the victim nor the narcissist, other than death.

Now that this part of the devil's affidavit had recalled this information to my brain, I typed into the Google search bar… *Malignant Narcissists and Schizoaffective Disorder* to see if the personality disorder was found to co-exist with the mental disorder. They can, I discovered; however, the narcissism is a permanent state, and the other is episodic, and can be controlled by daily medication to never appear.

Mr Greyson, after receiving both of our final hearing affidavits, witness testimonies, subpoenas, and the three expert reports (being the family justice report by Noelle Gordon, the substance abuse findings from Mr Jervis Fitzroy and Dr Ford's psychiatric assessments) asked for Ms Gordon to produce an updated recommendations report. Mr Greyson wanted her to speak with Dante's psychologist whom he had engaged after Judge Blake's request in March last year and consider the two other expert report findings.

Chapter 23
War and Peace Starts by Ripping Out a Heart

We presented for arbitration at ten a.m. I had my dad working with me as my McKenzie Friend, and my Mum, Anna Harper and Ivana were my supporting witnesses. Dante was represented by a barrister – Clarence Fuller, a young thirty-something man who wore the black gown and white wig. To me, he looked too young to be a barrister. Jackson Naylor was surprisingly absent. My opponent's witnesses were Charlotte and his mother, and we both wanted to cross examine Noelle Gordon personally. I also requested Dr Ford be available for questioning either by telephone or in person on the last day, as Dante didn't want to question her on her report.

I had booked two rooms at the Comfort Inn Hotel for the duration of the arbitration. One room was for my babysitters, Laurie and Fiona, to look after Christian during the day when Mum, Dad and I were at the hearing and at night if I had to work.

I had flown Anna in and put her up in a separate hotel. Ivana had provided Mr Greyson at the eleventh hour a hospital medical certificate stating she was not well enough to testify in these proceedings, so she was excused. I had no doubt that this was Dante's work.

I had not met Anna before, so it was interesting when you put the three of us girls together from Dante's past and present: there was a style to his choice of partners. We all had long hair, small builds, were around the same height, naturally pretty and had similar sized boobs.

We were all waiting outside in the foyer of the reception area to be escorted into the arbitration room with Dante's party on one side and me on the other. It was awful. Finally, a young lady appeared by the counter and requested that we all follow her down the hallway.

The room was set up just like a courtroom. Dante and his barrister sat on the right facing the judge and I sat on left with my dad. Our witnesses were placed in separate rooms. The Honourable Mr Greyson entered shortly after, and the proceedings began.

Dante bolted like a horse out of the starting gates, attempting to have Anna removed as a witness. His objection was denied. Clarence suggested we begin with the cross-examinations of my mother and then Dante's mother before I was up, as he believed they would be fairly quick leaving most of today focused on me.

The inquisition began! My mum was on the stand for a little over an hour. She was put under pressure at the outset over her recollections of conversations with me to do with the alleged violence in our home. Clarence Fuller made it hard for her to answer the way she wanted to, and her memory was not crash hot and sometimes she stubbornly didn't want to answer a question because she didn't know how. She was visibly flustered and frightened; at one point requesting a ten-minute break because she was having heart palpitations. Thankfully, from then on, Mr Greyson did stop Dante's barrister whenever he was agitating a subject for too long with my mum, having read in my affidavit that she had had a heart attack last year.

Dante's mother was called up. Clarence didn't want to question any of her sworn testimony, so it was my turn.

"Do you own a computer Marylyn?" I asked.

"No, I couldn't even work one if I tried," she said jovially.

"I notice your affidavit has been typed; was it done on a computer?"

"I think so, my son did it for me."

"When you say he did it for you, are you saying you hand wrote it and he copied it out?"

"No."

"Did you tell it to him, and he wrote it down and then produced the document?"

"No, I didn't."

"So, none of this is your own words then?" I said, feeling elated that I had just politely nailed her.

"My son produced it for me and asked me to sign it."

"Thank you, Marylyn, I have no further questions."

As she walked out of the room, I requested for her affidavit to be struck off based on the fact it had been fabricated by the applicant. Mr Greyson agreed.
I was to be on the hot seat now. Clarence, the barrister questioned me for 45 minutes starting with…

"What are five good things about Dante's parenting skills?"

I was taken aback as I couldn't think of one, so he had me lying to answer the question.

He chose to agitate subjects concerning travel logistics, my thoughts on the issue of drinking safeguards, my business and hours of work, my relationship status, and daily child-based routines and who did what in my family for Christian. We then broke for lunch.

They got stuck into me after lunch in the second round of questioning, asking me to describe the first and then the second alleged domestic violence incidents. I made sure I referred to the bill I paid for the window to be fixed the day after the first punch was thrown at me. When I finished recalling the second event, Mr Greyson stepped in asking, "Ms Prince, are you saying Mr Prince, in a state of complete intoxication, picked you up in mid-air and was able to throw you three metres across a room?"

"Yes, Your Honour."

"Ms Prince, I do not believe a word you have said; that is impossible," said Mr Greyson, raising his voice at me.

My heart raced, my blood shook inside my veins. I felt like I was going to pass out with my heart being ripped out by our arbitrator. My ears were ringing, and I couldn't hear the next question. I stared like a zombie into space.

"Ms Prince answer the question!" yelled Mr Greyson.

I was hyperventilating trying to breathe my way out of my panic attack. My hearing returned with a sharp shudder going from one ear to the other. I didn't regain my strength or dignity back, totally falling to bits for the remaining two hours of Dante's barrister's questioning of me.

Our arbitrator called it quits for the day at three p.m. passing comment: "Ms Prince is visibly unfit for more questioning so we will finish for today and resume at nine a.m. tomorrow morning."

I went back to the hotel and cried so hard at my utter failure.

"Dad I couldn't convince him Dante was violent to me."

"Ariel, you need to pull yourself together. You've still got two more days to get him to believe you."

"I can't do it Dad. I don't know how."

"You've got to grow some balls Ariel. Go on the attack, instead of being the victim. You've got to keep going, for Christian."

"I'm going to go to bed to lie down. I don't feel so good."

"Okay. Your mother and Fiona will sort out Christian."

"I closed the bedroom door behind me shutting away the whispers from the four of them in the kitchen.

The following day I requested that Anna be put on the stand first, citing she had to get home to her daughters. Mr Greyson allowed this request. It was my epiphany tactic in the wee hours of this morning, as I hadn't slept a wink all night from the nervous stress the arbitrator had implanted in me by his treatment yesterday. If I put Anna on the stand before the questioning of me continued, he would see another ex-wife claiming similar feats of appalling drunken violence and abusive behaviour. Mr Greyson had no idea what Anna was here to say as there was no written testimony in front of him from her. I had issued a summons for her appearance, so not even Clarence Fuller knew what Anna was going to declare.

Mr Greyson suggested I question Anna first to lead the testimony. After obtaining from her all the necessary prerequisites like name, association, whether she knew me, etc., I asked her, "Can you tell us about your relationship with Dante?"

She was eloquent, succinct, composed and explosive to say the least. She must have rehearsed her monologue for years with the hope of one day telling her history to a judiciary. We all sat listening to her story for twenty minutes.

I burst into tears at the bar halfway through her testimony because her experiences just about mirrored mine. I was in shock thinking to myself… *This is sick. He's sick. She has been coping it even with me in the picture, and she has 500 emails outside to expose what he does to help me.*

I stood up as Anna spoke about the emails… "Mr Greyson, I'd like to request whether Ms Harper can bring these documents in to enter in as evidence?"

"I don't think that will be necessary. I get the gist of Ms Harper's testimony and will make a note she was willing to give the communications into evidence to substantiate Mr Prince's co-parenting behaviour."

I then asked Anna to describe each of the assaults that she had endured at the hands of Dante, in depth. Anna took us through three events step by step. She said he was drunk on every occasion.

To finish up, Anna informed the court she had to seek therapy with a psychiatrist for years to deal with her fear of Dante. She described her parenting relationship as a 'living hell'.

Clarence Fuller declined to question Anna knowing any further questioning of her would continue to negatively impact their case.

"Thank you, Ms Harper. I know it must have taken a lot of courage for you to come here today. You are excused, and safe journey home," said Mr Greyson.

Anna left, and never spoke to me again even though our children were half-siblings to each other.

I was back on the stand again after Anna left. Clarence Fuller did his best to discredit me, painting me as a copycat wanting the arbitrator to believe I made everything up to look like Dante had a pattern of abuse. Frustrated he couldn't find something to use in my verbal testimony, he closed off his foray with, "Nothing further for this witness."

"Is there anything you want to ask of me Ms Prince, as you will not get another chance?" said Mr Greyson.

I saw in his eyes that he believed me to some extent.

"Yes sir… please, protect my son… and me," I said, bursting into tears because this was my very last shot at getting out of this hellish existence. He got up and handed me a tissue as my Dad gave me a big hug to comfort me.

"I can see this has been very traumatic for you."

There was a small break in proceedings allowing me to regain my composure and a much-needed cup of coffee. My father went to the men's toilet. Dante followed him. My dad finished his business and opened the toilet cubicle door to leave. Dante had been waiting outside the door silently. My father stood glued to the spot waiting for Dante to say something to him or move away from the opening. The two men were at a standoff anticipating a punch to be thrown.

Dante clenched his fists and bit down on his jaw, adrenaline running through his veins…

"Come on old man, take your best shot. You'll be on the floor quicker than you can sneeze," he said.

"At least you've picked on someone your own size, not a girl this time," responded Dad, in a smart-arse humiliating tone.

The men's door swung open with a loud bang. Two suits entered the toilet space breaking up the standoff. As Dad stepped out of the cubicle to manoeuvre past, Dante rammed his shoulder into Dad's chest to make sure my Dad felt pain. Dad took the assault in his stride commenting to the two suits as he left…

"Be careful boys, I think he's a sick pervert. I caught him lurking outside my stall."

Dante was up next on the stand. I cross-examined him for two hours. He grew visibly irritated and embarrassed minute by minute, as my questions pointed out the many flaws in him and his case.

Clarence requested he be allowed to redirect questioning of his own client. This was permitted and took up about forty-five minutes. It was obvious the two of them in the break had decided to take a different path, now moving the attention onto Dante's new stable family life and trying to show Mr Greyson the issues around travel now imposed by my move to Balmoral Beach. Furthermore, he wanted to highlight that his business hours at The Divorce Drs would make it hard for weekday time unless he was the primary custodial parent and Dante's proposed routine for Christian should he be awarded sole custody.

Day two of arbitration then concluded, on what seemed to be a round won by me.

Harvey called me that night to see how everything was going. My father answered my mobile…

"Hi Harvey, it's Desmond; she's in the shower, I can have her call you back."

"That would be great. How's she holding up?"

"Today went very well, but man to man, the best thing for Ariel is if Dante gets charged with assault again. Do you know anyone who could help me out?"

"I'll have a chat to a couple of guys I know who can handle themselves, as I know he's a bit of a boxer."

"Thanks mate. Please don't tell Ariel we've had this conversation."

"No problems Desmond, probably best she knows nothing. She's had to deal with enough," said Harvey.

"Before you go, could you let Ariel know I'm coming up tomorrow to support her. Do you think she'll be all right with that?"

"I'm sure she will. We'll meet you downstairs in the foyer at say 7.30 for breakfast, then we can all head over together," said Dad clicking off as Harvey agreed.

The last day was going to be a big day dedicated to cross-examination of Charlotte, Noelle, and Ms Ford. Harvey could tell I was nervous as hell as we waited outside the Arbitration Room door. The same young girl opened it for us to enter. Noelle and Ms Ford were escorted off to other rooms and Clarence proceeded in by himself.

Harvey grabbed my hand and bent down to whisper in my ear…

"You're strong and beautiful. You've got this."

He then kissed me on the cheek and as I pulled away to go inside, he said, "I'll be waiting out here for you if you need me."

The devil saw Harvey kiss me and was visibly enraged. Charlotte stupidly tried to coddle him grabbing onto his arm and stroking it. He flicked off her arm, aggressively growling, "Leave me alone!" under his breath at her.

He then stormed into the room, coming up behind me so I could hear his voice whisper ever so threateningly "I'll never ever walk away; you'd better get used to me."

Charlotte, who had been left behind in the foyer by her betrothed, shyly smirked at Harvey and scuttled off to the back seating of the courtroom as she was being called to testify first today.

Charlotte gave a glowing report during her examination about Dante's love for Christian and his wonderful way with her children. She testified there had been no violence during their relationship and that she found me to be the main instigator of conflict in their home. She passed comment that his past difficulties were all in the past and that she didn't believe he would ever hurt her, or their children. She did answer that they usually had a drink together a few nights a week which lined up with the alcohol testing results in Mr Fitzroy's report. She said that she had never seen him highly intoxicated, nor depressed, nor presenting with any type of unstable or risky frame of mind. Overall, in her mind they were a picture-perfect couple, with a business they worked hard in, and were currently endeavouring to conceive a baby to cement their union.

Noelle Gordon and Dr Ford were the two remaining witnesses to be cross-examined.

Initially the family justice report had gone my way. However, Noelle's second brief was less harsh on Dante, after speaking to his psychologist and consideration being given to Dr Ford's report indicating Dante was currently of sound mind with no risky disorders and the substance report showing no excessive alcohol consumption in the past four months. Her recommendations had gone from sole custody to shared custody, and from short daytime visits to graduating time, reaching a forty to sixty split in days once Christian turned six years of age. This second phase of advice did not align with either of our final proposed custody orders being sought. So, the brawl was colossal.

Noelle had gone soft on Dante, stupidly taking his word for it that he was no longer a risk and that his drinking had been minimised. The 'happily married' portrait had flipped her opinion, as now he apparently is a fallen angel no more, who has seen his cruel ways, and has engaged a therapist to help him manage his moods and dysfunctional outbursts for now and into the future. She now believed he would be a stable father to his son. Noelle, his psychologist, and the psychiatrist bought into his 'reborn, new man, new dad' crap! He was the charismatic actor after all!

None of the people involved saw the real him, as they had not been exposed to him long enough. They saw what he wanted them to see. It was going to be an enormous task to get Noelle to shift her perspective.

Clarence was first to cross-examine Ms Gordon. He went easy on her in his cross, not even going anywhere near her first report and the many concerns outlined. Instead, he chose to focus on questioning her around how she saw her new proposed visitation schedule working with a two-and-a-half-hour distance between us, and how to resolve medical disputes and schooling when the two households were very different. Inevitably, he was attempting to push for her to say – on all major decisions if the court found there were risks to Christian of any kind in my home – that Dante should be given sole custody and hence his client's proposed orders.

I was the last to question Ms Gordon and I knew I had to be tough and be able to work on the fly depending on her responses. I had prepped myself covering every possible answer to my questions as though this was going to be a championship debate. I had to fire on all cylinders…

"Ms Gordon, in your most recent recommendations, you refer to us as still having substandard defective communication. In fact, you have been alarmed by the extent to which we are prepared to discredit one another. Are you saying you do not believe any of the allegations?"

"No. It is not for me to determine whether or not they are true."

"In your experience, have you ever come across a case with this level of protracted antagonism?"

"The discord between the two of you is very high, but I believe this will fizzle out once this arbitration has concluded."

"So, you don't think Mr Prince will revert back to his, as you have put it, 'coercive control and menacing techniques', after this finishes?"

"No, he knows he has not reacted well to you, and believes he can manage his frustrations with therapeutic intervention."

"Would your opinion change as to your visitation recommendations if there was evidence put before this tribunal showing a previous relationship with the same level of hostile and abusive communication?"

"Of course. Past patterns can usually predict a future style. But with the help of therapy, communication can be managed better and hopefully abuse can be stopped."

"So if the level of dissention or abuse does not decline, what do you suggest?"

"Long-term bad blood is extremely detrimental to a child, so Christian would need to be placed in one home or the other permanently."

"So if this tribunal finds it reasonable to predict that the conflict will not subside, are you saying Mr Greyson should be looking at sole custody to one parent?"

"I'd hate to make that call at this stage, but ultimately, yes."

"Are you recommending our arbitrator place the importance of Christian's relationship with his father before his safety?"

"I am suggesting safeguards around Christian to assist with lowering the safety risks, especially in the father's care."

"Shouldn't there be no safety risks around a child when considering unsupervised visitation?"

"Yes. I believe Mr Prince has shown during his time with Christian these last few months that he has not posed any risks."

"So, withholding the child, taking off with him in public, kidnapping him from my home, being verbally abusive to me, and having a history of a significant mental disorder causing episodic insanity and a dysfunctional personality condition, plus a history of substance abuse, an assault charge and stalking and threatening to kill someone, poses no risks for you now or in the future?"

"I think it is all in the past."

"Would you place one of your children into the care of Mr Prince?"

"I will not answer that, as it is irrelevant."

"The very fact that you won't answer speaks volumes, Ms Gordon.

"Do you believe Mr Prince has a substance abuse issue?"

"He could, however, he says he isn't drinking heavily any more which shows in the alcohol testing and no illicit drugs have been detected in Mr Fitzroy's blood sample report in the last four months. Cocaine did show up in a hair follicle test but was present ten months ago."

"Have you ever known an alcoholic to just give up without intervention such as AA or rehab, or dedicated therapy?"

"It is not my field of expertise, so I cannot say."

"So last year you believed Mr Prince had a problem citing he had been drinking to excess for years and now you believe him, because he says so?"

"Yes. Charlotte told me he doesn't drink to excess in their home."

"What would you say if there was evidence before this tribunal, that Mr Prince swore he wasn't drinking to the extent I say he was in our relationship, but pay slips from his three employers show he had many sick leaves noted on a Monday?"

"I would conclude you were right as one could draw the conclusion that he was taking the Monday off due to being hungover from the weekend."

"Mr Greyson, I would like to draw your attention to the

subpoenaed material marked 'A, B and C' which are wage slips from Mr Prince's three past employers."

Mr Greyson stopped the proceedings, opened the material and quickly browsed through it. The room was silent. Dante moved a lot in his seat. "Continue with your questioning Ms Prince."

"So do you believe Mr Prince could take up drinking again in the future, say after this case is finished?"

"He could, but I'd like to think he won't because he has to care for his son."

"So when Mr Prince told you in his interview last year that he gave up alcohol for some twenty months, six years ago to focus on losing weight, that he did or didn't fall off the wagon since?"

"Alcohol is a risk with Mr Prince and can be managed with injunctions."

"I notice you have not recommended AA or even total abstinence from drinking for Mr Prince. Just to abstain from drinking when Christian is in his care. How do you propose zero intake is managed then?"

"Self-management and I'm sure Charlotte will ensure he doesn't drink."

"So you think he'll self-manage and his wife, who has informed the tribunal already that she drinks regularly throughout the week with him, will make sure there is no alcohol consumed for the twelve nights a month that you have placed Christian in their care?"

"If the court makes findings of risk regarding drinking then it is my recommendation to limit time to daytime visits."

"You have suggested a safeguard for Mr Prince maintaining regular contact with his therapist. What if he stops?"

"I recommend Mr Prince continue seeing his therapist until they think he doesn't need to attend any more."

"That doesn't answer my question Ms Gordon. What if *Mr Prince* decides he doesn't need therapy any more, doesn't this pose a risk to Christian?"

"Yes!" she said, getting agitated at my hammering.

"So do tell me, as the concerned parent here, how this arbitration process can actually achieve removing the risks around Christian regarding drinking and mental instability when Mr Prince himself in the past has stopped seeing mental health professionals because he didn't think there was anything wrong with him and he didn't need them?"

"You really can't guarantee Mr Prince will engage in therapy if and when it is needed," responded Noelle.

"You say that I am a risk to our son because my orders for sole custody and supervised time with Mr Prince shows I do not support the father-son relationship."

"That's right."

"Why is it your position to damn the female for seeking this type of parenting arrangement when there is clearly historic evidence supporting red-flag risks around a small child, and to the mother when the father is seeking the exact same order?"

"It is in the child's best interest to have a mother supportive of the father-son relationship."

"So you can't, or won't, see domestic violence as a good enough platform for not supporting an unsupervised arrangement?"

"I don't like your line of questioning Ms Prince. It is not up to Ms Gordon to determine findings of fact around domestic violence," interrupted Mr Greyson.

"Sorry… Ms Gordon, you state another risk to Christian that exists with both houses is that he will be emotionally damaged. Furthermore, you say that neither of us possesses insight into our own contributions, yet nowhere in your entire two reports do you note that I am the instigator of the hostility; you do, however, point the finger at Mr Prince. So why make this statement about me?"

"So that you both understand your role in mentally damaging your child."

"So, are you telling me to take the abuse, stalking, insults and controlling behaviour from Mr Prince to de-escalate the conflict?"

"In a way… yes."

"But aren't those behaviours in themselves domestic violence and against the law?"

"The two of you need to stop and make a real effort to co-parent for the emotional development of your child instead of focusing on the tit-for-tat contest."

"Should this tribunal care about my emotional stability and functioning?"

"I have noted a risk in your functioning as a parent under the aggressive stance taken by your ex-husband. I do consider the volatility between the two of you is likely to subside considerably after this matter has concluded. It is for Mr Greyson to decide what to do about this issue."

"What makes you believe that this will occur when Mr Prince's level of volatility with his other co-parent, Ms Harper, has never diminished?"

"I am not privy to the co-parenting dynamic with Ms Harper."

"Mr Greyson, I'd like to hand up a letter from my psychiatrist who has diagnosed me with adjustment disorder with mixed anxiety and depressed mood, DSM IN TR 309.28. Ms Gordon, can you tell this tribunal what this means for me please?"

"It means you have an anxiety disorder due to an identifiable stressor that causes marked distress and an impairment to normal functioning and if the stressor is removed, the disorder goes away."

"So what does this say to you with regards to my ability to function in co-parenting with Mr Prince?"

"That you will have great difficulty and could develop a long-term mental health issue."

"Thank you for that Ms Gordon. Moving on to my next subject... you know I have made allegations concerning Dante hitting Christian. You have noted Christian expressing similar words, and you are also aware of a child safety report. So why blatantly disregard the disclosure made directly to you by Christian?"

"Mr Prince emphasised he has never physically disciplined

either of his three children."

"So do you believe, with Mr Prince's history of physical violence and apparent amnesia where these events are concerned, that this could have actually happened to Christian?"

"There is a possibility."

"Furthermore, you have reports from Christian's kindy, showing he is displaying aggressive behaviour towards other children. From memory one instance outlined him hitting a child across their face. Is it conceivable this is learnt behaviour from his father?"

"Mr Prince said he has been taking Christian to boxing with him."

"Do you think it is appropriate for a young child to be exposed to such an aggressive sport?"

"No. It is inappropriate to be encouraging Christian to physically hit people."

"Do you think Mr Prince would be doing this to breed a mini-me version of himself as a fear and control tactic towards me?"

"I cannot answer that, but it could be the case."

"You have stated if anyone is trying to brainwash Christian, then it is occurring in my household, and the reason for this is because you say Dante spends relatively little time with his son."

"Yes, I believe I wrote something like that."

"In your experience is it normal to brainwash a child who is in your care to say things like 'Mummy bad, I hate Mummy', or 'I want to live with Daddy'? Wouldn't this mean I am brainwashing my child to say negative things about my own home?"

"Well yes, I suppose."

"Do you really believe I am stupid enough to do that?"

"No."

"So was this a mistake made in your report, or are you showing bias towards the father with no evidential support?"

Ms Gordon remained silent for a moment… "There is a risk in both homes."

"You have covered Christian's medical issues in your second report. I noticed that instead of addressing the issue pertinent to the care of Christian, which is that the father continues to ignore his son's medical conditions and blocks or ignores treatments; you chose to solely focus on calling me vindictive towards the father for telling you I was concerned Christian may develop similar genetic mental problems to his father. Why did you not address the real issue of medical welfare?"

"I don't think it is an issue. I believe Mr Prince will not be medically negligent."

"Why did you not reprimand Mr Prince anywhere in your second report about his clearly false fraud allegation, when he told you he did it to discredit me?"

"He acknowledged to me he did it as a response to all your false allegations."

"Mr Greyson, I'd like to point out to you the subpoena marked 'D' for this evidence."

"Thank you. I will make a note of that," said Mr Greyson.

"So because he told you, after he found out I had issued a subpoena to prove how vindictive his actions were, you saw it fair to tell this tribunal that *I* am the vindictive parent, not Mr Prince?"

"He came across as sorry for his actions."

"A narcissist can be magnetic and charming; painting flattering pictures to their audience to make you think they are great or innocent, when they are not, right?"

"Yes."

"Ms Gordon, can a narcissist be a good role model for a child?"

"A narcissist is unable to love anyone, even their own child and they are incapable of showing empathy and therefore incapable of caring for a child. But that doesn't remove the fact that they are a parent."

"Is a narcissist easy or difficult to co-parent with?"

"It is just about impossible from my knowledge. A narcissist doesn't care what the other parent thinks or what's best for the child."

"Do you believe Mr Prince could be a narcissist?"

"I am not a professional in the area, but I believe Dr Ford

didn't make any comments about this."

"But didn't you find a previous psychiatrist for Mr Prince's criminal case had identified that he suffered from a dysfunctional personality condition?"

"Yes."

"Are you aware of whether a personality disorder goes away?"

"They usually don't; they need to be somehow managed."

"Didn't Mr Prince tell you himself that he never sought treatment for this condition past the criminal review board's requirements? In fact, there was no treatment up until four months ago when a judge decided he needed to engage with a therapist?"

"Yes, it would seem that is the case."

"Can you see your recommendations are placing a child in the hands of a potential narcissist and you believe this is all going to go away once Mr Greyson, makes his ruling?"

"I can only hope so for Christian's sake."

"You are either naive or not very good at your job, Ms Gordon considering your answers here today so far."

"I think you are harassing the witness, Ms Prince. Control yourself and either ask a question or move on. Your statement is inappropriate and will be struck off the record," said Mr Greyson.

"Do you believe Mr Prince misuses communication channels to intimidate and bully me?"

"One could see it that way."

"Do you consider 718 emails since separation normal, excessive or obsessive?"

"It is extreme."

"Is it harassment?"

"Could be viewed that way, yes."

"And am I right that you believe Mr Prince will not harass me any more once custody is sorted out here?"

"I believe so. Everything should settle down if the two of you try and work together as parents."

"Would it surprise you to hear Ms Harper had brought over

500 communications she thought displayed abusive, bullying communication from Mr Prince into this tribunal?"

"That does paint a different picture and would be a concern."

"Do you believe on the balance of probabilities that Mr Prince was violent towards me?"

"Yes. It is possible."

"So why haven't you actually addressed this in any of your recommendations? You seem to say it is likely it may occur again, but you have recommended no safeguards."

"It is difficult. The only safeguard is to have the two of you ordered to not directly come into contact and that can't effectively work when co-parenting."

"So, is it in Christian's best interest to have his mother at risk of more domestic violence?"

"That risk is for the arbitrator to consider."

"You sent us to group coaching sessions in October. Why would you force me, a victim of violence, into the same room as my perpetrator to learn how to negotiate and compromise?"

"It is what Christian needs."

"But you do believe Mr Prince has been physically violent to me?"

"Yes."

"Don't you see the insanity of forcing an already traumatised victim into this position?"

"There is no other way, other than removing a parent's legal right to be a parent."

"I note you have not recommended Christian live with his father. Why not, considering you think he is a changed man?"

"There will always be many risks associated with Mr Prince, so Christian needs to be with the more stable parent."

"So, you say if the court decides to accept Mr Prince's orders today for Christian to live with him that they are placing Christian at risk no matter what?"

"Yes."

"You have recommended both Christian and I continue to engage with a therapist for the foreseeable future. Wouldn't that suggest you believe Mr Prince has been emotionally and/or physically abusive towards us so much so that we need therapy now and into the future?"

"Yes."

"So, a young boy needs mental health assistance to process acts of domestic violence towards him by his own father?"

"You are putting words into my mouth, Ms Prince. The two of you need some therapeutic assistance to help you cope."

"Lastly, if Mr Greyson finds facts pertaining to Mr Prince displaying the same level of domestic violence, abusive behaviours and threatening litigation in a previous intimate parenting relationship, would you change your statement that Dante appears to have gained better perception into his range of former problems?"

"Absolutely."

"I forgot. Would you remove all contact if Mr Prince has been violent towards Charlotte? Oh sorry, that should have been, if he is during their marriage?"

"I believe that would be my definite recommendation."

"And do you believe it would be fair for me to have to go through this entire process again if he is violent towards Charlotte?"

"No, it should be an immediate withdrawal of all visitation and custody rights."

"Lastly Ms Gordon, I am apprehensive as to your change in visitation recommendations. I put it to you that something doesn't gel. Has Mr Prince or any lawyer from The Divorce Drs referred you any clients since you first interviewed us?"

"That is privileged information."

"I want it on record; I believe Ms Gordon's most recent recommendations have been tainted by a possible professional relationship, creating a conflict of interest; you may have chosen money over my son's wellbeing, as I am aware you provide child psychology services in a private business capacity," I said.

My brain was working so fast trying to get out everything my gut was telling me from her contradictory answers.

"I'm insulted. I have acted as nothing but professional in my capacity as a justice counsellor for this matter. Where I may or may not receive referrals from has nothing to do with how I approach my custody advocacy role," said Ms Gordon, visibly upset.

"Mr Greyson, I request Ms Gordon's latest summary report be struck out, as clearly due to my questioning today, Ms Gordon has likely produced a biased report in favour of the father possibly for personal gain."

"Duly noted. I will make my decision on your request during my deliberation. Ms Gordon thank you for your time today; you are free to go," said Mr Greyson.

Dr Ford was the last witness to be cross-examined. Clarence was happy with her assessments; therefore, I was the only one leading questioning…

"Dr Ford, did you read any of the affidavits or subpoena material before producing your report?"

"No, I only read the family justice report dated the 19th of March, and an email from Mr Naylor."

"To clarify: do I have any type of mental disorder or condition for Mr Greyson to be concerned about?"

"No. You did not demonstrate any psychiatric disorder or other condition."

"Did you assess Mr Prince as having any instability or mental health disorders?"

"No," said Dr Ford.

"Your report did, however, identify Mr Prince has been previously diagnosed with schizoaffective disorder and a dysfunctional personality disorder. Is that right?"

"Yes."

"So in your professional opinion Mr Prince no longer has schizoaffective disorder?"

"He didn't present as having hallucinations or delusions. He did say he felt a little depressed over everything that was going on."

"How long would it take to ascertain if a person suffers from schizoaffective disorder?"

"At least a couple of weeks or more; it's difficult as an individual needs to present as delusional and depressive at the same time."

"Can you tell us what signs you would look for, for this disorder please?"

""Delusions such as having false or fixed beliefs, despite evidence to the contrary; hearing voices; sometimes incoherent speech; bizarre or unusual behaviour; depression; periods of manic moods; terrible sleep patterns, and impaired occupational, academic or social functioning."

"Thank you for listing these. I am concerned you didn't see any of these symptoms in the family justice report, like pts 4 through to 10, 23, 33 to 38, 56, 57, 80 to 90, 101, 106, 103, 122, 134 and the list goes on."

"It is not for me to conclude if your allegations are true; that is for Mr Greyson to determine," said Dr Ford.

"Why did you not identify Mr Prince with any existing personality disorder when, according to all medical journals, these disorders stay with you for life?"

"I do not have an answer for that," replied Dr Ford.

"If I believed Mr Prince was a narcissist, tell me in your experience, how long would it take to make this kind of diagnosis?"

"May I say that this type of disorder cannot be identified in the one hour allowed to produce the court brief that was requested by Ms Gordon. It takes months and sometimes years for a professional diagnosis of this kind."

"Humour me please, as I do have a point at the end of my questioning on this subject… what traits would you look for to determine if a narcissistic personality disorder exists?"

"Traits of a narcists can be an exaggerated sense of self-importance… fantasies of great success, power, and intelligence… believing they are special, and their actions are untouchable, godly almost… a sense of entitlement to things like people and money… a need for constant attention… they take advantage of others… they're arrogant, lacking empathy, and react to criticism or things not going their way with rage and retaliation," rattled off Dr Ford.

"What kind of history do they normally have?"

"Normally an abusive childhood; addictions to substances; mental instability; they're usually poor money managers and they don't hold down jobs or intimate relationships. They also blame others for their behaviour, and many have run-ins with authorities. Generally speaking, they're compulsive liars, and they are high functioning, dominant individuals usually in elite types of jobs due to the power provided to them by the role," explained Dr Ford.

"Do you think Mr Prince fits this description?"

"I could glean… some of these in Ms Gordon's report if they are in fact true accounts of events. Mr Prince did present as having a domineering attitude."

"So, now that I have brought this… oversight to your attention as a psychiatrist, do you think this tribunal should investigate this issue thoroughly considering my son's safety is paramount?"

"There are concerns when you put it like that."

"Are there safety concerns around a child being cared for by a narcissist?"

"Yes, the child is usually used as an intimate pawn quite negatively against the other parent, which always leads to physical and emotional welfare issues for the child."

"From your experience, are there welfare issues to a parent as well dealing with a narcissistic personality disorder?"

"I believe dealings can be cyclically abusive, manipulative and controlling."

"Your final point in your report said we have a highly dysfunctional intimate connection. Could this be entirely relatable to Mr Prince having a narcissistic personality disorder?

"A full assessment of both of you and your family dynamics would need to be conducted before I can answer that."

"If our arbitrator concluded from the evidence before him that

Mr Prince could be a narcissist and that the conflict originates from Mr Prince, would you recommend to place Christian into shared care across our two houses or minimise visitation for the wellbeing of our young child?"

"You cannot place a child into shared care when there is so much turmoil."

"One last thing Dr Ford, you say you spent one hour with Mr Prince, is that true?"

"Yes."

"Your report stated you saw Mr Prince from ten thirty to eleven thirty a.m. My question to you is, how could this be, when I went in at 11.09 a.m.?"

"I don't remember the exact times."

"Well luckily, I do, as I'm a bit of stickler for arriving early for appointments. I put to you that you really didn't bother to assess Mr Prince. You spent less than the required hour to produce this so-called expert report… in fact, less than forty minutes. It was probably a nice old cup of tea the two of you had together having some shop talk."

Dr Ford was silent, eyeballing me over her glasses. I waited, maybe thirty seconds, for a response and then wound up the cross examination…

"Thank you, Dr Ford. I do appreciate you taking your time out today to participate."

Dr Ford rose from the witness box, nodded at Mr Greyson and left the room.

"Well, that concludes the witness cross-examination," said Mr Greyson. Would the parties like to present written or oral submissions to conclude this arbitration?" asked Mr Greyson.

"I think the parties would like to end the matter as expediently as possible, so I recommend a short verbal closing statement," said Clarence Fuller, turning to obtain my agreement. I nodded as I just wanted the bloodletting to be finally over. Dante then whispered something to his barrister.

"I believe all the expert reports in front of this tribunal are saying there are no safety issues anymore surrounding my client.

The testing shows he has given up drinking to excess and is not abusing drugs. His therapist and Dr Ford believe he is of stable mind, exhibiting no mental disorders, and Mrs Gordon has recommended a significant increase in time for Mr Prince to spend with his son. My client has listened to everything that has been said during this arbitration and now wishes to move on and have a better co-parenting family unit for Christian. He has just informed me moments ago that he will accept all of Ms Gordon's recommendations in her second report," said Clarence Fuller, ending his submissions.

I sat glaring at Dante in shock thinking… *You have just dragged me through all this crap for eighteen months, and at the death's door knock you go from one extreme to another changing your mind… yet again!*

"Ms Prince, it's your turn," said Mr Greyson, looking at me impatiently while tapping his pen on the desk.

I pushed myself up from my chair, stood up straight, clasped my hands together in front of my stomach and began my last pitch…

"It is our responsibility as the adults in this room today to make decisions as to what is best for Christian Prince, a little two-and-a-half-year-old boy, who is stuck in the middle of a toxic parenting dynamic that I believe will never change. Both experts today suggest we should give Mr Prince the benefit of the doubt and accept that he is a changed man. But I argue his history shows he has not changed. He objectively can't change, as he has two co-existing dangerous and volatile mental health disorders being schizoaffective disorder and narcissism. Forcing Christian and me to be in a long-term intimate relationship with Mr Prince will have nothing but terribly negative consequences to our lives both physically and mentally. Finally, you must err on the side of caution and make findings of fact around domestic violence in this case which precludes you from issuing any other arrangement but sole custody to me. Thank you for listening," I said, signalling that I was finished.

My dad placed his hand on my back and gave me a pat letting

me know he was proud of me and to sit down.

"It has been an emotional three days for the parties involved and I do not wish to keep you much longer. I would like to take a little more time to deliberate on this case because of the amount of material and evidence given, so I will attempt to issue the arbitration award by the end of March… may I remind both parties that you are still able to come to custody consent orders, as arbitration awards are legally binding. Thank you," said Mr Greyson picking up his things and leaving the room through the back door, letting us know we were done.

I picked up my mountain of folders and put them back into my black suitcase and followed Dad out of the room, leaving Dante and Clarence inside having a heated discussion between them. Dad took my bag and walked back to the hotel by himself, while Harvey and I happily left the Arbitration Society's building together, hand in hand.

We made our way to the café across the street for a celebratory coffee. Dante and Charlotte came out of the building and crossed the road, coming within a metre of our table. I panicked, leaping up from my chair with my brain kicking into the fight-or-flight mode.

"Sit down Ariel. He can't do anything to you here," said Harvey as they continued to walk up the ramp of the car park beside the cafe.

"Don't put it past him," I responded sitting back down.

Within sixty seconds, Dante reappeared at the side of the building and spat at me before bolting back up the ramp. Harvey had his back to him, so he wasn't aware of what had happened until I jumped off my chair, screaming hysterically…

"That bastard just spat at me, look!" I said, pointing at my skirt where the phlegm had landed.

"Who?" said Harvey not understanding who I was talking about.

"Dante… he sprinted off up the ramp next door."

"He's on a whole different playing field than anyone I know," replied Harvey.

"Can we just go please?"

"Of course. Here's a napkin to clean it off before we go."

"Thanks," I said, trying to stop tears rolling down my cheeks as the adrenaline I had been running on was coming to a fast end, leaving me tired and emotional.

"He makes me feel so sick. I can never get away from him."

Harvey walked me back to the hotel and ordered the three of us room service for an early dinner as I was exhausted. Over a bottle of wine and pizza for us and chicken nuggets and chips for Christian, we sat on my king-sized bed, with Harvey and I discussing what had happened today, and Christian engrossed in the *Toy Story* movie.

Chapter 24
Life's Beauty is No One Gets Exactly What They Want

I had come out at the end of this litigation worse for wear, but proud, feeling like a gladiatrix. The last few years since I fell pregnant have felt like I have been in a serious car crash and now I was left permanently in strange pain. I am ultra-tired; my brain feels foggy and my head is always sore like there was no fluid mattress between my skin and the skull structures.

I had alleviated my increasing anxiety and stress over the last few months by ramping up my intake of wine and cigarettes at night. My mind and soul seamed tortured, sensing a constant threat of extinction. I often questioned my sanity when alone with my thoughts, imagining real monsters existing in human bodies and feeling frozen in time; physically unable to escape their torture. I feared these ruminations would never abate for the rest of my life.

The day after arbitration was like a new leaf turning over for me. I was able to focus all my energy on my new business, a life without litigation over Christian, and building a new life. My manager Linda had been a godsend. She had run the business as though it were her own since I took over in December last year.

Linda was a year older than me, with brown eyes and brown shoulder-length hair, attractive facial features and very small feet: size 5. She was a little shorter than me and had an endearing smile and mother hen qualities. I often compared us jokingly to the Ab Fab girls. We were a great team and fast became very close friends.

On my first day back on the job, she had compiled a new menu for me to consider to make my stamp on the café part of the business; she had also found more suppliers for the fine food grocery items; this with the view of grabbing hold of the opportunities I had briefed her with when I first took over the business. I was so impressed with Linda's proposal I instructed her to implement it in two weeks. I also offered to pay for Linda to complete a certificate in small business management to develop her skills. I'm a great supporter of higher education for women.

My blissful sleep that night was interrupted when my phone chimed after ten letting me know I had a text message…

TXT Dante: Get used to my way for the boy

I sent a copy of this text message the next morning with a plea to help me to Mr Greyson's email address and copied Dante in on it hoping to shame him.

I received a response from the Canadian Arbitration Society the following day politely letting me know I was not able to provide any further evidence on our matter as the hearing stage had concluded.

Dante didn't like my criticism of his behaviour to the arbitrator texting me…

TXT Dante: Fortunately, you're not very smart, you're a delusional liar. Get over your petty bullshit, and yourself, so you can finally start being a proper mother.

Despite being told I could not communicate with Mr Greyson I sent another email off in desperation with the subject line 'PLEASE HELP ME' and attached a snapshot of Dante's text. I didn't receive a response to this one.

Christian attended his therapy session dictated by Judge Blake the Thursday after arbitration with Abby Senden. I confirmed this with Dante in an email as I had to keep him informed on medical information.

Subject: Christian's Therapy

Date: 4 February

Moving forward, Abby will be working with me, not Christian on home-based behavioural methods to assist me to manage his aggression and anxiety, as she believes, like I do, that he is far too young to get benefit from sessions with her.

Ariel

Dante swiftly replied, like the prick he is, sarcastically informing me he was really encouraged I was seeing someone to get help for my issues. He also took great pleasure letting me know he and Charlotte bought a house together sending me photos of them standing in front of a sold sign. He also deliberately provided me with a wrong address for his new residence.

I thought, *He either thinks I'm really dumb or stupid, or it's just another mind game. Don't let him away with this.* So, I responded, very tongue-in-cheek…

Subject: RE RE Christian's Therapy

Date: 4 February

I see court has finished so you go straight back to being your normal narcissistic self. Nice work not co-parenting providing me with a fake address. I see your therapy has been an utter waste of time for you!

Ariel

Charlotte replied to me, like she's Dante's mouthpiece…

Subject: Address

Date: 4 February

I have bought this house, and for my own reasons am not comfortable giving you the address. Your email supports my concerns and distress over the fact that you would continue to stalk us, but for my husband's sake, I will provide the property's address – 112 Maple Glen Place, Cowichan Bay.

Charlotte Prince – The Divorce Drs

I thought to myself after analysing this communication… *He has her totally brainwashed. It's hilarious they're concerned about me turning up on their doorstep. What do they think I am going to do to poor little Dante? Shoot him? How I'd love to do that!*

Charlotte also flicked off correspondence to Abby Senden that thankfully did not endear themselves to her…

Subject: Christian Prince Therapy

Date: 5 February

Dear Abby

My husband and I are concerned Christian is unnecessarily being subjected to therapy as we believe Ariel invented all his so-called problems to assist her court case. We have been informed you are no longer treating our son. Can you please confirm if this is the case or what your plan for him is?

Charlotte Prince – The Divorce Drs

Dante's arsenal of control antics kept ramping up now his behaviour was no longer being scrutinised by a judicial representative.

He decided to sign me up to a divorce application sponsored by The Divorce Drs business. This application costs $150 a year to communicate with your ex-partner and $5.50 a month to store the information. In five days, I received 100 emails from this site, from both Dante and their marketing department trying to sell me their services. I refused to pay for receiving and sending parenting communication. He didn't care. He was enjoying strong-arming me.

If I had learnt anything from the last two years of litigation, it was that there is always two ways to skin a cat. Dealing front on sword fighting with Dante had me coming out the loser, as my soul could never play the same cruel game as his alter ego. I had to manipulate the tools he used against me.

Taking an alternative route, I personally phoned the divorce application's owner and followed up with a legal-sounding letter…

Subject: Subscription to your Divorce App

Date: 15 February

As discussed, please remove my details from your application immediately as I have not given you or my ex-husband permission to register me. Your registration process breaks the privacy laws. Please confirm in writing today that you have removed me from your database.

I also think from a personal point of view that emails sent from your system from my ex-husband that call me his 'spouse' are offensive.
Ariel Prince

For the next two months I breezed through my days at Ambrosia trying to keep myself busy waiting for the arbitrator's decision. The uncertainty was having a negative impact on my entire nervous system. I exhibited a roller-coaster ride of mood swings, anxiety attacks, insomnia, persistent coughing, weight and hair loss, and daily headaches with cold shivers down my head, like that feeling you get when a person pretends to crack an egg on your head.

I took the three days off work, from Good Friday to Easter Sunday, to spend with Christian, as I had been so busy with the litigation, and then starting in my new role as retail business owner, that I had hardly spent more than two hours a day with him. I was conscious that our time together may be dramatically changed by Mr Greyson, so I wanted to enjoy him as much as I could.

On Easter Monday we received an email letting us know, Mr Greyson would be publishing the arbitration decision at ten thirty tomorrow. My heart jumped out of my chest, as I thought… *Oh, my God, our fate is only twenty-four hours away!*

My body began overheating as my heart raced. My mouth went dry and my hands shook. Black dots feverishly appeared in front of my eyes, so I stepped out away for the front counter area and into the kitchen standing with my back up against the wall.

"Are you okay, boss?" enquired Linda.

Still conscious but fading, I looked towards the back of the kitchen where Linda stood cooking over the griller trying to pin her image to one spot.

"Linda, I think I'm going to pass out."

The black dots became larger, I slid my back down the wall placing my hand on the floor to cushion my fall. I crashed down at the entrance of the kitchen in full view of the café's seating area.

"Call an ambulance, Brooke, *now*!" yelled Linda as she ran to me.

Customers raced to my aid scrambling over my still body.

"Is she breathing?" asked Bob, one of our regular customers who came twice a day for a coffee.

Linda sat on her knees beside me putting her ear to my nose and mouth. "I think she is."

Linda said softly into my ear, "Ariel you're going to be all right. Stay with me. There's an ambulance on the way."

"Joey… call Ariel's parents," commanded Linda.

"Brooke how far away is the ambulance?"

"About ten minutes. The lady is asking for you to roll her over and place her on her side to keep her airway open."

Linda, Bob, and another customer Brian gently rolled me over. Brian took my wrist to check my pulse… "Her pulse is there, but it's faint."

My body began convulsing, shocking all the onlookers. Linda placed her hands on me attempting to stop the jerking movements.

"No Linda, you can't restrain her. Can you get some towels to put under her head?" asked Brian.

"I'll get them," said Joey.

He grabbed a large white towel from the storage area over the dishwasher. Brooke asked all the customers if they could move to the outside seating so they could ensure easy access for the ambulance officers' arrival.

The entire shop, staff, and customers were in shock watching my demise unfold. Many of my regular customers were aware of my struggles as my parents had told them in casual conversation, with many commenting that they could not believe I was still standing.

The ambulance sirens could be heard getting louder and louder and then they stopped signifying to everyone that they were on site. Moments later two paramedics came running into the shop with the stretcher and portable equipment.

"Ariel can you hear me?" asked a female paramedic.

I tried opening my eyes but didn't have the energy. I willed my mouth to speak but I couldn't project the voice in my head to come out of my mouth. Tears were streaming out of my eyes, but I wasn't physically crying; I was scared. My brain wanted to sleep, so I stopped trying to open my eyes and gave in to the blackness as my entire body lay like a tonne of bricks on the floor. There was silence, finally, for me.

The paramedics lifted me up onto the gurney and wheeled me out the front entrance to the ambulance. I was taken to the emergency department at the local hospital and bumped up the queue as an urgent priority patient. The paramedics thought I could have had a stroke or brain aneurism.

I was discharged from hospital two days later, with the conclusion drawn that I had suffered an anxiety attack.

I came home to the award sitting in my inbox since yesterday. I wanted to open it, but also didn't. My stomach was in one huge knot due to a growing fear inside me over our future. I clicked on Mr Greyson's email, opened the pdf file titled *Prince & Prince Arbitration Award* and sent it to my printer. Thinking there was enough time, I raced out to the kitchen, made a cup of coffee and on my return to my home office, the holy grail was sitting in the printer tray waiting to be read.

I read each page slowly, digesting Mr Greyson's thoughts on each relevant legal issue, the case law he was relying upon, and his thoughts on our overall presentations. Finally, on the back page were his binding custody orders. The first line read…

In the matter of Prince and Prince, I find in favour of the mother's orders, with a slight variation of an additional night to promote the father-son relationship once Christian Prince is six years old.

I took a deep breath and smiled, doing my best to contain my excitement as joyous tears rolled down my cheeks as I read through the full set of Final Custody Orders. Mr Greyson had accepted the very same orders I had put to Dante in September, eighteen months ago. That morning, my mind was off dancing on its own planet and singing, because I was finally set free from the agony of Dante's web. I called Mum and Dad, Tracey, Sophia, my brother, Harvey and Linda to tell them the news that I had retained custody of Christian.

This nightmare was finally over for ever! No more court, no more litigation, no more threats or gaslighting and, I was hoping, no more abuse or stalking. An ex-judge, and arbitrator has given him their legal answer, being: he cannot have custody. I had won against the malignant narcissistic Divorce Doctor. I felt like I was Little Red Riding Hood and I had just slaughtered the big bad wolf, all by myself, without the woodsman.

I had done, what I had to for Christian, now, Dante can suffer the consequences and lie in the bed he'd made.

It was time for me to celebrate, and I'm sure, for the devil to annihilate himself drinking for a long time!

I popped a bottle of Moet & Chandon with Harvey that night over an Italian meal at our favourite little Italian restaurant. Afterwards he chased me up the stairs to my bedroom, and we had wild sex until sunrise.

The very next morning, as I lay in bed next to Harvey, my mobile signalled an email had been sent in. I reached over to grab it from my bedside table and noticed the sender was Charlotte Prince…

Subject: Leave my husband alone

Date: 31 March

I ask that you now move on with your life, stop stalking us and please…LEAVE US ALONE! Dante tells me you have been begging him to reconcile over the past month, because your relationship with Harvey has ended. Your behaviour over these past two years has made me feel extremely uncomfortable. We now, without a doubt, classify your escalating levels of harassment as 'bunny boiler' territory. I am not going anywhere no matter how hard you try to break us up. The legal war is over with no more games to be played. I hope you find love, like Dante and I share. I beg of you, move on and leave us alone.

Charlotte – The Divorce Drs

How bizarre. She has gone absolutely insane, I initially thought.

"Can I ever get a break from these two?" I said to Harvey.

"Put the phone down and focus on us," said Harvey, pulling me back under the covers wanting to go another round in the bedroom before each of us needed to head off for work.

I stewed for a couple of days over Charlotte's catty trash talk to me. I knew I shouldn't, but I just couldn't help myself, reciprocating the intimate 'girly chat' with…

Subject: RE Leave my husband alone
Date: 3 April

For the record, I have no interest in getting back with Dante and have not begged him for anything. I do not stalk you. You're both way to ugly to be stalked.

Let's talk harassment. Wasn't it fairly recent you and Dante wrote to me, "try to abstain from being a useless moron." Real classy. I can't be a moron… I just beat your husband's arse over custody! Lol.

I only care what happens to Christian when he is spending time in your home. So, I advise, take real good care of my son. I'm sure you are aware of my capabilities considering Dante fears I'm going to kill him. Here are my words of wisdom to you – everything's in the manipulation. You think everything he wants you to think. Stop being so naive.

I wish you luck. He's all yours and I hope he does to you what he did to me. I'm sure I'll be hearing from you in the near future, when you call me, crying, so don't use my number until then.

Ariel

A couple of weeks later I received an email welcoming me to ArabLounge.com asking me to validate my email to inform me of my love matches. I considered it as spam and disregarded it.

My life had stabilised, and I felt ecstatically happy for the first time in years. I was full of optimism about my business and my sex life. Harvey and I had a loose dating arrangement, as I knew he was shattered over his marriage breakdown and that he may get back with Margot at the drop of a hat. So, we saw each other a couple of times a month.

He wined, dined and danced with me. It was the older man

with the desirable younger woman relationship. I got primal adult sex, totally focused on pleasuring me and my fantasies. No strings attached, as at this point, I really didn't like men. I only needed them to satisfy my sexual desires after the dry spell with my ex-husband.

I had lots of ideas coming to me after the arbitration decision came out. It was like positive karma was being sent my way opening up my entrepreneurial spirit pushing me to build my wealth position by cementing myself in this community. I made plans to expand my business into catering and fashion, and hopefully purchase the gorgeous house we were living in.

I drew up a business plan and sent off correspondence throughout the next few weeks, putting in motion some of my ideas. At night when I was working on my business plans, I noticed an increase in junk mail being sent to me from dating, sex and marriage websites. I thought this was random, strange and deliberate, needing my attention to stop this unwanted mail.

I clicked on one from DatingAgency.com to investigate. It was a UK site and up popped my name, a user ID, password, my date of birth, my gender and a button to click on to view my profile. I gasped upon seeing my picture and a description telling suitors I was…

Desperate and Needing a Fuck… My phone number was published along with a detailed description of my hair colour, height, interests, that I was overweight, religious, right wing, university educated and a hopeless dancer.

"Fucking bastards, this is crossing way over the line!" I said, so loud Harvey heard me from the front yard and came running in.

With Harvey looking over my shoulder, I clicked on a further six emails, from a lesbian site, a bondage site, a singles parents' club, a threesome chat group, and an Islamic and an Asian bridal agency. All had similar descriptions and the same photo. A couple even had my real address posted online.

"Argh… How dare they do this… arseholes!" I screamed, wanting to smash something to get the negative energy that was inside me dispelled.

I phoned my brother who was an IT expert and asked him to see if he could get me removed from the sites. He said he would see what he could do.

Harvey got back with Margot during the public holiday long weekend for Victoria Day. I wished him well and we remained friends. She had found out he was dating me and had taken me to Montreal for a dirty weekend recently. I received a surprise visit from her at Ambrosia after they reconciled, endeavouring to stake her claim over him, telling me they had never separated, and so Harvey was having an affair with me.

She rambled on for over an hour about how good their marriage was, and that Harvey often had these flirtations on the side. She had no idea I had seen many communications from her, sent to Harvey, on splitting the matrimonial assets and her admissions to sleeping with two other men. She was an absolute liar, and I thought she and Dante were two peas in a pod. I was sad though, thinking Harvey was choosing the deceptive ex-wife, because he didn't want two failed marriages on his dance card.

Once Margot left, I noticed Dante had sent me a text. He was letting me know he may be late due to traffic to pick up Christian from kindy. I decided the best thing for me to do was to drive out to the centre in case he didn't make it in time before it closed.

I was watching Christian outside in the sandpit, when I saw his car pull up, so I dashed out of his range, out of sight, inside behind a bookshelf across from the kids' bags. On his arrival, he asked Christian to get is bag. Christian followed his request. Then Dante went to pick Christian up. Our son repeatedly kicked and screamed uncontrollably, so much so that Dante dropped him. Christian yelled at his father, hitting Dante's legs with his fists saying…

"I don't want to go. I don't like you."

Christian was so distraught that the kindy staff intervened and took Christian away back to the sand pit to calm him down.

My heart sank as my worst fear had been realised… Something was happening to Christian at his father's home since

Mr Greyson's orders had rolled out two months ago, and I couldn't help him. Christian was trying to yell his way out of his misery. I wanted to run over to him, pick him up and run away with him. But I couldn't let Dante know I was there, as I was not supposed to be at the kindy, going by the arbitrator's orders.

I waited for Dante and Christian to leave. On my way home in the car, Margot sent me a message through Facebook.

MSG Margot: Just received an email from your charming husband and am waiting his return phone call. I told you I would get you back for screwing my husband. Your ex has also visited my house and left a package for my husband. Margot

I thought to myself... *I seem to have lunatics come out of the woodwork.*

I didn't respond. I was concerned my psycho-ex was linking up with Harvey's deranged wife, or ex-wife, I couldn't keep up with it all. I just needed them all to leave me out of their wicked entanglements.

Two weeks later when Dante rang Christian for their weekly phone call, Christian wouldn't take the phone from me, choosing to yell at me...

"I don't want to talk to Daddy! He's not nice!"

The following week Dante called again, and Christian said to him...

"I don't want to talk to you," and handed the phone back to me.

"You are poisoning and warping my son against me you bitch!" bellowed Dante at me and then smashed the phone down in my ear.

Christian had been displaying incremental increased mental health stressors such as frequent bed wetting, and saying he was feeling sick on the day when he was to go to his father's home. He was refusing to eat meals, dry retching when food was put in front of him and he was very anxious and defiant when I wasn't nearby.

I researched how children may react when there is a change in routines after custody orders are in place. Nowhere could I find reviews from people saying their children displayed this kind of physical repulsion tantrums. I admit, I was worried Christian was being ill-treated or he had the beginnings of some form of mental illness, but I could do nothing with my intuition, just manage him though his feelings the best way I could.

I held a birthday party at the house for Christian's third birthday. We had a face painter, magician and a Superman cake. Sophia and Tracey came with their kids, as well as a couple of relatives. Harvey turned up with three biker friends so Christian and the kids could sit on the back of Harley Davidson motorcycles for some cool pictures. Harvey gave Christian a Harley motorcycle jacket with a golden eagle on the back of it. It was on this day, I believe, that Christian fell in love with motorbikes, black leather jackets and aviator sunglasses. He was taking after his mum in this regard.

Harvey had finally separated from Margot. He tried to make it work with her for two months, but found out, after she caught an STD, that she was sleeping with their plumber. Margot had to tell Harvey about the affair so he could be tested. Thankfully, he was cleared and that was the final nail in the coffin of their marriage.

Harvey returned the evening of Christian's birthday to take us out to The Jungle Restaurant. Christian went crazy having a hell of a time in the indoor jungle park enabling Harvey and I to chat about things that needed to be said. He had hurt me, choosing to return to Margot, considering she was a cruel person. I mused that the men I have dated seem to choose nasty over nice and then when it doesn't work out, they return wanting what they gave up in the first place.

No wonder men shit me!

Chapter 25
Trying to Be a Hero

"Robbo how goes it mate," Harvey said cheerfully on his hands-free to his old footy mate driving back from the airport.

"Legend, great to hear from you," Robbo replied.

Harvey always got a kick out of being called 'Legend' by his old football mates, as it showed he was still well respected in the footy community.

"Hope you're ringing up to give me a hand," said Robbo, in a pleading overtone.

Robbo had taken the job of coaching the Tigers last year. He had been a great player in his time but found himself a little out of his depth with this assignment.

"I could be persuaded. But only for a short time as I have my state duties with the Masters games," said Harvey, knowing full well Robbo knew this, as Robbo was one of his star players.

"Would appreciate whatever you could give old mate. My record of zero from three means the board down here are looking hard at the new man." Robbo's voice sounded sad.

"Will be there for training Tuesday night; what should I wear?" Harvey asked, as he turned onto the motorway heading west.

"Maybe your national rep jumper and track pants mate as those legs of yours aren't the greatest," Robbo laughed.

"Yes, very funny. See you at four thirty on Tuesday" said Harvey as he hung up his phone.

Harvey was happy to help a mate, but his real intentions for doing this were different from his normal motivations. He had done some digging and found out The Divorce Drs had recently become a sponsor of the club. Harvey wanted to meet him, man to man.

Harvey's hair stood up on the back of his neck thinking about the aftermath he had witnessed in the couple of years after he had taken Ariel on the back of his Harley in the rain. In his mind, he saw her beautiful angelic face, which too often showed signs of intense crying and a bewildered sadness. Dante had changed her, stealing the positive light that once shone so brightly that she lit up any room she walked into. As a man in love with her since the day they had met, he couldn't get the images out of his mind of the violence she had described. *Fucking low-life prick!* thought Harvey. *If I find him, who knows what I'll do.*

Harvey was aware Dante was ten years his junior, and a kickboxer. But Harvey had a few stoushes under his belt, both on and off the football field. His nose had been broken seven times attesting to it.

Tuesday afternoon Harvey turned up to the footy ground early; his black Harley getting lots of looks from the young men entering the grounds as it roared. Robbo drove in and parked near Harvey. He swung his leg over the bike to dismount and placed his helmet on the foot peg. Robbo jumped out of his car and gave his old mate a very strong, hard handshake…

"Mate," Robbo said, grinning ear to ear.

Harvey put his arms around Robbo and squeezed him like a long-lost brother.

"You're looking fit, big man," Harvey said, as Robbo was all of six foot four, and still as toned as he was in his twenties.

Harvey removed his bag off the back of the Harley and the two of them made their way into the change sheds, chatting about old times along the way. Robbo ushered Harvey into an office marked 'Senior Coach' and motioned for him to take a seat…

"So," Harvey said, like a schoolteacher, "give me the rundown."

For the next fifteen minutes, Robbo talked about the older players not accepting him as coach, as the last coach had retired with a lot of success and had been at the club many years. His leadership group thought they ran the club, and the youngsters gave them more respect than they gave Robbo.

"So," Harvey said again, in the same tone as before, "want me to be the bad cop?"

"Yes, that's the way you operate," Robbo said, looking at the floor, nodding.

Harvey got changed in the office, grabbed a football and headed out to the grounds. He had taken Robbo's advice and had his national jumper on. This made him stand out amongst the others who were in an array of footy jumpers. Some of the players were already doing warmups and short kicking, but the whispering behind hands was obvious.

Harvey scanned the grounds for Dante or his car. No one standing around fit his description and there wasn't a red mustang in the car lot.

Harvey was startled when Robbo blew a whistle signalling for the thirty or so players to gather around…

"Gents," said Robbo, bouncing a football in front of him… "may I introduce Harvey who'll be taking some drills and assisting me on match day." Generous applause followed.

"Good evening ladies," Harvey announced, getting some sniggers from the younger boys in the crowd, "as my learned friend said, I will be getting to all of you individually, working with you, and I will, get the best out of you slackers," he yelled.

"Dickhead," said someone under their breath.

"Thanks to that girlie, all of you, four laps now, and back to me."

The team captain led out his team, following Harvey's command. Harvey met them after their first lap…

"Leadership group to me," Harvey bellowed, and led the six players to the middle of the ground to meet with him and Robbo.

"Need from you guys a summation of last week's performance," Robbo requested.

The next ten minutes led Harvey to believe these guys were coasting, and from the outside, they wanted Robbo gone. The leadership jogged off to finish running with the main group.

"They are fucking you over mate," said Harvey, looking into his mate's eyes.

"So what do I do?" asked Robbo.

"Leave it to me; you'll be surprised."

Harvey left and came back with three garbage bins, putting them in the middle of the ground.

"If any of you want to vomit, do it in these bins, not on the ground, as you all have to play on it," Harvey announced.

The footballs were put away and the team performed various running drills broken into four sessions only stopping to catch their breath, vomit or take in water. The footy team was exhausted at the end of training. They all moaned and groaned clearly expressing that they were not fans of Harvey. Throughout the training session, Harvey regularly scanned the grounds willing Dante to show up.

Harvey and Robbo followed the team into the change sheds. Harvey whistled between his fingers in the confines of the change rooms. The sound was deafening...

"Okay girls, decision time. Those who want to win on Saturday please be here at four p.m. on Thursday night. The rest of you can get changed and fuck off!"

A stunned silence came over the group.

Harvey and Robbo left the players in their dumbfounded silence and went into the coach's room to chat. The leadership group took it upon themselves to follow them, itching to complain about the training session and criticise Robbo for bringing in a new assisting coach. The last comment was from Dutchy, a well-built, guy of about five foot eight, and the oldest of the group...

"I have played with this club for ten years, won premierships with Plugger, the old coach, for your information Harvey, and he never treated us this way. So maybe it's *you* who should fuck off!"

By the time he finished his rant Dutchy was standing toe to toe with Harvey trying to be intimidating.

Harvey just grinned down at him saying nothing as he was at least six inches taller than Dutchy. After some time passed and neither of them moved, Harvey decided to show them all who's boss. He walked around Dutchy, opened the coach's room door and said loud enough for all team players to hear, "And also have a think about a new leadership group, as these pussies are not going to be running this club after Thursday night."

Harvey turned back around, glared at the footy players in the coach's room and the leadership group got up and left. Robbo's face was one of shock and horror. He didn't know what to say. Harvey gave him a wink as he walked out of the office to leave, signifying 'the bad cop' mission had been completed. This made Robbo relax and laugh a bit, shaking his head at Harvey's handling of the request, as he watched him leave.

Harvey started his bike and rode off, concerned that the real reason why he was there today hadn't shown up for the face-off.

Thursday afternoon came around quickly. Harvey led the Tigers training session again. In between plays he scanned the grounds and later that evening stayed back in the members' area for a glimpse of Dante, but nothing.

Harvey rang Ariel when he arrived at home that evening.

"Hi baby girl, how's it going?" Harvey said cheerfully.

Ariel launched in, not sparing any details telling him about Dante's latest antics and demands to change the orders to swap weekends so he could take Christian to a football game.

"So, Christian will be with Dante this weekend then?" Harvey asked.

"Yes, I agreed as I can't be bothered arguing, even though I had plans to take Christian to a theme park.

"Why do you ask?" I said, in an inquisitive tone.

"No reason. Tell me… what does Dante look like again?"

"I've shown you our wedding photo, but there's a recent one on his website. I'll send it to you on email."

"Thanks."

"Please don't do anything stupid," I said, worried that, if anything happened to Dante, I would be the prime target for the police.

"I can run fast," said Harvey with a laugh.

"I promise you I won't be doing anything stupid. Remember I'm a lover not a fighter. Much love." Harvey clicked off his phone not wanting to give Ariel any chance of probing him further about his intentions.

Harvey had hoped Desmond would do something about Dante. He had set up a meeting for him with the Agar brothers back in February. They told him Desmond had turned up at the pub, but he never approached the boys, and then they watched him drive off.

After seeing the dating cyberbullying, and then Ariel telling him she thought Dante might be hurting Christian, he decided to take action himself. Someone had to send this bloke a message to pull his head in, leave Ariel alone or else!

Saturday was game day. Harvey was putting his bag on the back of his Harley preparing to leave for the match.

"You going to be okay by yourself?" his best mate Tommy said, knowing what today was all about in Harvey's mind.

"Yeah matey, all good. Don't want to ruin these goods looks," Harvey said, brushing his face while posing like a Hollywood actor.

As he rode his bike to the grounds, he was oblivious to how fast he was going, swerving in and out of the Saturday traffic. His thoughts were miles away. The game butterflies were now fluttering and the thought of Dante finally being so close, and 'in-play' sent adrenaline through Harvey's veins.

Most of the crowd knew Harvey had arrived by the bike's exhaust echoing around the grounds as he pulled in. Harvey took his bag off the bike and was met by a small delegation of senior players. They were all wearing the club shirts and carrying their bags, looking keen to get on with the game.

"Really appreciate you helping us Legend," said Red, who had showed little natural talent, but lots of heart and aggression.

"I can't afford for you fellas to lose today. I have $100 on you against the opposition coach," Harvey said, looking across at Macca, the opponents' coach, who was getting out of his car.

"It's payable on the final siren, so don't think of sneaking off,' grinned Macca who then made his way to his team.

Harvey went straight to Robbo's office and found him pacing like a man in the waiting room of a maternity clinic.

"You too?" Harvey said pointing to the butterflies in his stomach.

"I'm off to watch the next quarter of the reserves," said Robbo as a way for self-distraction.

Harvey went outside the sheds to where the reserve coaches and Plugger sat. A cold shiver went down his spine when he spotted four men and three children in the members' box, just ten metres away to his right. The men all had beers in their hands. He immediately recognised Dante. Christian was mucking around with the other children. Harvey thought, *I wonder if he knows who I am?*

"It's the Legend," said Cornes, the reserves coach, with a huge grin. Cornes was a stocky man, who had played football for most of his fifty years and had a way with the English language that would make the most hardened blush.

"Looks like you might be able to ask for your match payments without flinching," said Harvey.

Cornes went through how the practice drills introduced on Thursday night had been a little confusing at first, but now the boys were doing them without thinking.

"That outside receiver thing is working a treat," said Plugger directly to Harvey.

But Harvey's attention was with the members' stand. He was transfixed on Dante. *Isn't he under court order not to drink with Christian there?* Harvey questioned himself… *This bloke's a piece of work… Clearly thinks he doesn't have to follow the law. I wish I had a camera to take a picture.*

The senior game started. Harvey stood with the other coaches, making suggestions periodically, but his mind was on the members' stand the entire game. He was staggered at how many beers these guys were consuming in front of their children.

Just to be clear in his mind it was Dante, at the break, Harvey asked Plugger, "Who are the blokes over there, mate?" pointing to the now very loud group of four. It seemed the children were no longer with them.

"That bloke is a local psychotherapist who sponsors us. Prince

I think his name is," he said, pointing at Dante. "The other is also a sponsor, but not sure what his name is. They get on the piss, knock the umpires, and abuse poor old Robbo for doing a crap job. Don't like them much, but they put money in the till."

It was obvious Plugger wasn't a fan.

One of Dante's group, a tall, athletically built guy, came over to speak to Harvey. He introduced himself as Joel.

"Are you Harvey? Played for the Tigers and senior league?" asked Joel, who seemed more sober than his mates on the side-line.

"Yes, that would be me," Harvey said, not making eye contact.

"Are you taking over from Robbo?"

"No, just helping out an old mate to deal with some attitude problems," replied Harvey, this time in a tone which left Joel knowing he had finished the conversation.

Joel left, and announced to his drinking buddies.

"That's him all right, still an arsehole," to which they all laughed out loud.

Harvey stared in the group's direction, arms folded and shook his head. He heard Dante say… "Ooooh!" and laugh.

The game started to turn in the Tigers favour. Harvey told Robbo to make some drastic player moves, which Robbo didn't question, although Plugger couldn't help himself…

"You're putting Weasel as striker? He's a backman, has been all his life," Plugger whined.

Just then, Weasel grabbed the ball and went towards goal. He advanced to the goalie and scored to the cheers of the crowd and his teammates. It was his first ever goal in ten years of football. The game ended in a three-goal win to the Tigers. As promised Macca came over and gave Harvey his winnings, albeit in small bills.

After the usual club songs and pats on the back, Harvey took his opportunity to go upstairs to the bar where he had seen Dante and his group go at the end of the match. Spirits were high and the two barmaids were flat out.

"Beer for the supercoach," said Plugger putting his arms around Harvey.

"Make it a lemonade; I'm riding the bike home."

"Stay at my place and have a few," said Plugger, his face beaming with pride.

Harvey heard…

"Saints don't drink, and their shit don't stink either," said by one of Dante's mates who had consumed way too much beer.

Joel came back over to Harvey.

"Don't mind them, they know fuck all about the game. Great move with Weasel to striker, he's proved himself with a goal. Who would have known?"

Joel continued to try and impress Harvey with his football knowledge, not letting supporters and players who interrupted to shake hands and congratulate Harvey take away his focus. Harvey didn't move as Joel continued to bend his ear. Dante and his group continued to consume beers and shots and got louder and louder. At one stage they even broke into a version of the club song.

Harvey asked Jerry, the club manager…

"These blokes always this rowdy?"

He nodded.

The crowd had thinned out with most of the players and supporters going out to celebrate. Red and Robbo were one of the last to leave.

"Come on Legend, come out with us," Red said, patting his friend Harvey on the back.

"No, be on my way soon," said Harvey, focused on his task.

Dante said loud enough for everyone left in the bar to hear, "Legend, what a joke!"

"Better than being a woman basher," Harvey said, at the same volume, staring down Dante.

"Oh shit!" Joel said, under his breath leaving Harvey's side quickly to return to his mates.

Jerry moved slowly to the edge of the bar and whispered, "What the fuck are you doing, there's four of them and they're half your age?"

Harvey continued his straight-edge gaze, as Dante rose, and unsteadily approached Harvey in his drunken stupor…

"*Now* I get it. You're the fucking knight in shining armour. Where's all your Hell's Angels mates?" Dante said smirking and as loudly as he could.

Jerry had now backed away and was poised to phone the police if any trouble started.

"Don't need them to deal with a wife beater," Harvey said.

Dante was now within striking range. His eyes had turned jet black, and he was shaping up boxer style, just like Ariel had described.

Joel grabbed Dante by the shoulder as Jerry said, "I'll call the cops if you don't take this outside," his hand over the receiver to dial.

"Come on mouthy, into the carpark if you're man enough, old man," Dante said, as he was being guided towards the door by Joel.

Dante's other mates were whispering about the wife-beater comments, as they had no idea what Harvey was on about. Joel knew what he meant. Harvey rose from the stool, picked up his helmet, bag and jacket and headed to the door and down the front stairs.

"You are a fucking lunatic," said Jerry, to him on his way out.

Jerry was now on the phone to Robbo and the boys who had left just moments before this hullabaloo started. Harvey walked over to his bike, where Dante's group was now standing facing him. He put down what he was carrying. The voice in his head coaching him, saying…

You have to land the first one.

Dante did some fancy Mohamed Ali style dancing, stumbling as the beers and fresh air took effect.

"You're in for the hiding of your life, old man. I'm gonna enjoy this," Dante said, slurring, and lunging forward with a right cross.

Harvey had time to lean back, avoiding the punch, and with

his left hand, struck Dante on the side of his head.

Dante fell to the gravel, and lay there for a moment, everyone thinking he was down for the count. Dante lifted himself up, swaying around attempting to face off again, but his posse of three took hold to control him.

"Fucking let me go. Fuck off!" Dante protested, trying to wriggle out of their grip.

Harvey felt his most vulnerable as he thought he might have four of them to deal with now. Jerry appeared at the top of the stairs, "Cops are on their way, gents."

With that, Dante's mates dragged him to their car and piled him into the back. They argued who was the soberest. Joel finally took the driver's seat and sped off down the road so the cops would miss them.

"You were lucky bucko. Go and buy a lotto ticket, and see you next week," Jerry said relieved he didn't have to jump in. He himself was too old to fight four young bucks.

Harvey started his Harley, let it idle for a while to warm up and with a loud roar, announced to the still night air he was leaving the grounds. He had done what he had come to do.

Harvey told Ariel the next day by phone that he had had an altercation with Dante at the sports club. She wanted to know everything, but Harvey thought it best, she not know, any of the details. It was a code he had learnt doing cage fighting many years ago, not to talk about your trophy wins. Harvey just wanted her to know he had gone in to bat for her.

Ariel asked if he would come forward as a witness to court for her if she needed him to in the future. Harvey felt uncomfortable getting more involved in the Prince custody drama, so he didn't answer.

Hervey would kick himself for this decision, later in his relationship with Ariel as he could have been her true hero changing her and Christian's world significantly, as well as his own. He just had no clue at the time, what level of complex insanity Dante functioned at, as he was just on the fringes of Ariel's life not being a player yet, in the madness, that was Dante.

Chapter 26
It's All About Me

It was business as usual on Monday for Harvey as he sat in his office going over his weekly calendar of meetings, reports and things to get done. He was still on a high from his triumph over the weekend.

His desk phone rang… "Some police officers are here to see you Harvey," announced Louise, the head office receptionist.

"Okay thanks."

What's this about? mulled Harvey, walking out of his office and down the stairs to meet his guests. He was hoping the impromptu visit wasn't because another one of his truck drivers had run someone off the road in one of their branded semi-trailers.

"Harvey, Constables Brown and Green,"' said the younger policewoman. Harvey thought *colourful names* to himself.

"Is this about one of my drivers?"

"No, we need to speak to you, in private please," said the older male officer.

Louise's' face turned white, and by her body language, Harvey knew this would be around the business quick smart as soon as he and the police went into an office. Harvey led the two officers upstairs to the boardroom and closed the door.

"Coffee, water? "enquired Harvey, trying to be pleasant.

"No thanks," came the unison reply.

"So, how can I help you today officers?"

The young female officer led off, "A club member reported a public drunken brawl at the Tigers club at around seven p.m. last Saturday. You were reported to be at the scene," she said, watching Harvey's body language closely.

"Yes, I know of the incident, and yes I was involved," Harvey said calmly.

"Did you strike a Mr… Prince?" said the female officer looking at her file for the name.

"I think you'll find he started it."

"Please answer the question," said the older officer.

"Yes, I did."

Harvey proceeded to tell, over the next thirty minutes, of the reason he was there and his take on what happened.

"Thanks for your time Harvey," said the young female officer after finishing writing up her notes.

"We are getting the club's CCTV footage to view, which will prove your statement correct or not," said the senior cop, officiously.

Harvey was relieved that this may soon be over, as he was now second-guessing his actions. The last thing he needed was to be charged with assault. It could negatively impact his job and Ariel's custody situation.

Harvey escorted the officers out of the building and waited for Louise's comments.

"You in some trouble boss?" she enquired, as a way to add to the rumours she had already spread.

"No, all good in paradise," Harvey replied, but knew there would be repercussions without a doubt, now the police were involved.

I stewed over whether or not, to confront Dante, about the weekend's event. I decided, because I had little knowledge on the facts about what had happened, that I needed to get Dante to admit to it. Then I could use it against him as a way of making sure he never dragged us back in to court again. The text I sent him read…

TXT Ariel: I have been informed you assaulted Harvey. Please explain yourself.

Dante and I were already crossing swords as we were in the throes of a huge disagreement over which school Christian was going to attend, and Dante was harping on that he wanted Christian living with him. He was in retaliation mode, being a total prick. Some of his most recent infuriating moves were that he hadn't allowed Christian to go to his very first kindy birthday party, and he had wanted to charge me a fee to spend time with our son on our country's National Day to take him to the parade, because Christian was in his care, not mine on the day. And, to top all these, Christian had expressed to me words to the effect, that his daddy had told him, 'he could easily make mummy die'.

Meanwhile, Harvey had to go on a road trip for three days for work. He was then off to Springdale to visit his kids. His countryside drive was interrupted by the mobile ringing through the speakers of the rental car.

"Just putting a call through, Harvey," said Louise, from his head office.

"Harvey Kane," he said, his mind coming back into business mode.

"Dante Prince, I don't think we have met."

Harvey was speechless, as this was the guy who wanted to take his head off last Saturday.

"Ariel says you and I have had an altercation. I know she's lying. I don't know why I'm even bothering to talk to you. You're just the gigolo she's seeing at the moment."

Harvey was about to interject, but Dante caught his breath and started again.

"Next time you see Ariel, just confirm we haven't met, so this isn't yet another false allegation I have to defend," Dante said, and then hung up.

What the fuck…! Is this guy mental? thought Harvey, and at the same time realising he had slowed to 60 km per hour on the freeway during the call, and there was a huge truck bearing down on him. He sped up, getting out of the semi's path.

Harvey took the rental car back to the highway speed and set the cruise control, trying to rationalise the last few minutes…

What just happened? Was I daydreaming? he asked himself out loud. The monologue in his head started going over information… *Ariel said he was a nutter and blacked out when he was drinking… but he had his mates with him. Surely, they spoke about it when they left. Does he really not remember I hit him, or is he playing me…? What the fuck is going on? Were they all so drunk, none of them remember? This is doing my head in! I need to focus on the road.*

In his office, Dante hung up the phone, and went on with his day, internally seething that Ariel was, yet again, making up false violence accusations against him.

This squabble led to our next clash…

A process server turned up at my door at seven p.m. on the Friday evening before the Thanksgiving long weekend, getting me to sign for more legal documents care of The Divorce Drs and Jackson Taylor. In the pile was a Form M, seeking an urgent hearing based on an 'extraordinary parenting matter,' plus a Form 32.1C requesting that the Arbitration Award be cancelled, and a Form 25 for a restraining order. The court date stamped on the bottom section was the 11th of October at the Western Community courthouse, giving me three days to prepare.

My brain was frazzled trying to come up with how he can do this and get into a court so fast as the paperwork had only been lodged seven days ago. I ran into the office with the documents reading the front page of his affidavit as I ran.

Under the heading 'Facts' on page eight of Form M was… ATTEMPT TO KILL ME AND MY WIFE.

"Fucking motherfucker!" I screamed out so loud, I'm sure the entire neighbourhood heard me.

Dante was alleging that I had hired a hit man to murder him. He gave a police event number, dated the 29th of September, just two days after my last communication to Dante that I was not agreeing to his demands to give him more time with Christian outside of our binding custody award.

A Detective Laurie Hall was the lead on the investigation. Dante had written that he had a recording of a taped conversation with the hit man called 'Fabio' and that he intended to play it in court. His application was processed as an 'emergency case' because the court believed him… that his family and himself, were all at risk of being murdered with me as the orchestrator! He was seeking that the court make an immediate ruling for a change of residence and for him to have sole custody, giving me two hours' contact with Christian once a week at a Family Support Centre.

I cried so hard the veins in my temple were bulging, and my neck was so sore I couldn't hold up my head. The lengths this man would go to, to remove me from our son's life was unbelievable. To me, he had now stepped up his game to an insane, psychotic level. He didn't get his way with the arbitrator nor with me, so he engages the criminal system to try me for an attempted murder, that I never did.

Oh, my fucking lord! Wait a minute… could this be Tracey's Fabio? I said to myself, my hands over my face. I picked up the phone and dialled Tracey.

"Hi. How are you going? How's life?" said Tracey, chirpily.

"I think Fabio has rung Dante telling him I hired him to kill him. Do you know anything about this? I can lose my son."

"What the hell!" said Tracey.

"Put Fabio on the goddamned phone, now!"

"I'll go get him," said Tracey.

"Fabio, Ariel wants to talk to you," said Tracey, handing him the phone.

"Nope. Tell her to fuck off!"

Right then, I knew he was involved.

"What the fuck did you do Fabio?" Tracey yelled at him.

"Tell the bitch good luck keeping her son now," he yelled, so I could hear him.

"Ariel, I'll ring you back," said Tracey.

"Tell Fabio he'd better start running as I'm going to fucking kill him if I lose my son over what he's done," I proclaimed, my voice sounding very serious.

Fabio and I had never been fans of each other. He and Tracey had met years ago at a nightclub. He had told her he was a stripper to pick her up. Tracey showed me a picture of him she had taken that night before she slept with him. He had long dark hair down to his bum and was muscly like a stripper, but with an awful patchy fake tan. I knew he wasn't a male entertainer with the East Coast Hard Bodies as I knew them all. After I told Tracey he was an absolute liar, she told him what I knew, so he didn't have anything to do with me from all those years ago.

Over the years their relationship was rocky as he loved to cheat on her and then get back together when Tracey found out. Unfortunately, Tracey married him, and they now had a daughter together. I am aware he broke her arm early on in their relationship in an elevator, accidently apparently, when she wouldn't go with him somewhere during a fight. I had loathed him then and now I really hated him.

I was feeling out of control at this point with all my emotions channelling to a darker shadow within me. I wanted to physically hurt Fabio and Dante, so they died excruciating deaths at my hands.

All my buttons had now been pushed beyond comprehension, with a heightened level of toxic adrenaline fuelling sinful urges I had not yet experienced in my life. My gut was telling me I could, unquestionably, physically hurt another human being without remorse. I had been pushed to my breaking point.

I picked up a letter opener out of the desk drawer, and slowly ran my finger over it fantasising that my beautiful black wings came out of my back again, giving me the guts to throw this dagger as hard as I could at the wall, picturing the target as being between Dante's eyes. I snapped out of my make believe and saw the letter opener wedged into the wall.

I had become a version of Dante.

Chapter 27
Bad Boys, Bad Boys, Whatcha Gonna Do?

That night, I asked Harvey to come forward with an affidavit attesting to Dante's assault to counter the fabricated attempted murder declaration. He refused pleading with me not to force him.

I didn't understand why he wouldn't help me. I got so mad, I dumped him over the phone.

After I finished working on my response material for that day, I walked up the stairs to Christian's room, kissed my son's forehead whilst he slept, contemplating what I would actually do for him. *Could my love for the devil's child, turn my soul into a dark beast willing to kill?*

I snapped out of this negative mindset which was out of character. Brooding, I went to my bedroom's outside balcony in the dark attempting to bring myself down off the trapeze wire.

Over the years, my mind had become most active at night when alone in the dark, smoking to calm my nerves. I catch myself inwardly talking, with two voices in my head and another background referee, which I know is me. One voice sits on top of my right eye reverberating behind my eyebrow and the other behind my left. The words are silent to the outside world, but sometimes they move my mouth or my hands with gestures trying to analyse things.

Tonight, I find me chastising myself, for not seeing this 'hit man' encounter being directed at me. It is his ultimate fear after all. He knows my assets can buy the services of many hit men, and he's been paranoid I could do it. He even tried to get a restraining order against me over a year ago expressing to the judge that he believed I would kill him.

Besides questioning myself on the day's events, I looked out into space blankly, hardly breathing; my stomach ached like someone was squeezing my insides. My stereo was playing 'Way Down We Go' by Kaleo. The lyrics prompted voices in my head in a pleading tone…

Why are you doing this…? Stop, please stop

I can't breathe… You're, going to kill me.

I feel like I'm having a heart attack… Stop, please!

If I die, I'll take you with me, you son of a bitch!

I took a drag of my cigarette and the voices continued, making my brain hurt:

I fucking hate you!

You lying son of a bitch!

A few seconds later:

Please let me go!

And then finally the darkness took over my delirious begging.

He needs to be fucking shot!

I climbed into bed and said a small prayer asking for God to help me. I knew I was having a mental breakdown. My body twitched for hours. Sparks flew through my veins before exhaustion took over my body to make it rest.

I awoke the next morning to my phone ringing at eight. It was Tracey…

"Hey, I'm so sorry about yesterday. I've gotten to the bottom of it," said Tracey.

"And what is that?" I snapped.

"The two of them are in cahoots."

My head was hurting so much with, I suspected a migraine, leading me grunt in reply, "Tell me then."

"Sophia and I went out the front for a cigarette when you had the kids in the pool at Christian's birthday. Sophia mentioned Charlotte had posted on her Facebook page that they were going to Mexico. I said jokingly to Sophia that it would be so easy to get Dante knocked off there as we had been there last year for a holiday and came across some people who would do this type of thing for very little."

"So how has this turned into Dante going to the police with a recording showing I hired Fabio to place a hit on him and his wife?"

"When I told Fabio about this stupid conversation at the party, he took it as a real threat and contacted Dante because he hates you. They plotted to make a call so it could be recorded with Charlotte in earshot to make it look like the hitman called Dante out of the blue."

"Why did you tell him about a dumb, stupid conversation in the first place?"

"I'm sorry Ariel… I told him you had nothing to do with it, and that it was just a throwaway line between me and Sophia, because we felt so bad for you. Fabio reckons I'm lying to cover up for you wanting him killed," Tracey said, becoming overwhelmed by tears.

"This is all so fucked up," I said pissed.

"I know, I'm so sorry Ariel. What can I do?" begged Tracey.

"If I lose my son over this Tracey… you tell that son of a bitch, I'm coming for him. He'll suffer my wrath for what he's done… he'll be hearing from my lawyer suing him for defamation. Better still… I'm sure framing someone for murder is a criminal offence. He and Dante will be the ones thrown in jail for what they've done. All hell is going to rain down on his fucking arse for getting involved in my personal business and putting Christian at more risk."

"I don't think he knew Dante's intention was to take the recording to the police."

"Well, more fool him. I don't give a fuck! He's just a wanker who deserves what he gets. Dante has screwed him, and now I will too. He's in so much deep shit, it's fucking hilarious."

I paused for a second to put together my thoughts…

"Tell him he's on tape telling the cops that people come to him to hire a hit man. The police will come looking for him real soon, especially when I ring them and give them his fucking address. I'll tell them the truth about his drug dealing and the illegal steroids. Let him know to look forward to a visit from the Hell's Angels, real soon!"

"Ariel he's going to go crazy if I tell him this," Tracey said, scared.

"Make sure you tell him today Tracey, over the phone, in person, I don't care how. He needs to know, and you needed to know what's coming, so you can make your own decisions."

"Shit Ariel. I'm worried."

"Don't you get it? He's put you in the firing line for this bogus murder plot too, as he's saying you approached him on my behalf. You could lose your daughter too. So just do as I ask, and I'll try and get us out of this."

"Okay. I'll do anything I can to help."

"I'll do my best to have him running in the other direction away from Dante in fear. Just get the hell out of his life Tracey."

I surmised after this call, that these were two sick men, coming together who share a passion for controlling and gaslighting their partners.

I placed a call to Laurie Hall, the detective appointed to investigate. He wasn't there so I had to leave a message.

I was so intensely wound up, my head felt like it was going to explode, and my gut feeling was that I was going to be so screwed in court. As today was Saturday, no lawyers work on the weekend. Leaving me zero days to find legal representation, as the Monday before the court hearing was Thanksgiving. How was I going to fight an attempted murder allegation without legal help? I was in trouble.

On Sunday I took Christian to spend some time with him at the beach. Christian loved the beach, and I found the wind and the ocean to be a calming influence on my soul. After about forty minutes playing on the sand, Christian was hungry, so we stopped off at McDonald's for lunch.

The large crowd in McDonald's made my inner emotions, which had been feeling trapped, turn into panic. I cracked under the pressure crying standing in the ordering line, being so mentally and physically stressed out exacerbated by the noisy chaos of the public.

People were staring at me, wondering, I suppose, why I was

crying at McDonald's, a place where their slogan is 'I'm Loving It'. Christian didn't understand and was pulling at my bag asking me,

"What's wrong Mummy?"

I picked him up and ran out of McDonald's coming to a stop on a bench outside the beer garden. Christian chased some birds and was being entertained by a busker nearby. I sobbed into my hands feeling sorry for myself and watched Christian through the gaps in between my fingers.

A male, about mid-fifties, sat down beside me.

"Hello," he said, "you look like you could use some help."

"I'll be fine," I responded looking up at him. I instantly recognised him as the man who owned 'Tarot Lodge' the crystal and clairvoyant shop in the arcade.

"Do you remember me?" I asked wiping my face and nose off with a tissue in my hand.

"Of course, you have been coming to my shop since you were a young girl. I think from memory you came in with your son about four months ago."

"I was looking for a pink crystal medallion to calm my soul," I responded.

"Ah yes," he said nodding… "now, on to more pressing matters. Do you mind if I read your palms?"

"No, please do," I said, holding my palms up to him.

He considered the lines for a short moment. I was worried and was trying to hold back my tears. I also couldn't believe he remembered me, all red faced and blotchy as I was now.

"Well, there is a lot of confusion here and you really need some help. Probably more than I can give you. Marleen is the one who can help you, but she's away on holidays. Do you want to come to my shop, and we can call her together?" he said, with the positive energy I needed.

All I could do was nod. I was blown away that this man knew I needed guidance from something in this universe. We got up together. He slipped his arm under mine, like a gentleman, helping me to steady my core. We walked over and I took

Christian's hand saying, "Come on bubba, we're going to a pretty shop inside and then we'll grab an ice cream."

Christian was happy with the plan. We waited inside the Tarot Lodge. I was pointing out all the beautiful, coloured crystals to Christian as a distraction while Dave whispered into the telephone. Dave then passed me the phone…

"Marleen can speak with you now."

"Hello. What is your name child?" enquired Marleen.

"Ariel."

"Why hello Ariel. Did you know your name means lion of God?"

"No, I didn't. That's probably why I'm a bit of lion sometimes," I said, chuckling as I found it funny considering my circumstances.

"I'm Marleen. Dave has given me his insights from your reading. Can you tell me when you were born and your son's name?"

"The sixteenth of May and Christian."

"And who are the two men in your life?"

"I'd say they would have to be Harvey and my ex-husband Dante."

"I see a large red lion on a coat of arms you must bow towards, and a very evil soul. I'm being told you need help, and you need to get your son away from him. He's going to really hurt him."

"What do you mean; how will he hurt him?"

"The spirits are telling me there is a real danger to you both. The dangers are different but have dire consequences."

"I don't know what to do; he has me back in court again. I can't get a lawyer in time."

"Can you get legal aid?"

"No."

"Have you spoken to a women's legal service?"

"Not recently as I used up my free hour for the last court round."

"Right then, give me your phone number. I will have someone call you within the next hour. Hopefully they can help you. You must get help, as there is imminent peril before you. He must be stopped," said Marleen.

"Thank you so much. I will take any help I can get."

"Please take care and keep your phone close by for the next hour." Marleen clicked off.

"Hope Marleen was able to help you," said Dave smiling at me like an uncle would.

"I hope she can. Thank you for your kindness."

We left and I bought Christian an ice cream on the way home at the shop that I had loved visiting when I was a child.

My brain and heart felt heavy as I was mentally digesting that two clairvoyants could see the devil energy and the possibility of Christian being his victim. My worst fear had been confirmed again this time by a well-established and highly regarded supernatural psychic.

I received a call from a lady named Imogen Delaney. She told me Marleen had contacted her. She was from a women's legal service. I immediately recognised her name.

"This isn't going to work; you know my ex-husband. He and his lawyer went into your room and spoke to you at the courthouse on one of our court days. I remember seeing your name on the duty lawyer's door."

"Oh really?" said Imogen… "off the record, can you tell me his name as I still might be able to help. I mean, I want to help you. Marleen told me what she saw."

"Promise me you won't tell him you have spoken to me if you ever run into him again."

"Yes. I promise you. My lips are sealed."

"His name is Dante Prince."

"Wow. Yes, I know him and Jackson well. Jackson and I are actually good mates. He's told me his partner was in a protracted legal case that no judge wanted to touch."

Imogen went silent for a couple of seconds and I didn't know what to say.

"Oh my God! You're the ex-wife they've all been talking about," she said excitedly.

"Yes. That's me."

"Shit. Give me a couple of hours. I'll make some calls and have one of my colleagues contact you."

A roll of names was already going through her head quickly to determine a suitable fit.

"Thank you and please don't tell him."

"I won't. Us girls need to keep together. Don't worry, I'll find someone," she said, hanging up.

The next phone call I received was from a lady named Penelope and the following day I was sitting in a barrister's office, on a public holiday, the day before my court hearing, thanks to Marleen and Imogen.

Penelope Lore had jumped to my aid, no questions asked and for free. Penelope was a huge advocate in the field of women's domestic violence, having been a victim herself during a twenty-year marriage. She had gone to law school as a mature-aged single mother and came out a barrister in her forties.

The universe had responded, sending me a legal angel and renewing my faith in a higher god.

On Tuesday we stood in front of Judge Darby who had presided over Dante's ill-fated restraining application against me. After the formal representations were given, it was on.

"Why are Mr and Ms Prince back in my courtroom, Mr Naylor?" asked Judge Darby.

"Your Honour, I'd like to hand up this police report marked as 'Exhibit A' outlining an investigation into the attempted murder by the respondent, on my client and his wife. We'd also like to tender this recording into evidence as 'Exhibit B' to play to you so that you understand the urgency for the orders Mr Prince seeks today," said Jackson as he handed the evidence up.

"Is this true Ms Lore?"

"Your Honour, the father has fabricated this allegation. Ms Prince, under no circumstances, has tried to murder her ex-husband," replied Penelope.

"Right then, can you play me this recording?" asked Judge Darby passing the USB stick to his associate.

The associate plugged it into the court's audio equipment and pressed play. The recording switched for everyone to hear with bated breath…

"Can you just give me a moment mate. I need to pull the car over," I heard Dante say.

"Yeh sure," said the man's voice.

It sounded like Dante's car had come to a halt. There was a couple of seconds of silence and then Dante's voice…

"Can you repeat to me what you just said? I didn't quite hear everything, and I would like my wife to listen in, so I'm putting you on loudspeaker."

"I'm ringing to let you know I have been approached by your ex-wife, Ariel, to engage a hit man for her. I know she's been trying to stop you from getting access to your son and I don't agree with it."

"Who are you?" Dante asked.

"I'm Tracey's husband, Fabio. We meet a few years back."

"And when is this hit supposed to happen?" asked Dante.

"When the two of you go to Mexico next month."

"How did Ariel approach you and how did she know I was going to Mexico?"

"I don't know mate. I just think this is all wrong. Tracey asked me how easy it would be to get in contact with a mate of mine in Mexico to find someone."

"Thanks, mate, for this. Can I call you if I need any further explanation?"

"Yeh, you've got my number now," clicked off Fabio.

"You've got her honey," we heard Charlotte say sounding excited, "You've finally got her."

"Did you turn off the recording?" said Dante.

The recording finished.

"Ms Lore, I am outraged to hear your client would do such a thing. Has a Notice of Family Violence been filed, Mr Prince?" said the judge addressing Jackson.

"No, Your Honour, we have filed for an urgent restraining order with non-contact injunctions and for the respondent to refrain from coming within one hundred metres of Mr Prince and his family including Christian Prince, who is the son of Ariel and Dante Prince," he said looking down going through his paperwork in case the judge wanted a copy.

"Right then, I believe this meets the threshold to issue a temporary restraining order until the police investigation makes their findings."

"No, Your Honour, this is not fair; my client is innocent, and you are clearly finding her guilty here today. Furthermore, you are punishing a victim of violence by removing the very son she has been fighting to protect through the courts for two years… against a man who is known for violent outbursts, stalking and abusive, controlling behaviour. This is a tragedy and injustice at play!"

"Control yourself Ms Lore! I find your emotional outburst to be offensive and disrespectful to my position. I place it on record that you are on notice… that one more of these wild eruptions will have you in front of a disciplinary board."

Penelope sat down, conceding defeat for the time being.

"You Honour, my client also seeks for the arbitration orders made in March to be set aside, giving my client sole custody until the mother is charged or otherwise by the state."

The judge read the Form 32.1C with the entire courtroom silent for a few minutes.

I sat there broken, my left eye twitching. I felt gutted thinking, *He's unstoppable, so entrenched in getting his way that his maniac brain fabricates the unthinkable without a care for the repercussions, meeting legal requirements to get everything removed from me in one fell swoop. He's actually brilliant, like a criminal savant!*

Judge Darby exhaled heavily in contemplation looking up at the parties before him. Penelope could see he hadn't made a conclusive decision on this request, so she jumped up in my defence…

"Your Honour, my client has not been charged with any crime and until such time as she is, you cannot disband binding custody orders set by a tribunal. Can we ask that you have them set to the side only in the interim, as if you discharge them these parents will be back fighting in court after my client is found innocent?" said Penelope.

"For the interim Ms Lore, I agree with you. But I must protect the entire family from such a serious allegation. Where is Christian Prince now?"

Penelope turned around to get my instructions.

"He is at his child care centre," said Penelope.

"I order the child Christian Prince be picked up from the child care centre by his father by four p.m. today and the child is to remain in Mr Prince's care until such time as Ms Prince has been found guilty, or not, of attempted murder," said the judge.

"No disrespect Your Honour, but I urge you to be cautious. You personally have already made findings that Mr Prince has been very dishonest to this court and yourself just last year," pleaded Penelope, knowing her timeframe to overturn this mess was closing.

I burst in tears, covering my face, realising this morning was the last time I'd see Christian until all this mess was over. How long that would be was anyone's guess. Dante had just ripped my heart out to let me know I'll never win against him!

"Ms Lore, will you please ensure my associate is informed once the investigation into Ms Prince is finished, so I can bring this matter back to court to determine what is required in the long term?"

"Yes, Your Honour," replied Penelope, feeling gutted she had not stopped this train wreck.

"Mr Prince, if you have been dishonest to this court in any way, you will not get away with it twice," warned Judge Darby, looking straight at Dante.

"Parties are dismissed," said the judge, smacking down his gavel and removing himself from the courtroom.

I sat dumbfounded in my chair; the black mascara mixed with my tears staining my cheeks in the shape of streaks of lightning. Penelope was saying something about going to the Victorian Court of Appeals to enter an application for Judge Darby's decision to be overturned. I didn't really hear much of what she was saying, as my hearing was going in and out, with my heart racing, in a state of uncontrollable panic.

Penelope wanted to walk me to my car, but I said, no and thanked her for her services, and then excused myself to go to the ladies' toilets as I didn't want to talk to anyone. I ended up stumbling out of courthouse ten minutes later, mentally fragile and completely unglued, possessing half the strength of the person I used to be, before Judge Darby decided to remove Christian from me.

Dante was outside the courthouse with two officers. I saw him point at me and then the two men walked towards me. I said to myself, *This is it; they're going to arrest me.*

"Ms Prince, I'm Detective Hall and this is Detective Nile; we'd like you to come to the station with us for questioning."

"Okay," I responded, and followed them into the building next door.

I was interviewed for maybe an hour and told the detectives everything I knew. They were very pleasant, and didn't play good cop, bad cop with me. They could see I was distressed, but cooperative. I gave them Tracey and Fabio's address and phone number, and Sophia's mobile number.

I left the police station scared as hell and drove straight home. I wanted to run away with Christian, but I'd have a warrant issued for my arrest on top of attempted murder. I went home and cried myself to sleep. My subconscious mind toyed around with the fact that I had been sucked in further to the insane vortex that was Dante, with the paralysing thought, that there was only one way out if I wanted my life back, as he was never ever going to leave me alone.

Chapter 28
Casualties of Negative Intimacy

Harvey, my parents and Linda had been ringing me repeatedly trying to find out what had happened in court yesterday. I hadn't answered my phone to anyone. I sent each of them a text message letting them know I would talk to them tomorrow after work.

I just turned up to Ambrosia the next day like nothing had happened. It was Linda's day off, so at least no one else at my business knew that I was in court yesterday. Harvey rang me from his car while he sat in the car park outside Ambrosia. He asked me if I could spare thirty minutes to come out and talk to him. I agreed and went out to the car park.

"Come for a ride with me."

"Where to?"

"I want to take you somewhere."

"I've only got fifteen minutes so it will need to be close by."

"Okay then, I'll have to change my plans and take you somewhere close by then."

I opened the door to his Mercedes, got in and we drove off. There was no conversation between us along the way. I was so mad at him and the court and the universe. Harvey pulled up at the beachfront. We got out of the car and walked over to a park bench that looked out over the beach.

"I love you Ariel. I've loved you for so long," Harvey said as he took my hand.

'So why wouldn't you help me?"

"You of all people should understand. He could get me fired and charged with assault if I stand up in court and open this can of worms."

"I lost Christian yesterday," I said tears sprouting up in my eyes again.

"You *what*?" exclaimed Harvey.

"The judge believed him and gave Dante sole custody. I'm not even allowed to see Christian until the investigation is over."

"I'm so sorry Ariel. I had no idea this would happen."

"I told you, I needed you, but you wouldn't listen."

"There's got to be something we can do?"

"Yes… appeal or wait till it comes out that I didn't hire Fabio."

"I won't let you down again. I love you and I want us to be together. Please take me back and we'll do this, together?"

"I never had you in the first place Harvey. We were just casually dating."

"Would you consider a more permanent relationship with me then?"

"I don't know. I don't have the brain space left to think about this," I said studying his face. I was having trouble trusting him and the thought of being in another serious relationship wasn't on my radar.

"Okay then… Well, how about you give me your answer on New Year's Eve? That'll give you nearly two months to think about it. I'm going to be in Springdale to see the kids. I'd love for you to come and spend the evening, plus a few days with me."

"I'll let you know. Now, I need to get back to my shop," I said abruptly as I was uptight about being away for too long during peak trade.

Harvey and I continued to speak on the phone, but we didn't catch up one on one. Over the next couple of weeks, the detectives went about their business trying to qualify the events outlined in Dante's statement. They phoned Tracey and Sophia who had both gone in and been interviewed.

I got a call from Tracey the first weekend in November to tell me the police had turned up wanting a statement from Fabio three times in the last week, but he had done a runner when they first came to the house; had ditched his mobile phone number and hadn't been home since. She was happy as she didn't want to be with him any more.

Christmas was forty days away. I was home relaxing in the

evening having a red wine and late dinner by myself watching the shimmer patterns gliding across the water. Life was quiet without Christian and I missed him terribly, but I had soldiered on with my daily routines hoping he would come home soon. Dante had not flared up once since court. He had won; I had lost.

My phone rang. The number was silent, but I picked it up.

"Hello, Ariel speaking."

"I was hoping to get you," said a male's voice on the end of the line.

"I'm sorry, I don't recognise your voice. Who is this?"

"Never mind. I was ringing to say g'day and I wanted to let you know your profile sparked my interest."

"What profile?"

"Oh, come on, stop toying with me," he said sounding a bit irritated.

"I'm sorry, you have the wrong number," I said and hung up.

He called again two days later at around the same time of eight p.m.

"Ariel, I just want to get to know you. Don't hang up."

"I'm sorry, I'm not on any sites. Please don't call me."

I hung up.

A week later at nine p.m. I had another private number call me. I didn't answer it letting it go to message bank. All that was left on the voice message was heavy breathing.

The next morning at eight thirty, my phone rang.

"Hi. Ariel speaking."

"I know where you live."

It was the same man again.

"How do you know where I live?"

"You live across from the beach and have a couple of big rocks in your front yard." he said with no hesitation.

He was right.

"Leave me alone and please stop calling me."

"What if I want to get to know you?"

"Stop calling me."

"We will meet. Ciao for now," and he hung up.

I was petrified this bloke was stalking me and was going to turn up at my home. I told Mum and Dad what had been happening. Dad suggested I call the police. I didn't want to be involved in two police matters; that's all I needed. One for attempted murder and one for stalking activity.

I decided to break my lease and move. I let the real estate agent know of my intentions that afternoon, organised for an agent to place my old house in Victoria on the market, and I began searching for a house to buy in the area that was on a hill and had ocean views.

I found one suitable and scheduled a viewing for the following day. I loved it, made an offer of $700,000 and it was accepted. Unfortunately, the building and pest inspection came back a week later with extensive asbestos, so I crashed the contract.

On my way home from work I had the same real estate agent contact me to let me know he had just been giving a new listing. I went to the viewing after work. The house sat on 1,065 sqm, was a battle-axe block and had a large fully fenced back yard. It was a two storey, half brick, half-timber Milton style home with a huge pool, a granny flat downstairs for Mum and Dad and four rooms upstairs. Internally it was painted a crisp white and the bathrooms had recently been renovated. The floors were polished wood and the deck on the second floor had views of the surrounding countryside. I was sold on the view alone.

It was a bonus the property had been built like an internal fortress. No one was getting in and nobody could see the house. I could be stalked no more. I made an offer that evening with the contract to go unconditional on the 10th of January and settlement seven days later.

A few days later, I was standing at the back wall in Ambrosia fixing the homeware display when I spotted Detectives Hall and Nile walk into my shop stopping at the front register. I admit, my blood pressure dropped through the floor realising this was it. They were either going to handcuff me and take me away or tell me the investigation was over.

I asked Taylor to come off the floor and take over at the register so I could speak to the police. I didn't want to be further interrogated in front of customers and staff. The only staff member who knew why the police would be there was Linda.

Walking out the back into the kitchen area, I whispered in Linda's ear, "The police are here."

Linda's eyes widened as she stared at me registering my words.

"Right then. You go. I'll take care of out the front and get Alistair to finish making these lunch orders."

"Thanks."

"If you need a witness, I can come with you."

"If I need one, I'll come and get you. Can you call Mum and Dad and let them know the police are here?"

"Got it boss!"

I walked up to the police who were now waiting at the couches near the flower kiosk.

"Hi. Can I help you Detectives?" I said as confidently as I could muster.

"Do you mind if we ask you just a few questions?" said Laurie.

"No, but can we talk away from my shop?"

"Sure, how about we sit outside?" said Detective Nile.

"Okay. Would either of you like a drink?"

"I'd love a flat white," said Detective Hall.

"I'll just have some water," said Detective Nile.

I called Joey over and asked him to sort out a round of drinks. Then I followed the police officers down the aisle with my stomach in knots worrying about what was going to happen.

"We've just got a few questions for you before we close the case," said Laurie.

I nodded, waiting for the interrogation to begin. Detective Nile seemed to be the designated note taker.

"Did you plot to kill Dante Prince in Mexico?" asked Laurie.

"No."

"Have you approached anyone to organise a hit on Dante

Prince?"

"No," I said flatly.

"Did you give a man named Fabio money to take out a hit on your husband?

"No."

"Thanks Ms Prince, we just needed to confirm you hadn't conspired to murder Mr Prince. We'll be closing the case, noting the allegation was unfounded. I'm sure this has been a stressful time for you," said Detective Hall.

"You have no idea how much damage this bullshit report has caused me. I lost custody of my son," I said brimming with tears because it was all over, meaning I could get Christian back.

"Is there anything else you wanted to add to our report?" asked Detective Nile.

"I have a question. When did you realise that I didn't do any of this?"

"We intercepted a suspicious message from Fabio to Dante a couple of days ago saying words to the effect that Fabio wanted $25,000 paid upfront and a further payment of $25,000 to lie to put you behind bars," said Detective Hall.

"So, who's framing who here, and are there any repercussions for making a false police report?" I asked.

"We can't tell who's the instigator and we really don't have time or resources to waste on more fruitless outcomes going after them. Sorry. I know that isn't what you wanted to hear. Is there anything more before we close this off?" asked Detective Hall.

"Where do I start? I have a lot to say as I'd love you to know about the type of person you've just been played by and what he's done to me," I said with courage and determination, wanting the authorities to know everything.

I was with the police officers for a total of two hours. They were gobsmacked by my story. Laurie picked up on the cyberstalking and the stalking on the telephone as being possible criminal offences.

At the end of the meeting, he told me he would follow up on the internet stalking to see if there was anything he could do, and requested I send him copies of the emails I had received from each of the websites to start his investigation.

By the time the police left Ambrosia, the shop was in full swing and I was elated to know Christian might just be back by Christmas. I dashed off to the toilets before coming back so I could freshen up and splash some much-needed cold water on my face, as I had sporadically cried to the officers during my emotional tirade about Dante's historic abuse.

I felt positive as Laurie's investigation, I had no doubt, would lead straight to Dante.

I called Penelope and told her the good news. She in turn wrote to Judge Darby's associate. Judge Darby then issued orders in chambers the following day for Dante to return Christian back to me at nine a.m. on Saturday outside the Western Communities Police Station and he resurrected our custody arbitration orders. He also dismissed Dante's restraining-order motion, revoked the temporary injunctions, and suspended Dante from his family justice counsellor appointment, until the Attorney General's office conducted a review of his actions.

Christian was returned and I was so appreciative of having him in my life again, having gone through this ordeal. He was a very special child who was needing a safe haven to shield him. He was returned to me, like a wound-up ball of stress, clinging to my side for a few days, until he realised, he could relax as he was back with Mummy for good.

The Christmas rush was extra exciting for me, as everything had flipped back to the way it was meant to be. The downside was I was a little stressed, as three staff came down with the flu the week of Christmas and I had a cook on leave. This placed enormous stress on the full-time staff to do extra hours. I also worked every day from six thirty a.m., doing the food preparation, covering the exiting cook till close every night, with late-night shopping.

My only day off was Christmas Day and our arbitration orders had Christian sharing the day between Dante and me. At least Christian had Christmas morning with me and was able to open Santa's presents as soon as he woke up. Christian was just old enough now to understand who Santa was and the traditions of Christmas. It was a joyous time for the two of us.

Harvey rang me on Christmas Day from Springdale and asked me again to spend New Year's with him. I baulked as I didn't think I could spare the time away from my business with so many staff unavailable. Christian was spending Christmas afternoon through to New Year's Day with Dante, so I told Harvey I would think about it.

On Christmas night, I felt ill and assumed I had caught the flu off a staff member. I had all the flu type symptoms: aching bones, sneezing, a headache, and a stiff neck. Over the next few days, I lacked energy, had a runny nose, and a sore stomach to add to my list of ailments. I also had cold shivers running over my head and down my neck regularly like that feeling you get playing that game as a child when someone pretended to crack an imaginary egg on your head.

These shivers resulted in dizzy spells. I was also overly emotional. I was not feeling well by any stretch, so I reconsidered Harvey's suggestion to take a few days off and spend some time in Springdale, Newfoundland with him.

I told my staff, two days before New Year's Eve, that I was taking a few days off and would return in the new year on the 3rd. It was my intention to make a surprise visit to Harvey, calling him from the airport in Newfoundland on the morning of the 31st once I had arrived to let him know I was there.

He was really surprised to receive my call as he was supposed to be on a plane heading back to surprise me on the mainland. I thought while waiting for him to pick me up: *He is genuine. That was sweet of him to come back for me.*

Harvey took me to the Riverwood Inn for a New Year's Eve dinner. It was very romantic, overlooking the river. We dined on a delicious seafood banquet, consumed a couple of cocktails and a glass or two of wine and finished the night off with a to-die-for, exquisite chocolate liqueur dessert. As the fireworks started, we moved outside to watch. It was a truly magnificent display, with lots of cheers from the guests.

It was cold out, so Harvey hugged me from behind as we watched the bursts of colour appear and disappear across the sky. The display went for about fifteen minutes and it seemed like the whole of Springdale was there to watch.

Harvey then took me for a stroll along the riverbank stopping near the wharf where we kissed, and he professed his love for me. We then returned to the inn and had a glass of champagne.

As I clinked my glass with Harvey I thought, *It's going to be a new era for* us. *I'm leaving all the trauma and crap behind. There is nothing more he can do. I'm sure of it.*

I felt dizzy after the glass of champers, so I excused myself to go to the little girls' room. I splashed some water on my face as I seemed to be overheating with my heart racing so fast, I could hear the beats in my ears.

My head was suddenly hit like a sledgehammer, smashing tiles. I fell to the ground narrowly missing the white porcelain sink on my way down. My sight was blurred so I couldn't see if anyone else was in the bathroom with me.

I regained my senses after some time and slowly made my way back to the table stumbling around the packed restaurant like I was extremely intoxicated. I was crying and cradling the side of my head above my right ear with my hand. Harvey jumped to his feet when he saw me navigating the crowd and came quickly over to me.

"What happened? Are you all right?" he said, sweeping me up into a protective embrace.

Several waiters came over wanting to assist. The surrounding guests kept on going with their celebrations probably believing I had just passed out drunk.

"I don't know. Am I bleeding? I think I was hit over the head," I said slowly trying to get the words put together and out of my mouth… "Never felt like this before. What's wrong with me?"

"We need to get you to hospital!" said Harvey frantically.

All this commotion was occurring in slow motion to me, so the time felt like an hour, but was only a minute or two from my exit from the toilets.

"Can you pass me that handbag?" requested Harvey to the waiter.

"Thanks. You have my credit card, please charge anything outstanding to it and bring it back to me. Can you call for a cab please? We'll be waiting outside for it."

Harvey carried me out of the restaurant and into a waiting green-and-black cab.

"Central hospital please as fast as you can," instructed Harvey to the cab driver.

We were at the emergency section of the hospital for about three hours. This time is an absolute blur to me as I felt like my brain was shutting off.

Being New Year's Eve there were lots of people in emergency. I was taken through all the general checks. I was in so much pain; I was incoherent and pretty much unable to put sentences together, just sporadic describing words.

"What hurts?" asked a nurse.

"Head's on fire," I said, as I went into a painful spasm, curling up into the foetal position.

I said this over and over to the nurses and doctors coming in and out of my emergency cubical. I was being asked questions I couldn't answer because my brain wouldn't kick into action due to the tremendous pain. I was fitting so much my stomach hurt as much as my head. It was a chore to remain awake. All I wanted to do was sleep.

"We ran tests to see if Ariel has meningitis. Results are negative and her bloods show nothing sinister. So, I'm not really sure what's wrong," said the emergency doctor.

"She's been under enormous stress these past few years so maybe it's a bad migraine?" Harvey responded.

"Could be. She seems okay physically. I wouldn't rule out a neck strain. It would be best just to take her home. She probably needs some rest. Here's some panadiene forte and endone for the pain. If she gets worse, please come back and see me," said the doctor.

Harvey organised a cab back to his father's house. I feel asleep in the taxi.

Harvey's father was up watching the early morning news on TV and was startled by Harvey's dramatic entrance into his home, carrying a female in his arms.

Harvey carried me into the bedroom and put me to bed then he filled his father in on the night's events.

"Well, I hope she's going to be okay mate. I'm off to play golf," was all Harvey's father could reply. He was miffed over this unknown girl in Harvey's life.

I woke up a few hours later still in pain, although the full body spasms were less severe.

Harvey was excited I was in Newfoundland with him as he wanted to show me around his hometown. I knew he didn't comprehend how ill I felt. To him there was nothing medically wrong with me.

He wanted to take me to Main Street for brunch. I didn't want to leave the bedroom but said yes as I didn't want to disappoint him. I took the tablets prescribed, threw on a pair of jeans, a T-shirt and a jacket and left with Harvey.

We walked around the tiny shopping village near Aspen Road stopping off at various local stores for about forty minutes. I had a seizure concentrated in my head, stumbled and fell to the ground on a corner street. Harvey helped me up.

"I feel like I'm going to black out."

"You'll be right. How about we stop into a café for a coffee and breakfast? Food will make you feel better."

I vaguely remember going to breakfast and to a Christmas shop.

We then went back to Harvey's father's house at my request. I feel asleep on the couch in the living room. When I woke up mid-afternoon, my brain felt like I was having electric shocks pumped into it every few minutes. I couldn't hold my head up straight and I was in a state of distress over my mortality.

Ryan and Anastacia, two of Harvey's adult children, turned up at the house to meet me. I was totally embarrassed as they tried to converse with me, but I was unable to make a good impression feeling the way I was. I asked to leave the table to lie down as I couldn't cope any longer with all the people, the noise and my failing body.

After Harvey's children left, I begged Harvey to take me home. Harvey was upset at the thought of me leaving early and his holidays being cut short. But he organised our return flights for the morning.

Harvey's father, having worked previously at the airport and knowing the ground staff, was able to organise me a wheelchair as I could no longer hold myself together upright to walk. At the airport, I was given priority access and whisked off to the wheelchair lift to board the plane.

I passed out on the plane shortly after take-off. Harvey cared for me the entire plane flight home. He was my white knight.

I don't remember touching down at the Comax Valley Airport. My father picked us up and Harvey carried me from the car, up the stairs and into my bed.

I woke at about seven p.m., going into the master en-suite to go to the toilet. After I had done a wee, I stood up and went to pull up my underwear. Upon standing upright, I saw a heap of black stars in front of my eyes and the sledgehammer hit me again.

I fell to the marble floor. Harvey heard the crash from the kitchen downstairs where he was with my parents.

"Ariel are you okay?" he yelled out and waited a few seconds.

I couldn't respond.

He ran up the staircase, turned right into my room, scanned it and realised I wasn't there. He opened the double doors into the en-suite finding me on the floor knocked out. He checked my pulse determining it to be faint and slow. He couldn't see any areas I was bleeding.

Rolling me onto my side into the safety position Harvey then picked up the phone in the bathroom and called for an ambulance.

"Denise, Desmond!" Harvey yelled out.

Seconds later Harvey met them at the top of the stairs explaining what was happening. My mother became distressed and wanted to see me.

"I don't think that's the best idea," said Harvey.

"I do need you to put together a hospital bag for her. Can you do that for me?" Mum nodded biting her lip with worry.

"The two of you will need to get Christian out immediately so he doesn't witness what may unfold here. I suggest you take him out for an ice-cream."

"Right then Denise, you organise Christian and I'll get the car ready."

Christian stood at the garage door holding my mum's hand, "Bye Mummy, see you soon," he yelled out looking around waiting for me to come to the top of the stairs to say goodbye.

"I'll contact you as soon as we reach the hospital," said Harvey looking straight at my Dad from the top of the stairs.

"Come on Christian, what flavour ice cream do you want to get?" said Denise leading him into the garage to leave.

"Chocolate please nanny."

The paramedics arrived about ten minutes after and attended to me in the en-suite. They repeatedly questioned Harvey about my use of recreational drugs and checked over my body for signs of injection points. They didn't believe him that I had never taken any type of drugs before. Harvey knew I was totally against drugs and that I was proud I had never succumbed to their allure like my brother and friends had.

The paramedics thought, because of my incoherent presentation, that I was a druggie. The paramedics treated me the entire time labelling my condition as that of an overdose.

"Do you have stomach pain Ariel?" I heard a voice that seemed like it was miles away as a blurred blue image stood over me with no face.

I think I nodded.

"What about chest pain?"

I starred up at the scary dark-blue scarecrow-like outline and moved my eyes side to side as I tried to make my voice say no. I physically had no ability to speak.

"Do you feel like you're going to vomit?" the voice asked.

"Yeh," I heard the voice in my head say.

My face began perspiring suddenly. Then the sledgehammer came down on my skull again.

"She's having a seizure, Tony. Harvey you'll need to move outside please."

One paramedic was on their knees beside me counting the duration of the seizure and the other two were preparing the gurney.

"One minute, seventeen seconds."

I was rolled over onto my side again by the paramedic. I lay as limp as a wet rag on the cold floor unaware of my surroundings with no thoughts in my head. Time was frozen for me leaving me in a limbo black room with no door or windows just a breeze dancing over my body. I breathed in and out irregularly and slowly in short breaths like a dying creature going through the motions of taking in that last beautiful intake of life.

"Ariel we're going to lift you up on the bed," said a paramedic.

Their words sounded distorted to me, but my brain got the gist of what was about to happen. I was lifted into the waiting ambulance. The siren was turned on and the call made to the hospital of my impending arrival.

"Not too sure, probable drug overdose. Could be an aneurism, a stroke, hard to tell. She's incoherent and having seizures. We're administering morphine, blood pressure 98 over 56, temperature 38.5. Arrival time three minutes. Recommending Category 1 or 2 admission."

"I need you to try and stay awake Ariel," a woman kept repeating to me.

I was boiling and all I wanted to do was curl up into a ball.

On arrival at the hospital, I was scooted off into the emergency ward as a Category Two patient, possible drug overdose or brain condition. I was initially seen by an ER Doctor and was hooked up to all the necessary machines.

I was semi-conscious but not much help with information as I was dizzy, lacking energy and every so often my brain would light up on fire and I would convulse on the bed keeling over in pain in the foetal position.

A couple of nurses came in and out over the next hour taking blood samples for drug testing as well as a complete blood count test and an ECG. I was given tablets for pain and nausea and had trouble holding myself up to swallow them.

The nurses seemed totally oblivious to my actual state and went about their activities as though I was a naughty child not doing as I was told. It was humiliating as I struggled to be conscious and stay alive fighting this chaos going on in my brain.

"My head's on fire," I kept repeating to the nurses when I was in between fits of pain and as they were asking me questions.

"Do you know where you are Ariel?"

"Yes."

"What day of the week is it?"

"Head."

"Who is the prime minister?"

"On fire."

I was suffering a mass of trauma shocks inside me. The consciousness inside me was distraught over being asked these stupid questions instead of being asked how I felt for them to be able to fix me.

My hands were intermittently freezing up into a claw like position for a few minutes at a time and my left-hand side of my chest felt like it was being crushed, restricting my ability to breath.

"Why is she talking slowly? Does she normally react this way to pain medication?" I heard a female voice say.

"I have no idea," said Harvey.

I hadn't realised Harvey was in the room. I couldn't see him. I moved my hand slowly off the bed using all the energy I had, in a gesture to hold his hand. Harvey saw what I had done and swiftly took my hand in his, like we have always done to show our affection.

Placing his hand over my tensed-up claw he asked, "Is she going to be all right? The doctors in Springdale just thought this was a strained neck and referred her to a physio."

"We're not quite sure what's happening. The test results are inconclusive showing many abnormalities. But we do know she hasn't had a heart attack and all her major organs are stable. We're waiting for a private bed to be allocated so she'll be moved out of emergency and into a hospital wing," replied the nurse.

The paramedics came in and apologised to Harvey that they had made the wrong assumptions and that they felt terrible for treating me as a junkie case.

After a few hours, a Dr Ferrier was appointed to oversee my admission into the intensive care unit of the hospital as the ER staff were not equipped to further explore my condition. The emergency staff were concerned, whatever I had, maybe a life-threatening illness, as tests ruled out a drug overdose. I was placed in a room next to Dr Ferrier's office which was opposite the medical reception desk.

Dr Ferrier ordered morphine injections to be given straight into my stomach every four hours to alleviate the pain that was coursing throughout my entire body now. The seizures subsided after twenty-four hours. I was heavily sedated and either stared into space or slept.

Further tests revealed I could have any one or a range of four major brain conditions: an aneurism, a stroke, a tumour or a TBI. I was watched every second of the day as I lay almost lifeless in my hospital bed infrequently coming to but with not enough energy to move or speak.

I heard a lot of voices coming in and out of my room but was unable to understand what was being said. I did know my son visited a couple of times as his was the only voice that laughed in all the drama.

Day two of my hospitalisation, I was sent for head scans.

Day three, I was in and out of consciousness and having blood tests every four hours. My blood pressure was ridiculously low, and Dr Ferrier was concerned about my heart rate.

Day four, I had a dye injected into a vein searching for abnormalities.

Day five was another CT scan. A bright red lesion showed up

on screen indicating the existence of a mass the size of a twenty-cent piece hovering over the top of my spine and under my skull or the craniovertebral junction. Another red area was at my front temple on top of my right eye.

I was still not coming out of the comatose-like state which worried Dr Ferrier. He decided these lesions were a lead and needed to be investigated. I was prepped for a brain biopsy to determine whether the larger mass of the two was an abscess or tumour.

A hospital orderly picked me up and placed me into a wheelchair strapping me in so I wouldn't fall out. I was pushed down a path of corridors for what seemed like a long time. The harsh fluros above penetrated my eyelids hurting my pupils and overwhelming my fragile senses.

Eventually I was led into a white sterile room with a glass window and two technicians on the other side of the glass. I was placed on and secured into a chair in the middle of the room in a white straitjacket so I couldn't move.

I was freaking out internally but couldn't express any emotions as I had severe brain fog. I opened my eyelids for a few seconds. I'm sure they showed I was petrified as I glanced at a large round 3D type machine with a huge, oversized needle protruding from a computerised arm.

A technician said to me over a loudspeaker, "Ariel please try and remain still. The machine to your left is going to move over your head to create a three-dimensional image of your brain. You will not feel anything, I promise."

About twenty minutes later the needle started to be positioned close to the back of my head. Tears started rolling down my face. I wanted none of this. I was screaming inside my head…

"Stop! Don't do this. Please."

I had a sick sense of horror overwhelm me. I needed to get out. I willed myself to get up and squirm my way out of this harness. I couldn't. I went into a violent rage in the chair, summoning everything I had in me.

A red light in the corner went off like a siren whirring. The machine came to an abrupt halt within centimetres of my skull. The needle retracted quickly from near my head. Medical staff ran into the room to contain me, so I didn't harm myself further.

After ten minutes, when I had visibly shut down, the team began preparing for the procedure to be performed again.

Dr Ferrier had requested for Dr Becker, a neurosurgeon, to be flown in from Montreal to have a look at my case. He was hoping to have the results of this biopsy for when she arrived today. Dr Becker arrived as the second procedure was about to begin with the needle poised at the back of my head.

She looked at the scans showing the red masses…

"Stop, stop the procedure. It's not safe," said Dr Becker to the technician.

The technician stopped the robotic arm.

"The mass is below thousands of nerves and is likely pressing on all of them. There is no way you can get to this lesion without severely damaging the brain. It's too risky. She could end up paralysed or in a vegetative state."

This procedure was called off.

Day six, Dr Becker decided to treat the lesions in my head as if they were a cancer with infrared light photoimmunotherapy. My blood pressure was getting weaker by the day which was concerning Dr Ferrier.

Day seven, I was given more infrared treatment. I came to for a small period in the morning and was able to talk to Harvey. I found it hard to keep my eyes open so my lids fluttered during our chat and I couldn't look up at him. I stopped mid-sentence and feel asleep again.

By two fifteen that afternoon I was sitting up in bed with my eyes open. My brain was foggy, like I could feel dense clouds in my forehead. I had little energy and felt like I was going to vomit.

"I need to tell you some things," I said to Harvey. "Get a pen and paper please."

"Sure!" said Harvey scrambling through my laptop bag and pulled out the items.

"There's an A4 orange envelope in the bottom of my wardrobe containing everything including my will."

"Baby, please don't talk like this, you're going to get better."

"My passwords are Benji01 or 2475 or 60609."

"Are these to bank accounts or bank deposits?"

"It's all in the envelope," I said distressed that he wasn't writing it down.

"Okay."

"There's a safety box in the ground behind the shed. The key is 2866."

"I want you to pay out the mortgages with my life insurance," I began to cry but kept going as I needed to get this out. "You must fight to keep Christian, whatever it takes. Promise me you'll do this?"

"I promise," said Harvey.

"And you'll look after Mum and Dad. You all live in the house and raise him," I said entrusting him.

"Did you write it all down?" I asked, slowly as my brain was finding it difficult to get the words out. My head fell onto my left shoulder and my eyes closed as I had no more strength to fight my need to sleep.

Harvey had been at the hospital every day coming in and out, fitting his work schedule around my hospitalisation. Each day through chatting with the medical staff, Harvey let out little bits of my story and life events over the last few years. He expressed his concern over my mental state and the high levels of stress I had been under.

Dr Ferrier sat in his office on day seven, mulling over my illness and the various life events Harvey had told him about. He began to view my condition from an entirely different perspective in case the photoimmunotherapy didn't work.

He thought to himself: *This could be PTSD related or a combination of it, and the past head injuries from the violence by her ex. The points of collision could be the exact point the lesions are showing.*

Day eight, Dr Ferrier instructed the nurses to give me various antibiotics and for non-steroidal anti-inflammatory drugs; pain management pills, an antidepressant and I was put on oxygen. He figured he would blast my body all at once to damage any bacteria so my body's immune system could attempt to fight whatever this bubble was that was shutting me down.

Harvey sat in the chair beside me as he had done every night. He had bought KFC for his dinner and was watching the evening movie '*City of Angels*' on TV. He sporadically looked over at me willing me to wake up from this nightmare. Like the movie, he saw me as his angel, his fallen angel.

The movie's theme song 'Angel' came on moving him to tears as the realisation hit him that just maybe he might have to walk out of here without me by his side. He listened to the words of the song, really feeling them; the hairs standing up on his neck as it all rang true.

He cried for the first time over me. His strong calm front cracked as the enormity of losing the girl he had fallen in love with a decade ago engulfed him like a sucker punch to the gut. He turned the TV off at the end of the movie and sat in the dark watching the heart monitor beeping off and on and the lines going up and down across the screen, and eventually falling asleep before midnight.

I didn't know if I were awake or asleep, in a dream or not; I felt an enormous pressure in my head, and I was shaking, like my body would explode at any minute. I saw nothing but black and my heart was heavy, depressed heavy.

"God, if you're there, please take me," my inner voice said, desperate for the almighty God to say something back to me…

"Please, I beg of you. I have no fight left."

I relaxed, my head fell resting on my right shoulder on the pillow and I felt myself exhale praying to God one last time…

"Take me before the devil does."

Beep, beep, beep, beep, beep, beeeeeeeeeeeeeeee… went the heart monitor.

At 2.49 a.m. the rhythmic green line on my heart monitor went flat, showing a cardiac flatline. My heart and soul had given up on this life.

Within a few seconds, two nurses came running into my room, flicking the lights on as they ran, and going into lifesaving mode.

"Check the machines?" said one nurse.

They both ran around the bed pulling out cords and looking at the machines.

"Nothing here," said the second nurse.

"Call in Doctor Ferrier. I'll start CPR."

Harvey had awoken to his worst nightmare and was being shuffled out of the room by a third male nurse.

"You'll have to come this way," he said ushering Harvey out the door.

"No, I want to stay with her. Please let me stay."

He stood his ground, and another male nurse ran in grabbed Harvey's other elbow and dragged him out.

"He did this to her! I'm going to kill him, if it's the last thing I do!" shouted Harvey.

The doctor flew in through the door.

"Give it to me!" he said wanting information.

"There's no reason for this to have happened," said the nurse.

"No equipment malfunctions. They were last checked twenty minutes ago. Blood pressure was low but no real change."

"How long for CPR?" the doctor asked.

"About a minute and half," said the nurse compressing my heart.

Dr Ferrier checked the computer readouts handed to him by the nurse.

He made a risky decision, grabbing the intracardiac injection from the hospital tray and plunged it into my heart muscle in the fourth intercostal space between my ribs.

A bolt of electricity went through my body lifting me up off the bed and down again as oxygen flooded my lungs.

The medical staff froze to where they stood, either staring at me or glancing up at the heart monitor wanting to hear the 'beep' sound and see the green electrical pulse line shoot up to signal that they had saved my life.

Everyone in the room waited; the voices in their own heads silently willing me to breathe.

I didn't want to come back…

But my lungs filled with a rush of air, restarting my heart. God didn't want me quite yet and seemed to have another plan mapped out for me.